SCHEMES
BOOK
1

KINDRED SCHEMES

R. K. HARRINGTON

Lady River
PRESS

FIRST EDITION

Cover and Interior Designed by ebooklaunch.com

Edited by Lebowitz & Daughter

ISBN: 979-8-9986055-6-7

Published by Lady River Press, LLC

P.O. Box 5868, Arlington, Virginia 22205

Library of Congress Cataloging-in-Publication Data has been applied for.

For my husband:
Without you, this book would never have been inspired
nor executed. You are truly amazing.

For my sons:
Thank you for being lovely humans. Keep being you.

For my mom:
I owe my love of romance books (or books, in general) to you, even
if I did get in trouble for reading under the covers on occasion.

For my friends and family who supported me along the way:
You will never know how fully I appreciate all the reads, re-reads,
late night conversations, and encouragement.
Thank you from the bottom of my heart.

For my editors:
I am very lucky to have had your guidance
and advice for my first book (and many more!).

CHAPTER 1

London, 1809

Oh no, here he comes, the lascivious Lord Finch and his merry band of drunken fools. Alaina looked out at the crowded ballroom, her eyes connecting with the group of men making their way toward its center. Alaina had only been at the ball for a quarter hour before this particular disaster struck, the leers of the men making the hairs at the nape of her neck prickle. It did not escape Alaina's attention that Lady Barbara, Lord Finch's sister, accompanied the group, and wore a sly smile. Hopefully, this latest encounter would be short. Surely, Lord Finch would not want to be rejected twice, let alone in front of a large crowd.

Alaina looked to her right to find her parents close at hand, thankfully, and she stood a little straighter knowing she would not face this alone.

The group of men seemed to move in unison before coming to a halt a few paces before Alaina and her family. A group of onlookers formed a circle around them as if ready to enjoy the ensuing spectacle, Lady Barbara taking her place in the throng. Alaina struggled to focus on the faces of the onlookers as she held her head high, ready to meet Lord Finch and his friends with as much dignity as she could muster. She hoped to project a more serene exterior than she currently felt, her heartbeat accelerating to such a degree that she could feel the blood rushing in her ears.

Lord Finch stepped to the fore of the now halted group, and gallantly bowed to Alaina before speaking, his voice so loud that Alaina was sure people arriving in carriages outside could hear.

"My dearest *beautiful* Alaina," he started, clearing his throat before continuing, "You have set upon me quite a conundrum. I fear I have fallen madly in love with the idea of having you as my wife, and I feel you should be happy with such an arrangement. I am quite the catch, you know, especially for someone from the country, and one who likes to *read*."

From behind him, Lady Barbara piped up with an added insult, "Amazing, really, that Alaina found her way out of the library to be here." Laughter rippled through the crowd.

Alaina cringed at his easy use of her given name, devoid of any honorific, and seethed at the mockery of her character. Lord Finch and his sister sounded ridiculous, pompous, and conceited.

Alaina was frozen in place, her lips trembling in rage, and when no comment ushered forth from her lips, Lord Finch rejoined, unfazed by the one-sided nature of their conversation. "I find myself at an impasse. Shall I continue to press my suit with decorum, or should I make my feelings known to the whole world, so that you may not so easily dismiss them as you have in the past?"

A warmth crept up Alaina's neck and touched her cheeks, giving her pale skin a glow, although one not easily perceptible in the dim light of the ballroom. She turned once again to where her parents stood, only to find that her father had disappeared, and her mother's pale face was drawn in embarrassment as she watched her eldest child with dismay. Oh, how Alaina wished her father would have stayed; his tall frame was intimidating to a crowd, and his familiar umber eyes were always reassuring to her.

Resolved to put a stop to this farce, Alaina turned back to Lord Finch and remarked, her voice distant and strange sounding in her ears, "Lord Finch, it seems my earlier rejection of your suit did not deter you in the least, but I ask you to have a care for your surroundings."

As the words left her mouth, Alaina watched Lord Finch's face change, his outwardly serene expression making way for something more sinister. His smile twisted into an outright leer, and his pale green eyes seemed to burn of their own accord, the candlelight no longer just a reflection in them. He lowered to one knee and reached out his hands in supplication as he sneered, "Please, will you marry me, my *lady*?" The emphasis on the last word ensured that Alaina felt the insult.

Lord Finch was quickly joined by his friends, their idiocy knowing no bounds, all of them dropping to their knees in a chorus of marriage proposals, each more mocking and infuriating than the last. Soon laughter rang loudly in Alaina's ears as the men and then the onlookers seemed to find amusement in her predicament. Her world blurred through a sheen of tears, the faces of the laughing men—now resembling something like demons—the only clear points in her vision.

Alaina glanced about to find her mother and threw herself into her open arms, shielding her from the worst of the crowd. The two women made their way to the outer edge of the ballroom and quickly to the front entrance, only stopping a moment to gather their cloaks before heading out into the cool night. Her father, having had the forethought to make his way to the exit, met them in the front drive, where he had already called for their carriage to be brought around, and not a moment too soon.

The Sinclair family hastened into the carriage, a pall falling on them as the conveyance made its way onto the main thoroughfare and toward their London townhome. Alaina squeezed her eyes shut, focusing on the clip clop of the well-matched team of four, grateful for the silence of her parents, as she let tears make their way unchecked down her cheeks.

⁂

The morning light poured into the front parlor, and Alaina noted yet another dreary day. It was one of many in the past fortnight.

"I want to go home!" exclaimed Alaina. She snapped her book shut and leveled a hard stare on her sister, Evelina.

"You are home. I do believe we are safely ensconced in our family's town-home," Evelina countered, looking around the room as if to check that she was correct.

Alaina huffed a bit at her sister's flippant comment. "You know what I mean, Evelina. I want to go back to our home in the country."

"Now, Alaina, I know your run-in with Lord Finch may have put you off the London season, but running away to the country will not solve anything," Evelina said gently.

"Oh, I beg to differ, dear sister," Alaina fumed. "I shall be able to escape into my books with everyone of import stuck here in this cesspool of a city. If I am going to be mocked for being a country bookworm, I may as well live up to the moniker and enjoy myself!"

Evelina rolled her eyes heavenward and shook her head. A silence stretched between the sisters. Feeling the strain of her emotions, Alaina pushed off the settee and began pacing in front of the window.

Alaina presented quite a vision, backlit by the soft light of windows behind her. She was slender with dark brown, almost black, eyes that could sparkle with joy, glitter with rage, or shine with tears. The sage green capped-sleeve day dress she wore was a bit lower-cut than her girlish dresses of the past, the neckline scooped low across the top of her bosom. The empire waist of the gown highlighted her shape, and the dress flared ever so slightly on from the rib cage. Her hem brushed the floor, covering the simple leather boots chosen for warmth, which made little sound as she traversed the narrow space in front of the window.

"Alaina," Evelina tried once more, "One lord and his heinous sister poking fun at your love of books was only to salve their hurt at being turned down so early in the season. There are plenty of eligible gentlemen who think intelligence to be a virtue."

Alaina continued on in silence, not looking once at her sister. In contrast to Alaina, Evelina's dress showed her younger age, with a higher neckline and more voluminous shape, but the pretty pale pink fabric was just as fashionable as Alaina's. Despite her youthful garb, everything else about Evelina made many question if she and Alaina were actually born on the same day. It often astounded people to learn Evelina was not yet old enough to be out in society.

Finally, Alaina spoke once more, her anger getting the best of her. "It is absurd! It just does not make sense that I am to feel ashamed by the ridiculous actions of some overbearing, pompous, and foolish lord and his drunken friends," Alaina raised her voice just a bit, rubbing her temples to stave off the impending headache before turning from the window to look at her sister again.

Evelina, who was seated on the nearest couch, averted her gaze. She chose to play with her embroidery instead of meeting her sister's pointed stare. "Alaina, you cannot let yourself be run out of town by some ignoramus. Your books can only provide so much comfort. And, although our acquaintance is limited in London, I am sure you will make fast friends soon. Mama and Papa always have fond stories to tell of their time in London. I am sure your first season here will be no different."

Another pause hung in the air without so much as an acknowledgement from Alaina, before Evelina changed tactics. "Besides, you love to dance!"

"And what if my next dance partner turns out to be just like Lord Finch and his friends? The whole lot of them are just awful!"

Just then, the sisters heard the front door of the townhome open, letting in noise from the street and the lilting voice of their mother, Lady Charlotte Sinclair, Countess of Norwich. As the door closed, both sisters could hear grunts of assent from their father, Edward, as their mother talked without stopping. The subject of the discussion was of little import, just parties and all manner of rumors from the goings-on of the ton.

Edward and Charlotte entered the front parlor, where Charlotte quickly approached her daughters, ceasing her incessant talking to greet them with affectionate hugs and kisses.

"Girls, how wonderful to see you *both* in the parlor," Charlotte proclaimed, sure to give a sidelong glance to Alaina. Her mother had been pestering her for the better part of the week to give up her sulking and rejoin society. From Charlotte's telling, Alaina would think there were friends to be found around every corner in London; this had yet to come true.

"Be careful, Mama, you might scare Alaina back upstairs to hide, or even worse, back to the country," Evelina needled.

"Oh, my darling, people have totally forgotten about that embarrassing display by Lord Finch and his friends." Charlotte gave a reassuring hug to Alaina, only stopping to clasp her shoulders and look into her eyes with motherly affection, a slight frown knitting her brow. Alaina was not one to lack confidence in any scenario, but a London season could be quite intimidating, and this one was proving unusually difficult.

Even though the Sinclair family had arrived early to prepare for the season and to allow Alaina to attend the first few balls in what they thought would be a low-stakes environment, she had been beset on her debut by Lord Finch and his sister, Lady Barbara. What had seemed like normal societal behavior quickly turned into unwanted and cruel attention when Edward turned down Lord Finch's inappropriately timed marriage proposal, just three days into Alaina's first season. After that interaction, it was clear that the Finch family was only out to improve their own status through association with the Earl of Norwich and his newly arrived daughter.

The last embarrassment had come in the form of a mocking proposal from Lord Finch and all his cronies. Through the whole ordeal, the Sinclair family struggled to renew old acquaintances in London; twenty years in the country had isolated them and their daughters. But it seemed to Alaina that London was only an extension of the small-minded society in the country, where women having opinions were shunned, and reading was mocked. Only, in London, you could not easily escape prying eyes. To Alaina's despair, she found that no one other than her family cared to know her for who she was and what she thought. She felt like her only value was as an ornament on whoever's arm would tolerate her.

"Your mother is right," Edward stated, stepping further in the room. "This should be a time of celebration and merriment! Let us forget the past few weeks."

"Oh, Papa, if only it were so easy," Alaina countered.

"At my age, it is easy to forget how tough the London season can be," Edward smiled. Crow's feet at the corners of his eyes told the happy story of his marriage, parenthood, and life. He certainly had made it a point to see the best in most situations, imparting that spirit to his daughters.

Alaina and Evelina briefly regarded their parents. Both of them in that moment wished for the same kind of love and companionship Edward and Charlotte shared; a love that could conquer all of society's ills, whatever they were.

Edward and Charlotte presented quite a pair, Edward's dark hair, eyes, and dazzling smile beautifully contrasted against Charlotte's petite stature and fair coloring. Both parents, even in their middling years, still dressed at the height of fashion and it was easy to see how they may have captured the eyes of the ton in their younger years.

Alaina and Evelina shared much of both their parents' features, presenting a perfect blend of the two; their stature was from their mother, eyes from their father, and their strength of will and character from both.

"Now, if you ladies will excuse me, I have been neglecting our estates' books in town and need to see to those with my steward. I am sure you have much to discuss without me intruding," Edward said, with looks to each of his daughters and finally his wife.

"Bye, dearest," Charlotte chirped, placing a kiss on his lips and gracing Edward with a soft smile.

"Bye, Papa," Alaina and Evelina echoed, as he approached the doorway and disappeared from sight.

"Now, darling, what has you so worried? I am confident you will have a wonderful season and will find love when the time is right." Charlotte turned to Alaina. "The Mansfield Ball tonight is a wonderful place for a fresh start."

Before Alaina could answer, Evelina chimed in, "I think Alaina struggles in leaving the rest of the season to chance. Look at how her debut was set on its head by one buffoon and his awful sister. I mean, I cannot fault her for preferring her books, where characters cannot jump off the page and change the course of one's life."

A faint chuckle escaped Alaina before she responded, "That is about right. Why are young ladies so at the mercy of society's dictates and men's attentions?"

Charlotte paused for a moment before answering. "It may be that a lady has to appear to be at the whim of men and society, but we are not *totally* powerless. Besides, even the best men need a little nudge in the right direction. Your father was certainly enamored with me, but he did not have a mind for marriage at the time. It was lucky I was able to nudge him toward what was best for both of us."

"Well, how do you suppose I nudge *all* of society? After the start I have had, I would be surprised if anyone would want to be associated with me," Alaina countered with a huff.

"Not all of society, dearest, we just need to attract the attention of someone specific, a gentleman who is eligible and from a good family. Honestly, every family makes their own machinations to that end. It would seem your father and I forgot what London was like, you must forgive us. This season in London has only served to remind me why we spend most of our time in the country, away from the barbarism of a select few," Charlotte stated simply, with a shrug of her shoulders.

Evelina inserted herself with a mischievous grin. "I may have an idea. Now, I know you have a dislike of any perceived manipulation of events, but what I am thinking may work."

Alaina fidgeted uncomfortably under her sister's regard, and did not feel much better when she turned her attention to her mother, who was also smiling. "Ok, so what does this plan entail?"

"Well, I hear the Duke of Ashford is in town for the season, and he is looking for a wife. Apparently, he finds it time to settle down, which makes him motivated to take a wife. As an earl's daughter, you might be able to gain his favor," Evelina rattled, her voice reaching a high pitch of excitement. "Besides, the gossip papers are usually unkind, but he gets high marks all around, especially in the looks category. That includes being kind-hearted."

"I do not see how I would ever hope to garner such attention; it seems I only attract the men who are toads," countered Alaina, chewing her lip before continuing. "And it all seems a little underhanded to me, fixing my attention and designs on one who *is* truly looking for a match, when I am just trying to avoid the next embarrassment."

"Oh, pish posh!" Charlotte exclaimed, "You *are* looking for a match. *You* just think you will stumble into a love match without any work." Charlotte paused only to hold up her hand to stay her eldest daughter. Alaina's mouth clamped shut. "And why should that match not be one of your choosing?" Charlotte asked.

Evelina shook her head slightly, as if to disagree with her mother, and took a different tact. "You want to have fun, right? Dance? Laugh? Avoid any potential Lord Finch imposters?" Evelina questioned, a giggle of affection barely contained.

"Yes, I do," Alaina said, her voice small, with a slight nod of her head, barely one of assent.

"Well then, it seems we have a target, as it were. Now to teach you how to be subtle, aloof, and charming all at the same time. Time to put your opinions aside, just for the time being. Are you ready?" Evelina inquired, already ten steps ahead in planning.

Alaina groaned, briefly wondering if her family's machinations would make the whole of her season better or worse.

Christopher squinted into the sunlight streaming through the trees in an effort to see the person at bat next in cricket. He was also unsuccessfully trying to avoid the pestering, bordering on heckling, of his best friend, the Duke of Ashford.

"Why can you not attend the Mansfield Ball this evening?" Graham Wallace, the Duke of Ashford, almost yelled across the clearing, breaking Christopher's concentration on the game. Graham looked too pleased with himself for the timing of the question to be ignored. He smiled rakishly, his straight, white teeth glinting in the sunlight. Tanned, clear, and radiant, his handsome face was ever so slightly smug as he taunted his friend to distract him, the two men on opposing sides. His garb was well-tailored and stylish, but partly discarded or in disarray because of the game at hand, his jacket left on some bench close by, his white sleeves rolled up even in the cool air of the day, his snug tan breeches tucked into worn, but still perfectly polished, riding boots. If they had not been friends since Eton, Christopher may have been jealous of Graham's perfect good looks, money, and confidence.

Christopher Kendall, the Marquess of Rochester, straightened in exasperation and regarded Graham, who was standing ever so slightly off the pitch line. "You know I hate social gatherings. I have no wish to even be *rumored* to be attached to a young miss, let alone converse with those who would wish for such an occurrence. Also, as a duke you should have no trouble garnering the attention of any lady of your choosing in your quest to find a wife; I don't know why you feel you need me there accompanying you on your foolhardy mission."

"What is it? Are you senselessly committed to bachelorhood? As for me, the mission is not foolhardy, as you describe it. Everyone needs an heir, and why should I not be in search of a comely wife while I am still young and handsome enough to snag one who would actually not detest my advances and want me only for my money? You should consider that, my friend. We are not getting any younger. I am truly surprised," Graham continued, his hand on his chest as if truly wounded. "After all our time as friends, and all the holidays spent at Ashford with my family. You would think I would get a bit more enthusiasm when I asked you for a small favor." Graham beamed with a glitter of mischief in his eye.

Graham's needling garnered no response from Christopher. He certainly would not let his friend know how close he had come to the truth; after watching his own parents, Christopher was convinced marriage was not for him. In his opinion, it was easier to fall into a bad union than a good one. For now, he could ignore the implications of not having an heir, something that seemed to bother his friend much more.

"Will you pitch already?" Ned, the next up in cricket, hit his bat on the ground before once again resuming the proper stance, tearing both men from their conversation and back to the game at hand. Christopher turned toward the batter, prepared, and let the ball fly, only partially committing to the game as he weighed his friend's request. His pitch was easily fielded by Ned, allowing the other team to score, and Christopher grit his teeth in frustration.

"Come now, Christopher. You will be at the Mansfield Ball to provide support. Everyone knows I am seeking a wife since those damn gossip papers published my courtship with Lady Bella last season. Everyone assumes I am even more determined this season to find a wife. No one will care a whit about what you do, as long as you do not show any prolonged interest in a lady." Graham was proving relentless.

Christopher ran his fingers through his strawberry blonde hair, almost golden in the afternoon sun, and squeezed his clear blue eyes shut against the brightness and the impending doom of attending yet another high society social gathering. Christopher was similarly dressed to his friend, his navy-blue coat still on, tapering to his waist, where breeches of the same color hugged his hips and thighs until they disappeared into brown riding boots, worn from use, like Graham's.

He straightened his tall, broad shouldered and athletic frame, coming to terms with the fact that Graham was going to wheedle yet another season of playing the extra wheel out of him. It was in Christopher's mind that he should have turned down the welcoming arms of Graham's family all those years ago at Eton. If he had done so, he would not have to deal with all the simpering belles of the ball and their meddling relatives intent on a match. He would not be convinced or tricked into marriage by anyone when all it would lead to was a life of unhappiness. Seeing his parents destroyed by a loveless marriage had done much to convince him.

"I will attend this ball," Christopher acquiesced, pointing at his friend. "But if I am beset by ladies and their parents this evening, you will need to convince someone else to ensure you are not courting the season's worst fortune hunter."

"That is all I ask," Graham said, putting his hands up in mock surrender and looking supremely pleased. They had been friends for a long time, and through all that time, Graham had always been self-assured, in part due to his impending dukedom, and in part because he was just that confident. Christopher was the only one of his friends who occasionally did not fall over themselves to do the duke's bidding. It appeared that, this time, he had failed in that regard.

Christopher was dreading the upcoming Mansfield Ball, but more immediately, he was regretting his upcoming loss in cricket. Stubborn and competitive almost to a fault, he concentrated on the matter at hand. Graham may have just convinced him to spend yet another evening out in society against his will, but he was not going to lose at *cricket*.

Winding up the pitch, Christopher put his whole force behind the throw, intending to have Graham beg off and not even make a swing. However, Graham was equally competitive, which usually worked to their collective advantage. Graham swung with all his might, sending the ball careening toward Christopher too quickly for him to react appropriately. The ball struck his eye, knocking him to the ground. Christopher first wondered if this would get him out of the ball this evening, before succumbing to the impending darkness.

At some point, not too much later by Christopher's estimation, as the sun was in approximately the same spot, he opened his eyes to find all his friends, including Graham, leaning over him in a rather tight circle.

"Please accept my sincerest apologies," Graham said, looking sheepish, if still a bit amused.

"I think it was the fall backward," someone chimed in from the back of the crowd of faces staring down at him. Graham rolled his eyes heavenward as if to communicate that such a statement was idiotic. Putting out his hand, Graham helped Christopher to his feet.

Christopher touched just above his eye where the ball had hit and felt a stickiness that could only be blood. From what he could tell, he had a nasty gash, but no swelling, thankfully. A cold compress should stop the bleeding and then he should be as good as new, if a bit ghastly looking.

"Well, I think that means the cricket match is over then chaps," Christopher stated flatly. The crowd of gentlemen dispersed rather quickly, leaving the two friends to regard one another in the midday light.

After some stilted silence, Graham queried, "Do you wish to nurse your eye this evening?"

Christopher raised both his eyebrows, a quick sting reminding him of the cut. "Are you saying you would relieve me of my duty to your family? After all your caterwauling?"

Graham looked a bit sheepish. "I was hoping to have your company, but seeing as I just sent a pitch directly at your head, I would understand if you swore me off for the whole season."

Christopher sighed. "Graham, you have the strangest ways of convincing people to do as you please. Despite the seemingly minor injury to my eye, I did give you my word."

A grin broke out on the duke's face, and he seemed to take Christopher's last statement as an affirmative answer. "I was thinking of arriving at Mansfield House this evening around half nine, would that work for you? I would offer to send my coach to pick you up, but I figure you will want your own transportation in case you are swarmed by a hoard of lovely young ladies."

"I do believe I can find my own way to the ball, and having my own escape route would be preferred," Christopher stated as he regarded his friend with a fair amount of incredulity.

"Come now, your eye will all but guarantee people, especially the young ladies, will avoid vexing you," Graham chuckled.

Christopher rolled his eyes. "How could I say no to such a good friend, especially if the future of his family is at stake," he replied. "But, if I should have to entertain any questions about my eye, I shall take them to task before I come for your hide."

Chapter 2

Alaina swayed to the music, finding the tune irresistible even as her palms, ensconced in her gloves, dampened. She inwardly strived to keep a furrow from her brow. The crystals of her midnight dress sparkled in the candlelight of the ball. Her curls, piled high on her head, kept time with the small orchestra. She looked out over the dance floor and took a deep breath, hoping that her appearance looked serene, despite the rapid beating of her heart.

Despite all the reassurances from her mother and sister this afternoon and their supposed fool-proof plan, Alaina was nervous. Yet, she found it difficult to shake the feeling of hope. The feeling that something serendipitous was in the air this evening. Alaina turned back toward the refreshment table and tried to look interested in the various treats. Refusing to take yet another glass of lemonade, lest she be in the ladies retiring room by half nine, Alaina feigned being in search of something as she moved down the length of the table and back again before looking once more at the door.

Maintaining an eye on the door, but trying to seem aloof at the same time, Alaina caught an awkward stumble coming toward her. She barely side-stepped the man's bumbling approach and her quick action nearly caused her to topple the whole refreshment table. Alaina gave a quick sigh of relief when she only gave the table a gentle bump, setting the glasses and dishes on the table to shaking, but her solace was temporary. This *gentleman*, if he even warranted the title, had clearly been drinking too much before his arrival and had almost caused the both of them to be covered in foodstuffs. *Would the foolishness and bad luck of this season never end?*

Thankfully, the gentlemen halted just short of the table and seemed to go about his business without a care. It was Lord Finch's drunken display and her lack of action, not far from her mind, that gave her the courage to confront this latest buffoon. Alaina refused to be forbearing with yet another fool!

"Usually, a person can wait until arriving at a ball to partake in *libations*," Alaina gritted through her teeth, loud enough that she was sure the man could hear. "There are always plenty supplied at these sorts of functions, if you are capable of waiting. And you run less risk of embarrassing yourself or others."

The target of Alaina's remark seemed to only partially acknowledge her statement, a grunt escaping him as he continued to look at the spread of snacks, finally settling on a small, candied fruit and popping it unceremoniously in his mouth. Not to be ignored, Alaina stomped her slippered foot in an unladylike manner.

The gentleman finally turned to face her, and Alaina was taken aback by the steel-blue eyes that pierced her as if they were made of ice, a small cut marring his otherwise perfect brow.

"Pardon my uncoordinated approach, my lady. I assure you I would never tip the table and ruin your *beautiful* dress." The quip seemed to insult and compliment at the same time; Alaina could not be sure.

Alaina's initial anger turned to shock as she made note of the man's crisp speech, one certainly not marred by drink. The about-face in her perception caused her words to tumble from her mouth with little thought. "I was just worried that… Well, what I mean is…"

The man's eyes swept the length of Alaina, as if finally assessing the person before him, while he pressed her to finish her thought. "What? Were you worried I was already in my cups? That I am a drunk? I assure you I just slipped a bit on the floor. I am not usually so clumsy."

There was something about the man, a challenge in his eyes maybe, that compelled Alaina to speak before he could turn away. Unfortunately, she could not find an appropriate topic and her mouth outpaced her mind. "I am sure you have quite the story with your eye."

"Pardon?" the gentleman countered, taking an ominous step toward her. Alaina immediately regretted her statement, wishing to fall in upon herself as his glacial eyes once again stared at her with enough intensity to freeze her in place. Alaina was taken aback by his height, finding it difficult to not tip backward to meet his eye in the crowded ballroom.

He was impeccably dressed, his dark gray coat and breeches tucked into tall black boots, contrasting with a silver waistcoat, white shirt, and cravat. Alaina could see that everything was expertly tailored, his coat tapering to his perfectly flat stomach, and his breeches hugging his narrow hips enough to make Alaina feel the color rising in her cheeks.

Alaina cleared her throat as she searched for her next words, coming up with only a measly reiteration of her question before remembering herself. "Your eye? I do apologize, sir. I did not mean to offend."

A chuckle escaped the gentleman's lips, as if in disbelief at having to converse with her, and he promptly set her upon her heels. "Is that your idea of polite conversation?"

"Y-es, I mean no, not really. It is just that it looks like it hurt," Alaina stammered, standing as tall as she could manage, only barely making it to his shoulder. She refused to yield any ground, even if she could not find her voice.

The man's eyes narrowed, and it felt to Alaina that many moments passed before he spoke once more. "And I bet you are curious as to how I came by the injury. It seems like your curiosity got the best of your manners."

Alaina's disbelief at his directness caused her mouth to drop open, and she was rendered momentarily speechless. *He was lecturing her!*

The man crossed his arms across his chest, and leaned in a bit, as if to make sure she heard him. "You know the saying: curiosity killed the cat."

Alaina felt warmth rise to the tips of her ears and she regretted ever opening her mouth, but then she noticed a twinkle settled in his eyes as a quick chuckle escaped his lips. He was laughing at her, or the situation. Either way, his reaction perturbed her, and she snapped, "What has you so amused?"

The man's voice belied the twinkle in his eyes. "Who says I am amused?"

"W-well," Alaina started timidly, before she squared her shoulders and pressed on. "I cannot say if you are or not, but it is my usual experience that laughter indicates pleasure in something."

Now the gentleman let out a more full-bodied laugh. "I fear pleasure and amusement are two separate concepts, at least in my mind."

Alaina's brow furrowed as she mulled his last statement. The man's eyes darkened as they stood in silence, and Alaina's confusion deepened. Alaina opened her mouth but was stayed by a familiar voice.

"Yoo hoo! Alaina, darling, I simply must introduce you to someone."

Alaina saw her mother fast approaching, her rich amethyst gown shimmering as she made her way through the crowd. She was joined by a stately lady, petite with lustrous ebony hair and alabaster skin, setting off her stylish silver dress. She glanced back at the gentleman and saw he was calmly waiting as if to continue their repartee, or possibly just to observe the upcoming introduction.

Alas, it was time to greet the new arrivals, and she plastered a pinched smile on her face. "Mother, how delightful for you to join me. I thought you would be enjoying your time with the other chaperones."

"My dear, as the ballroom got more crowded, you appeared as though you might be swallowed up at any moment." Charlotte looked askance at the gentleman. "Not to mention, I have met the most wonderful and interesting woman, and I thought I should introduce you."

Turning to her new companion, Alaina's mother continued, "This is the Dowager Duchess of Ashford."

Alaina felt a flicker of disbelief cross her face, but quickly bowed her head and executed a graceful curtsy, hoping her quick motion covered her face and emotions. How had her mother even found the dowager at the ball, let alone garnered an introduction? "It is wonderful to make your acquaintance, your grace."

The dowager quickly took both of Alaina's hands in her own, stepping closer and leaning in as if they were old friends. "Please, my dear, as I have already told your mother, you must call me Eleanor. I am not one to stand on ceremony with people, as long as I like them. Your mother and I were just getting equally bored sitting with the old biddies over there and we struck up a conversation. I just had to meet her daughter as well."

"As you wish, Eleanor. I would be honored if you would do the same; please call me Alaina."

"Your mother tells me your initial foray into society has been *eventful*. Lord Finch making such a fool of himself, and his sister egging him on like that? There are some in society whose manners are lacking," Eleanor paused, giving Charlotte and then Alaina an exasperated look. Alaina heard a scoff from the man behind her and felt insulted once more that he would include her in that group of ill-mannered lackwits. It was all she could do not to turn and glare at the gentleman.

Without giving Alaina or Charlotte time to respond, Eleanor continued. "Never fear, my dear. After the first few weeks of the season, gentlemen with more decorum tend to grace us, and the riffraff find themselves at the gaming tables instead of the ballroom."

Alaina was about to respond when, unexpectedly, the dowager duchess peered past her and addressed the gentlemen who had been Alaina's verbal sparring partner. "Christopher, where is my son off to? I had expected you both to be strutting around the ballroom together like a pair of peacocks."

Alaina's eyes widened as she suppressed a groan of embarrassment. *She had been sparring with the Duke of Ashford's friend!*

"How rude of me," Eleanor quickly course-corrected. "Alaina, I know you and Christopher were speaking when your mother and I joined you, but I doubt you have been properly introduced; Christopher is not one for such formalities. May I present Christopher, the Marquess of Rochester. Christopher, this is Lady Alaina Sinclair, the Earl of Norwich's daughter, newly arrived from their country seat for the season."

Alaina was glad the lighting in the ballroom was low, because her discomfiture was acute. Alaina felt a raw heat suffuse her whole body, hidden beneath the midnight hem of her dress, all the way to the crown of her head. She hoped the marquess did not notice; it would not do to have him report back to the duke on her actions. Her skin tingled with embarrassment as she met Christopher's eyes to acknowledge the introduction. *What a blunder!* This man was the duke's friend, and they had been practically at each other's throats.

"Nice to make your *formal* acquaintance, my lady," Christopher rejoined.

"And you as well, my lord," Alaina choked out what she hoped to be a graceful response.

Turning his attention back to the dowager duchess, Christopher answered her earlier question. "Eleanor, your son left me to fend for myself just after we arrived. I am sure he will be with us shortly." Christopher finished his answer and moved his regard back to Alaina.

Still embarrassed by their unfinished argument, Alaina had trouble finding her tongue. Just when she thought she might burst from mortification and rattle off something about how the weather had been so pleasant today, there was a commotion to their right. A tall, dark-haired man approached through the crowd, his all-black ensemble only broken by his white shirt and cravat, tailored to show his tall and slim frame. Based on the amount of attention he attracted just by walking through the crowd, Alaina guessed him to be the Duke of Ashford. When he quickly approached the dowager duchess, placing a peck on her cheek, any remaining doubt was erased.

"Mother, how pleasant to see you at this ball. You should have told me you were going to be here; I would have escorted you." A quick nod to Christopher and a sheepish smile seemed to convey an apology, though Alaina could not fathom for what.

"Nonsense, darling, I can make my own way to these events. How am I to catch up on the latest happenings if I am linked to you all evening?" Eleanor seemed like she would have been tickled by the duke's escort, but Alaina had little time to consider this. "May I present to you Lady Alaina, the daughter of the Earl of Norwich, and her mother, the Countess of Norwich."

The dowager motioned to both Alaina and her mother. The Duke of Ashford's eyes lit up as he casually swept Alaina's person. Alaina felt herself blush at his perusal and was captured by his rakish smile. The duke's height rivaled that of the marquess, and Alaina found her eyes drawn to both.

"A pleasure, ladies," the duke addressed both of them, keeping his eyes fixed on Alaina as he executed a very courtly and graceful bow for their benefit. Alaina and her mother returned his sentiments and curtsied to complete the circle's formal introductions.

Alaina was unsure of just how to continue. She looked amongst her companions and found the duke and marquess studying her with different looks. There was a glean in the duke's eyes that was calculated and sure, at ease with the situation. However, Alaina felt equally drawn to acknowledge and continue her exchange with Christopher. Breaking the connection with the duke, she glanced toward the marquess, who seemed to be brooding or wary, Alaina couldn't quite tell.

Seeing her attention drawn in a different direction, the duke glanced to his side to find his friend intently staring at Lady Alaina.

"Christopher? Do you know Lady Alaina?"

"Yes, but not much longer than you," came the marquess's smooth reply. "We were engaged in quite a tête-à-tête before your mother and the countess arrived to rescue her."

The duke's brow furrowed slightly as he looked between the two, barely missing the quick glare that Alaina tossed Christopher's way.

A gentle throat clearing broke the silence as Eleanor entered the fray once more. "Graham, darling, do you not think that it is time to liven up the party with a bit of dancing?"

The duke stared blankly at his mother for a moment or two longer than Alaina thought would be required to grasp his mother's meaning, before he turned to her and executed a crisp bow once more. "Lady Alaina, would you do me the honor of the next dance? That is if it is not already spoken for by someone else."

Alaina pointedly ignored the marquess as she smiled a bit too brightly toward the duke. "There is no one else, your grace, and I would be most honored to be your partner for the next dance."

"Well then," the duke said, presenting his arm to Alaina, "Shall we line up with the other couples?"

Alaina placed her hand on the duke's proffered arm and did not even glance in the marquess's direction as they passed him on their way to the dance floor. She would worry about the marquess later; it was time to impress the duke.

Chapter 3

Being swept around the ballroom in a waltz had its advantages. Alaina tried to focus on her partner. The first dance with the duke had been marvelous, but almost the entire time, she felt the weight of the marquess's stare. Alaina could imagine him brooding in displeasure at the edge of the ballroom, lying in wait to flay her for her rudeness. And yet at every glance, his eyes were never in her direction. The duke was gracious and kind, and seemed to be genuinely interested in what she had to say — or was that just wishful thinking? *Yes, a waltz allowed her to avoid looking toward the marquess too often.*

"I do hope you like to ride?" The question from the duke brought her back from her thoughts. Looking up at such close range was just as difficult with the duke as it was with the marquess, but she managed to glance up and reply to his question without too much pause.

"Actually, my sister is the more accomplished equestrienne. I know the basics, of course, although Evelina always mentions that I look almost petrified every ride." Alaina saw no point in being coy; riding was certainly not her favorite past-time, but it was a good way to spend time outdoors with her sister.

"Oh," Graham cocked an eyebrow. "Well, perhaps you could join me for an easy ride in Hyde Park. We could just enjoy the sunshine and the company. My sister could join us. She loves to ride, is married, and would provide a proper chaperone."

"That sounds very nice, as long as you understand that my lack of riding skills is not false modesty on my part, your grace." Alaina looked into the duke's eyes and saw a twinkle; clearly, he had a kind heart. He was handsome and seemed to enjoy real conversation.

"Of course, my lady. I do not think you are the type of person to put on airs. It is quite refreshing." The duke smiled and Alaina felt a little flutter in her heart.

The music ended as Alaina and the duke completed one last turn around the ballroom. Each of them stepped back to acknowledge the end of the dance with a bow and curtsy, right near the mothers and the marquess. Graham looked upon Lady Alaina with a broad smile, one that reached his eyes. Lady Alaina, suddenly faced with such interest and the presence of the marquess, averted her gaze and gave the duke a timid smile. As the duke led them completely off the dance floor toward her mother's side, he quietly commented, "It would be uncouth for me to request yet another dance this evening, but I hope to call on you tomorrow?"

Alaina glanced to catch his eyes, so dark and yet so earnest. "Of course, a call tomorrow would be most lovely. I expect you know where the Norwich townhome is?"

"My mother certainly does, whether before this evening, or through her conversations with your mother." They had arrived at their party, and the duke passed one last sparkling smile to Alaina before delivering her to Charlotte and joining his own mother.

"What a marvelous couple you two make," Eleanor beamed.

"I most heartily agree," Charlotte emphatically answered. Alaina's mother was not one to gush, but apparently herself and the dowager had made the decision to become family over the course of just two dances. "Do you not agree, my lord?" This time she was addressing the marquess.

"They do make a handsome couple, very much in sync during the dance," Christopher responded. The marquess paused as if to ruminate on some thought, and then said, "They most assuredly cannot dance anymore this evening without tongues wagging, but I would be honored with the next dance, Lady Alaina."

Christopher turned to Alaina, meeting her questioning eyes with almost a dare, as he held out his arm in supplication.

Alaina met the marquess's eyes, wary of his intent. If their argument before was anything of an indicator, it might be best to limit their interactions lest the marquess take tales of her poor temper to the duke. However, as she looked around the group in an effort to forestall such an event, she found no excuse ready on her tongue.

"I would be honored with the next dance, my lord," Alaina responded, her voice small and flat, as she tried to present a calm, uninterested demeanor. Her hand found his arm, and the marquess led her onto the dance floor.

Just before Christopher left Alaina to the line of ladies to start the contradance, he leaned in and his breath tickled her ear. "It was cricket."

Alaina, confused by the statement, did not say anything until their first turn together. "What was cricket?"

"The eye," the marquess quickly replied. "You seemed rather curious about my injury, I thought I would enlighten you."

A few moments passed as each of them made their way in between other couples, before they could converse again.

"And here I thought it was none of my business," Alaina remarked, as her face remained placid.

"Technically, it is not your business, but I could not have you thinking I got into a brawl," Christopher started, a line of couples walking between them. "Forgive me if my reaction seemed rude. You see, I had just been called out by someone who suspected I already had imbibed more than enough for the evening, and that was after a friend dragged me to this affair after a run-in with a cricket ball."

"And that gave you license to insult someone you did not know in the least?" Alaina responded, a little louder than intended.

"I was just pointing out the obvious," Christopher countered. "You *were* being rude."

"And you think the way to counter a perceived slight is with a real one?" Alaina bit out acridly.

"Perceived? You called me a drunk and then noted my unsightly appearance," Christopher growled.

Alaina and Christopher had stopped almost nose-to-nose in the center of the aisle, and both quickly realized that they were blocking the procession of couples. Stepping back into their places once more, Alaina tried to assess the marquess's implacability, his furrowed brow a clear indication of his continued morose mood.

Christopher continued the dance in silence, presenting his arm as required for their own procession down the aisle of couples, and Alaina could see a muscle work in his jaw before he finally spoke. "I fear, my lady, that we find ourselves at an impasse. As it is not necessary for the dance, shall we avoid speaking to one another further?"

Worried that if she denied his olive branch, the marquess would ruin her chances with the duke, Alaina cautiously accepted. "You have a deal, I shall try and enjoy the rest of the dance, but I shall trouble you no further lest I be subjected once more to your forthright *observations*."

⁎

Leading Lady Alaina through the dance had a heady effect on Christopher. Just moments ago, he had been ready to flay her for even talking to him, so loathe was he to even be in this insipid place, but it was a rare lady who chose to stand toe-to-toe with him when he was in such a mood. Her spunk in that moment had been enough to keep his attention fixed upon her, convinced at the next opportunity *he* would finish what *she* had started. But, as he watched Graham dance with Lady Alaina, taking care not to stare, he was surprised to see vivacious smiles and easy laughter, when she had practically scowled at him only a few moments earlier. It was in his mind that the lady may be yet another two-faced fortune hunter, and one who had accidentally exposed her true colors to someone deemed less than eligible.

And now that he had a moment with the lady, he had bungled his attempt to learn the truth of her character. He had been unable to put aside his personal compulsion to spar with the lady, and he had gleaned no useful information to aid his friend. It would be easy to assess her as an ill-tempered shrew by their interactions, certainly, but he had been hesitant to fight with Alaina, and brash in his offer of silence. Now, Christopher would never figure out more about her character to protect his friend.

Casting a glance to his right, keeping his eyes guarded, he looked over Alaina with curiosity. Obviously, this lady had many facets: impertinence, unease, the ability to beguile his friend. The question was, which one was real?

Glancing quickly over his shoulder, he caught the duke regarding Lady Alaina with a similar curiosity. Christopher just hoped that his friend was not blinded by her beauty. Her looks were to be admired, but both of them had dealt with their fair share of empty-headed or ladder-climbing ladies. There was no guarantee she did not fit into either category, regardless of Charlotte and Eleanor's new friendship. It was often the mothers who foisted their deficient daughters upon an unexpecting gentleman.

Christopher and Lady Alaina once again found themselves in the starting position of the contradance. *What a shame it was not a waltz, so he could be closer to Alaina,* he could not help but think, the wish coming from a dark recess of his mind.

Meeting Alaina's eyes, Christopher could not help but admire her vibrance despite everything that had transpired. Alaina nearly dazzled, her eyes twinkling in the candlelight of the room. Christopher could tell she loved to dance, her grace unmatched in the currently dancing couples.

Christopher escorted her a few steps down the aisle of dancers, in accordance with the steps of the dance. Still having found no further words to speak, he was surprised by the reaction of his gut to this small slip of a woman, his mind fighting his body as he tried to recall their uncomfortable interactions. *He was here to help his friend root out any bad apples. Besides,* Christopher reminded himself, *he had no desire to get married in the least.*

One final turn in the dance brought Christopher and Alaina face-to-face. Christopher met her eyes, seeing a shift in their dark depths, one that did not speak of anger, and he was left with a sense of wonder. But just as quickly, she glanced away, and he lost the window to her soul, leaving him with a sense of disappointment. Never had he felt the need or desire to see what thoughts lay beyond a lady's eyes until he had laid eyes upon Lady Alaina.

Well, this would certainly not do. Time to keep himself focused on the task at hand, finding his best friend a good match. It would be better if anger had remained in the place of whatever else he had just felt. Christopher mentally shook himself from his reverie and made the gracious step forward to receive Alaina and see her back to her mother. *It was time to make an exit.*

———✦———

A jostle in the carriage brought Christopher back around to the conversation at hand.

"It seems that you did not need an escape after all, my friend," Graham commented, earning only a non-committal grunt from Christopher.

"Well, what do you think?" Graham seemed to be on edge, regarding his friend with an intense stare. Christopher had never seen him in such a fervor over a lady. Lady Alaina must have made quite an impression.

They were headed to White's, their favored gentlemen's club, for the rest of the evening. Graham, having apparently found the only young lady he was going to pursue, at least at this point in the season, orchestrated a quick exit from the ball, much to Christopher's delight.

"Well?" Graham asked once more, Christopher's rumination having kept him from answering in a timely manner.

"I must admit she is beautiful," Christopher said. "But…"

"I was expecting that," Graham interjected, a flippant quality to his voice. "And that is why I just have to bring you along."

Christopher rolled his eyes. "But you barely know her! Do you even know anything about her family? I have heard nothing of them. And besides, she was very uncouth."

"Uncouth how?" the duke chuckled, doubtful of his friend's assessment.

"Well, if you must know, she made mention of my eye," Christopher admitted, feeling foolish even as he said the words.

A barking laugh escaped Graham. "And here I thought the eye would keep the ladies from talking to you at all. Turns out it was a conversation starter."

"Stop making light," Christopher stated. "I know she was all smiles and laughter with you, but she was quite cross with me."

"And I am sure it had nothing to do with your behavior?"

Christopher was quiet at that.

"I suspect her anger may have been provoked," Graham continued through the silence. "Well, you have never had my charm."

Christopher felt sufficiently needled, and attempted to change the subject. "But you still do not know much of her family."

Graham shrugged. "Not hearing about someone prior to the social season is usually a mark in their favor."

Nothing more was said between the gentlemen. Christopher deemed his friend impervious to advice, no matter what he claimed, once he set his mind on something; this seemed to be one such case. Maybe it would get Christopher out of any more social outings this season.

The carriage stopped outside of their club, and both Christopher and Graham hopped down, carrying their hats casually. As they entered the front door, they were met with another din of noise, one not so different from the ball in volume, but certainly different in character. The club was loud, filled with smoke and the smell of whiskey – an atmosphere ripe for the debauchery of the late hour.

Usually, Christopher found this type of scene calming and comfortable. With the type of crazed activity occurring, he could simply fade into the background and be left to his thoughts. He had never been one to have difficulty tuning out the world around him, that was, as long as it did not involve him directly. This evening, however, the sense of familiarity and calm was elusive. He could not help but think of a pair of brown eyes dancing with amusement in the candlelight, luminous skin showing a hint of rising color as she talked, the quiet strains of a waltz playing in the background, while a certain young lady danced around the room, smiling up at… *his friend.*

Christopher shook himself, this time adding a physical flourish, to change the track of his mind. It would not do to be distracted by the lady's beauty; Graham had brought him along to determine her character, and the suitability of her family.

"Shall we head to the back, possibly find a quieter corner?" Christopher suggested. The duke could only nod his assent, since the noise in the room was enough for Christopher to have to yell, and still barely be heard.

As the two moved through a series of rooms, each with shelves of books, some with gaming tables, and some with groups of women entertaining gentlemen with laughs and more, they slowly made their way toward the back of the club. Finally, they were able to find a room, smaller than the rest, at the far corner of the building, only half-filled with people and smoke. It was quiet enough to hear a companion talk.

Christopher and Graham took seats by a window overlooking the back alley and motioned to the nearest server for two drinks.

"I have another favor to ask of you," Graham started, as two cut crystal glasses were put on the table. Christopher assumed the brown liquid sloshing in each was brandy, and was happy when a decanter of the same was placed on the table.

Taking a sip of the liquid and finding it to be his preferred drink, Christopher sat back and warily eyed his friend. "The last time you asked a favor, I was embarrassed to be the fifth wheel in your matchmaking scheme, which you were sure would require my assistance. During the course of the evening, I determined you need no such help."

"I most certainly do. You are my voice of reason! Look what happened last season with Lady Bella."

"You mean when you dragged me about with the same purpose as this season, and then refused to listen when I told you Lady Bella was merely feigning interest in order to make the true object of her affections jealous enough to propose? Ah, yes, I can see how I am your source of reason."

"But I have certainly learned my lesson. I promise to take your advice this season," Graham gave his friend an amused half-smile, mirth showing in his eyes, and waved his hand as if to wipe away the current subject. "Actually, the favor I ask is almost just a continuation of the last. I would like you to accompany my sister and me to call on Lady Alaina and her family tomorrow."

"Why would you need me to do that? I am not a suitable chaperone, and it sounds like you have some agreement with your sister to help you in that manner, considering you are bringing her along. I would again just be the odd one out." Christopher really just wanted to take a day to wipe Lady Alaina's eyes from his memory so he could be the support his friend needed to make a match.

"Nonsense! You and my sister could provide company for one another. Besides, after my cousin Percy caused a ruckus at my country estate over the holiday season, my sister's husband has been loath to have her out and about without additional escorts while he is in the country. I feel like between the two of us, we can quell his concern without drawing too much attention." Graham seemed distracted for the moment, looking at his glass of half-finished brandy.

"What did your cousin do exactly? I do not think you ever filled me in on the details, just that he has made it clear that he is happy to be next in line for the dukedom, but annoyed to not be *the* duke." Christopher had been trying to get these details from his friend running up to the start of the season, since of course this was one of the main reasons to be taking a wife. Graham needed to produce an heir to the dukedom, or many of them, to ensure his family's holdings did not fall into his squandering cousin's hands. Christopher had met Perceval Wallace, or Baron Wallace, on a few occasions while they had all been at Oxford together. His cousin was a year or so older than Graham, but being the heir to a second son of a duke meant he was always second best, or at least felt it. Percy's father had been given a generous living, even for a second son, but made nothing of it, and died early, leaving Percy with his many gambling debts and a household in shambles. Percy had made it clear that he was jealous of the ease that Graham found in life, but Christopher was surprised at how malignant the jealousy had become over the years. It had been nearly a decade since they had all graduated, and Percy seemed to be doing well in society from all appearances.

Graham took a deep breath and sighed. "It was Christmastime, and as you know, we usually host a grand party at our country estate, with a small family gathering prior to the event to allow for ample time to catch up. My mother is not one to leave family off the list and let the gossipmongers speculate on the state of affairs for the family, so I acquiesced to inviting everyone, and that included Percy, who acted most horridly."

"But it is not unusual that Percy is unpleasant. That happens every year," Christopher interjected.

"Well, you would feel differently if you had been there. It was different from other years, more…"

The sound of a clearing throat interrupted Graham, and both men turned to see who had intruded on their conversation.

"Charles!" exclaimed Christopher. He rose from his chair to clasp his own cousin in a hug.

Graham paused for a moment before he too rose to greet his friend's cousin. "Charles, fancy meeting you here." The duke's voice was flat.

The newcomer, an equally tall but lankier version of Christopher, returned their greetings. "Christopher, your grace, it is nice to see you both."

A silence hung in the air, but Christopher was quick to fill it, motioning for his cousin to take a seat in the remaining chair in their corner. "Charles, I did not realize you were in town for the season. You should have sent word."

"Well, dear cousin, I could say the same," Charles teased. "I am surprised to see you here for the season, and out in society it seems. I wonder if you have found it time to take a wife."

At this, Graham piped up. "Well, he is not really looking for himself; I am in need of his cynicism as I venture into the game of matrimony."

"But what he fails to mention is that even if I offer advice, he would not take it," Christopher rejoined, shooting his friend a pointed look.

"Of course I would. I need your guidance. Who else would tell me I should be wary of the most beautiful and charming lady at the ball?"

"Like I said, you know nothing of her family!"

"It is just because she dared talk to you," Graham countered. "And she mentioned your injury. I forgot to ask, did you have to tell her how you got it?"

Charles cut in. "Wait, wait, whose family? And I was wondering what happened to your eye, but I thought it rude to mention."

"See?" Christopher remarked, thankful to prove his point. "Charles thinks it uncouth."

"You need to let it go," Graham replied. "She was probably just concerned. I found Lady Alaina quite charming."

"Lady Alaina?" Charles asked, trying to keep up with the conversation.

"Daughter to the Earl of Norwich," Christopher answered quickly. "But Graham is smitten and nothing I say will deter him, so we can change the subject. How are things with you this season, Charles?"

Charles seemed surprised to have the conversation turn to him so quickly. "I am in town on business. Seems that even when you have people to manage things for you, every so often a shipment or two of goods requires my personal attention."

"Ah, yes," Graham interrupted. "Christopher had mentioned you were making a good turn at becoming a successful merchant. What is it that you trade?"

"Mostly spices and silks," Charles answered, adjusting his cravat as he settled into the chair a bit more. A server came by with an empty glass for Charles.

"No trouble, I hope?" Christopher inquired.

Charles cleared his throat and squirmed in his seat, but answered smoothly. "No issues that are out of bounds of normal business, I assure you."

Christopher was thankful for the turn in conversation. He hoped it would steer clear of Lady Alaina for the rest of the evening, for he could not trust his mind to stay as honorable as his intentions. Grabbing the decanter, he filled their three glasses before drinking a healthy portion of the burning liquid. If he were lucky, enough brandy would dull any further mention of the ball.

Somewhere in White's the clock chimed two o'clock in the morning. Charles rubbed his eyes, trying to focus on the sloshing brown liquid once more. Several hours after arriving, he found himself decidedly alone. Charles quickly threw back what remained in his glass and made to rise from his chair, but a voice stopped him.

"Calling it quits already?"

Charles did not have to turn to see who it was, and resettled himself in his chair just as Percy took the chair opposite him, the chair ironically occupied by the man's cousin, the Duke of Ashford, just thirty minutes prior.

"To what do I owe the pleasure of your company?" Charles said, feigning congeniality.

Percy seemed to catch Charles's tone. "Come now, my friend, surely I am owed a better greeting."

A tight smile remained on Charles's face as he responded. "Forgive me, between my oft-ignored correspondences and your near-constant throng of flaky investors, I would have expected you would have harbored the frosty feelings."

Percy waved his hand with an air of confidence. "Nonsense, I am just bad at writing 'tis all. As for the investors, the noncommittal group to date has infuriated me just the same. I am glad to have run across you in London, what good luck."

"Hmm." Charles placed his hands on his knees, silently hoping to escape Percy's company. However, another gentleman quickly took the spot that Christopher had occupied earlier, flopping into the chair.

"Charles," Percy started, seeming to ignore that one's wish to leave, "May I introduce you to Lord Richard Finch. Finch, this is Charles Kendall, the trader I was telling you about just the other day."

Charles felt heat rise in his face at the slight of the man's introduction, one without his proper title, but refused to dignify it with a correction. The men were equal in the eyes of society, even if Percy held onto unrealistic ambitions.

Richard turned an almost predatory smile on Charles. "Nice to meet you, Charles. Percy tells me you trade all over the world, amazing how you work so hard."

Charles gritted his teeth, all of a sudden wishing for a whole bottle of brandy to appear on their table. "Nice to meet you as well," he responded minimally.

Only a moment of awkward silence fell before Percy seemed to once again take on the role of facilitator. "So, Charles, what are you finding turns a good profit in trade these days? Or are the rumors true that you are in London to get your business on better footing?"

Charles cleared his throat in an effort to clear his head; he was intent to leave, and was wary of being lured into a longer evening with inane prattle. "You should not believe everything you hear. Things have not much changed. Silks are always in demand, especially in London, and spices always turn a profit. And I am surprised at you, Percy, bandying rumors about when you know how much damage they can do. If I were to believe everything I heard, I would be worried to look behind you and see a runner ready to haul you away to debtor's prison, but I know that could not be further from the truth."

Percy's eyes narrowed as Charles spoke, but only momentarily. Richard cut through the silence after Charles' answer. "Sounds like good business, certainly enough for a good drink and a game of cards now and then, am I right?"

A grunt escaped Charles, which the other two gentlemen seemed to take as one of assent.

It was not long before a fresh decanter made its appearance on the table, each gentleman with a fresh glass, and cards were in Charles's hand. A few sips of the brown liquid, and any thought of quiet twilight hours at home fled from Charles's mind; he would play just a game or two to be polite and then be on his way.

Chapter 4

"Are you really going to wear your riding habit?" Evelina queried.

"The duke made a point to ask to call today and go for a ride in Hyde Park. I see no reason to get dressed twice, and I do not expect any other callers. With the duke around, no one really approached." Alaina finished up the final touches to her outfit, adjusting her cuffs in the mirror, while Evelina looked over her shoulder from the four-poster bed. Alaina looked at her reflection and her mind drifted to last evening.

The duke seemed kind and genuinely interested in her. Their two dances had been magical; his debonair grace around the ballroom had lifted her spirits and made her feel even a bit giddy. It did not hurt that her mother and the dowager duchess had hit it off perfectly. The only thing that weighed on her mind was the interaction with the marquess. Alaina had thought the evening was going well, but when the duke left quickly with his friend, Alaina's thoughts raced wondering at the reason. Perhaps the marquess had swayed the duke to leave early, and even to not call today as he had promised. Alaina knew she had not put her best foot forward, but how was she to know she would be arguing with what appeared to be one of the duke's closest friends? And it was not like he had acted pleasantly either.

An unladylike snort escaped Alaina's nose.

"What is that for, Alaina?"

"Nothing," Alaina replied. She had not had the courage to tell anyone of her blunder with the marquess, preferring to focus on the positive; the duke would call today. "Just making sure I am properly dressed."

She may not like to ride horses, or be very good at it, but Alaina certainly enjoyed a good riding habit and this was her favorite. It was a deep plum color, with the edges trimmed in black ribbon. The collar was flat with no lapels, and the deep plum skirt was slim enough to hint at Alaina's physique. One final adjustment to her black hat, adorned with a deep plum ribbon, and Alaina looked the part of an accomplished equestrienne.

"No need to fuss over your outfit so much, you know it is your best riding habit. The duke is sure to be taken with you, just as he was last evening." Evelina fidgeted, ready to be done and go downstairs to await visitors in the parlor; it was her one glimpse into the London social scene at her age, and she was excited for callers.

"Alright, shall we?" Alaina turned from the mirror, resolute to meet the day. She hoped the duke would show, as promised, for a ride, otherwise this outfit would be for nothing and it would look ridiculous should they have any other callers.

Alaina and Evelina descended the stairs from the second floor of the townhome. When the sisters reached the bottom, they crossed the small foyer to the front parlor. Once there, Alaina and Evelina took up the books they were currently reading to await guests.

Alaina sat near the window on a settee in order to best see the street outside as well as soak up any sun London had to offer, her book all but forgotten next to her. As it was, today was a bright, sunny day, a welcome change from the weather of the previous few days. She did not expect any callers other than the duke and his sister, but what of the marquess, would he be in attendance? She shook her head to clear the vision of his brooding look, and wished to ignore the flutter she felt in her stomach, the way her heart skipped a beat when she thought of the marquess's piercing blue eyes. He wanted nothing to do with her anyways, their arguments made that very clear. Pushing back the thought that he was the cause of her jittery demeanor, she refused to give the marquess one more thought. Alaina was determined to focus on the duke.

Her mother, Charlotte, had certainly been industrious in making friends with the duke's mother, Eleanor, which put Alaina at ease. Alaina forced her memories to those couple dances and interactions with the Duke of Ashford, a smile forming on her lips. She had fully expected the duke to be dull, or self-centered. He was certainly handsome, but also charming and intelligent, with a brilliant smile to light up the room. Not to mention his interest in her, and his promise to call after so short a time, but with no embarrassing theatrics or rudeness.

Alaina was pulled from her reverie by the sound of the front door opening. She quickly glanced out the window. Sure enough, Alaina saw three beautiful horses outside tied to the back of a large and well adorned carriage. Alaina assumed this was the duke and his sister. She did not consider the significance of the third horse before a quiet knock sounded on the partially opened parlor door.

Alaina and Evelina slowly rose from their chairs to face the door as Arthur, the butler, announced, "Lord Wallace, the most honorable Duke of Ashford, his sister, Lady Ramsbury, the most honorable Countess of Carlisle, and Lord Kendall, the most honorable Marquess of Rochester."

The last name nearly stopped Alaina's heart. The duke had not mentioned bringing anyone other than his sister.

The three entered the room, the duke and marquess following Lady Ramsbury and executing crisp courtly bows to both Evelina and Alaina. Both men's gazes rested on Alaina. The sisters were sure to execute curtsies in kind, acknowledging both the gentlemen and the lady who graced their parlor. Alaina forced her eyes to remain on the duke, but she could not ignore the weight of the marquess's stare.

It was the duke who made the first greeting. "Lady Alaina, it is wonderful to see you on this fine day. I am happy you were able to receive us, and I hope you are ready for a ride. I do apologize for bringing along an extra guest," he made a quick motion with his head to indicate the marquess. "But he is a dear friend and fancied a ride in Hyde Park this morning. I hope that is ok?"

"Most certainly," Alaina said, a little too quickly, her throat just a bit tight, but not enough for her companions to notice, she hoped. "And may I present my sister, Lady Evelina. She is but a couple years younger than I and not out in society just yet, or I would have made the introduction last evening. We are so glad to have you, and as you can see," she quickly motioned to her outfit, "I am ready for our ride."

After a subtle clearing of Evelina's throat, Alaina rejoined, "And this is Lord Wallace, Lord Kendall, and Lady Ramsbury." Alaina motioned to their newly arrived guests, meeting Evelina's eyes. Her sister quickly smiled, curtsied again for good measure, and gave a pert acknowledgement of the introduction.

Alaina met each of her guests with what she hoped was a bright and confident smile, ignoring the butterflies currently in her stomach, and the blue-eyed reason for their presence. "Thank you so much for coming. Lady Ramsbury, it is nice to make your acquaintance. It is nice to see you again, Lord Kendall."

Alaina quickly met the eyes of the marquess, his stoic demeanor giving nothing away as to his mood, and Alaina could only hope that their interactions on their outing would not resemble their thorny conversations at the ball.

"How pleasant to make your acquaintance, Lady Alaina. I am so grateful to be able to join in on the ride today," Lady

Ramsbury bubbled as she crossed the room, a wide smile gracing her face. "I am just happy my brother decided to actually join us for the season this year after what happened last year. My mother is absolutely thrilled she was able to meet you last night, and is most hopeful my brother is able to settle down this year."

An uncomfortable sound, a cross between a grunt of disapproval and a cough one might make if a piece of food was lodged in their throat, escaped the duke. Alaina turned her attention to the duke, finding his usually confident smile a bit lopsided. As she met his eyes, he shrugged. His sister raised her eyebrows and put her arms akimbo. "Well, she is in need of grandchildren!"

"Georgiana, I am embarrassed to say in such company that you could also provide her grandchildren," Graham said.

"Hmph! You know what I mean," Lady Ramsbury countered. "*Heirs.*"

Alaina continued to smile, forcing her attention to remain on the duke for a few moments before acknowledging Lady Ramsbury's greeting.

Alaina thought the lady looked much like her brother and mother, with porcelain skin, dark hair and eyes which practically danced with delight. Each of her newly arrived companions were well dressed for the ride, Lady Ramsbury's riding habit matching her own in flair and style, but in a deep peacock color, a feather of that bird gracing the pert hat sitting jauntily on her head. The duke looked resplendent, from his crisply starched and tied cravat, white to match his shirt, all the way to his shiny black knee-high boots. But it was the marquess that Alaina found holding her gaze, their eyes melding across the short expanse of the parlor.

Lord Kendall, the Marquess of Rochester, had hair with a hint of red in it, the sunlight catching it, almost making it shine. His eyes, between green and blue, caught the same morning light as his hair. His garb very much matched the duke's, the only difference the color of his coat and breeches, a deep emerald which gave his hair an extra flair. As she had noted at the ball the previous evening, the marquess stood even with the duke, but his broad shoulders made the duke seem almost scrawny. Alaina found the marquess's eyes inscrutable, and turned her gaze to Graham's sister.

"Lady Ramsbury, I am most pleased to have met everyone at last night's ball as well." Alaina practically giggled, trying to ignore the exchange about providing heirs; she certainly understood precocious sisters, but was able to stifle her laughter, and merely return the duke's regard with an amused grin. At the same time, she heard a chuckle just out of her range of vision, toward the door of the parlor. As she shifted her glance to find the source of the sound, she was presented with the slightly reddened countenance of the marquess, and the straight face of her butler, Arthur. Clearly, the marquess had not been able to contain his mirth in the slightest. Alaina certainly hoped the two friends had a good-natured relationship. If not, how cruel to laugh at a friend after such a gaffe from his sibling!

Trying to gain control of the room, Alaina quickly changed the subject. "Would you all like me to call for some biscuits and tea before we take our ride?"

"There is no need for refreshments before our ride. I am most eager to be outside and we had such a wonderful breakfast. I find that I am not hungry in the least, but thank you for the kind offer. Shall we be off?" Lady Ramsbury was first to respond, clearly used to being in charge of a household. The duke and marquess did not seem phased by the lady's attitude, and simply both looked to Alaina for her assent.

"That is a wonderful idea. I will just call for my horse to be brought around front, and we can head out on our ride," Alaina spoke with a little more ease now, having seen Lady Ramsbury's confidence around both the duke and marquess.

"Have a wonderful ride, and maybe after, we can have refreshments and tea? I am confident you will all be hungry then," Evelina said. Alaina and Evelina exchanged a sisterly glance, and Alaina could see she was eager to join in on the activity, but alas she was too young to be out and about without a parental chaperone.

The duke finally spoke. "Well, that is a wonderful idea, Lady Evelina. I look forward to our post-ride snack and tea. Georgiana, shall we?" He motioned for his sister and the marquess to precede him out the parlor door and toward the front of the townhome, each accepting their gloves from the butler on their way out. The duke presented his arm to Alaina, and smiled down at her warmly, meeting her eyes with a sparkle of mischief.

It was really quite a lovely day, and what better activity to enjoy it than a ride on horseback in the middle of Hyde Park. The four riders seemed at ease, grouped together with two horses in front and two in the back. As she had expected, Alaina was most comfortable in the back pair of horses, feeling quite inadequate as a rider next to the other three in the group. They truly seemed one with their animals, but Alaina was never able to fully relax, her hands gripping the reins with vice-like strength, and the legs in her sidesaddle never quite comfortable. The duke realized this early in their ride, and decided to fall back to meet her, requesting walks for his horse more often than needed to allow Alaina to rest a bit. While they walked their horses through a grove of trees, they were able to chat as a group.

"I hope you will see fit to call me Georgiana, no more of this lady stuff," Georgiana shot over her shoulder.

"That is most kind. I will certainly do such and expect you to dispense with the formality as well. Please call me Alaina."

"Well in that case, I guess I should give you leave to call me by my given name as well. Please call me Graham," said the duke, cocking his head a little and glancing sidelong at Alaina with his charming lopsided smile. Alaina smiled back at the duke, pleased with Graham's attention, having enjoyed the ride and conversation so far.

"I give you leave to call me Alaina, your grace, er, Graham," Alaina said softly.

After what felt like an eternal pause, the marquess stated quite quickly, "And as a member of this little riding group, I give you leave to call me by my given name as well. Please call me Christopher." His statement was almost gruff, and he seemed to be waiting for her acknowledgement.

"The same to you, my lord. Please call me Alaina."

"Christopher." The marquess corrected, this time adding a teasing grin to his face, one that actually reached his eyes.

"I apologize… Christopher," Alaina responded, feeling as if she had a stone lodged in her throat. She was perturbed that Christopher's eyes had such an effect on her, and hoped no one else in the group could sense her discomfort.

"What is your favorite part of your family's country estate, Alaina?" Graham questioned.

"Oh, uh," Alaina started, finding solace in his benign question and the change of subject. "I guess you can already tell that it is not riding around the grounds on horseback, that would be Evelina. I am partial to a few spots along the edge of a pond. On particularly sunny days, I prefer to sit underneath this one large oak tree and read, but on other days, I like to sit out on this large boulder that stretches a bit over the edge of the pond. If the water is high enough, I can put my feet into the pond and soak up the sights. I often bring my journal, or a book, or both."

Alaina looked over at the duke to gauge his reaction, worried he may make too much of her reading like Lord Finch and his sister, but he appeared almost like he was trying to imagine the scene she described. As he smiled broadly and maintained eye contact, Alaina continued. "Sometimes I find the country inspiring enough to write, sometimes I need to just read and think, and sometimes I just like to be."

"That sounds quite nice. I often find myself trying to find the perfect spot to read or just take in nature. Most people imagine men as only involved in sport, hunting, or gaming, but I certainly like my time to relax alone in the country."

"I do not remember much of that introspection you speak of when we were kids. If I remember correctly, you were always terrorizing the grounds with Christopher," Georgiana needled her brother.

"Quite right. If you remember, though, I have grown up since then, Georgiana," Graham chided.

"Ah, yes, I seem to remember you and Christopher are now grown men, looking to take wives, as you should," Georgiana returned his banter.

"Not this again, Georgiana," Graham warned. "Besides, I am the only one of us currently looking for a spouse. Christopher much prefers his bachelorhood."

Alaina stifled a giggle, recognizing good-natured sibling banter. She and Evelina had much of the same relationship, teasing one another, sometimes for maximum embarrassment, but totally understanding each other. She caught a quick protruded tongue and wrinkled nose from Georgiana, directed at Graham, and sighed, turning forward in her horse to find Christopher observing her intently, a shielded look in his eyes. Maybe Graham's comment had bothered him in some way, but the reason eluded Alaina.

Alaina was about to chastise him about keeping his eyes forward, and how rude it was to stare, when a commotion just in front of Christopher caught her eye. Just as the sound reached her ears, a group of riders emerged rather recklessly from a dense cove of trees.

"Look out!" Graham cried out. Georgiana pulled her horse to a quick stop, with Graham easily pulling up next to her. Alaina tried to stop her horse as well, but with the commotion from the other horses galloping past, her horse spooked and attempted to flee the noise, unfortunately in the forward direction. The quick reaction of her horse forced the reins from Alaina's hand, and she lost control. Finding purchase in her horse's mane, Alaina closed her eyes and clung to her horse with only hope that the horse would stop. As her horse galloped wide of the offending group, Alaina heard an accompanying rumble of hooves come up beside her. A strong pair of hands quickly gathered the reins that had slipped from her hands and pulled the frightened horse to a halt. Too afraid to open her eyes until the earth stood still, Alaina assumed her savior to be Graham, but was surprised to find Christopher's blue eyes looking at her with something akin to concern. Alaina watched as his eyes traced her face, and she felt surprised to find warmth in his countenance. The connection between herself and Christopher seemed unbreakable, and Alaina felt something warm build in her chest as she looked at the gentleman who she, just a few moments ago, might have thought of as an adversary.

"Are you quite well?" Christopher asked, a muscle in his jaw working, as if in anger.

Alaina could only nod in the affirmative, and she swallowed hard to calm her panic as Christopher led her horse back to Graham and Georgiana.

As they passed the reckless horse riders, Christopher took a breath as if to call out, but Graham seemed to beat him to the punch. "Ho there! Did you not see our group while you were galloping through the trees? You could have easily toppled two ladies, coming upon us as you did."

Alaina immediately recognized two of the three riders: Lord Finch and his sister, Lady Barbara! The third rider was not familiar to her. Alaina found herself wishing the earth would open up and swallow her whole; nothing good could come of interaction with those siblings, no matter their companion. Unfortunately, Alaina was not so lucky. However, the mystery of the third companion was quickly put to rest.

"Cousin, how delightful to see you," the lead male rider of the group called out. He certainly looked familiar to Alaina. "These are my companions, Lord Finch and Lady Barbara Finch, his sister."

Lady Alaina stiffened in preparation for the encounter, and forced her head high.

With almost no choice in the matter, the duke made the polite introductions. "Percy, you are familiar with my sister and the marquess, but I would like to introduce Lady Alaina, daughter of the Earl of Norwich. You quite nearly toppled her from her saddle. Lady Alaina, this is my cousin, Lord Wallace, and his companions as he has introduced them."

With the introduction of Lady Alaina, the second man, Lord Finch, made his way to the fore of the group. "Lady Alaina, we meet again," Lord Finch smiled, a leer that made a woman feel unclean and uncomfortable. Alaina gave a shiver at the perusal.

It was Lady Barbara who cut in next. "Lady Alaina, I am afraid I barely recognized you without your nose in a book."

Before Alaina could answer the insult, Christopher practically growled, "Levying insults about improving one's mind through reading is usually done by those who are found lacking."

Alaina stifled her surprise, and elected to answer simply, "Lord Finch, Lady Barbara, pleasant to see you both again. I am doing quite well, thank you."

At Alaina's unease, and Christopher's response, Graham seemed to think it best to keep things quick as well. "We were just about to turn for Lady Alaina's family townhome. Good day to you, cousin."

Alaina was stuck in a terrified trance, but could still notice the narrowing eyes of Graham's cousin as the duke turned his horse around to venture back the way they had come. Alaina strived to keep pace with the duke, Georgiana and Christopher falling behind them.

Georgiana was the first to speak. "What is Percy doing here in London?"

Graham sighed. "Georgiana, I am sure he is here to do what every other nobleman does, to enjoy the social season."

"I seriously doubt that, Graham, not after Christmas," Georgiana rebuffed.

Graham shook his head and seemed to grit through his teeth, "We can talk later, Georgiana, I do not wish to ruin the rest of the ride."

Georgiana fell silent once more, and the group plodded along without the levity of before. The close encounter had set them all on edge.

"So, how do you know Lord Finch?" Christopher asked, after a few moments of riding in silence.

"Obviously, we have encountered each other in the early part of the season." Alaina did not feel the need to freely share her humiliating experience.

"Why, yes, that is clear. How did you meet and why such a cold greeting?" It was Georgiana's turn to prod.

"Well," Alaina sighed, fortifying herself to tell a quick version of the first weeks of her season. "I met Lord Finch at my first ball of the season, and he took quite a possessive course of action. He asked for more dances than was proper, and called upon me the next day only to suggest that a quick marriage was in my best interest. I had to claim illness for him to leave me alone."

"And I hope that you turned him down straight away?" Graham leveled a questioning glance at Alaina. This certainly was not the conversation she thought she would be having with the duke.

"I was so stunned that my father had to plead a moment for me to escape and then turn him down himself, making the excuse that a match so early in the season would not serve either of us."

"What happened then?" Georgiana pressed.

"Well, Lord Finch seemed quite embarrassed by the rejection, and once I was back out in society, he initially avoided my presence and my family's presence, which did not particularly upset us." Alaina paused, and she swallowed hard before she continued, "Eventually, though, he worked up the courage, or enough drink, to make a public spectacle, this time joined by his foolish friends, with Lady Barbara cheering them from the crowd. My parents and I had to flee the ball."

Christopher let out a laugh, and Georgiana giggled. Alaina fell silent to await their mocking to commence, but after a few moments, Graham spoke up in a soft voice. "I am sorry to hear that Lord Finch and his sister caused you such grief, but I might add that anyone who keeps company with Percy automatically falls out of favor with us. And ignore their laughter," Graham indicated Georgiana and Christopher. "It is not directed at you. I have to admit, to watch one of Percy's friends embarrass themselves would prove quite amusing were it not at the expense of another."

Alaina nodded her head, and attempted to change the subject. "Now how about tea?"

"Yes, tea would be lovely," Georgiana acquiesced, and the group continued home to the Norwich townhome.

Tea proved to be uneventful, thankfully, and Evelina was treated to some afternoon fun with their newfound friends. Refreshments were plentiful, but as the time in the day grew short, everyone seemed spent, and Georgiana even had to suppress a yawn. They decided to make their goodbyes.

The riding companions bid Evelina farewell, and they all headed to the front steps of the townhome as the Ashford carriage was readied. Graham clasped Alaina's hand in his own and executed a bow before bringing her gloved hand to his lips. "Until we see each other again."

"Thank you," Alaina murmured, touched. Graham handed his sister into the awaiting carriage. Georgiana graced Alaina with a broad smile and a wave before she disappeared into the coach.

Christopher was the last to alight, but not before he paid Alaina farewell. He mulled over the afternoon's events, and was surprised to find the threat to Alaina's safety had affected him more than just a mere acquaintance. He had felt an overwhelming urgency to gather her in his arms and ensure that the terrified, haunting look in her eyes once he had stopped her runaway horse would never again take root. Taking her hand in his own, Christopher paused as he bowed over her hand, and could not resist the urge to place a gentle kiss on her knuckles.

Alaina was jolted by the whisper of breath across her skin. She hoped he could not feel the acceleration of her pulse. Almost unable to breathe, Alaina whispered, "Thank you for everything."

Remembering his defense of her against those who ever seemed to be her tormentors, Alaina added, her voice more forceful than she intended, "You did not have to defend my honor, I can do so myself."

Christopher looked into Alaina's eyes and paused, before dropping her hand, his gruff reply belying his words. "I am sure you can, although you should not always have to. It was truly nothing, or at least nothing I did not already owe you."

With that, Christopher practically leapt into the conveyance and Alaina watched as her riding companions left just as quickly as they had arrived.

CHAPTER 5

Slap!

Lady Barbara smacked her gloves in her hand as she stalked through the front door of her family's townhome. Percy and her brother, Lord Richard Finch, followed on her heels, but both held back a bit as the tirade continued.

"It seems Lady Alaina foils us at every turn. First the humiliation of her rejection, and now she has set her sights on the Duke of Ashford!" Lady Barbara exclaimed.

The men remained mute, as the butler collected their outer garments and hurried off to put them away.

"Well?!" Came Barbara's final exasperated question.

It was Percy who braved a response. "Well what? How were we supposed to know that we would happen upon *her* at Hyde Park?"

Lady Barbara let out a huff and rolled her eyes, turning on her heel and leaving the men to stare at one another in the foyer. Once she made it to the parlor, she heard a shuffle of feet as her brother and Percy came out of their trance to follow her.

Percy entered first and straightened his jacket before making another attempt to placate Barbara. "My dear, it was just a coincidence that Lady Alaina was there with Graham. He is no closer to matrimony than he was last season."

Barbara, who had been angrily tapping her foot as she waited for some explanation from her brother or her would-be fiancé, stopped and strode toward Percy.

"And what makes you think that, *my dear*?" Lady Barbara sneered. "There is no guarantee that Graham will fail once more this season to secure a match. With Lady Bella last season, I had her ear as a 'friend'; but if Lady Alaina is the object of your cousin's desire this season, I am afraid I will have no sway there. We can no longer delay! My parents demand that I marry someone with money and status, and the Duke of Ashford and his future wife, whoever she may be, stand in your way."

Percy shuffled from one foot to the next uncomfortably. "Like I said, I will find some way to supplant Graham, some scandal, or… Well, something. You will be my duchess very soon, but we must remain calm."

"Lies!" Lady Barbara exploded, throwing her hands in the air before leveling a threatening finger at Percy. "You know as well as I do that you coming into the dukedom through schemes is unlikely, but you could at least make your move and extort some sort of better living from the man. I have delayed my parents for five seasons on the promise that I could secure my own future. Am I a fool to think that you have some sort of brilliant plan to upend the duke's life enough to see your own situation improved? Or is it that you are not willing to do what is necessary?"

Barbara's final outburst brought a moment of silence to the room, the only sound the crackling of the fire and the ticking of the grandfather clock in the corner.

Finally, Percy spoke in a quiet voice. "Barbara, my love, I promise this is the season."

"Do not 'my love' me. You have no plan!" Barbara yelled.

"But I will have one soon, and possibly, we can even exact revenge upon Lady Alaina in the process," Percy cajoled, his statement punctuated by a brief bow and an uncomfortable clearing of his throat. "I must take my leave of you both, but I hope to see you this evening."

No goodbye ushered forth from Lady Barbara or Richard, and Percy unceremoniously left the townhouse rented by the Finch family for the season.

Without Percy as his shield, Richard found himself the recipient of his sister's glare, but did not miss his opportunity to needle her. "Well, dear sister, I fear any further tongue lashings and Percy will find himself another lady. And I thought you loved him."

A huff came from Lady Barbara, and she finally gave up her post, flouncing into the chair nearest the fireplace. "I did love him once, but that was when his promises to me were not so empty. Now I am just a spinster hoping to convince our parents that Percy is not a complete waste of a match. They need to see that my future is secured before they consent to anything, even if they know there are no others waiting in the wings. I fear I have misaligned my hopes and dreams with that man. And I fear no amount of tongue lashing will see him on his way; you know Percy has few friends in London, and we are the only ones who entertain his visions of grandeur," Barbara sniped.

"I think that is because you like the idea of being styled as something more than a baron's wife," Richard spit back at his sister.

"If you remember, dear brother, it is our parents who demand we climb the rungs of society. They forbade me from marrying Percy without a better living promised. Besides, you dislike the idea of having such a person as a friend? May I remind you that you could not even garner the attention of a bookish, country mouse?"

"She is an earl's daughter!"

"She was new to town, and you blew your opportunity. Even with our little stunt designed to embarrass Alaina, no one of the ton seems to care that she is not truly one of them. It is amazing that someone so new to London society would be so easily accepted. Why, the Duke of Ashford has even settled his attention on her."

"Percy will find a way to turn things around for the better. We will find our family's position improved in society, mark my words," Richard said, seeming to need to hear the words out loud.

"I wish I had such confidence," Lady Barbara said with finality, waving one hand toward her brother. "Now leave and crawl back into whatever gaming hell you came from this morning. I am sure you will find some other poor fool to swindle before the day is finished."

"Do not mock me! A game of cards is an honorable way to pass the time, and a bloody good way to make money," Richard protested.

"If I find a use for your talents in treachery, I will let you know," Barbara snarled, turning her head in a final note of dismissal.

Richard needed no further prodding to leave, muttering under his breath. He left his sister in front of the fireplace, rubbing her temples in frustration. *How was she going to convince Percy that now was the time to extort money from the duke. There could be no further delay!*

"I cannot believe his cousin was so reckless and callous to have come through the trees so quickly, almost directly on top of you. And then, to not even apologize. Think of who could have been injured! Think of the horses that could have been injured, all due to a few idiots!" Evelina raged, reaching a rather loud decibel.

Alaina cringed. "I know, dear, it is quite upsetting, but luckily no one was harmed, and all the horses seem no worse for wear. Bartholomew spooked a bit, but he recovered nicely," Alaina assured Evelina of her own horse's safety, fibbing only a little about how disastrous things *could* have been if not for the quick actions of the marquess. Evelina truly doted on all their horses, but Bartholomew had been her horse since he was a foal.

"Of course," Evelina spoke, as if almost reassuring herself, "I am just happy that everyone returned safely."

"Especially your horse," Alaina ribbed, giggling a bit in an attempt to break the mood.

Evelina gave a half-hearted giggle, and took a deep breath. "Now, you must tell me all about your time with the duke. Was he charming? Does he seem smitten? Will he call again? It seemed like you two were getting along nicely at tea."

Alaina reached across the span between the wingback chairs by the fireplace and clasped her sister's hand affectionately. "Slow down, Evelina, it was really only our second meeting. The duke was kind, so different from Lord Finch, thank goodness."

"Well, how about his sister? She was so pleasant," Evelina continued.

"Georgiana was quite pleasant as well, and the marquess, well…" Alaina paused. The marquess had not been quite as ornery as their initial meeting, but quiet and reserved. Alaina could not deny the electricity between them, but he also seemed to despise her. Besides, if Graham's statement was true, Christopher was not in want of a wife. Graham was, though, and he certainly did not hate her.

"The marquess? Oh right, well what is he like?" Evelina plowed ahead, unaware of her sister's ruminations. "He seemed to me like he did not want to be there!"

"Well, I do not think he did," Alaina wondered out loud. "It seems the duke drags him along quite against his will. I did not tell you, but last night he was so surly and pompous! I was sure he would convince the duke to avoid me at all costs."

"Avoid you? Why?"

"Well, I may have been quite contrary myself," Alaina answered sheepishly.

"You?" Evelina poked. "Never, I would not believe it."

A chuckle escaped Alaina. "Ah yes, my reserved demeanor is infallible."

"Quite." Evelina paused before reiterating the question, "So?"

"So what?"

"What is the marquess actually like? What was he like today?"

Alaina thought once more, remembering his defense of her, something even Graham had failed to do, and her mind reeled from confusion. "I do not quite know what he is like, certainly more than he appears."

⚜

"So, are you worried about the fact that your cousin is in town?" Christopher probed. The situation at the park this morning had been upsetting, but purely coincidental. Still, Christopher felt he had only heard part of the story from his friend.

Graham left his spot at the mantle, looking into the flames, to pace the room. "I do not think it unusual that he would be in London for the season, but Georgiana insists he is up to something worse, maybe even following us around town."

"Where is Georgiana?" asked Christopher. When they had returned, both men had quickly retired to Graham's study, where they filled glasses of brandy, and Georgiana had begged for reprieve.

"She is upstairs resting, or so she says. I imagine she is writing to her husband to tell him of the day's events and her suspicions. She was quite adamant that Percy was up to something. I just think it was bad luck." Graham stopped pacing and faced his friend. "So, are you prepared for another evening of avoiding young ladies wishing for just a dance? Alaina and her mother will be attending the Stamford Ball this evening."

"I would assume so," Christopher answered blandly, not wishing for yet another evening of parading about with Graham.

"You are coming, yes?"

Christopher released a sigh. "I guess. I fear I see more facets of Alaina's personality by the minute. First, she is rude to me, then all smiles for you, and then today, showing a bit of backbone with your cousin. What type of friend would I be to leave you to your own devices?"

Graham smiled broadly. "Yes, she is marvelous, is she not? And that story about Lord Finch! How terrible for her to go through. It is amazing she decided to finish out the season after that."

"It is," was all Christopher chose to say.

"Well, as things are, I do not believe I need your help any longer with Lady Alaina, but with Percy on the loose, I could still use your support."

Christopher found his doubts about Alaina were overshadowed by the situation with Graham's cousin. "What is it that Percy did to make you so on edge?"

A sigh escaped Graham. "Like I said, he caused a ruckus at the family gathering portion of the festivities over the holidays. Percy overheard my sister and her husband talking about some renovations they were planning up in Cornwall at their estate and Percy became enraged. He started raging about how we had all this money that frivolous renovations could be completed with no thought to others who had less. He then had the audacity to threaten that *when* he came into the dukedom, he would quit being so generous with the staff and would sell the holdings so he could invest them in his shipping company. Something about having to work for his money. If I had to guess, he has debtors at his heels."

"Hmm, that explains Georgiana's reaction to seeing him in the park. Why did you not tell me sooner?" Christopher asked, and then thought to be a bit more reassuring. "I am sure *'when'* is just an empty threat. Percy was always a spineless weasel."

"I can only hope that is the case, but my mother and sister are quite shaken by it all. I would have told you last night, but Charles had impeccable timing," Graham grumbled. "I fear where you are perceptive of *most* people and their character, you have a blind spot for your cousin.

My dastardly cousin, Percy, may be more overt in his intentions and poor character, but do not forget, Charles tortured us through Eton."

"That was just fooling around, you have to believe that. Besides, we are all grown now," Christopher countered. "He is my only living family. And we have only been in touch since my uncle, his father, passed a couple of years ago. I do not want to punish him for something that was done when we were but adolescents."

Graham blew out a breath and scrubbed his hand through his hair. "Yes, I know, I know. Let us hope that my paranoia over Percy is just clouding my judgement of all cousins, including yours."

"Thank you," Christopher said quietly.

Graham left his now empty glass on the sideboard and approached the large ornate wooden desk that overwhelmed its corner of the room, especially with its piles of papers left for too long without proper attention. Graham sighed and unceremoniously dumped himself into the chair behind the desk, looking intent to deal with the disorder just now.

"It seems like you have a full afternoon," Christopher chuckled, taking another sip from his cup. Graham had never been one for extreme order, but even for him, his desk was untidy. Papers littered every corner, causing him to have to haphazardly shuffle things out of the way. After a moment of watching, Christopher noticed Graham had not found what he needed. "Is there something important you cannot seem to place? I would say I could help, but you have quite a disorderly pile."

Graham paused in his search to give his friend an exasperated look before continuing. "It seems I have misplaced my ring. If I am to respond to these correspondence and invoices, I would need that."

"Your family ring?" Christopher questioned, placing his hand on his pinky to ensure his own was in its rightful place. "I am surprised you do not wear it at all times."

"Well, it barely fits on any of my fingers, and honestly, I do not like the feel of baubles on my hands. It gets in the way of riding," Graham explained.

The shuffling of papers continued, the crease on Graham's forehead deepening until he finally located the ring. It was a gaudy piece of jewelry with the large Ashford crest on it, speaking to the age of the title and its time in the Wallace family.

"Aha! Found it! See, with a desk this messy, the ring is in a safe space."

Christopher looked at his friend, who continued to shuffle through the mess on his desk. "Well, now that you have all you need for an afternoon of fun, I will leave you to your business, and I will see you tonight."

Already distracted by the mess of papers, Graham gave a quick wave. "See you tonight."

Christopher walked out of the room, shaking his head in amusement; some things never change. Graham was lucky his disorganization contained itself to his study.

CHAPTER 6

Alaina craned her neck in an effort to see from the ballroom to the front entryway, earning a discreet but stern elbow from her mother.

"They will be here soon, darling, I am sure," was all the assurance Charlotte provided her daughter, being sure to smile at passersby as they entered the Stamford Ball.

Alaina forced a smile and tried to remain calm, casting only surreptitious glances toward the door, pausing now and then to take in the sights. The Stamford Ball was quite spectacular, if a bit peculiar as far as balls went, with the ballroom almost directly at the front door.

The corner nature of the house allowed for two large wings, one directly to the left, the other just to the right of the front entrance, the ballroom acting as a centerpiece. Bordering the large ballroom were alcoves, some with doors leading into rooms of both wings. A dome of glass windows and doors graced the back of the ball, leading out to expansive gardens. Large chandeliers graced the ceiling space with a soft light, and candelabras were placed strategically on tables throughout the room to root out any remaining darkness, making it feel as if the room was glowing.

Anticipation got the better of Alaina as she glanced once more toward the front door, the smile on her face becoming more painful by the second. An eddy of questions filled her mind in anticipation of meeting the duke and his mother at the ball. And yet, her stomach fluttered as she considered the other person who may be in attendance, the marquess.

Charlotte, sensing that her earlier reassurance had not hit its mark, turned ever so slightly to her daughter. "I am sure the duke and his mother will approve of your appearance and will be pleased to see you in attendance.

Alaina had chosen one of her more costly gowns, its primary color ivory, which complemented her ivory skin beautifully, especially in the candlelight. The dress was simple in cut as well as color, with a bodice closely fit to her bosom. Rather than simply cut straight across, a slight dip in the middle provocatively showcased Alaina's natural curves. The flair at the neckline was countered by a simple flared skirt, which remained slim, and small sheer cap sleeves adorned Alaina's shoulders. The simplicity of the color and silk fabric of the dress was paired with intricate beading. Small lines of clear beads trailed along the sleeves, almost seeming to flow onto the bodice, where they were joined by seed pearls sewn into the delicate fabric, almost giving the appearance of a shortened corset. The skirt was then finished with the same beads, gradually growing larger in size as they reached toward the hem. In the candlelight, the dress from head to toe gave the appearance of the stars falling from the heavens to join the earth. Her hair was in a soft upswept coiffure. Her lady's maid, Cecilia, had taken great pains to place each of her dark curls in perfect concert to give her the air of a goddess, with soft tendrils framing her temples and spilling from the crown of her head, reaching halfway down her back. The lustrous nature of her hair rivaled the dress.

Alaina's mother had opted for a darker, midnight shade to represent the night, with the dress fitting close to her body, but more conservative in its cut. The dress was also beaded with similar seed pearls to give the illusion of a starry sky, taking quite a literal interpretation of the ball's theme.

Standing together, it was easily noticeable that their dresses had been made by the same seamstress with the same idea in mind, making it obvious to any observer that they were closely related. And it was certainly easily observable that the women remained at the edge of the ballroom, their excitement palpable.

Christopher looked around the foyer, the crowd at the front door overwhelming even for someone of his stature. As he looked out over the throng, finding few to block his way, Christopher's eyes finally came to rest on a head of lustrous dark curls. Even without seeing her face, he could see her twinkling eyes and soft smile in his mind, causing his stomach to clench and his heartbeat to rush in his ears.

Clearing his throat and straightening his coat, already impeccably placed on his broad shoulders, Christopher was about to start making his way through the sea of people, forgetting every moment in the afternoon he had convinced himself he was attending the ball in service to a friend, or at least providing escort for his friend's sister, when a voice brought him up short.

"It is quite crowded in here, Christopher, I do hope we can find some space in the ballroom to enjoy the evening. With this crowd, it is doubtful we would even be able to readily see Lady Alaina," Graham said as he glanced briefly over his shoulder.

"I believe I see Alaina up and to the left, just inside what I presume is the start of the official ballroom." Christopher motioned over his friend's shoulder toward the general direction where he had glimpsed the halo of curls, no doubt belonging to Lady Alaina.

Graham took the lead, guiding his mother, the dowager duchess, through the crowd gently, trying to avoid the press of people where possible and offering his apologies whenever he had to interject through groups to make his way toward the ballroom proper. Christopher was close behind, with Georgiana following confidently at his side.

As they approached what Christopher had rightfully assumed was Lady Alaina, both her and her mother turned toward the door, as though looking for someone. *Most certainly that someone was the Duke of Ashford*, brooded Christopher.

The duke's eyes missed Alaina's as hers settled on the group. Unable to gain the duke's attention, Alaina glanced over his shoulder to see Christopher looking intently in her direction.

Their eyes locked, and a sudden and unexpected feeling hit Christopher low in his gut and caused his heart to race. He broke their connection and found Georgiana was looking at him oddly. Such a look would most certainly be joined promptly with an uncomfortable inquiry, one he would not allow, so Christopher sought to have the first word, if not the last. "I do believe we have been successful at locating Lady Alaina."

"Indeed?" came a short and sweet reply from Georgiana, her lips barely containing a smile and question. Tapping her brother on the shoulder, she brought his attention around to Lady Alaina and her mother, Charlotte, just a few yards away.

Graham quickly smiled at the approaching ladies. He executed a quick bow. "Forgive me for my delay. Christopher mentioned that you were over this way, but it was so difficult to see. I was sure he could have been mistaken, but I can see he has most certainly found the most beautiful ladies in attendance."

Alaina offered her own observation. "Your grace, the crowd at this point in the ballroom seems too great, it is a wonder you were able to see us at all."

"Please call me Graham, my lady, just as I said this afternoon," the duke said in a teasing tone, one Christopher was certain was accompanied by a rakish smile. The marquess's hand flexed ever so slightly as he watched his friend take the lady's hand in his own and place a kiss upon her gloved knuckles.

Eleanor had been observing her son's actions with obvious affection, and dropped her hand from his arm as she approached Charlotte. "It is so wonderful to see you again, Charlotte. I hope you had a less exciting day than the children did. It seems they had quite the experience in Hyde Park."

"Eleanor, I most certainly have no stories to compare with what I heard from my daughter. We can hope that any further outings will be altogether boring."

"Alaina, Lady Charlotte, how nice to see you. I must say your dresses do look oh so lovely. You both practically sparkle in the candlelight," Georgiana gushed. "No wonder Christopher was able to pick you out from the crowd."

Christopher was quick to acknowledge Alaina and her mother, ignoring the thinly veiled gibe from Georgiana and executing a courtly bow. "Ladies, it seems the journey from the front steps to here has left me in need of refreshments. Please excuse me." And with that he turned on his heel and made his way back through the crowd, Alaina's tinkling laughter raking over his senses. *He was here in service to a friend. He was not in want of a wife, not now, and maybe not ever.*

"Your furrowed brow gives me worry, my lady," came the duke's voice, breaking Alaina from her moment of perturbation at

Christopher's swift departure. It seemed nothing had changed in his opinion of her.

Trying to focus on the present, she turned her face up to the duke, having most recently been staring at his broad expanse of chest as they swept across the dance floor. "My apologies, your grace. I am just surprised they have already played two waltzes this evening."

Graham met her eyes with a glint of merriment and roguishness. "My lady, what makes you think I did not request such a course of songs in order to be close to you throughout our dances together?"

"Surely you jest, your grace. It is my understanding that all the pieces picked for this ball are carefully curated by the hostess herself, Lady Stamford." Alaina met Graham's eyes with a certain amount of puckishness of her own, putting a hand on her chest in jest.

Graham threw back his head to let out a burst of full laughter, and Alaina grimaced, self-conscious of the duke's display. As the dance ended, she glanced about the room to see if any stares were directed their way, thankfully finding none. Graham led her to her mother's side at the edge of the dance floor. From what Alaina could see, Charlotte and Eleanor had become fast friends.

"Mother, Lady Charlotte, I fear I have all but exhausted my dances with Lady Alaina and must entrust her to your care," the duke said, gracefully acknowledging both women. As Alaina settled next to her mother, Christopher and Georgiana returned from the far side of the ballroom.

"…Surely you cannot think that. Marriage is not such an awful venture," was all Alaina heard from Georgiana.

Christopher's response was low, almost inaudible, as the pair rejoined the group. "There will be no matchmaking from you, Georgiana."

One look toward the back of the ballroom told Alaina that the musicians were taking a quick break, leaving time for a bit of conversation.

"What were you two talking about?" Eleanor interjected.

"Oh nothing," Christopher replied. "We were just debating the benefits of country air."

Georgiana hurriedly added, "Yes, we were talking of the country air and its ability to test out a couple's true compatibility. Sometimes the season in London leaves much to be desired."

The marquess cleared his throat, and to Alaina's ear seemed quite uncomfortable. Looking around the group, no one seemed to know what to say after such an odd statement. After what Alaina thought to be an interminable amount of time, she opened her mouth to say something, although not entirely sure what, when Georgiana queried her directly.

"Alaina, would you join me for a quick turn about the room?"

"Sure, Georgiana, it seems we are at a good break point in the music." Alaina joined arms with Georgiana, missing the mothers' approving looks, the duke's kind attentions, and an odd look from Christopher.

As they walked the perimeter of the room, Georgiana chattered while Alaina followed her lead. Alaina heard something about garden parties, and the Ashford estate, its many good qualities. With the cacophony in the room, she was barely capturing snippets of the constant stream of thoughts from Georgiana, such that she was surprised when she was asked a question.

"What do you think?" Georgiana looked to the side to catch Alaina's eyes.

"Of what?" Alaina questioned back, hoping her lack of attention did not seem rude.

"Of a garden party?"

"Sounds lovely."

"Good, then I shall start planning." Georgiana seemed to continue on with their promenade with renewed purpose, picking up the pace to traverse the remainder of the room.

"When will this party be, may I ask? It seems like you have months until the weather warms enough to truly do it right," Alaina observed. They were so early in the season; there were still some months of cold weather to make it through.

"Oh, no dear, I plan to have the party within the month. The Ashford Estate is beautiful all year round, with plenty of space even indoors should the weather be too ghastly. If we are lucky, we will be able to enjoy the grounds with a bit of snow before things turn too warm. But do not fret, with strategically placed fireplaces, the Ashford gardens can be lovely and comfortable at least for a stroll. To be perfectly honest, I am already a bit put out by London this season anyways. It is absolutely dreadful to be here alone at the moment, and…" Georgiana paused, as if remembering something upsetting, turning her face into a sorrowful mask, eyes looking far away.

"Are you thinking of the encounter with your cousin?" Alaina questioned. The only confirmation she got from Georgiana was a slight nod. And without realizing it, they had arrived back at the group, making a full circle around the room in what seemed to be record time. It was Christopher that greeted Alaina first.

"Lady Alaina, I would find it a great honor if you were to join me in the next dance." He spoke abruptly, less of a question than a statement.

Looking to Georgiana, Alaina found herself looking into twinkling eyes. "My dear, I do believe you were asked a question," Georgiana needled Alaina good-naturedly, having recovered from whatever melancholy had affected her.

Turning back to face the marquess, Alaina assented to his request. "It would be an honor, my lord."

The walk around the ballroom had perfectly filled the dead time in the music, and Alaina could see the musicians setting up for the next set. Accepting Christopher's arm, he led her onto the dance floor, saying nothing, although taking great care to guide her through the crowd to the proper spot on the floor for the contradance. As they set up in lines opposite one another among the other couples, their eyes met, and Alaina felt a flutter in her stomach, similar to the beginning of the ball. As the music began, they met in the middle of the aisle.

"I do wish to thank you again for this afternoon, Christopher," Alaina started.

"Like I said, there is no need to thank me," Christopher stated flatly. "It is what anyone should have done. Rudeness like that should not be countenanced."

"Ah, yes. You seem to have an aversion to such behavior, it seems," Alaina teased.

Finally, through his gruff exterior, Christopher chuckled. "I fear it is something that I cannot let pass without a comment."

"I must ask," Alaina said cautiously, "Would it be possible for us to start over again? I fear we may have both misjudged."

"Both?" Christopher feigned an affront, a smile finally breaking on his face.

Alaina shook her head, and let out a chuckle of her own. "Yes, both. Now do not claim offense so soon."

Christopher grunted assent and led her through the steps of the dance in comfortable silence. As soon as it was their turn to join in the center of the column of couples, Alaina placed her hand just on top of Christopher's, feeling a warmth spread up through her fingers, her body tingling at every point of contact with the man next to her.

Christopher felt once again stunned into silence. He had convinced himself that it was his duty for the season to determine the character of any lady Graham took interest in, and yet she had caught him off-guard.

Clearing his throat, he attempted once more to start a conversation. "So, Alaina, from your description the Norwich country estate sounds like quite a gem. Very well kept, if I were to guess."

Alaina gave him an oblique look, but answered his question. "I do love the country. It is serene and quiet, perfect for enjoying nature."

"Sounds lovely," Christopher agreed. "I expect there are not too many neighbors either."

"Actually," Alaina countered, "there are quite a few estates that belong to those of the peerage nearby my own family's. We even have our own balls from time to time, but they do not compare to what I have seen in London."

"Hmm, interesting," Christopher said, considering how best to proceed.

Alaina let out a giggle. "How is that information interesting?"

"Well, uh… I guess I find it interesting that one who is so enamored with the country, and has sufficient neighbors, would feel it necessary to travel to London to find a husband."

Alaina halted briefly as they promenaded down the aisle of dancers, and then continued, her voice tight, "I fear I do not know what your observation may mean?"

Even hearing the edge in her voice, Christopher pressed on, reminding himself his line of questioning was necessary if he was to determine her real motivations. Graham was much too trusting and had been fooled in the past. Christopher ventured a guess that genuine affection often resembled the attentions of a lady out for money or flirting for other ends, like Lady Bella. "I just find it strange to brave a season, when a perfectly suitable gentleman could be found nearer to home."

"Well, if you must know," Alaina gritted her teeth. "Lord Finch is not the first person to be narrow-minded in his vision for a perfect wife. There are many in the country who feel the sharpness of my mind is a detriment. I thought London would be better, but I was a bit disappointed at the start of the season."

"And now?" Christopher asked.

"Now, I have made better acquaintances, or at least I thought I had. The duke and his family seem like wonderful people. It would be a shame to leave now."

"Why a shame?" Christopher pounced.

Alaina mused, "My logic must be muddled because I fear that I am missing why it would be odd for someone such as myself to use the London season to meet new people and possibly make a match."

A few moments passed between them. Christopher was unsure of just what to say, and Alaina seemed deep in thought.

Alaina's eyes widened, then narrowed, as she watched Christopher from across the aisle, couples weaving in and out of the lines. Once the marquess and Alaina rejoined, Alaina hissed, "Am I to guess that you're prying about the state of my family's country estate and then prodding about why I would come to London instead of making a match closer to home is an attempt to determine if I am a suitable match for your friend?"

Christopher opened his mouth to offer a hollow rejection of that claim, but it seemed Alaina was incensed enough to continue without waiting for an answer. "How dare you! My family has no need of the duke's wealth or position. Did it occur to you that I may be in search of something more than a good match? Someone to respect and love me for myself? Is it so hard to believe that my experiences in courting have been less than ideal in the country, and I am just happy to find someone in the duke that is kind and thoughtful?"

Christopher noted the high color in Alaina's cheeks and felt a pang of guilt for his line of questioning. Having taken his interrogation to the extreme, he had once again offended the lady and could offer nothing to placate her that was not a lie.

As the dance ended, they both bowed to the other, after which Christopher closed the space to offer his arm and escort her back to the group. As they walked back, Christopher adjusted his cravat, suddenly feeling it too tight. He was ashamed and hoped he would find some words to take away the hurt he had imparted, but his tongue remained still. The marquess delivered Alaina back to the group, and watched as she forced a smile on her face, one that did not reach her eyes.

Only a few moments passed before Alaina turned to her mother. "I fear I am spent from all the dancing. Would it be possible for me to rest a bit in the ladies' retiring room?"

Her mother looked to the group. "If you would excuse us, Alaina and I need to find a place to sit and rest for a bit."

Eleanor was quick to understand. "Actually, Georgiana and I could join you. It certainly is about that time in the evening."

As the ladies walked away from the two men, Graham turned to Christopher. "Well, I would say this evening is a success. Lady Alaina is absolutely lovely this evening and truly a delight, but I would ask, what did you say to take away her smile? You are supposed to be helping me, remember?"

"I was just…" Christopher started, but was interrupted.

"Christopher! Graham!" called Charles, and he approached the men through the crowd. "How nice it is to see you here; the Stamford Ball is always the talk of the season, and this one is no different."

Graham nodded in greeting, his face impassive.

Christopher plastered a smile on his face and returned his cousin's greeting. "Charles, how splendid to see you here! Are you here with anyone in particular?"

"No, no, just mingling with members of the *ton*," Charles bubbled. "I find it is good for business to come to these events, and this one is my favorite. At least here, the company is always interesting."

Graham still held his silence, leaving Christopher to carry the conversation. "I take it you have found a few investors for your shipping company this evening? From the rumors I hear, you have all you need."

Charles shuffled from foot to foot and cleared his throat, but continued on brightly. "Well, there is never such a thing as too many investors, eh? I have not had much luck this evening, but the night is still young."

Graham broke his silence. "Not so young. I hope you have been enjoying the festivities."

Charles was slow to respond, his eyes narrowing ever so slightly. "Yes, your grace, I find that the evening is proving enjoyable. And it appears that you are also having a wonderful time. Who was that lady that was leaving as I arrived?"

"Lady Alaina," Graham answered curtly.

Christopher was quick to cut in, "Graham is on the hunt for a wife, and Lady Alaina has caught his eye."

"Well, I can see why," Charles said. "She is beautiful."

Graham's eyes darkened, and even though Charles's comment irked Christopher as well for some reason, he opened his mouth to break the tension. Just then a familiar figure approached.

"Cousin! What good fortune to see you here. I trust you are having a pleasant evening," Percy exclaimed as he stopped to converse with the men.

Already in a dark mood, Graham wasted no time with pleasantries. "Percy, I did not know this was a public ball. I am surprised they would let you into such an occasion."

Percy attempted a haughty look and sniffed as if annoyed to have to answer to such a barb. "I was able to secure an invitation. I am a baron, you know."

"We are aware of that fact; you seem to flaunt it like a dukedom." This time it was Christopher's turn to land an insult.

"Maybe someday it will be." Percy chuckled as he leveled the thinly veiled threat at Graham. Too cowardly to stick around after such a comment, he quickly added, "Have a good evening, gentlemen."

Graham and Christopher watched Percy retreat into the crowd. "Well, your cousin seems like a piece of work," said Charles.

Christopher was shocked when Graham growled, "It seems that is the lot of cousins. If you will excuse us, Christopher and I need to check on our companions."

Graham had already started walking away when Charles responded, seemingly unperturbed by the insult the duke had delivered, "I would want to make it back to Lady Alaina posthaste myself. She is a gem."

Christopher tried to ignore his cousin's ill manners, choosing to attribute them to an admiration of Alaina's beauty and nothing more. He quickly fell in behind his friend, giving only a weak smile to his own cousin before he allowed himself to be swallowed by the crowd. Catching up to Graham, Christopher was quick to reassure him. "I am sure Percy would not do anything to insult your family here, not with so many people."

"You give him too much credit," Graham countered.

"Well, we can still try to find your mother, sister, Lady Charlotte, and Alaina if you wish to err on the side of caution," Christopher acquiesced.

"That was my plan."

The two men set about making their way through the throng of people. Unfortunately, though, at the edge of the ballroom, Graham was stopped by a boisterous man, who clasped his hand in a jovial greeting. The man was quite a bit shorter than Graham and Christopher, and about as round as he was tall, with thinning hair and a bulbous nose from years of excess drink. Christopher quickly recognized him as the host of the ball and, seeing no way for Graham to quickly extract himself, Christopher quickly sidestepped to make his way to the ladies. Even with his earlier statements of reassurance to his friend, Christopher had a growing suspicion that Percy was up to no good.

<hr>

Alaina was thankful for the break in the retiring room, even if she had no need of the actual facilities. *How dare Christopher?!* Finding it hard to justify her anger toward the marquess, especially as a close friend of the duke, she had made an offer to start anew, and he had gone about interrogating her about her intentions! Perhaps what made his line of questioning smart more was that he was at least partially correct in suspecting her of scheming, but only to make the acquaintance of the duke. It was true that she wanted a love match, but setting about to orchestrate a meeting at the Mansfield Ball did not speak kindly of her character.

Alaina hoped that a bit of time away from the marquess would let her temper reach more of a simmer, and the dowager and her mother seemed more than happy to take their time.

However, Georgiana seemed oblivious of her plight and, having grown impatient, pulled Alaina out into the hallway. It was certainly a quieter place than the ballroom with lower, softer light emitting from small sconces placed far apart on the walls. The ladies' retiring room was located far down the hall to allow for maximum privacy, which left it quite desolate. The only people in the hall were ladies coming and going from the room. As Alaina and Georgiana walked down the hall with a mind to rejoin the party, someone stepped out from one of the many alcoves just in front of them, causing both Alaina and Georgiana to stop short. Recognition was immediate.

"Percy!" Georgiana exclaimed, more irritated than scared. "What in the world are you doing here? You seem to be lost." Georgiana crossed her arms in an attempt to look intimidating, although Percy towered over both of them.

"Well, cousin, I have found you, which was my aim, so I am not lost at all," Percy responded contritely, placing a hand on his chest in mock hurt. He then turned his pale face and leering attentions to Alaina. "My lady, I do feel the need to pass along the regard of my friend, Lord Finch. He would be most put out to have missed an opportunity to see you, but I fear your rejection of him so early in the season has caused him a fair amount of heartbreak."

Georgiana seemed unmoved by Percy's statement. "You had best leave us alone, Percy. I would not want Graham to find you harassing us in a dark hallway. Graham has no care for your friend's misfortunes in matrimony. On the contrary, Alaina's rejection of Lord Finch only improves his opinion of her."

The cousins continued to argue, leaving Alaina no opportunity to cut in and defend herself. "Well, dear cousin, that may be the case, but I am sure even your brother would not be able to make any lady his wife if a rumor about her virtue were to circulate. And who knows? Maybe Lord Finch took such *liberties* with you, Alaina. He *was* quite smitten."

At this, Alaina interjected, matching the outrage on Georgiana's face. "My virtue?! How could you even think to bandy about such lies? No one would believe it!"

"Oh, dear girl, you know how society can be with these things. All it takes is a suggestion, there need be no truth in it," Percy mocked, his smile filled with venom.

At that moment a looming presence appeared behind Percy, causing Alaina's heart, if not her head, to silently rejoice. *Christopher!* Feeling the change, Percy turned to find the marquess glaring at him from an uncomfortably close distance.

"Two times I find you accosting friends of mine in one day, Percy. I think it is best you remove yourself from this hallway, posthaste, before I feel the need to remove you myself," came Christopher's barely controlled order, rage seething between his teeth.

"As you wish," Percy bowed toward Christopher and then to the ladies, being sure to leave them with one last threat. "Remember, dear Alaina, what damage a rumor can do. Good evening."

All three watched him walk down the hall and disappear around the corner and into the ballroom, half-expecting one more snide remark. When he was gone, Christopher turned to Georgiana and Alaina, "Are both of you alright? Graham had sensed something amiss with Percy's presence here tonight. I am glad I was able to escape our host to see to your safety. I imagine Graham will be along shortly as well."

Georgiana turned a concerned eye toward Alaina, in shock after that ordeal. Percy's cruelty knew no bounds. "Christopher, I fear that I am quite put out by the experience. To encounter my scoundrel of a cousin twice in one day is too much. I wish to go warn my mother, who I imagine will want to leave immediately. Can you escort Alaina back to the ballroom and let Graham know we will want to retire from the party shortly, so he can call the carriage around? Alaina, should I give your mother the same message?"

Alaina quietly replied, "Yes, please do."

Georgiana, having received the affirmative answer she expected, nodded to Christopher, and silently turned on her heel to retrieve the mothers.

Christopher offered his arm to Alaina, but when she did not immediately take it, he leaned closer to try to catch her downcast eyes. The guilt from his forceful questioning still weighed on his mind. While he may be the last person she wanted to offer comfort, Christopher still hoped to cheer her up, especially after this latest Percy encounter. When she did finally look at him, what he saw ripped at his heart. Her eyes were glittering with barely controlled tears.

"Do you think anyone would actually believe a rumor Percy or Lord Finch conjured about me?" Alaina asked, almost in a daze.

"A rumor? About what?"

Alaina swallowed with difficulty, a lump in her throat making it difficult to speak. Finally, she croaked, "Percy implied that… he said, well, he said, 'maybe Lord Finch took liberties'… with me."

Christopher made a low sound in his throat, and Alaina could not fathom what it meant. It was a few moments before Christopher formed words. "I fear that Percy will go to any lengths to hurt Graham, without a care for collateral damage. The only comfort I can offer is that up until now his threats have been empty; Percy is a coward."

Alaina did not feel the least bit consoled by this statement, still paralyzed and in no hurry to return to the ballroom. Christopher could see that she was trying to collect herself before seeing the crowds and his friend. Without thinking, Christopher took her hand in his and squeezed, attempting to reassure her.

The physical connection had an unintended effect, shocking both Alaina and Christopher into awareness of the other, all prior insults and arguments forgotten in that moment. The brief glances and flutters now combined as the tinder for something that had been burning under the surface.

As if drawn by a larger force, Christopher took a single step and then another, closing the distance between them. Alaina walked into his embrace, their bodies melding together. Christopher's hands rested on the small of her back, the warmth of his hands seeping through her gown. Alaina rested her head on his chest for just a moment, and was comforted to hear the beat of his heart, one that seemed to be racing just the same as her own. When she pulled back, Christopher saw anxiety reflected in her eyes.

"Try not to worry. Percy is one for empty threats," Christopher said softly.

Alaina nodded her head slowly, but Christopher was sure Percy's threats were at the front of her mind. Yet, he was unsure of what to do to reassure her. As time crept along, Christopher became more aware of where their bodies connected, and his body betrayed his intention to merely comfort. Unable to stop himself, Christopher's hands first rested on her shoulders and then he gently cupped Alaina's face, his fingers gently stroking her cheek. His steel-blue eyes bore into her umber orbs and their breaths mingled until he finally lowered his lips to hers. Each of them surrendered to the moment, and Alaina found her hands in Christopher's hair almost unbidden, her body pressing more fully against his. Alaina was surprised to find iron-hewed thighs resting against her own through her skirts, and an unfamiliar tingling suffusing her core. The kiss was tender and electric, starting a flame inside both of them that threatened to consume.

Christopher pulled back abruptly, the chagrin over his actions acute. Alaina was a lady, first and foremost, and without any intention of offering marriage, he had no right to be stealing kisses and wanting more in dark hallways. If they were discovered, he would find it hard to maintain his bachelorhood. And that did not say anything as to his relationship, his duty to Graham. *Tasked with providing a voice of reason and then ending up in a tryst!*

"Alaina, I am so sorry for my actions. I never meant to… I did not think…" He started and stopped a few times, trying to find the right words, and then decided, "It is time to get you back to the party, back to Graham."

Shocked and embarrassed, all Alaina could do was quietly place her hand on his arm as he led her back to the ballroom. She felt a void where she and Christopher had touched just moments ago, and an even bigger hole in her heart. From lecturer to savior, callous to comforting, Alaina did not know which way was up with Christopher. And what of her plan to find a man who was suitable, someone like the duke, someone who was actually looking for marriage? Her head and her heart disagreed on much, but they could agree on one thing: the Stamford Ball could not end soon enough.

Chapter 7

Alaina stared out the front window of the parlor, focusing on nothing in particular. There were few passersby on the street so early in the morning. Alaina took a breath and closed her eyes, letting the light of the day warm her, her arms wrapping herself tight in an effort to banish the chill completely. The book she had chosen as her escape, the latest volume of *Mountville Castle*, was momentarily forgotten on her lap. Alaina picked at her modest mauve day dress, its pleated chiffon accents of pale pink gracing her throat and cuffs, providing the gown's only adornment. Alaina's choice of a simple bun met perfectly with the simplicity of the dress, and her mood.

Alaina had been thankful that they had decided to leave after the run-in with Percy, and *that kiss*. She had felt like a coward as they had made for the front door, but it was all she could do to steady her voice when she came face-to-face with Graham. Her initial shock and, dare she think, *pleasure* after the kiss with Christopher had morphed into thankfulness at not being discovered by anyone in the ton. Surely the scandal would have sent her parents running for the country and would have left her reputation in tatters. That was provided a rumor started by Percy did not do its own damage. To think that someone would be so cruel as to falsely indicate she had intimate relations with anyone, let alone someone she could not stand in the least!

Totally in a daze, Alaina missed the quiet knock at the door, but a gentle clearing of the throat that followed cut through her reverie and she looked back toward the open parlor door.

"Father," Alaina murmured, breaking into a smile, as she got up from her seat at the window to meet him. "What brings you to the parlor this morning? From what mother tells me, you have been quite engrossed in managing the estates, I hardly thought you had time."

"Now, now, I hardly think I have been so absent from this household as to not hear that my eldest daughter has caught the eye of this season's most eligible bachelor." After a quick pointed look from Alaina, Edward continued, "Your mother has been keeping me posted, although I think it fair to say that if it should not work out between the duke and yourself, your mother will have at least made a lasting friend of the dowager duchess."

Alaina giggled. "She and Eleanor have certainly become very close in the last few days. I half expected the wedding to be planned already with how much they talk, but truly they seem to have become the best of friends."

Alaina, having closed most of the distance between herself and her father, stood awkwardly, unsure of whether Edward planned to stay or go. The earl seemed a man on a mission, but what exactly it was eluded Alaina.

Finally making his way into the room, toward the pair of chairs before the fireplace, Edward cleared his throat. "Are you alright, Alaina? You seem a bit unlike yourself this morning."

Alaina huffed, wondering how long he had really been observing her at the door. She had been sitting near the window for quite some time and had not even opened the book in her lap. Choosing to avoid the heart of her father's question, Alaina countered with barely contained contempt, "It is amazing that anyone can find love in this city."

"Ah, yes, my dear, the London season can be tough, but you have been through that part already. From what I hear, the duke is quite smitten with you," Edward said, picking up the poker to stoke the fire.

Staring into the fire, newly rekindled, Edward appeared happy to wait in silence.

Eventually, Alaina spoke. "So how did you know you were in love with mother?"

"Well, simple really. I just saw her from across the room and our eyes met. Luckily for the both of us, we were quickly introduced, and conversation just seemed easy."

"I was hoping for something a bit more *helpful* than that," Alaina sighed, finally placing her book on a side table with a clunk before pacing along the wall next to the fireplace, coming to a stop a few paces from her father at each turn. "Did you not doubt you were in love for a second?"

Edward turned toward his daughter and met her eyes, as she had stopped her pacing and was waiting, hands clasped in front of her skirt, a slight frown on her face. "Alaina, my dear, everyone has doubts, but most of the time those doubts come about in love because one overanalyzes. From what your mother tells me, you and the duke get along splendidly well, and his family is quite pleasant to be around. She says you have been so happy these last couple of days, and that is a start. Sometimes love comes about at once, like it did for your mother and I, and sometimes it comes with time. You need to be patient."

"I know love can take many forms, it is just…" Alaina paused as her mind wandered once more to the embrace with Christopher, not quite sure how to continue. She thrust her reaction away in favor of her logical plan. "It is just that I seem to have gained the attention of the duke, and he is charming, and kind, and we have the most wonderful conversations, but I am still unsure if the connection is really *there* or ever could be."

"Well, not every love story is the same. Maybe it will take time for you to know your mind and your heart with the duke. I mean, it has only been a few short days. It may turn out that he is *not* your match," Edward stated.

Alaina glanced toward the floor, hoping to avoid her father knowing everything about what the last few days had been like. In particular, the kiss from the marquess had been surprising and unsettling. It had been so unexpected that she had no time to think in the moment of its implications, but since then her mind had been filled with unwelcome thoughts. How was it that she could find such pleasure with someone with whom she seemed to consistently argue? What if they had been caught by someone in society? Would she be forced to become an outcast? Was it the magic of the ball? Alaina's fear of Percy and Christopher's rescue? Or was she just *wanton*?

And all that was not even mentioning the fact that the marquess had seemed outwardly so unaffected after the moment had passed. He had easily seen her back to the ballroom, into the care of the duke. He had then gone back to escort her mother, the duke's mother, and Georgiana to the front foyer to meet them in order to retire for the evening, all the while giving no indication of any of it meaning anything to him. Meanwhile for her, the kiss had been all she could think about.

Not wishing to expound on all the events of the previous days, she merely rejoined, "Perhaps you are right. Love at first sight is not so common, I would think."

"Certainly, my darling daughter," Edward stated. "All you can do is follow your heart. I am sure whatever man you choose to marry will feel like the luckiest on earth."

He crossed the small distance to where his oldest daughter stood and brought her into an affectionate hug. Alaina returned the hug with fervor and when she pulled back from her father's embrace, she found his eyes misty and brimming with pride.

Edward cleared his throat. "Well, I should leave you to your musings before any callers should find me all emotional over the prospect of my daughter finding a husband and a wonderful life outside of the confines of our family. That may put a damper on any courtship." He must have thought better of his last statement and added, "Although, you know I am glad to lend my assistance if the need should arise to show someone the door."

"Of course, Father," Alaina smiled, watching as he exited the room.

"Well, I have no idea of what to expect from today," Alaina sighed, sitting once again on the front sofa, trying to occupy her mind with a book instead of the duke, Christopher, and that kiss!

***

"Graham, for the last time, you do not need me to join you on any more outings," Christopher practically growled, as he looked at his friend across the parlor. Graham and Georgiana had joined him for breakfast. It was Christopher's thought that they would just depart from the Rochester townhome when they were done and, hopefully, leave him in peace.

Georgiana was the one to answer Christopher's protest. "Christopher, you have seen Percy's maleficent motives up close, and I fear that our interaction last night was not even the worst of it. *I* would feel better if you were to join us today."

Christopher sighed and looked between the siblings, ruminating on how to say no to Georgiana, when she added,

"And, if I were to guess, Graham prefers to have you there to keep me from monopolizing Lady Alaina's time. He may have certain questions to ask her today."

Finally, Graham broke his silence. "Georgiana, I would beg you to keep your conjectures to yourself."

"Am I wrong?"

Graham snorted, but did not answer, and Georgiana broke out into a self-satisfied smile.

First Christopher's presence was to provide additional protection in case they should run into Percy, which was unlikely, and now it was to provide a walking partner for Georgiana, so she would not invade any bit of privacy between Graham and Alaina. Both valid, but thin reasons.

It was in Christopher's mind that the last thing he wanted to do was to see Alaina today, or ever again. Last night, he had been convinced that their kiss had been borne out of the moment, out of his concern for a lady in distress, but when the kiss still plagued his mind this morning, he was forced to admit that being in her presence may be ill-advised. Christopher certainly did not want matrimony; he had watched his parents make each other miserable.

Never mind the fact that he had been in a passionate embrace with his friend's love interest a mere twelve hours past. Did it make it better or worse that Christopher's mind continued to wander to that dark hallway even as they sat here talking of Graham's courting activities? The whole situation was mad!

"So, can we count on your support today?" Graham asked, and Christopher felt his resistance melting, or maybe it was that he did also want to visit Alaina. The war between his mind and his body, for he would not admit that his heart had anything to do with it, felt like one he could not win. And so, he capitulated, to his friends and to himself.

"Lucky for the both of you, or maybe unfortunately for me, I have no other plans this morning. Shall we be about it, then?"

⚜

Alaina was eventually joined in the parlor by her sister and mother, after the pair's much later breakfast. Evelina and Charlotte seemed perfectly capable of carrying on an animated conversation without much more than a short assent here and there from Alaina.

It was just before noon when Arthur entered the parlor to announce the duke, his sister, and the marquess. Arthur may have been as discreet a butler as they came, but he passed an affectionate stare to Alaina. She truly could not remember a time in her life when Arthur was not present, and she had come to value him as a friend and a kind of second father figure.

After the brief introduction, all the presented persons entered the room, with the duke sweeping in first, hat in hand, and the marquess and Georgiana entering second. Each of the gentlemen gave a brief bow to the ladies in the room, with Charlotte, Alaina, and Evelina repaying the gesture with curtsies of their own. Alaina pointedly avoided making anything but brief eye contact with Christopher, attempting to focus almost all of her attention on Graham and Georgiana. *If he could ignore the kiss, as he seemed so inclined to do, so could she!* Even with that effort, she had a prickling sensation that told her Christopher's eyes rarely strayed from her person. And yet, after a quick glance toward the marquess, Alaina found him focused on the sibling pair.

After pleasantries, Graham was quick to offer an outing. "I hope you are prepared for a walk. It is quite brisk today, and your dress certainly seems quite delicate. I hope you have a good cloak?"

Alaina found it difficult to focus on the duke, the kiss with Christopher and her embarrassment at the front of her mind. She pushed aside those thoughts and gave a quick answer. "Your grace, I assure you my outerwear should suffice for an outing. I assume we are headed to the park?"

A look crossed Graham's face and he expounded on their plans. "Why yes, Alaina, I was planning on taking a walk through Hyde Park, if it is ok with your mother? Christopher and Georgiana can provide us with a proper chaperone arrangement."

Charlotte quickly gave her assent. "Alaina has been hoping you would call today. I am certainly ok with the outing and will await your return. I assume barring anything too exciting, we can have refreshments for you when you return?"

"Yes, that would be most delightful. Shall we?" The duke turned toward Alaina, offering his arm to punctuate his question.

"I would be delighted. Arthur will most certainly have my cloak and muff at the door waiting for us."

They all made their way out of the parlor. Having successfully avoided eye contact with Christopher for the whole of the exchange, Alaina found her eyes roaming over Christopher's broad shoulders and crisp dress as she and the duke followed behind the marquess and Georgiana, her mind wandering to their kiss once more. It was easy enough to consider the kiss they had shared the previous evening when the marquess's attention was not focused on her person, but it was Alaina's most fervent hope to avoid any conversation with Christopher. Thinking of his body pressed against hers was one thing, but having to find words in his presence would be quite another task, and one Alaina would most likely fail.

⎯⎯⎯ ⚘ ⎯⎯⎯

"I just do not see how that is relevant," Georgiana said, not bothered by her brother's discontent.

"How is it not relevant to determine the size of the gathering that is supposed to be happening at *my* estate in a few weeks' time?" Graham countered. Alaina could certainly tell that he was annoyed with his sister.

"Oh, dear brother, you always say it is the family's estate. Why is it suddenly such a concern that I am using it to plan a small gathering you would hardly notice at any other point in time?" Georgiana paused ever so slightly to deliver this final point, and gave her brother a flippant smile before turning forward again and continuing down the path.

Alaina heard Graham sigh and witnessed an ever so slight shake of his head. He obviously was annoyed with his sister, but not angry.

"She does have a point, Graham," Christopher added.

Graham fixed his attention on Christopher. He cleared his throat, leveling a pointed stare complete with a raised eyebrow. Christopher quickly turned back to face forward, getting the hint that he was not to interject.

Alaina had not known what to expect from this outing, but she was certainly surprised by the turn of events. Conversation had flowed easily out of Georgiana about the weather, the play currently at the Royal Theater, and this latest conversation about the garden party. Graham, usually confident and quick to engage in conversation and banter with his sister, was unusually quiet. His engagement on the matter of the garden party and his perceived annoyance only grew more pointed with Georgiana's constant needling and interruptions when he had tried to engage with Alaina in any type of conversation.

"Come along, Christopher. I feel my brother is quite annoyed with us at the moment," Georgiana chirped as she dragged Christopher along the path, giving Graham and Alaina a bit more privacy.

Another sigh from Graham brought Alaina's concentration back to her companion, who to this point had rigidly led her through the park on their walk. Feeling a certain relaxation of his posture and softening of his arm muscles under her hand made Alaina curious. Tilting her head to the side to get a better glimpse of her escort, she caught him staring intently at her.

"Is everything alright, Graham? I hope you are not too put out by Georgiana's garden party. When she asked me if it was a good idea at the ball, I thought nothing of it being an inconvenience."

"Alaina, my dear, everything is alright, and the garden party is of no consequence to me. It was just striking that my sister chose today to unnecessarily needle me at every turn. She knows I was hoping for a comfortable, somewhat private walk in the park."

"Oh," the small word escaped from Alaina's lips as she broke the stare between them, suddenly uncomfortable.

Graham gently placed his hand over the hand Alaina had rested on his arm and squeezed, starting up again with their walk, now at a sufficiently far distance to not be overheard by Christopher and Georgiana. Alaina was surprised, as she had not even realized they had stopped walking.

"Alaina, I apologize if I make you uncomfortable," Graham started. "I was quite hoping that my need for a semi-private audience would be met naturally today, and that the reason for it would come out during the normal course of conversation, but it seems that Georgiana had other plans altogether."

Graham's hand remained overtop her own and she remained mute, really unsure of how to best respond to such a statement. She was truly happy to be with the duke, to have him showing interest in her, just as she had hoped and planned. He was sweet, kind, and respectful of her person, of her mind. But the close enough proximity of Christopher tied her stomach in knots, the memory of their interlude wheedling its way into her mind at the most inopportune moment. His glacial eyes, looking at her as if he could see through to her soul. It was unsettling. There was no opportunity there, his snarky remarks on marriage and obvious distaste for her made that quite clear.

Graham forged ahead. "Alaina, have you enjoyed my company over the last several days?"

It was this question that she could not avoid. "Why yes, your grace, I certainly have enjoyed our time together, even with some moments cutting the interactions or events short."

"Good, I had hoped you felt the same as I did, that the last few days have been most pleasant. I do share your consternation that we have not been able to spend more time alone in conversation, but I do hope we can continue to get to know each other over the course of the next few weeks and months." Graham paused, and Alaina could tell that he was wondering how to continue. "Would I be permitted to embark on a more formal courtship with you, Alaina? Not engaged, obviously, that will come with time if we each wish it."

Graham again stopped them on the trail, in a small copse of trees that provided a bit of coverage and space, away from any prying eyes in the park. The duke faced Alaina and clasped both of her hands in his own. They locked eyes and Alaina could see the earnest plea for her time, her person, and maybe her future.

Alaina hoped that Graham could not feel her pulse race. She certainly was touched by his interest. He was kind, and genuine, and it did not hurt that he was handsome. But, Alaina found it difficult to banish the prior evening and her scandalous interlude with his best friend. She had been so worried about the threat of a rumor from Percy about her virtue. Alaina could only imagine if they had been caught! It was not like the marquess was in search of a wife, or even liked her. Their kiss seemed to have no effect on him, either after the ball or even on their outing. And every other interaction, from their first meeting, was confusing at best and confrontational at worst. It would be silly to let their connection, whatever it was, mar a wonderful courtship with the duke.

Pushing the kiss and all other thoughts of Christopher from her mind, Alaina responded kindly, steeling her emotions. "Why yes, Graham, I would like that very much."

Trying to remember her father's sage advice, Alaina smiled and reveled in the moment, convincing herself that it was best to give the duke a chance. Graham released a breath as a smile appeared on his face. "Well then, Alaina, I have accomplished my most fervent wish for the day."

After a slight pause as they regarded one another for a second or so more, it was back to the walk. "Unfortunately for us, Alaina, I feel we should rejoin our companions up ahead. They seem to have stopped to wait for our slow plodding." Graham pointed up ahead on the pathway where Georgiana and Christopher were still within sight.

"And may I suggest that on our next walk we take our mothers along? It seems that Christopher and Georgiana are much too interested in inserting themselves into our conversation," Graham stated matter-of-factly.

Alaina was more than happy to concur on that point. "That sounds like a good idea to me."

Without the marquess around, Alaina could hope that the memory of their kiss would fade, and her courtship with Graham could flourish. All Alaina could hope was that Christopher's silence on the matter meant he wanted to forget their kiss the same as she.

CHAPTER 8

Alaina took in the sights at the Bond Street Bazaar, shifting the packages in her arms as she followed next to Georgiana. The countess chattered incessantly about what was needed for the party: a seemingly endless list. The cacophony of sound, from the hawking of vendors to ladies and their maids haggling over prices, made it difficult for Alaina to hear exactly what the countess was saying. Graham had insisted that if they were to be out and about in London, he and Christopher should both join them, for safety, and the marquess's presence was stretching Alaina's nerves more tightly than she cared to admit. Alaina had certainly welcomed the past week without Christopher as a shadow.

True to his word, Graham had engaged her in more private outings over the past week, including a couple of walks in the park with both of their mothers, one walk with Evelina and Charlotte, and even one afternoon tea with Georgiana in tow. Alaina found a small smile on her face as she remembered their witty conversations and the duke's solicitous nature. He was kind, intelligent, and an overall wonderful person. However, Alaina often found herself imagining another pair of eyes, ones the color of the ocean, in moments of silence, in her dreams, and haunting her at every step. Alaina's smile turned to a grimace as she realized it was the first time she had seen Christopher since the walk in Hyde Park, and now she was faced with the object of her wandering thoughts.

The past week had disappeared quickly. When she was not spending time with the duke, Alaina found her time commandeered by Georgiana with all manner of party planning.

The first order of business was to send out formal invitations, which Alaina helped Georgiana pen. The next day of planning had consisted of mapping out a few days of activities, including rides about the grounds at the Ashford estate, some luncheons and teas complete with card games or charades, and culminating in a small garden dance at the end of the third day, leaving the fourth day of the gathering to be relaxed as people took their leave of the Ashford estate. The idea was for the country gathering to last only four days total, so that the impact to everyone's social season in London would be minimal.

With all the details of the party set, Georgiana had declared their need for an outing to acquire all the necessary supplies. Alaina had thought it merely an excuse for her to leave the Ashford townhome. Without chaperoning duties, Georgiana had attended fewer society events in the preceding week, and seemed a little perturbed.

At the bazaar, Alaina was amazed by the crush of people and wares. Each stall was filled to the brim with all types of trinkets, and Alaina found it difficult to imagine needing much else for the party in the country.

"Gentlemen, would you mind overly much if Alaina and I stopped at the dressmaker and the milliner?" Georgiana chirped, a triumphant smile marking her face after a full day of shopping.

Alaina leveled a perturbed stare at her companion. "Georgiana, we agreed no additional wear would be required for this event. Not only is there not enough time for anything to be made before we have to travel to Ashford, but I am quite sure the men do not want to tag along with us for that." Alaina felt acutely uncomfortable with the idea of shopping for clothing with Graham and Christopher in attendance. The only shopping she had ever done in her life had been with her mother and sister; not even her father joined.

"Alaina, you must at least look for something special for the dance on the third evening. And besides, five days is plenty of time for the dressmaker and seamstresses to make a few day dresses as well. Everyone has already procured their wardrobes for the season, so I imagine the shops are in need of some business."

Sighing, Alaina resigned herself to an acutely uncomfortable trip to the dressmaker's shop. Even if Alaina's enthusiasm was lacking, Georgiana did not seem to notice as she hurried off in the direction of Madam Benoit's. Alaina was quick to follow, not wishing to be separated from her only female companion. Graham and Christopher followed at a distance.

Georgiana made it to the door of the shop and looked at the group and then to Alaina.

"Shall we, Alaina?" Georgiana motioned to the door. "Graham, you and Christopher can wait outside and stand watch in case any brigands seek to accost us."

"Yes," Alaina answered, as she met Georgiana at the door, glancing back sheepishly toward Graham, pointedly ignoring the marquess, before entering just ahead of Georgiana.

"So, how long do you think they will be in there?" Christopher asked.

"With Georgiana, who knows," Graham chuckled. "As a child, whenever she and my mother went out shopping it felt like the whole afternoon passed before they returned."

Christopher groaned and shuffled his feet, looking up and down the street. A couple caught his eye.

"Look who it is," Christopher pointed.

Graham looked up and set his jaw. "Percy and his lady."

The walkway was busy, but certainly not enough to hide their presence. Both men stood their ground as the Baron and Lady Barbara approached.

A brief nod of acknowledgement was all that was offered before the insults began. "Ah, cousin, what are the odds we encounter you?" Percy remarked, then he addressed Lady Barbara. "My dear, I am sorry to have our outing ruined."

Lady Barbara sniffed and raised her head a bit. "Certainly not something we could have anticipated. No matter, I had planned to go to the dressmaker, and so I am here. I will leave you all to talk, just do not come to fisticuffs in the middle of the street."

Barbara made her way into the shop, a small tinkling bell punctuating the silence between the three gentlemen. It was Christopher who attempted to fill the quiet as they waited.

"So, Percy," he started, "you and Lady Barbara are often in each other's company. Shall we offer a congratulations?"

Percy's eyes narrowed a bit, but he responded blandly. "No congratulations are necessary. We just encountered one another on the street moments ago and were just chatting when we came upon the two of you."

"Ah," Christopher responded, his brow furrowing in confusion. Graham remained mute.

After what felt like minutes, Percy clasped his hands together. "Well, gentlemen, like I said, I was on my way to the, uh… the milliner myself for new boots when I happened across Lady Barbara. I should be on my way."

And with a glare and a tip of his hat, Percy made his way around Christopher and Graham and continued down the street.

⁕

Alaina had been looking over the velvets on the back table when a tinkling of the bell alerted her to the front door. Looking up from a deep emerald bolt of fabric, Alaina half expected to see Graham and Christopher enter the shop, but was surprised to see Lady Barbara filling the portal.

Georgiana was across the shop, in animated discussions with Madam Benoit about a number of dresses for the party. Her attention had not moved to the front door yet.

Like a serpent, Lady Barbara moved silently through the many tables piled high with stacks of fabric, until she came face to face with Alaina.

"Lady Alaina," the lady sneered.

"Lady Barbara," Alaina answered flatly. Lady Barbara continued to stand in front of Alaina, her glare never wavering. Hoping to avoid another confrontation, Alaina attempted to make polite conversation. "So, are you shopping for a particular event?"

Lady Barbara let out a huff and hissed, "Please do not put on airs as if you care a whit for what I am doing. If I were more suspicious, I might think you were trying to determine what ball I would be attending, so you could embarrass my family yet again; maybe even flaunt your courtship with the duke."

"Lady Barbara," Alaina said in a gentler tone. "It was never my intent to cause you or your family pain. It seemed to me …"

Lady Barbara interrupted Alaina with a sharp retort. "Oh, save it! I do not care to hear any of your mewling. Just go back to your books and leave me alone."

Alaina caught a motion out of the corner of her eye, and was relieved to see Georgiana approach.

"Why, Lady Barbara, I am surprised to see you and Alaina conversing at all. I cannot imagine there would be much to say, or, I guess, much *nice* to say," Georgiana interjected, her tone overly cheery, as she moved to stand beside Alaina.

Now outnumbered, Lady Barbara seemed a bit reluctant to continue her attack, and her silence was quickly overshadowed by the chatter from Madam Benoit. "Oh! Mon dieu! Lady Barbara, I do apologize for not seeing you when you first entered! I have just finished with Lady Georgiana, if you have a particular interest in anything?"

Lady Barbara's demeanor quickly changed, and she turned a smile toward the proprietor. "Madam Benoit, you are so kind. I had come in to see if I could order a few more evening dresses…"

Lady Barbara receded to the back of the store in animated conversation over the latest styles or something of the like.

"Alaina, are you all right?" Georgiana asked softly.

"I am now," Alaina answered, sure that her encounter with Lady Barbara could have been much worse. "I must thank you for your timing. I fear she was about to tear me to shreds."

"Well, I should apologize for not even seeing her enter," Georgiana disagreed. "I should have been over right away. She did not say anything overly hurtful?"

"Nothing, thankfully. I understand her not being able to forgive me for rejecting her brother's suit, however ill-conceived, but I had hoped the outward animosity would simmer to quiet disdain," Alaina finished.

A tinkling of the bell on the door once more announced the arrival of more guests in the shop. This time it was Graham and Christopher, who wasted no time in approaching Alaina and Georgiana.

In a hushed voice, the duke inquired, "I hope you ladies fare well?" He looked to Alaina, where his gaze lingered, and then to Georgiana.

Alaina gave a slight nod, and Georgiana was quick to stop any further questions. "We are quite fine, thank you. I take it from you joining us in the shop that something is amiss?"

"Yes," was all Graham said.

Christopher expounded further, "Lady Barbara was accompanied by Percy, who made his way to the milliner after the lady entered here. I fear any of your planned stops are tainted."

"Oh, well, I have no wish to encounter Percy nor stay here with Lady Barbara," Georgiana said quietly. "Alaina, would you forgive me if I cut our trip short? Maybe you can come back later with your mother?"

Alaina wanted to assure her new friend that there was nothing to worry about, even if she had no real need for a new dress. "Of course, Georgiana. Maybe I can even bring Evelina along, she was quite put out that she could not join us."

"Perfect," Georgiana chirped. "Then shall we be off?"

The group nodded in assent, and began to make their way to the front door. Alaina found that she still held onto the bolt of velvet, a beautiful deep emerald, and moved to straighten the fabric on the table. She looked up and was surprised to find Christopher rooted to his spot, an intractable look on his face.

Alaina's thoughts raced; their arguments, their kiss, Christopher's brooding stares, and his shows of concern all muddled in her head as she made to move past him.

"Are you *actually* ok?" came Christopher's question, as his hand softly cupped her elbow, the touch enough to shock Alaina and stop her in her tracks. His hand barely touched the inside of her arm, and yet a shiver ran up her spine as the heat seeped through her sleeve.

Finding herself unable to move, as if Christopher held her in a vice grip, his steel-blue eyes searching hers, Alaina sought to keep their interaction short. "Yes, I am quite alright. Lady Barbara had no time to cause any trouble."

Alaina watched as Christopher stepped back, breaking the featherlight touch that seemed to sear Alaina's sleeve, before he responded, "Well, I find it is best to avoid those like Lady Barbara all together."

Alaina chuckled, "I do believe you have mentioned that on several occasions. But based on your advice, I might find myself shunning all of society."

Wishing to avoid any conflict, their many arguments weighing on her, Alaina moved around the table in an effort to follow Graham and Georgiana, but she was stalled by Christopher as he said, "I do not wish to avoid everyone… And I would be the first to admit that sometimes my first impressions are flawed."

Alaina was shocked and unsure of the meaning of Christopher's statement and found herself tongue-tied. She attempted to change the subject and cleared her throat, hoping it would keep her voice even. "We should be going, my lord."

"We should," Christopher replied softly, both of them still rooted in place. "I just hope you are able to finish your shopping at a later time. Maybe you can even have a dress made with that velvet that had you so enraptured."

Alaina started a bit at his statement, the timber of his voice almost a caress, sending a ripple of awareness through Alaina's body. Unsettled by her reaction to Christopher, Alaina took a few quick steps and joined the rest of the group, who had gathered at the front door. She felt Christopher's presence behind her, but did not look around, afraid of any further flip of her stomach. She was happy to follow the group out of the shop without further delay. If Alaina thought to forget Christopher through the force of time and space, she had seriously misjudged.

***

"What gowns are you going to have for the garden party?" Evelina asked again, a huff accompanying the question as if she were certain her sister was ignoring her out of spite.

"Huh? Oh, yes, the dresses. I am afraid we will have to return tomorrow with mother, maybe you can join us this time."

"How wonderful!" Evelina exclaimed. "Mother had promised to take me once I heard you were going shopping. But wait, why must you return tomorrow?"

"Lady Barbara interrupted our outing, and Percy, it seems, was occupying the next shop on our list. Georgiana felt the day finished," Alaina sighed.

"Oh, how awful!" Evelina exclaimed. "I assume she did not apologize for her past behavior and ask to be fast friends?"

"No," Alaina stated flatly. "Thankfully Lady Barbara had no chance to say much of anything, but it definitely put a damper on the afternoon."

"I can imagine," Evelina agreed.

Alaina made no more effort to engage in conversation, gazing into the fireplace absently.

Evelina paused for a moment before she inquired, "Alaina, are you quite alright?"

"Yes, I must just be a bit tired. Georgiana seems to have boundless energy," Alaina offered as an explanation, turning her gaze toward her sister ever so slightly.

"Oh, she is probably just as spent as you!" Evelina rejoined, keeping her tone light and teasing. Still, Alaina did not seem entirely present in the room mentally.

"Is everything ok with your gentleman?" Evelina tried once again to draw her sister out of whatever abyss had swallowed her.

"Who?" came Alaina's reply. The question seemed to snap the spell, and Alaina turned to look directly at her sister, the question still hanging in the air.

"The duke, silly. You know, *Graham*. The one who has been treating you to the most wonderful experiences in London," Evelina ribbed.

"Oh, yes, everything is perfect. This week has been truly wonderful. It's just..." Alaina paused.

"Just what?"

Alaina took a deep breath, heaving it out before she answered simply, "Well, the marquess joined us this afternoon."

"Ah," Evelina said. "Did his mood ruin the afternoon?"

"No, no, nothing like that," Alaina corrected.

Evelina opened her mouth as if to ask further questions, but a knock sounded on the door. Without waiting for an answer, the handle turned and in through the door came their mother, Charlotte, carrying a full tray of tea and biscuits. Evelina jumped off the bed and relieved Charlotte of the tray, allowing Charlotte to close the door behind her. How she had opened it would remain a mystery to both sisters.

"So, girls, I thought you might want some tea to warm you up after a day like today, and Alaina, I wanted to hear about your adventures in town." Charlotte moved across the room to sit right in front of the fire. "We also need to discuss our plans for next week. I cannot believe the party is so close at hand!"

"Well, today was not as exciting as you think. We just went from shop to shop, following Georgiana as she stocked up on games, candles, stationary, and all manner of things for the gathering in the country. I fear we may need to go back for dresses. Lady Barbara interrupted our visit to Madam Benoit's, but nothing too terrible happened." Alaina recounted their day, silently praying for no additional questions.

A look of worry crossed Charlotte's brow, but she continued cheerfully, "Well, we can all go together tomorrow.

I am sure Evelina would like something new to wear as well." Charlotte received an enthusiastic nod from her youngest. "A garden party at the end of February? It is definitely something new, but it should be magical as long as there is not too much snow, if any, and the weather is not too frigid," Charlotte mused. "Surely Georgiana knows what she is doing."

"I do not care if it is too cold; I am just excited to be able to attend! I appreciate that the rules are a bit more relaxed in the country. I have been so bored in London." Evelina waved her hand to dismiss her mother's worries.

"Well, I am excited we can all participate. Your father is going to stay in London to tend to his books and solicitors, so it shall be just the three of us. Eleanor and I have been talking about travel arrangements. She insists that we can all travel together. I feel like that may make the journey more fun. How does it sound to you both?" Charlotte queried.

"That would be delightful!" exclaimed Evelina.

Alaina seemed to ponder the question overmuch and then asked a question of her own. "Would the marquess be joining us as well?"

"Well, it is possible. I assume he is invited, correct? Why would you ask?" Charlotte queried, a perplexed look passing over her face.

"I just feel that we would be awfully cramped in one carriage is all. As it is, with the duke and his family and us that would be six people!" Alaina blurted.

Charlotte clucked at her daughter. "Alaina, I am sure Eleanor would not have us traveling together if it would not be comfortable. Besides, maybe the marquess is traveling on his own."

"It seems like the duke and the marquess are ever together," Alaina said quietly.

Alaina got up from the chair she had been sitting in and once again stood at the mantle, gazing into the fire. Evelina and Charlotte exchanged a concerned look.

Assuming the same as Evelina, Charlotte tried to reassure her daughter, but misplaced the source of her unease. "There will be plenty of time for you and the duke to continue courting in the country, more quieter moments like this past week. I am sure the marquess will not intrude."

"Yes, I hope so." Alaina sighed and turned to face both her mother and sister, who were staring at her with concern even still. "I must just be tired; I am so sorry for being out of sorts this evening."

"My dear," Charlotte began, gently placing her teacup in the saucer. "I know today must have been a tiring day, especially with the cold weather *and* Lady Barbara. We should let you rest."

Charlotte put the tea service back on the tray, leaving the tray for Alaina if she should need it, and quietly ushered her youngest daughter out of the room. Charlotte paused at the door to look once more at her oldest child, who had turned her attention back to the fire. She thought better of saying anything further and figured heading to the country might bring her out of the doldrums. It would at least be far away from the likes of Lady Barbara.

Much later in the evening, Alaina startled awake and looked around her room, her heart still racing from the nightmare that had plagued her sleep. The fire was still burning high and the clock on the mantelpiece showed the time to be just shy of midnight. After her mother and sister had left, she had forced herself to drink some tea, feeling it warm her up completely. Then, without undressing, she laid down on top of her comforter to rest, planning to stay up and read in the parlor once she had warmed up.

Apparently, she had fallen asleep, completely missing dinner. She imagined her mother had checked on her, found her sleeping, and left her alone. But now that Alaina was awake, she was hungry, and hopeful something was left in the kitchen as a snack, so that she could go back to sleep. Putting on house shoes over her stockinged feet, Alaina grabbed a candle, lighting it from the fire. She quietly made her way out of her room and downstairs, contemplating the dream that had awakened her.

She had been at a ball of sorts, but the people around her were a blur. An image of Graham and Georgiana formed in front of her, with Georgiana whispering in Graham's ear. He was looking at Alaina both aghast and angry. She stepped forward to try to explain, only for them to disappear into the crowd. Then, as if by magic, Christopher appeared, and when she tried to run to him, he put his hand up to stop her and then laughed at her. And then everyone at the ball laughed at her, their faces seeming to emerge from the blur she had seen before. She began to turn around to look for anyone for help and only saw her family turned from her in shame, her mother crying on her father's shoulder, and her sister, Evelina, red with embarrassment. She had woken with a cry in her throat and tears stinging her eyes, glad to find that it was just a dream.

Once downstairs, she headed straight to the back of the house and into the kitchen. The stove was cold, but on the small table was a plate of scones and biscuits beside a pitcher of water. Alaina found a glass in one of the upper cupboards and filled it with water, grabbing a few biscuits before retreating from the kitchen and back toward the staircase at the front of the house.

Balancing everything and the candle proved difficult, but Alaina was able to make it to the staircase, when a soft light from the front parlor doorway caught her eye. She poked her head into the parlor, surprised she had not seen it on her way to the kitchen. In the parlor, a lone candle sat on the small table between the two main chairs in front of the fireplace. The flames in the fireplace had burned down to embers, as if someone had accidentally fallen asleep. A chill had begun to creep into the room, and Alaina stepped inside the parlor to get a better look, shivering as she did so. As she moved closer to the fireplace on the far side of the room, she saw her father's profile and heaved a sigh of relief, as he appeared to have taken up refuge in one of the wingback chairs facing the fireplace.

Depositing her candle, snacks, and glass of water onto the table beside him, she reached out her hand and gently shook his shoulder to wake him.

"Papa," Alaina whispered, trying not to startle him.

Edward's eyes slowly opened and for a moment he seemed confused at his surroundings. But as he looked around, his vision cleared. He took stock of the clock on the mantle, and he turned his head, catching Alaina leaning over his shoulder. "My dear, what are you doing up so late? I was just in here relaxing after a grueling day with my estate manager and solicitor and I must have fallen asleep, but I never imagined anyone would be up at this hour. Is everything ok?"

"I fell asleep quite unexpectedly and slept straight through dinner. I was just grabbing a snack and saw the light from the parlor. I will have to say you scared me a bit."

"Sorry dear," Edward apologized and then added, "Missing dinner is quite unlike you."

Alaina paused and then came around to sit in the chair opposite her father. Closer to the fire, it was still warm enough to sit and talk for a few minutes.

"Well..." Alaina started, unsure of where to begin, or really what to say. "I guess I am a bit excited... and anxious about the visit to Graham's estate in the country."

"Oh, well, you and Graham have gotten on so well these past two weeks or so, I see little reason that you would be nervous about that, unless his family has been unkind? At least you and Georgiana seem to be getting along quite well. From what your mother says, the dowager duchess..."

"Yes, no, she is quite a good friend. I have really enjoyed her company, and the dowager duchess is quite nice as well," Alaina interjected quickly, wanting to avoid any thought in her father's mind that Graham or his family had been unwelcoming in any way.

Edward looked across the small table at his daughter. "Alaina, my darling daughter, I hope you feel you can talk to me about your concerns. I promise to not even mention them to your mother, although we rarely keep secrets from each other. As long as you are not in danger, I will defer to your wishes." Edward left the statement there, preferring not to pry.

"Papa, I fear…" Alaina paused and chewed her lip.

"What is it that troubles you?" Edward asked, his voice soft.

"I fear that I may not be perfectly sure that the duke is the one for me, and I feel terribly that I am letting our courtship drag on with such doubts," Alaina admitted.

"Drag on?" Edward questioned, almost rhetorically. "Two weeks is such a short amount of time, you could hardly be accused of drawing out your time with the duke unnecessarily. Like I said before, not every love story starts with a lightning strike. You need to let your heart find its way."

"I suppose," Alaina acquiesced, but the bent of her dream still weighed on her mind, and her response came out taciturn. How was she to explain that Christopher had been at the center of her thoughts?

But Edward was not finished. "However, I shall leave you with a warning; do not delay once you have settled in your heart and mind how you feel. Once you are sure, more time just serves to complicate matters of the heart."

Alaina nodded slowly. She understood how more time could complicate matters, and made a promise to herself that by the end of the garden party, she would have a decision. No matter how her mind wandered to Christopher, Alaina was determined to discern her true feelings for Graham. She owed it to herself and to the duke to be honest about her heart.

With renewed resolve, Alaina got up from her seat and gave her father a quick kiss on the cheek.

"Thank you, Papa. Goodnight."

Edward watched his oldest walk from the room, smiling to himself. He was not one to offer his own opinion on matters of the heart, at least not out loud, but if he knew his eldest well enough, he could predict the outcome.

Raucous laughter rang through the Finch townhome, and glasses clinked in celebration, all sounds of merriment grating on Lady Barbara's ears. "To our good fortune, and Charles's bad luck!" Percy jeered, and the target of his comment threw back the remaining contents of his glass.

"Deal another round, Percy. Let's see if your good fortune holds," came Charles's retort, a little slurred, his face reddened with drink.

Richard clasped Charles on the back in a show of encouragement. "I knew you were not a quitter. You never know when the cards will turn around. The night is still young."

Another round of laughter peeled out of the men, so loud that Lady Barbara thought it might rattle the windows. She stifled a yawn and rolled her eyes. "You men. It seems all you care about is a game of cards and endless brandy."

Her statement did little to quell the joviality, as Percy chided, "Come now, Barbara. Your brother assures me that your parents are not going to be home until the 'morrow. We are free to have some fun."

Barbara strode over to the table where the men were setting up another game of loo, her arms crossed and a scowl on her face. "You assured me that we would be married this season, that I would have something to come to my parents with to convince them of our match. All I see is a drunken fool who is going to let a garden party in the country seal his fate."

That statement had a sobering effect on Percy. "Barbara, let us not talk about that here, especially in front of our guest," he said, motioning to Charles.

Charles seemed oblivious as he looked at his hand of cards. "A garden party? How dull…"

Percy was quick to interject, "Quite right, my friend. I fear Barbara worries for no reason."

Barbara's brother, Richard, cleared his throat. "Alright, let's play, gentlemen. What is the wager?"

"Can we not just play a friendly game of cards this evening? You came close to cleaning me out last night at White's." Charles chuckled but could not cover the whine in his voice.

Lady Barbara scoffed and walked away, perching herself on the settee by the fireplace as she watched the men. Only Charles's presence kept her from berating Percy further; it seemed that nothing she said spurred him into action. For several moments, the only sound in the room was cards being placed on the table.

"You know, not all garden parties are dull," Charles said, almost absently. "There was a story bandied about when I was young, of a garden party with a fair amount of drama, if rumors were to be believed." Charles placed another card on the table before he continued. "Apparently, some tenants were in the midst of a feud during a party my parents were hosting. Well, normally those things would be of no matter, except for the fact that one of the tenants decided to release the pigs from their pen. The pigs made their way all the way to the party, through the garden doors and into the center of a game of charades! Needless to say, the game was cut short."

A chortle escaped Charles as he laughed at his own story, distracted enough to miss that he had once again lost at cards. Eventually, a frown knit his brow, and he scrubbed his hand over his face.

Richard was first to speak. "I feel your bad luck streak continues, my friend. You should be grateful we are playing with nothing more than pride at stake."

Charles grunted, and then tried to stifle a yawn. "Well then, I fear I must retire for the evening and hope a new day brings something better."

Abruptly standing from the table, Charles bowed to both gentlemen, neither Percy nor Richard seeming to care about Charles's quick departure. Charles walked unsteadily toward the door before he appeared to remember Barbara's presence.

She watched as Charles approached and bowed drunkenly in front of her.

"I wish you a pleasant evening, my lady. I do apologize if our presence so late in the evening was bothersome," Charles said, the slur of his word slight but noticeable to Barbara. "I hope you can convince Percy to take you to the garden party; it seems a silly thing to let decide one's future."

Barbara watched as Charles stumbled out of her parents' townhome. A smile made its way to her face for the first time this evening.

"I had hoped all evening that you would smile, but now that I see it, I fear I am not going to like what it entails," Percy stated flatly, as he shuffled the cards mindlessly. Richard was half dozing in his chair.

"But you heard Charles. A garden party is a ridiculous thing to worry about; all I would need to do is to convince you to accompany me," retorted Barbara.

A murmur came from her brother. "But you are not even invited to the party; how can you expect Percy to accompany you?"

Barbara exchanged a look with Percy, who drew a breath, and blew it out slowly, his cheeks puffing as he did so. "I fear, Richard, that your sister can be quite convincing. It seems we are going to the country."

CHAPTER 9

Orchestral harmonies reached Alaina's ears in the duke's box at the Royal Theater, and her smile widened as she took in the actors and actresses on the stage in all of their glamour. It was certainly much different from anything she had seen in Norwich.

Alaina's heart fluttered in excitement, though she found her nerves stretched taut at the presence of the one behind her. She could hear the marquess's deep chuckle, even if the substance of his conversation remained elusive under the music. Straightening her back and shifting about in her seat, Alaina forced her mind to thoughts of her own companion, the duke, and the spectacle in front of her.

On this particular evening the group included the duke, Alaina, the dowager duchess, Alaina's mother, Christopher, and Georgiana. The box was a generous size and contained two rows of chairs, four in front and four toward the back, with Graham and Alaina taking the front of the box for the best view, flanked by their mothers. Christopher and Georgiana offered to sit behind the couple, affording the marquess a full view of Alaina.

Christopher found it difficult to avoid studying the lady who had occupied his thoughts for the better part of the past two weeks. She was dressed in a deep teal creation, with a simple, slim silhouette, the neckline fashionably low, causing her breasts to swell almost over the edge at every breath. The sheer, elbow-length sleeves gave him the impression of a nightgown. The vision of Alaina in that dress made him imagine the body underneath, much to his chagrin. He could only imagine slim, strong legs and rounded, but not soft, hips, leading up to a slim waist and perfect bosom. The thoughts of her body seemed to haunt him throughout the play, the heat of his imagination making its way through his body, a spreading urge starting in the pit of his stomach. But what bothered him most was the intimacy the lady seemed to be sharing with his best friend.

The graceful curve of her neck, leaning over to listen to Graham, and then the crinkle of her eyes and nose when she laughed at some inanity Graham had whispered, made him wish to share those moments with her. Sitting behind the couple, Christopher wished to be able to gaze upon Alaina's dark eyes, pools so deep he would be lost in them; he wanted to whisper in her ear and see her laughter, to catch her scent, one that was already wafting to his nose, soap and roses. He imagined her eyes full of merriment, a small smile or laugh playing across her face as she watched a humorous part of the play. But it was Graham that Alaina turned her smiles on, with whom she shared her laughter and light.

If his friend had not seemed so enamored, or the lady so inclined to return his friend's interest, he would certainly be getting to know Alaina better, even if he was not interested in marriage. He wished to free her soft hair from its coiffure, and watch the curls cascade down her back, the play of dark curls across her back and around her perfect face, her face flush with desire. It seemed that in the week since they had last met, she had grown even more beautiful. It was from these thoughts that Christopher required the occasional prodding from Georgiana in order for him to keep up his end of their conversation.

Alaina felt the heat of Christopher's gaze, but a few surreptitious glances back toward Georgiana and Christopher made her feel like it was only her imagination, since he always seemed to be engaged elsewhere, either looking at the stage, talking to Georgiana, or just glancing about the theater. It certainly left Alaina unsettled, but she was determined to enjoy the play and her outing with Graham, who looked resplendent in a subtle black coat and waistcoat, with a crisp white shirt and cravat, matching black trousers, and tall boots. Graham's tall stature, dark hair, and brown eyes gave him a mysterious air, especially given that he was dressed in all black, save for his shirt. Graham was most certainly handsome, but it was Christopher that Alaina could not stop thinking about.

It seemed that at the slightest glimpse of Christopher, Alaina's heart raced. It was the memory of his concern, his defense of her person, that *kiss*. Her mind constantly fought her heart; the marquess was not even looking for a wife, and his behavior was unpredictable to say the least, so why should she even ponder their connection? But at every turn, her eyes sought Christopher's. Her heart yearned to be safely wrapped in his arms, their bodies pressed together. And tonight was no exception.

Graham, his sister, and his mother had escorted Alaina and her mother from their townhouse by carriage. The duke's carriage was large and spacious, certainly large enough to fit three across on each side, with plush deep green benches and interior upholstery. Even with such accommodations, Christopher had met them at the theater, just inside the front door, a little to the side to remain out of the way of the main entrance. Even with his inconspicuous placement, Alaina had seen him immediately, and she had the feeling that Christopher had seen her too.

As Christopher had moved to meet them upon entering, their eyes connected, even from such a distance, to devastating effect. His glacial eyes seemed to stare into Alaina's soul, emanating a warmth she was not sure was possible for their color; it was almost as if a fire burned behind those sapphire-blue orbs, the blue part of the flame when you first start a fire, hot and intense. His strawberry blonde hair was crisp and neat as always, his face handsome, with a strong jaw and nose, the dimples in his cheeks only evident when he smiled.

And to Alaina's amazement, he had held her gaze almost the whole of his approach, only breaking it to quickly survey her from the top of her head to her toes, causing her discomfort, especially in sight of the duke, something she had hoped was not readily evident. Once he was within shouting distance of the group, the trance broke, and he politely greeted the ladies, starting with the dowager duchess, leaving Alaina to be greeted last, almost coupling his greeting to her with the duke's.

Before making their way to the Ashford box, they held polite conversation, talking of the weather the past week, and something about biscuits. Alaina found it hard to concentrate. Where the duke was confident and well dressed, handsome in his own right, Christopher was glorious. His coat and trousers were a dark charcoal grey, with a deep blue waistcoat and cravat, and a crisp white shirt. His dark boots reached to his knee, completing the elegant, if not slightly rugged, look. Every piece fit snugly to his person, from his broad shoulders to his narrow waist and muscular thighs. Christopher was certainly well dressed, but it was his stature and demeanor that captured her attention. He was ever so slightly broader of shoulder than the duke, even if both stood about the same height. The marquess carried himself with an easy grace, almost seeming to swagger toward the group as he approached, and he stood relaxed but poised during their greeting. It was not to say that the duke was not athletic and graceful, but Christopher felt magnetic.

Dragging her thoughts back to the present, Alaina considered the second act of the play in front of her, trying to ignore the feeling that she was being watched. If she had chosen that moment to turn in her seat, she would have seen the truth; Christopher seemed enraptured by her, for he had felt the connection too when she had entered and they locked gazes. He had felt powerless to break it, even as he approached the group. He had made a point to avoid her this past week, with hopes of putting their kiss behind him; his friend was looking for a suitable wife, and he was not. He felt he had little to offer Alaina, and felt it best for her to find a connection with someone like Graham. Especially if it was not in Christopher's heart to marry just yet or ever. Alaina deserved that commitment, one which he could not offer. That did not stop his thoughts. As he had watched her being led on the arm of his best friend, Christopher could not help but drink in all of Alaina. Her eyes sparkled and glittered, emotions of trepidation, wonder, and, dare he say, happiness, played through those deep pools of dark honey that seemed to want to swallow him whole. He felt that if he kept staring, he may drown.

Before either Alaina or Christopher realized, they had reached the second intermission, the lights in the theater coming up ever so slightly as the sconces were turned up, and attendants scattered throughout the establishment. Georgiana was the first to break into conversation.

"Well, Alaina, what are you thinking so far of your first London theater experience?" Georgiana asked.

Alaina turned around to meet Georgiana's eyes. "Well, I must say there is nothing to compare it to in the country. I am truly honored you all chose to bring me along. I am enjoying myself immensely." Alaina gave a shy smile to the duke. As

Christopher was pondering the couple's attachment, a messenger was shown into the box where they were seated, reaching across the marquess to convey a letter to Graham. Obviously, it was something important in order for it to interrupt an evening affair.

Graham quickly opened the sealed letter and read it, his eyebrows gathering as he did so. Christopher, watching, saw that it must be grave news indeed.

"Would you excuse us, ladies?" Graham addressed the group, leveling a stare at Christopher. Both the duke and marquess quickly stood in their chairs, making their way around the edge of the box to the back, close to the curtain leading to the hallway. It was not so far away to give them complete privacy, so they conducted their discussion in whispers.

"What is it, my friend?" Christopher started.

"Well, it seems that some of the tenants on my country estate are having issues with thievery of livestock, and destruction of some of their equipment. Nothing major, but worrisome enough to warrant some attention from me, to see if these are separate incidents or something more nefarious at work," Graham said.

"Do you really think it could be something worse than just some shenanigans from kids or accidents?" Christopher asked skeptically. Graham's estate manager was certainly thorough, and it seemed possible that he was reporting minor, unrelated incidents.

"It is possible, although it could be feuds among the tenants that need to be addressed. Who knows? Francis Locke, my steward, was insistent that it requires my immediate attention, and he is certainly one I trust; he is not one to exaggerate in the least."

"Well, when will you leave?" Christopher asked, almost sure from his friend's face that this would cut the evening short.

"I can ride out there this evening and be there just shy of tomorrow evening, if I go on horseback. I would leave a smaller carriage to bring my belongings. If it truly is as Mr. Locke says, I should attempt to be there as soon as possible."

Having seen the quiet exchange between Graham and Christopher, along with the oddly timed message, Eleanor moved slowly to stand just beside them and queried, "I assume all is not well, my dear." She looked at Graham with concern.

"No, mother. It seems the country estate is seeing some suspicious happenings that require my attention immediately," Graham sighed. Over his mother's head he could see Lady Alaina. "It appears my evening will have to be cut short."

"Well, I think Alaina will understand, dearest. Just be sure to say your goodbyes, but as you say, you must be on your way. Please be sure to bring someone along with you for protection. Maybe Christopher can go with you?"

"Well, Mama, I had hoped Christopher would stay in London to look after you and Georgiana and provide escort for you to come out to the country in a few days' time for the garden party. I will bring along someone from the stables, so I am not alone though." This last statement from Graham seemed to do much to ease Eleanor's worry for her only son. She clasped his hand briefly, silently wishing him well, as she made her way back to the front row, electing to sit directly next to Charlotte, since Alaina had decided to stand and look over the orchestra for a better view.

Graham turned his attention back to his friend. "Christopher, I hope you can spare some moments in the next week to look after my mother and sister, and…" After a short pause, he added, "…and Alaina as well. I would like to see them all safe and sound and delivered to the garden party."

Christopher gave Graham an affirmative nod. "Of course, I am at your disposal this evening. Keeping your family safe is something I would do at any time, so I can also provide them escort to your estate in a few days as well."

"Thank you." Graham glanced again at Alaina and then back to Christopher. "You know, I was quite surprised that formally seeking a wife in society turned out to be not as stressful or devoid of fun as I had thought, or at least it's much better than my attempt last season. You should maybe reconsider your position on the subject."

Without waiting for a response from his friend, Graham quickly made his way to Alaina to explain his sudden departure. Christopher watched as Graham clasped Alaina's hand first to his heart and then touched her glove-covered knuckles to his mouth in a kiss of farewell, but not goodbye. Alaina gave Graham a radiant smile and a quick nod. The duke then made his way to Georgiana. She gave her brother a quick hug in a show of sibling affection and then watched as Graham almost raced out of the box. In the back of Christopher's mind was the thought that Graham was not telling him everything.

"I just do not see why Graham had to leave so quickly. We will be in the country in a few more days. Can he not deal with these matters then?" Georgiana was again lamenting the course of the evening after the final act of the play. The group had made it through the throng to their carriage and was now slowly making their way to the Norwich townhouse.

"Georgiana, you know that Graham takes his responsibility to the Ashford estates seriously, and if Mr. Locke says it is important and to be dealt with immediately, Graham is not going to question it. We can only look forward to seeing him at the party," Eleanor chided.

"Ah, yes, the garden party." Georgiana cocked her head toward Alaina, who was sitting opposite her in the coach, flanked by Charlotte and Christopher. "Alaina, have you gotten your dresses yet?"

Alaina was happy for the benign turn of the conversation, and she answered easily. "Evelina and I go tomorrow for our fittings. It should leave a few days for packing and preparing. We shall have great fun on our carriage ride to the country!"

"Oh, yes! We will make the best of things without Graham," Georgiana said brightly, her chatter filling the carriage. "Now with the six of us…"

"Six?" Alaina interjected, confused.

Georgiana answered quickly, "Well, Christopher will be joining us, silly."

Alaina felt her throat constrict uncomfortably. She practically squeaked, "But I am sure the marquess would want to take his own conveyance."

Alaina felt Christopher stiffen beside her and braced for some sort of retort from the marquess, but was thankful when none came.

"No, Graham was most insistent," Eleanor said, in a tone that brokered no argument. "We can never be too safe. It has certainly been an eventful year so far, starting with the holidays."

"What happened during the holidays?" Alaina questioned.

"Oh, well dear, that was none other than excitement caused by Percy," Georgiana stated, looking as if she were to continue, but then her mother chimed in again.

"Yes, well, we do not want to dwell too much on the past, now do we? Just better to be safe." Eleanor left the statement as if to end the conversation about it.

"Ok, no need to dwell on things," Georgiana stated with a flip of her hand. "So, Alaina, Christopher is our escort, and that makes six. Does that clear up things?"

Alaina sat back, hoping that the seat of the carriage would swallow her, as she replied, "Yes, that is perfectly clear, thank you."

After a few minutes of silence in the carriage, the rich timbre of the marquess broke the silence. "Do not worry, I should not bother you all with my presence overly much."

Alaina felt like his statement was directed at her and her alone, but Eleanor was the first to speak. "Oh, Christopher, do not worry yourself. Your company has always been welcome to us; in my heart, you are my other son."

Happy to let Eleanor speak for the group, Alaina held her tongue and could only wonder at the wanderings of a particular gentleman's mind as the carriage ambled along the London streets.

Christopher refocused on the mantle as the clock chimed the hour of 2 o'clock and he scrubbed his hand over his face. The amber liquid in his glass had been largely forgotten as he had sleeplessly wandered around his townhome since returning from the theater, eventually settling in his study. Christopher had convinced himself that the week of not seeing Alaina was peaceful, happy, and exactly what he was looking for in his life; there was nothing missing at all.

Christopher had spent his time keeping up with correspondence, reading, riding in Hyde Park, and enjoying his lack of participation in the London social scenes. At times, visions of Alaina, her lustrous burnt-umber curls bouncing as she danced, an easy smile on her face, her dark eyes sparkling in the candlelight, had filled his mind, always to be suppressed. *It was only her beauty, nothing more, that held his mind, and that attraction would pass.* He had done his duty and at least determined Alaina to be worthy of his friend, no matter their tumultuous interactions.

And yet, when he had seen Alaina after just a week, Christopher had been mesmerized all over again by her presence, and had listened intently as she, Graham, and Georgiana talked of politics, the latest novels, or whatever crossed their minds. Watching their easy interactions left him tongue-tied and awkward. He was either saying the wrong thing or somehow saying it the wrong way. It seemed that Alaina had preferred their time apart, judging by her reaction this evening. She had practically balked at his being a member of their traveling party to the garden party. And he had sought to guard his heart from further angst with his surly response. Christopher could only hope that the trip to the country would pass without any bitterness between them.

Christopher sighed and again reshuffled papers on his desk in an effort to put Alaina out of his mind, but the memory of every touch, the feel of her rosebud lips on his as their bodies fit perfectly together, crowded his rational thoughts. Christopher refused to give in to his yearnings, and he picked up the only letter he had not responded to since returning home.

Dear Cousin,

Since we are both in town for the season, I was hoping you may have time to spare for a family dinner or two. While there may have been animus between our fathers, I hope we can put that to rest.

Let me know at your earliest convenience if you would be amenable.
Respectfully,
Charles

Nothing in particular had kept him from responding to the letter, but since seeing Charles at White's, Christopher's life had been distracting and full or responsibilities. If only Graham had not been forced to leave to take care of issues with his tenants, he could ask him advice about Charles. Christopher did not wish to shirk his only living relative, but when Graham had doubts about a person, it was best he listen. *Perhaps it was just that his mind was muddled with the intoxicating vision of a lady.* He would call upon Charles as soon as he was back from the country. Finally finding something to close out the evening, Christopher penned a quick letter to Charles to that effect, sealing it quickly to be sent in the morning.

Throwing back the brandy left in his glass, Christopher stood and banked the fire in his study, striding from the room and upstairs in search of the peaceful sleep he was doubtful to find, the vision of a set of twinkling eyes hounding his every step.

Chapter 10

The slowing pace and jostle of the carriage indicated to its occupants that they approached their final destination at last, each of them craning their necks to see out the window. Alaina could see the marquess on horseback and forced her mind to think of Graham. She clasped her hands tighter in her lap to keep them from shaking as she took in the densely forested drive of the Ashford estate, thankful to bring the journey to an end, but terrified of what the coming days could bring for her heart.

Across from her, Eleanor and Georgiana seemed to bubble with excitement, clearly happy to be headed toward their ancestral seat in the country, and chatting quietly about the country gossip. Evelina and Charlotte were looking out the opposite side of the coach in wonder at their new surroundings. This gave Alaina some time to contemplate her mission.

After the discussion with her father, Alaina was determined to glean her compatibility with Graham at this party. She would put the marquess out of her mind. Their interactions, though engaging, seemed to end in awkwardness, or bickering, or in an embrace in a dark hallway, begging to be discovered. He was not even inclined toward marriage, and he was Graham's best friend. It would be in her best interest to ignore him.

In the last few days, it had been easy for Alaina to ignore Christopher. Georgiana and her mother had only come to call once more to finalize travel plans, staying only for a short tea. As became custom in those few days since the duke's departure for the country, Christopher had escorted the dowager duchess and the countess to the Norwich house only to wait outside on the steps. Though the marquess's behavior was odd, neither Eleanor or Georgiana seemed bothered, and so it was left at that.

The day before they were scheduled to leave for Kent, Alaina had been to the dressmaker's shop with her mother, sister, and father to have the final fittings for their new attire. Madam Benoit had certainly delivered beautiful dresses for both of the sisters, and with a day to spare for their trip. It had been a relief to Alaina that any further outings to the dressmaker's had not been in the company of the marquess, and yet, she also felt the weight of disappointment.

The remaining packing had been done later that evening, in preparation for an early morning departure in the duke's conveyance shortly after breakfast. The plan was for Eleanor, Georgiana, and Christopher to stop by the Norwich townhouse to pick them up before heading out of London toward the Ashford estate near Kent. Alaina had been the first awake and ready for the journey, taking a breakfast to give her energy for the trip ahead, but not much, too anxious about the upcoming proximity to Christopher.

The two-day journey had been uneventful, and Alaina had been saved from having to face Christopher in the carriage, as he had opted to go on horseback, claiming that he could not protect the group whilst sitting in a carriage. Only a few times had she caught a glimpse of him riding in front of the conveyance, seemingly engrossed in his surveillance of the country road and its immediate surroundings. When they had stopped at an inn the first night, Christopher was quick to retire to his room, claiming exhaustion from the ride.

In one instance, as Alaina had been taking in the countryside, she had felt her eyes drawn to Christopher's form where it lingered. When she had dragged her attention back inside the coach, pondering such questions, Alaina caught Eleanor's curious stare.

"Beautiful countryside, yes?" had been Eleanor's only question, accompanied by a wistful smile. Not waiting for a response from Alaina, the dowager duchess joined in an animated conversation with Evelina and Georgiana, both of whom had chattered throughout the entirety of the trip. Both seemed equally boundless in energy, and Alaina giggled remembering the hours of amusement provided by just the two of them covering a range of subjects, from the party, to horses, to society. It had been truly pleasant to feel part of a larger family.

"What is it, dear?" Eleanor punctured Alaina's thoughts again, this time reacting to the giggle that had escaped her in her reminiscence.

"Oh, just remembering this trip with fondness. Georgiana and Evelina truly did keep us entertained," Alaina answered.

Eleanor seemed to agree, a wide smile gracing her face. "They certainly do not need our help in conversation, do they?"

"I do believe we have arrived!" Georgiana exclaimed, just a moment before the carriage came to a halt. When Alaina looked out the carriage window, she could see that it was true; they had arrived. Ashford Manor was an imposing sight, its columns looking large on its façade. Mature shrubs and trees softened the face of the building and surrounded the front walkway. The tree-dappled late morning light spotted the front drive, and Alaina felt calm despite the dramatic edifice.

⁎

Christopher brought his horse to a stop just ahead of the carriage in the wide entryway of Ashford. Dismounting, he quickly turned to the carriage in order to provide assistance to those disembarking. The footman was setting the small step in place when Christopher arrived at the open door. The first to alight was the dowager duchess. Eleanor accepted his outstretched hand with a smile and stepped down, looking up at the large facade of the Ashford Estate as she moved toward the front door, seemingly sure of her place in the world. Georgiana followed, stepping down briskly to catch up with her mother.

Alaina had moved toward the door when she spied Christopher, offering assistance to both Eleanor and Georgiana. She hesitated ever so slightly before accepting Christopher's outstretched hand. As she stepped down onto the small step, she found herself entranced by his gaze, unable to avoid meeting his eyes. Alaina had hoped to offer a quick thanks to Christopher for the assistance and be on her way, much like the two who preceded her, but she was unable to form any words. In her distracted state, she missed the step with one of her feet and descended unnaturally, at a pace that sundered the outward display of grace she had hoped to convey. Her fall would have been worse had Christopher not caught her around the waist and set her down easily. He was quick to step away once he was assured of her stability, and briskly turned around to offer his assistance to Charlotte and Evelina.

Alaina found herself short of breath, both from the near-disastrous tumble and the contact between herself and the marquess. She quickly brushed her skirt, ensuring it was in its place and, turning her head down to hide her embarrassment, made her way toward Eleanor and Georgiana. Alaina was unsure of what they had seen of the interaction, but she was sure of one thing: Christopher's hand had left its mark on her waist, and she could still feel it burn through the fabric of her dress. Ignoring him was going to prove difficult.

Christopher finished handing Evelina down and closed the door to the carriage, allowing it to make its way toward the stables. As he watched the carriage slowly make its way out of sight, he took an uneven breath in, shoring up his emotions for what was to be a long four days.

If he were being honest with himself, he had almost been too late to save Alaina from certain disaster as she faltered down the steps; he had been so distracted by her nearness. The whole journey he had been content to ride astride, ignorant of the goings-on in the carriage, but never quite able to shake the feelings he got just knowing Alaina was in close proximity. His distraction had been so acute on the journey that the mere sight of her, and the look in her eyes, had made time stop, if just for a moment. Her unexpected tumble had caught him by surprise, but he had sighed in relief as he was able to right her just the same, assured she had taken no injuries.

Her nearness in that brief interaction had struck him like lightning. He had essentially picked her up by the waist to save her from the fall, making their closeness acute. His head had been quite close to her hair, if only for a second, and the smell of soap and roses had been heady. He had felt a quick tightening in his lower belly and, not trusting his reaction should he continue to attend to the lady, had brusquely placed her on her feet, and turned to assist her mother and sister. Alaina had moved to the front door shortly thereafter, giving Christopher time to collect himself.

"Yoo hoo, Christopher, are you coming inside or do you plan to go out for a ride? My mother wants to get everyone settled," came a reminder from Georgiana that he was not alone, not even close to it, and needed to steel himself against the upcoming few days.

He slowly turned and headed toward the house without a word, taking a deep breath, more determined than ever to ignore the lady. His sanity depended upon it.

⁕

After being settled in their rooms, Alaina, Evelina, and Charlotte had gone about unpacking and hanging their dresses in the provided wardrobe. They had left quite early in the morning from the inn and had gotten to Ashford just past the lunch hour. That being the case, a simple tray of food and tea had been prepared and sent to each of their rooms, the rooms themselves connected by a series of doors. A quick check-in with her mother and Evelina found both of them yawning and half asleep from the journey, so Alaina returned to her room, quietly leaving each of them to rest before dinner.

Alaina found she could not eat much more than a nibble on the corner of a sandwich, the tea at least warming her. After a time, she stood from her chair by the fireplace and walked to the window. Her room, much like her mother's, Evelina's, and all the other guests', she imagined, was well-furnished and comfortable, lending a homey air to an otherwise ornate surrounding. There were high ceilings and rich wall coverings, long drapes on each of the two windows flanking the fireplace, which was set almost in the center of the room. Two pale blue and navy wingback chairs and one ottoman were set in front of the fireplace to leave a warm place for a guest or two to pass the time. The bed was directly across from the fireplace, a large four-poster, with thick sapphire velvet drapes that could be used in the evenings to keep out any drafts, currently pulled back and tied with gold decorative rope. The bed was one of the only feminine touches of the room, with a crystal blue coverlet, and decorative pillows piled to match.

At the window, Alaina stared out at the view. An expansive estate stretched as far as she could see, with lush green hills rolling toward the horizon, the expanse dotted with copses of mature trees. She could see what looked to be an orchard in the distance. Just below her, a little difficult to see from the third floor where she was ensconced with the other guests, was the stables. Every now and then she would hear a horse nicker or whinny, the soft crunch of gravel underneath their hooves peaceful, reminding Alaina of home in Norwich.

She closed her eyes to shut out the day and just listen to the quiet of the country, when a feeling crept up her spine, as if she were not alone. She opened her eyes to find Graham and Christopher outside her window, looking to be readying for a ride, both atop horses. Graham's black stallion was already turned toward the back of the property, heading to a path that disappeared quickly down a hill, and Christopher was on a strong-looking chestnut horse.

Christopher had stopped for some reason before following Graham, and caught sight of Alaina standing in her window. Close enough to see that her eyes were closed, he had kept the horse under a tight rein, feeling almost desperate for her to acknowledge his presence, the heady feeling of her in his arms still fresh in his mind. That memory overpowered every other doubt; in that moment, Christopher just wanted to see her smile at him, and him alone.

Alaina opened her eyes and found Christopher's. She felt a shock as he gave her a crooked smile and his eyes twinkled with mischief. Alaina felt frozen in place, surprised by his reaction, and she raised a hand to wave, a soft smile coming unbidden to her face. Christopher returned her gesture with a nod of his head, finally turning in the direction where Graham had disappeared, kicking his horse into a gallop to catch up to his friend.

Alaina inwardly groaned and lay down on the bed, worried about how dinner would go. She closed her eyes to once again shut out the world, hoping a good rest would clear her head.

***

"Christopher, you look absolutely resplendent. It looks like the country ride did some good for both you and Graham," Eleanor chirped as she swept into the parlor, where guests were starting to collect prior to dinner. "I just saw Graham in the hallway, and he looked much more chipper than when we arrived. I expect that is something to do with the ride this afternoon, and something to do with the anticipation of better company."

"Yes, I am sure it is," Christopher gave Eleanor a tight smile, hoping it passed for something warm. She had always been like a second mother to him, and in no way did he want to seem ungrateful or put off by her presence.

"Well, not to worry, I think more of the guests should be arriving for dinner shortly, and you will have more young people to converse with," Eleanor stated simply, as if sensing his unease.

Christopher chuckled and shook his head, striving to allay any of Eleanor's hurt. "Lady Eleanor, I assure you that your company is quite enough for me. I am afraid I will only know a few of the souls attending."

"Pish posh, you have nothing to worry about. You look wonderful and I am sure any lady who joins us this evening will be agog." And with that Eleanor detached herself from Christopher, making her way around the room, pausing only briefly at the pianoforte to adjust a flower in the vase that decorated the instrument. A candelabra also rested atop the piano and complemented the lighted sconces around the room, giving the air a warm ambiance.

Christopher surveyed the room, finding it much as he remembered from when he was a boy. Usually when he visited Graham at Ashford, they spent their time riding through the grounds or in Graham's study on the other side of the house. As a boy, he remembered that this parlor in particular was in close proximity to the large dining room and was used by Eleanor to entertain guests when it was a small, non-familial gathering. A few sideboards were spaced strategically around the room, each with decanters of whiskey and wine, so anyone could easily access a refreshment without disrupting the socializing occurring in the room. It was not expected that people would stay in this room much beyond waiting for dinner, so only a handful of elegant chairs of varying patterns, all with soft rose-hued tones, were scattered along the outer walls. The pianoforte was in the corner, with a harp beside it, for musical entertainment. The floor was largely left bare save for runners at the edges beneath each of the sideboards and some of the chairs. This allowed for the center of the room to be used for whatever whim struck the dowager duchess, like charades. Christopher had often played charades with Graham and his family on holidays from school, when his family was not up for having him at home, or when he chose not to join his family. Tonight, it would allow for good mingling.

Christopher placed himself toward the opposite side of the room from the pianoforte, near one of the sideboards, and fixed himself a brandy, waiting for the other guests to arrive, or really one guest in particular. This afternoon he had been surprised to find Alaina standing in a window directly above the stables. Graham had not seen her, or had been too intent on the ride to notice, but Christopher had felt desperate for her to see *him,* and his heart had leapt when she had waved.

The rest of the ride in the afternoon had been invigorating, with fresh air and a bit of a chill to bring clarity to Christopher's thoughts. That afternoon, Christopher had chosen to ponder the first time they had met, at the Mansfield Ball. The range of emotions that played across her face had perturbed and amused him at the time, and now he held them close to his heart as a vision of Alaina fully as herself. Not only had her face, with her long lashed umber eyes that seemed to glow in the candlelight, and her full winsome lips, either curved in smile or pursed in thought, caught his attention, but her confident stature and grace also came to his mind. He may have been initially annoyed to be caught in the throes of the season, much less a conversation with a young miss, but to deny that Alaina's lithe, athletic build, subtly displayed in a simple and bewitching frock, was alluring would be untruthful, to say the least. He had noticed her pert, full breasts, shown with just a small amount of cleavage over her low-cut bodice, long graceful arms, and, from what he could only imagine, long, lean, and strong legs to match. The vision kept him company more hours of the day than Christopher cared to admit.

Since he and Graham had been out for a vigorous ride, there had been little talk, allowing Christopher ample time with such thoughts. Only toward the end of the ride was he required to recount the last week to his friend, leaving out many of the more personal details, just giving a report on everyone's safety and the uneventful trip out to Ashford.

Christopher and Graham had known each other almost their whole lives, and had become fast friends in school; it was this that made Christopher pause and ruminate over the implications of his own thoughts. Graham had been his lone friend at Eton, and he had quickly offered his own home as a refuge away from Christopher's increasingly unhappy one. He had convinced himself that his fascination and attraction to Alaina would pass; Christopher certainly had no intention of interfering with his friend's courtship of the lady. That thought, however, did little to calm his racing mind.

In the parlor, more of the party's attendees had started to arrive. It was his understanding that there would be twenty in all, an equal matching of gentlemen and ladies, though he was unsure of the exact guest list. As the parlor became more crowded, Christopher withdrew to the far corner by the pianoforte, lightly touching the keys as he tried to remain nonchalant, waiting for the one who haunted his thoughts. Soon, Christopher watched as Georgiana walked into the room followed by her guests of honor.

"My wonderful friends, may I welcome you to Ashford Estate! I know most of you are well acquainted, but may I be the first to introduce Lady Charlotte, Lady Alaina, her eldest daughter, and Lady Evelina, her youngest daughter. They hail from Norwich, and are the wife and daughters of the Earl of Norwich, Lord Sinclair." Georgiana finished with flair, the Sinclair family surrounding her as they acknowledged the rest of the guests.

As Georgiana made the introductions to each guest personally, Christopher moved forward, unable to see Alaina from his vantage point at the back, as she was much shorter than some of the gentlemen currently blocking the way. He did catch sight of Graham and his mother on the other side of the intimate group, both of them involved with the introductions. Christopher heard Georgiana finish with the formalities, and the group seemed to disperse, gentlemen making their way to a few of the sideboards for drinks, while the ladies seemed to collapse on Georgiana, Alaina, Charlotte, and Evelina in salutations. It was at this moment that Christopher caught sight of Alaina. She was smiling at her newly introduced companions and chatting. She seemed so happy and at ease, and Christopher wondered if she shared any of his trepidations for the evening.

He had just a moment to take in the sight of her before she made eye contact. She was garbed in a rich velvet sapphire gown. Since this evening was indoors, she had opted for the low-cut evening gown she had procured from Madam Benoit's dress shop just a few days prior. The bodice of the gown dipped quite low in the front, almost exposing the rosy peaks of her breasts, but dipped even lower in the back, exposing the graceful column of her neck and upper back. The skirt was simple but narrow, and grazed her hips and derriere ever so slightly, letting the imagination do the rest. The sleeves were almost iridescent, a stiff chiffon of the same color that covered her whole arm, collected by a simple cuff, with silver buttons. The sleeve itself was translucent, so even as it covered her whole arm, it gave the observer a vision of graceful limbs, slim and strong. In society, this would not be deemed indecent, but it was certainly a departure from the demure frocks he had seen her wear in Hyde Park. It made Christopher wonder if she wore any chemise underneath, doubting it was even possible, making his mouth go dry.

The ladies had been twittering together when they finally noticed Christopher's presence, having unknowingly inched ever so slightly forward.

Georgiana was the first to speak. "Oh, dear, I seem to have missed introducing you, Christopher. Ladies, this is Lord Kendall, Marquess of Rochester. Please do not set your sights on him though, he detests the very *idea* of commitment. Christopher, I expect that you heard all my introductions earlier?"

Christopher gave a noncommittal grunt, tearing his eyes away from Alaina and acknowledging the rest of the group politely. He was happy that a grimace did not cross his face at Georgiana's barb. Everyone seemed satisfied with the brief introductions, and the ladies parted like the sea around him, making their way across the room to the musical instruments in the corner to inspect them. He could hear Georgiana giving the group a tour of sorts.

Graham stayed behind and he greeted his friend warmly. "Christopher, I trust you were able to get some rest after our ride. This past week in the country has made me loathe to return to the stifling air of London at the end of the party, even if it means being done with these tenant issues."

"Yes, I find the air much more invigorating here. I am not sure I rested so much as just enjoyed being here again. I know it has only been a couple of years since I made a proper visit to your country seat, but it feels longer," Christopher said. "What do you think is at the root of the mischief?"

"I am not sure I would say mischief, per se, but there are too many coincidences to be ruled only unfortunate accidents." Graham paused and scrubbed his hand through his hair. "A broken plow here, a stolen cart there. Tenants have been blaming their neighbors, and some have gotten into rows. I have mostly been playing mediator, but I feel there is something more to these minor offenses."

Eleanor walked over to the two young men, and Graham placed a peck on his mother's cheek.

"Lady Eleanor, it has been *ages*," Christopher greeted her with a short bow and a smile.

Eleanor waded into her next statement with care. "Oh, Graham, I have missed you this last week. Might I trouble you for an escort to dinner? I wish to hear how things are going on the estate."

After a moment of silence, Graham answered, "I would be delighted. I think Christopher was slated to escort you, so we can just swap." Turning to his friend, he asked, "Christopher, I pray you will deliver Alaina safely to dinner."

"Of course," was all Christopher said, swallowing uncomfortably. Even the short walk to the dining room seemed a daunting task.

After what felt like an eternity, Georgiana proclaimed that dinner was ready for them, and deftly paired people, bringing Alaina over to Christopher last. Christopher silently accepted his charge and stretched out his arm to offer her escort to the dining room. Alaina placed her hand on his forearm, and they made their way to the hallway.

It took a considerable effort from Alaina to ignore the sinewy muscles of the proffered arm as Christopher deftly led her to dinner. Her fingertips tingled and she felt that sensation creep up her arm and down her back. They only touched at the one point, but their connection did much to bring to her mind a different moment, one she had been both yearning for and wishing to forget. Christopher and Alaina were followed only by Georgiana and her escort, Lord Blackmore. Graham and Eleanor then led the procession, as true hosts. Each of the pairs were generally spaced out, allowing for quiet conversation as they processed along the long corridor, passing sconces every few steps.

"Alaina, before you flay me for a perceived grievance, it was Eleanor who requested time with her son. It seems she has missed him this past week," Christopher said. "I will deliver you safely to Graham's side for dinner. Let us try and remain cordial on our short walk. That should not be too hard?" Christopher questioned.

"Of course, my lord," Alaina stated, her tone flat. "I cannot imagine we would have any time for a row."

Christopher chuckled, "I fear it seems to take no time at all for us to ever be at odds, but let us forget that. And, I beg you to remember that my name is Christopher. I promised to not bother you overly much on our journey, and I will strive not to do so here. I hope we can let the next few days pass pleasantly."

"You think it is so simple? It must be nice to have such an easy disposition. You bother me without even saying a word."

"I bother you without…" Christopher started, but his voice faded, as if realizing Alaina's intended meaning. Christopher cleared his throat and continued, "We must both endeavor to forget that particular *interaction*."

"You do not think I have tried?" Alaina questioned. "And imagine my surprise to find you are not the least bit affected."

"Ah," Christopher said, and they traveled in silence a few paces more.

Just before reaching Alaina's place at the table, Christopher leaned over and whispered, "It matters not what I feel, but what is right, and there is nothing more to it. Graham has certainly found a gem."

Alaina had no time to respond as they finally reached her place at the table to the left of Graham, who sat at the head of the table, his mother directly across from her. Alaina watched silently as Christopher pulled out her chair. She settled herself primly on the edge of the seat, hopeful that no one would notice her burning cheeks in the candlelight. She was momentarily relieved as the marquess moved to take his own place at the table, but found her eyes surreptitiously watching as he sat and conversed with his own dinner partner. Turning her attention to the duke, Alaina forced a bright smile and was happy to lose herself in easy conversation.

Only a few times did she find her attention once again drawn toward the other end of the table, always to find Christopher in animated conversation. *For one so opposed to social gatherings, he seemed to be enjoying himself. And what was she to make of that statement of his? Was he affected the same as she? Was it his commitment to remain unmarried? Was it his friendship with Graham?*

CHAPTER 11

After the awkwardness at dinner on the first night, Alaina resolved to make the best of her time at Ashford, not necessarily avoiding Christopher, but avoiding one-on-one conversation. She wanted to get to know Graham and ultimately her heart. In this, Alaina's conversation with her father was never far from her mind.

Unfortunately, the next two days passed with little time spent with Graham, who seemed to be spending more and more time dealing with tenant issues. It almost seemed that every time Graham and Alaina were engaged in private or semi-private conversations, Graham's steward would appear with some sort of pressing matter. Graham had not yet confided exactly what was happening, but from what she could gather, some serious mischief was being levied on the tenants, possibly even thefts and violence, and they had yet to find the perpetrator. Alaina thought it may have been a conflict between tenants, and had offered such a suggestion, but Graham's reaction had firmly put that option out of her mind. On certain occasions, Graham even sought out Christopher to accompany him in his investigations. On these such occasions, Alaina could breathe easily, knowing she could easily engage with the group activity without having to be aware of the marquess's presence.

It was the times where the duke did not seek his friend's council that set Alaina's nerves on edge. She was both angry at Christopher and angry at herself. She was angry at Christopher for saying some nonsense about 'what is right,' but leaving her to wonder about his feelings for her. It would be easy enough for any person close in proximity to get the wrong idea, ruining her chances of determining if she and the duke were a match at all. She was also angry at herself for her heightened reactions, both to his statements, and to his mere presence. The marquess had made it quite clear he was not interested in her, or really marriage as a general concept, but Alaina found it difficult to categorize his actions as uninterested. She had always been one to take a person's words at face value, and she was questioning her own instincts.

On the third full day of the garden party, the group enjoyed a luncheon toward the back of the manse in a room that buttressed the courtyard. It was situated between the wings of the house that stretched far to either side of the entrance, perfectly symmetrical. Since it was toward the back of the house, the room was quite large, which could cause loud echoes in conversation, making it seem filled with more people than it truly was. The windows in the room were floor to ceiling, flooding the space with light even in the winter months. The table, extremely long, was set lengthwise along the windows, with the guests situated more to one side, to allow for more intimate conversation.

The guests were now enjoying the second course, conversation filling the cavernous space, from time to time with peals of laughter. It was the rare occasion that Alaina was seated next to the duke at the head of the table, and they both were engaged in easy conversation about the afternoon activities.

"So, I know you do not prefer to ride, but it would be an excellent way to show you the grounds. I have not had the opportunity to do so yet, and would be honored if you would allow me to act as your guide," Graham proposed. Alaina considered for a moment his earnest and hopeful expression and thought the idea would be delightful, even if her lack of riding skills required a slower pace.

"I would be delighted to accompany you," was her easy response, joined by a smile.

"Well then, we shall plan to leave immediately following lunch," Graham stated, as if relieved to finally have some time to show Alaina his estate.

Just then, the door at the fore end of the room opened, and Graham's steward, Francis Locke, walked in and quickly made his way to where Graham sat at the head of the table. The same scene of the past two days played out yet again, with a quick whisper in Graham's ear, a furrowed brow from Graham, and a hurried apology to Alaina.

"Alaina, you must forgive me yet again. It seems I must attend to some business." Graham sighed and gave Alaina a longing look before quickly standing from the table and offering a brief apology to the group. On his way out of the room he tapped Christopher on the shoulder and made a quick motion for him to follow.

As both men exited the room, Alaina heaved a sigh, upset once again to have her plans for the afternoon fouled. At this rate she would neither spend quality time with the duke nor see the grounds of his estate. She was at least relieved Christopher had been called to duty by his friend, saving Alaina from an afternoon of angst about their interactions.

Georgiana had been seated across the table, but only a few chairs down from the couple, and had heard their conversation. Seeing her friend's disappointed expression, Georgiana offered to salvage the afternoon.

"Perhaps I can show you the grounds after lunch?" Georgiana queried.

Alaina responded with a half-smile, "That would be lovely, Georgiana. Thank you."

"Good, we will bring your sister along with us; I know she has been wishing for a ride. She may leave us in her dust, though."

Alaina giggled, "Evelina certainly has a way of leading the charge, at least on a horse." Maybe it would be a pleasant afternoon after all, Alaina thought, attempting to buoy her own spirits.

Graham and Christopher quickly walked through a few back hallways, usually reserved for the servants, making only one stop in the estate's armory for their pistols. They found their way out to the stables through a side door on the west wing of the manse. With only one barn hand currently in the stables, as the others were taking a quick lunch, it was easier for the two friends to quickly saddle their own horses. It was only after this was accomplished, and they were on their way to see to the trouble, that Christopher inquired about the issue.

"What is it this time?"

"One of the barns used by a group of tenants for storage and livestock is burning," Graham answered quickly, his mind fast at work.

"It seems to have escalated then?" Christopher asked, already knowing the answer. Until this point the disturbances had been modest in comparison; a few stolen chickens or pigs, vandalized and broken farm equipment, but nothing more dangerous. Each time the culprit or culprits had eluded getting caught.

After riding some time in silence, Graham postulated, "It is possible the fire is an accident, but I am doubtful, given the course of the last week and a half."

Needing no further explanation, the two men continued on horseback until they could see a thin thread of smoke behind a copse of trees. As they approached, they could smell the acrid smoke and a faint smell of pitch. Passing under a large oak tree and onto a well-worn trail, used for carts and small foot traffic, both men could see the barn just ahead.

Neither Graham nor Christopher could see the flames, just billowing smoke. A few people could be seen throwing buckets of water on what they assumed was the last of the flames or burning embers.

Christopher and Graham brought their horses to a halt right in front of the barn, quickly tethering them to a nearby fence that seemed untouched by the fire.

One of the men, who had been putting out the fire, came out of the barn's large bay doors and mopped his brow with a soiled handkerchief, catching sight of the approaching gentlemen. The man was short in stature and wore what looked to be well-tended clothes, including a white shirt loose around the neck, and brown trousers held up by suspenders. The man looked a bit beleaguered and sooty from the fire, but his face lit up when he approached Graham and Christopher.

"Ho there, your grace! We appreciate the help, but I think we have the fire well in hand," came the man's quick greeting and explanation, all with a happy tone, considering the circumstances.

"Tobias, that is good to hear. I am thankful that the fire was caught early," Graham proclaimed, as he clasped the man's hand in friendship. "May I present my friend, the Marquess of Rochester."

"An honor, sir," Tobias acknowledged Christopher, and each man bowed his head in respect and greeting.

Graham took a moment to survey the scene, allowing Tobias to lead him through the barn to get a full picture of the damage. Nothing was as extensive as Graham had expected, given the report from Mr. Locke. He had thought to find the barn in tatters, but from what he could see, minimal damage had been done to the boards on the outer wall, with no structural damage. The animals had been evacuated easily into the attached run-out, and the equipment was thankfully stored on the far side of the barn.

"From what my steward said, the barn was burning to the ground." Graham addressed Tobias, who was also looking over the damage, mentally taking note of the repairs that would be required.

"No, we caught the fire early and were able to take advantage of the nearby water pump to put out the flames quickly. To be honest, I am not completely sure how you heard of it so quickly. I was so distracted by the fire that I had forgotten to send a messenger until just now." Tobias scrunched his brow.

Graham was about to inquire further when one of the men who had been helping Tobias ran around one of the stalls. "Father! You have to come and see this," exclaimed the young man.

As they all came around the stall door, it became clear what had caused the fire. In the middle of a pile of hay lay a glob of black, easily discerned as tar, and certainly the source of the fire. The edges of the sizable blob were still smoking but the hay surrounding was soaked, due to the recent firefighting activities.

"Well, at least we can confirm it was no accident," Christopher stated plainly, having remained mute until that moment.

The young man who had made the discovery looked obliquely at the two well-dressed gentlemen. "I already knew that, sirs. I saw two figures run from the barn and smelled the smoke shortly thereafter. I had been wheeling a cart of grain and was too far away to see them well, but it appeared to be a man and a woman. I quickly sent my little brother for help and set about putting the fire out myself."

Graham and Christopher exchanged glances. "Could you describe the two you saw?" Graham asked.

"I was pretty far down the trail when they ran out, and once I smelled the smoke they were long gone on their horses. I would have run after them, your grace, had I known."

"No way to have known what they were up to, um, sorry, I do not think I caught your name?" Graham responded.

"Henry, your grace. I am Tobias's son, and my little brother is Jacob. He ran quickly for help, so really I think we have him to thank."

"It sounds like there are many people to thank. I appreciate your efforts," Graham smiled warmly in thanks to both men.

"That, and a bit of luck," stated Tobias, almost half to himself. Everyone in the group seemed to take a moment to consider what could have been the outcome had Henry not been close by to tend the fire quickly after it started. The only salvation was that there was still work to do to see the barn safely into the night, so there could be little time to dwell.

Tobias and Henry once again joined the group of people working to clear out and replace the charred hay, mumbling their goodbyes to the duke and marquess. Christopher and Graham then made their way out of the barn and approached their horses, stopping to thank other tenants who had dropped their day's tasks to help put out the fire.

"It is unfortunate that we have no better description than a man and a woman on horseback," Christopher lamented.

"Well, we at least know something. I always thought it unlikely that it was a collection of unrelated events that caused my tenants to panic, but now I can be sure there is something more nefarious afoot. And this mystery couple is to blame for all of it."

"Let us just hope the barn burning is all they get up to today," Christopher murmured almost to himself, as he followed his friend back to the manse.

***

Across the estate, nearer to the orchards, Alaina gingerly picked her way across a trail that looked almost abandoned, with overgrown vegetation and rocks littering the rut between two lines of trees. It was obvious that at some point this had been a main thoroughfare for surveying the grounds and moving goods, but it had since fallen into disrepair through lack of use. It was unfortunate they had not chosen whatever path had obviously replaced this one, for it was causing her to be quite slow in her progress.

The tour of the grounds had started out normally enough, but even before they were out of sight of the main house, Georgiana's horse had slipped a shoe. She returned to the house, vowing to return as quickly as she could with a new horse, directing Alaina and Evelina toward the path they were currently traversing. Evelina had been itching for a full gallop across the fields she had seen through her windows the past few days, so she quickly bounded ahead of Alaina on the trail, cresting the small hill just ahead, taunting Alaina to "keep up!"

Alaina now found herself alone in the woods, which was peaceful aside from the treacherous nature of the trail ahead of her, coupled with her normal trepidations on horseback. As she was guiding her horse around yet another large stone on the path and looking ahead to a thorny bit of overgrowth, Alaina heard a crackle of branches. She stopped her horse and looked through the trees, straining to see what or who was there. Alaina half-expected some woodland creature to skitter across her path, but she could not shake the nagging feeling that she was not alone. Hoping it was her sister, she called out.

"Evelina? Is that you? You know how I dislike being frightened, especially on a horse," Alaina attempted to sound calm.

There was no answer and no further sounds from the woods, but the eerie quiet was almost more unsettling. As Alaina looked around, hoping to see something, she felt a prickling on her neck, and her heart began to beat faster.

"Who is there?" she called, sure there was someone there. Again, there was nothing more than the breeze through the trees in response to Alaina's question.

Just as Alaina was about to chide herself for being paranoid, a large black stallion bounded toward her and her horse from the dense copse of trees. Alaina was able to pull her horse back just as the other passed in front of them, narrowly avoiding a collision that would have sent Alaina airborne. Her horse regained its footing and did not appear to be spooked overly much; *thank goodness for being given the most even-tempered horse in the stable*, thought Alaina. Alaina watched as the stallion ran a little way up the trail then disappeared into the trees, obviously spooked by something. It had a full complement of tack, saddle, bridle, and reins. Maybe someone had been thrown and was hurt?

Fighting the urge to flee, Alaina dismounted and was leading her horse toward the thicket when a woman emerged, looking disheveled. The woman's hat was askew, a few twigs protruding from her hair. Her riding habit didn't look torn, so Alaina assumed she was largely uninjured, just shaken from the fall from the black stallion that had just bounded through the trees. The woman stood looking about before turning toward Alaina, and recognition was immediate.

"Lady Barbara?!" Alaina exclaimed.

Lady Barbara's eyes narrowed, and she advanced on Alaina wordlessly. Alaina felt cornered, and without a stump to once again mount her horse, she was stuck facing Lady Barbara alone and on foot. Trying to diffuse the situation,

Alaina forced her tone to be cheery. She refused to let Barbara see her terror in meeting anyone, let alone her nemesis, in the woods. "Are you hurt? I am guessing your horse got the best of you; I fear I am no stranger to that. Surely you want to retrieve your horse before he gets too far afield." Alaina's voice lost its volume as the other woman approached, stopping just short of Alaina and her horse.

Lady Barbara looked back toward the black stallion, happily grazing in a nearby clearing, and shrugged before she turned back to Alaina. It was then that she finally broke her silence. "Out and about alone, Alaina? It is strange that the duke would let you out of his sight and let you traipse around Ashford without an escort."

"I am not alone, Lady Barbara, I assure you," Alaina said weakly, as she swallowed hard against her fear.

Lady Barbara once more looked about, as if she were looking for anyone to prove Alaina's claim, and then chuckled, "It appears you do not have anyone to save you today, Alaina. I have been frustrated at our last few encounters. Now it appears we have all the time in the world to *chat*."

The emphasis on the last word made Alaina's skin crawl, and she took a tentative step back toward her horse; maybe if she could get a foot in the stirrup, she could hoist herself up. Surely Lady Barbara could not chase her on foot.

But Lady Barbara saw her motion, and closed the distance between them, grasping Alaina's arm before she could turn toward her horse. Her next words were spit out in anger. "You think you can escape on your own?! You have humiliated my family at every turn, you have been saved at every interaction, and now I shall have my own form of revenge without society's prying eyes."

With Lady Barbara so close, Alaina took stock of the fact they were of equal size, for up until then Lady Barbara had loomed large, Alaina's bully and tormenter. It was also apparent that Lady Barbara would never cease in her mission to avenge her brother for what was an insignificant slight, nor would she ever cease to hate Alaina, for *any* reason. No matter how passive or even kind Alaina was to Lady Barbara, it would never stop. It was this that finally caused Alaina to erupt, the long-held anger at her treatment this season bursting forth unchecked. Pushing with all her strength, Alaina surprised Lady Barbara, throwing her off balance. Lady Barbara lost her grip, and stumbled. Her eyes burned with fire as she landed squarely on her backside.

Alaina capitalized on her moment of surprise and quickly placed a foot in the stirrup, her arms barely finding purchase on the saddle as she tried to hoist herself up. Lady Barbara quickly righted herself and came after Alaina with intent, but the sound of approaching riders stopped her in her tracks.

There was no time for Alaina to react as Lady Barbara turned and ran for the glade where her horse still grazed, throwing one last verbal volley over her shoulder. "This isn't over, Alaina!"

Alaina felt a rising panic, as the sound of hooves signaled that the group of riders was almost upon her. She struggled to find her seat in the saddle and whirled her horse around in the path just in time to see Graham and Christopher gallop through a thicket and come into view. Alaina breathed a sigh of relief and quickly looked around for Lady Barbara, intent on alerting the men of her presence, but she found no trace of the woman.

The gentlemen had stopped just short of her position when she heard the sound of an easy trot from the opposite direction, and espied Evelina.

"Alaina! What happened to you? I know I raced ahead, but I had expected you to catch up to me ten minutes ago." Evelina seemed concerned, and Alaina watched her sister's eyes widen as she caught sight of the duke and the marquess.

Christopher and Graham had joined them on the tight trail, Graham in front, Christopher close behind. Before Alaina could respond to her sister, both men spoke.

"Alaina, are you alright?" Graham calmly asked, Christopher's identical question just behind the duke's.

"What is going on?" Evelina gathered quickly that something was amiss.

Graham opened his mouth, but it was Alaina who answered first. "I am ok, I think," she said, as she rubbed her arm where Lady Barbara had held onto her. "I am thankful you all are here now, you have impeccable timing, really." A nervous chuckle escaped her lips before she continued, "I just saw Lady Barbara, and she… well, she…"

Alaina felt her throat close up, and her fear of what could have happened took over as her body shook uncontrollably.

As if he could wait no longer for an explanation, Christopher interjected, "She what?"

Alaina took a steadying breath and attempted to continue. "She seemed quite angry with me, but that is not so unusual. She seemed happy to find me alone, and she grabbed me, but I was able to push her away. I fear I only escaped because of your arrival. Why is she even here?"

Finally, Alaina looked up and saw the shock on Evelina's face and ominous looks from Graham and Christopher.

It was a few moments before anyone said anything. Finally, the duke took charge. "Alaina, Evelina, can you follow Christopher back to the house? I have to go visit some neighbors and alert them to the goings-on of the afternoon. With Lady Barbara's appearance, I fear Percy is at the root of all the mischief on the estate, and now they are threatening bodily harm!" Graham practically growled. After a pause he continued, "I hope you forgive my abruptness, but trust me, it is for your safety."

Evelina and Alaina both sat in stunned silence and could only nod in agreement as Graham steered his horse past Christopher, giving his friend a look and nod.

Christopher was quick to motion for both Evelina and Alaina to precede him on the ride back to the stables, Evelina taking the lead. The sound of plodding hooves filled the silence as the group picked their way along the trail.

Evelina spoke first. "So, it seems all the issues Graham has been called away for are related to his cousin?"

Christopher was slow to respond. "Yes, most of them have been vandalism or theft: a broken plow here, a missing sheep or two there, nothing to alert us of any real danger. But we had just come from a fire at the barn when we met with Georgiana and she said you were out riding alone. Trust me, if I had ever had any reason to suspect, if I had known…"

Alaina and Christopher's eyes met, his steel-blue ones delving into hers, and he finally finished, his voice choked, "I would never have let you out here to ride alone, *never*."

Alaina held his gaze for a few seconds more and then turned in her saddle. The look in Christopher's eyes seemed to say too many things at once: anger, fear, possession. It was too much to bear, and they rode on in silence as Alaina wished for the solitude of her chamber to settle her mind.

***

"What on earth happened?" came Georgiana's question as the group pulled up to the stables, and disembarked from each of their horses, clearly done with their ride. Georgiana pulled away from her freshly saddled horse to meet Alaina, Evelina, and Christopher, a furrow marking her brow.

Christopher answered, "Evelina and Alaina got separated on their ride and Lady Barbara made an appearance. I was thankful that Graham and I found her in time before something worse happened."

"Worse than what? What was she doing in the woods on my brother's estate?" Georgiana questioned, but a shake of Christopher's head stalled any further inquiries.

Alaina and Evelina did not say anything and looked a bit shocked at the turn of the afternoon. Georgiana quickly intervened. "Well, then, I say we retire to one of the private family parlors and rest while things get sorted."

Georgiana ushered the ladies inside through the side door of the stables, and Christopher followed quickly behind, but took his leave almost immediately. He would not be joining them, as he had more important matters to attend. Christopher first went in search of Graham's steward, Mr. Locke. Knowing this was one of the few times Christopher could question the man alone, he made sure to search the whole house to find him, but had no luck. Christopher then checked in with the butler to find Graham still out on the estate, probably visiting his neighbors to warn them of the afternoon's events and the suspicion of who was to blame.

Frustrated, Christopher returned to his guest room, placed along with the other guests in the east wing, opposite from the wing with the stables. Georgiana had given Alaina and her family lodgings in the other wing, since they were more than merely guests. He expected it was not just Alaina's planning assistance, but the fact that she may soon be family that had prompted the decision. At the moment, Christopher was both relieved and perturbed by their physical separation. If their rooms had been closer, he would be more apt to run into Alaina and would have an excuse to talk to her. His worries about displaying emotion were eclipsed entirely by the panic he had felt to learn that Alaina and Evelina were out exploring the property alone.

He could not shake the urge to find himself in their wing for one reason or another, just for the chance to see her. It was madness. Was it just lust and their proximity? Deep down he was coming to admit to himself that was false. His body wanted hers, to be sure. When Alaina was near, his belly clenched and his manhood seemed to have a mind of its own, but he also yearned to know all her thoughts, her plans, desires in life, and to laugh at life's inanities together. Christopher sighed and moved absently to stand at the window in his room, knowing in his heart what he wanted, but feeling as if he may have missed his chance.

From the first, Christopher had found himself forcing Alaina away, only to be pulled back into her orbit. He could never expect her to entertain him as a suitor now, not with his behavior and his proclamations against any proper form of attachment. Not to mention the fact that his friend, his charming friend, was courting the young lady. They seemed to get along well, and Christopher was perturbed to find himself jealous that her smiles were reserved for Graham. No, there was certainly no chance for Christopher to convince Alaina of his worthiness.

CHAPTER 12

"Is this not the most exciting thing?" Evelina said, barely able to contain her excitement as she and Alaina made their way to the courtyard for the final ball with their mother, Charlotte.

Evelina was so excited to be attending her first ball, more than happy to take advantage of the looser social strictures in the country, and seemed unperturbed by Alaina's silence. Luckily, Alaina did not need to speak much as Evelina bubbled over with excitement and anticipation of the evening's activities.

Alaina harbored many worries in her mind, not the least of which was Lady Barbara and Percy out and about on the Ashford Estate, the wake of their destruction exposing their desperation. Truly, Alaina had no idea what would have happened if no one had been close by to rescue her today. But Alaina was resolved to enjoy the last evening of the party, and she had forced herself to focus on her preparations, which brought another concern to the forefront: her dress.

Madam Benoit had assured her that it was the fashion all ladies in society wore. Unlike her dress on the first evening of the country gathering, her frock on this occasion was high-backed, even going so far as to having a mock collar at the base of the neck. However, it was the front of the dress that was cause for concern. The neckline was low, revealing ample parts of her pert breasts, and even more of the cleft between them, where the neckline dipped even lower. Most of the dress was made from the velvet that had interested her in the dressmaker's shop. The skirt was pleated with a chiffon of pale pink, almost giving the illusion of an entire skirt underneath, or even glimpses of her shift. It was an enchanting illusion, one that had raised her mother's eyebrows, but had not caused an outright protest.

Alaina had tried to convince herself internally that her scrutiny of her appearance had nothing to do with Christopher's comments, but standing in her room alone and studying her reflection in the mirror, she knew it had everything to do with Christopher. Since this afternoon, Alaina could no longer hide from herself that it was Christopher that her heart beat for, even if he refused to act on his feelings. When the duke and Christopher had appeared on the trail, Alaina's eyes had only been for Christopher, and she had been surprised by the relief she felt due to his presence alone. In that moment, she knew that to continue with the courtship with the duke would only serve to hurt. But Alaina did not want to ruin the party and planned to speak with Graham on the morrow, after the guests had left. Her decision did not make her heart leap with joy, as it was clear that Christopher was not in want of a wife. *Even if he was, she could scarcely hope that he would be interested in her.*

Georgiana had enlisted Alaina's help in planning the events for the past few days, but had been adamant that the decorations for the final ball be left to her. Apparently, Georgiana had been envisioning this type of party for quite some time and wanted it to be a surprise, even from her mother and Graham. Alaina and Evelina had absolutely no idea what was in store for them. Alaina forced a smile, determined to enjoy the evening; she was certainly curious what was in store.

"Well, I guess we are almost there. I do hear some music up ahead," Charlotte leaned in to add to the conversation, hoping to reassure both her daughters before joining the other guests.

Alaina sighed as they rounded what she assumed was the last corner, seeing wide glass doors ahead and a glow from the outside. Evelina almost squealed in excitement as they approached the open doors. Stopping just past the opening, Alaina, Evelina, and Charlotte stood in awe for a few moments, taking in the wonderland before them. Just to their left was a small refreshment table with sweet treats and what looked to be a warm mulled wine. As this was a sizable manor, the courtyard was quite large, and a path wound its way lazily toward a well-lit dance floor, where a soft minuet was being played by a small contingent of musicians. A small group of benches was placed almost directly ahead, not too far from the refreshment table and far enough away from the music to allow conversation. It seemed at every turn was a tower with a good-sized flame, making the courtyard warmer than Alaina had expected. Their breath was visible in the air, but the glow of torches and candles scattered throughout the garden made it almost feel like an indoor ball from a bygone era. Some of the plants in the garden showed a layer of frost or had hanging icicles, twinkling in the light of the courtyard, giving a feeling of magic.

A click of heels on the stone pathway leading to the dance floor caught Alaina's attention and she looked up to see Georgiana coming to greet them, looking dazzling in an amethyst brocade, with a high back reaching up to her ears as the neckline flared under her chin. A keyhole neckline teased a glimpse of her pale skin, shining radiantly in the soft light. Where the fabric of the dress was complex, the cut of the skirt was simple, falling almost straight to the floor. Alaina thought that Georgiana really did look like the queen of the ball.

"Georgiana, you are a vision. We must thank Madam Benoit for her handiwork. And just think what your husband would think to see you. He would most assuredly be agog," Charlotte said graciously, motioning to Alaina and Evelina as well. Even Evelina, who was garbed in a more youthful cut with a higher neckline and fuller skirt, looked enchanting in her ice-blue silk dress. The fuller sleeves and skirt allowed for heavier undergarments to keep her warm where the lighter fabric could not.

"I thank you for the compliment, Lady Charlotte, and I would agree that Madam Benoit outdid herself. I would like to welcome you all to my winter garden party!" Georgiana said cheerily, wrinkling her nose ever so slightly as she smiled broadly at her newfound friends. A slightly different look, something more forlorn, passed along Georgiana's face before she smiled once again. "I imagine my husband would be as you say. I am hoping you will all meet him at some point in the future."

Georgiana's smile faded ever so slightly. Choosing to ignore that subject for now, Alaina spoke first. "Well, as the queen of the ball, maybe you can show us your creation. From what I see, it is quite enchanting."

"Of course. Most of it is self-explanatory," Georgiana said, motioning to their immediate surroundings. "But I must say the dance floor is my favorite part. Come with me."

Georgiana turned and led the pair of sisters and their mother along a winding stone path toward the music. From the entrance of the courtyard, only a small part of the dance floor could be seen, but as they followed the path and made it past the dense collection of frosted and dormant plants, the full floor came into view.

"Wow," was all that came from Evelina's lips. Alaina looked over at her sister's face and smiled at the wonder she saw there.

Alaina was the next to pay a compliment. "I am truly impressed by your imagination, Georgiana. Everything is breathtaking."

"Indeed," remarked Charlotte. "I fear this party will outshine any I may attend in the future."

A parquet floor had been set up in the garden, large enough for ten or so couples, plenty for the number of guests at the country party. The quartet of musicians, two violins, one cello, and a viola, were at the far end of the dance floor, and a handful of couples were taking part in a waltz. Georgiana craned her neck to see over the couples, finding Graham deep in conversation with Christopher. Both men looked quite stern, but a glance toward the entrance to the dance floor brought a smile to Graham's face and something slightly different to Christopher's. Catching Georgiana's motion to join them, both of them made their way around the edge of the dance floor, avoiding the fray, joining the group in a few moments. Graham sank into a deep bow. "Ladies, with what beauty and grace I see before me, the party can now officially begin."

Evelina giggled as they all sunk into curtsies to match Graham's bow. Christopher bowed as well, murmuring his welcome.

"Alaina, may I have the honor of this dance?" Graham asked, offering his arm.

"You may, sir," Alaina smiled, taking his arm and letting him lead her a few steps as they set up for the next dance.

"Evelina, it would be an honor if you would join me," Christopher said as he offered her his arm. Evelina graciously accepted, and Christopher led Evelina in the same direction as Graham and Alaina. Georgiana and Charlotte were left to stare after each of the couples wistfully, and for the same reason: husbands that were not in attendance, whether by choice or not.

———————✤———————

The evening of dancing flew by for all the guests, the magic of the atmosphere seeming to accelerate the passage of time, none more so than for Alaina and Christopher. Alaina shared a pair of dances with Graham before being swept away in a waltz by Lord Blackwell, a friend of Georgiana's husband who also attended school a year ahead of Graham and Christopher. It seemed that no sooner was Christopher without a partner, that Alaina was occupied in a dance or in conversation, and vice versa. Finally, Alaina found herself alone at the refreshment table, able to catch her breath for the first time since arriving.

"My lady, we need to stop meeting like this," came a rich, low voice behind her, almost like a caress.

Alaina turned to find Christopher smiling at her, a twinkle in his eyes, apparently amused at his own wit.

"And what has you so amused?" Alaina pressed. She had wished for and dreaded the moment she may be alone with the marquess.

Christopher cleared his throat, and his eyes darkened with something that made Alaina shiver, before he breathed the word, "You."

Alaina stuffed her elation, and let her skepticism guard her heart. "I amuse you, sir?"

"Not so much that, but I would admit that I cannot stop thinking of you," Christopher added, and Alaina felt her insides twist in a knot.

"Surely you jest," came her parry. "Pretty words just tumbling from your mouth because of the magic of the evening."

"No, never that."

"How can you say such things? I was sure that you hated me once," Alaina challenged.

"Hated you?"

"Yes, hated me. We argued at every turn."

But Christopher pushed back, "I admit, yes, we argued, but I found myself enthralled at our every interaction. And there was your courtship with Graham to consider. I could not act on anything before…"

"And now is the appropriate time?" Alaina asked. She felt her heart leap, but was cautious.

Christopher was slow to respond, but then the words came out in a tumble. "No, I know that this is an inopportune moment, but I cannot seem to help myself. At dinner, at the dress shop, our kiss at the Stamford Ball; it was like I was consumed by something."

Alaina struggled to calm her breathing. The memories he had recalled tumbled about in her mind. Christopher's eyes feasted on Alaina, from her hair to her toes, his slow perusal of her person a loving touch, a gentle caress. Alaina noticed that his breathing matched hers and she wished that her mind did not feel so jumbled. When she finally spoke, her tone was gentle but cautious. "So, am I to understand that your thoughts on marriage have changed?"

Alaina watched as Christopher set his jaw, and she did not wait for his response. "I will take your silence as a 'no.' Am I to assume that your original statement is correct? I do only amuse you?"

Christopher opened his mouth, but in the next moment the couple was swallowed by the rest of the partygoers as they gathered around the refreshment table. Georgiana was among the group and was quick to interject, "Alaina, Christopher, what are you doing all the way over here? The musicians will be playing their last set soon, and I would have you both on the dance floor!"

The group seemed oblivious of the couple as they grabbed glasses of punch and treats before once more retreating to the inner garden as strains of music reached Alaina and Christopher's ears.

Christopher presented his arm to Alaina, and she stiffly accepted. They walked in silence along the path to the dance floor, and found themselves quickly set upon, Christopher finding himself paired with a lady of Georgiana's acquaintance and Alaina paired once more with Lord Blackwell. They each passed the rest of the evening with stilted smiles and forced conversations, wishing for the evening to end.

Alaina flounced once more in her bed as the clock in her room chimed to remind her that sleep eluded her for yet another hour. Her interaction with Christopher weighed on her, the elation of his admission mixed with disappointment; the marquess had no interest in a wife. His feelings on the matter did not change the fact that in the morning, Alaina would need to sever her connection with the duke, an undesirable task, but necessary. Graham deserved someone whose heart was not already captured by another.

⚜

Christopher stood by the window in his room and stared at the moon, numbly watching it peak in and out of the clouds that traversed the night sky. His mind was occupied with his interaction with Lady Alaina, one left unfinished. Christopher chided himself for his tongue-tied interaction. *To imagine that he left his thoughts on marriage unsaid, even when Alaina asked him a clear question. The thoughts roiled in his mind. He was still wary of the institution to be sure, but on the other hand, the idea of being without Alaina for even a moment caused an ache in his chest.* He could only hope that tomorrow would give him another opportunity.

Chapter 13

Alaina found herself wandering the halls of the Ashford manor the next morning, a bundle of nerves and anticipation. She knew she had to end her courtship with the duke, and had no wish to hurt Graham or his family. However, it was her unfinished conversation with Christopher that weighed most heavily on her mind and her heart.

Since the prior evening had been the last night of the party, most of the guests had departed early in the morning, directly following a buffet-style breakfast. Unlike the previous few days, there was no set time for the meal, and so Alaina, Charlotte, and Evelina had only encountered one other guest, Lady Drake, Georgiana's friend from Cornwall. They had eaten in relative quiet compared to the previous evening, each person only contributing niceties and small talk about the weather and other such things. Alaina had been relieved that Graham had not made an appearance.

Georgiana had invited the three of them to stay on for a few days after the party since, in her words, the party planners needed rest following such an event. This allowed Alaina the freedom to roam the house. Charlotte and Evelina had gone back to their chambers after breakfast, each claiming exhaustion from the night before, leaving Alaina to her own devices near the library. It had been in Charlotte's mind, at least, that Alaina may need some time to reflect, or just to read and be with her thoughts. In truth, Alaina had no intention of remaining stationary; she was too worried to sit still.

It was also her most fervent wish to talk to Christopher and finish their conversation, if for no other reason than to put the matter to rest, one way or the other. Though wandering the halls could be construed as nosy or untoward, Alaina felt that it increased her chances of encountering Christopher, even if that meant also a chance of encountering the duke. When her mother and sister had made their way to the stairway leading upstairs, Alaina had feigned in the direction of the library, simply passing the doors, making her way slowly down the hall in the direction of the stables. Pausing every so often to look over a portrait of some previous duke or duchess, or a landscape painting, Alaina tried to appear calm and without purpose. However, on the inside, she was jittery, hoping that at every doorway to a darkened parlor or bend in the hall, she would see Christopher. She was equally nervous to encounter the duke.

As Alaina rounded the last corner before the door to the stables at the end of a long hallway, she heard muffled voices. Feeling her feet pick up speed she began to search for the source, even poking her head into a few of the open doorways on her right, only to find darkened rooms, each appearing to have a slightly different purpose or décor. Alaina had just found yet another sitting room, this one so decorated in a rose motif that she could envision herself in the middle of a bouquet, when the door to the outside stables opened and the muffled voices became clear as Graham and Christopher entered the hallway.

The sudden change in sound and situation startled Alaina, and she could feel herself blush at the possibility of being caught snooping. Before she could exit the rose parlor's door completely and turn around, she heard the voices stop, along with the accompanying footsteps.

"Alaina?" came the surprised greeting from Graham.

"Graham," Alaina quickly righted herself and turned around, bobbing a curtsey in quick acknowledgement and turning the same to Christopher, who was situated directly beside the duke. "Christopher."

"Well, is this not a pleasant surprise? Forgive my manners, I was just flummoxed to see the person who was just on my mind," Graham said, recovering from his initial shock. "I had hoped to seek an audience after I cleaned up from my ride, but it seems fate has decreed this to be the opportune moment, Alaina. Would you do me the honor of an audience in my study? I would also like your mother there, if possible. Christopher, would you be so kind as to fetch Lady Charlotte? I assume she is in her room?"

This last question had been directed to Alaina, who nodded her affirmation. Before Christopher could respond,

Graham presented his arm to Alaina and started to lead her back down the hallway she had just been exploring. Christopher followed along in silence as they all made their way toward Graham's study, located just opposite the main staircase. No one spoke, each lost in their own thoughts and anxieties. As they passed the stairs, Alaina heard the click of Christopher's boots steer away from them and ascend the large marble staircase to the upper chambers, obviously intent on seeking out Lady Charlotte for the upcoming conversation.

Graham's study was just across from the breakfast room, and he left Alaina's side briefly to greet the scattered few guests still eating breakfast before departing. As Alaina watched Graham easily converse, totally at ease in his own home, she thought about the possibility of sharing a home with someone; standing at their side, and laughing at some inanity or giving a teasing look to them when it suited her. The difficulty in this rumination was that Alaina could only picture standing by Christopher's side. Graham was a wonderful, caring, and handsome individual, but she had waited too long, taken too much time to know her heart and her mind. Alaina may never get the opportunity to tell Christopher how she felt. And now she was faced with the fact that there may never be any formal connection between her and the marquess. It was possible that the machinations of her mother and the dowager duchess would have still seen her entertaining courtship with the duke, but from the first, Alaina had been drawn to Christopher. Standing on the precipice of a possible proposal from the duke, Alaina knew what she had to do, but wondered if she had the courage.

It was possible that after today, Alaina may never even see Christopher again. He had looked stunned by her question on their possible future, and his lack of answer on his thoughts of marriage had been a response on its own, and though he seemed interested in her, perhaps without the force of the duke's friendship, Christopher would not seek out her company on his own. That thought gave Alaina pause. Doubt crept into the back of her mind when she thought of Christopher; maybe he only wished for a dalliance, all his beautiful words said for every purpose except for marriage.

Alaina heard a pair of footsteps approaching from behind. Turning only enough to confirm who approached, Alaina averted her gaze, suddenly unsure of what she should do, and acutely aware of what heartbreak may lay in the future, both her own and that of the duke.

Graham also saw his friend and Charlotte approach, and deftly excused himself from his guests, making his way back to Alaina's side, seemingly unaware of the tension that to Alaina felt obvious.

Presenting his arm again to Alaina, Graham cleared his throat. "Shall we?" He motioned toward his study.

Alaina nodded and followed ever so slightly behind Graham, keeping her hand on top of his arm. A surreptitious glance over her shoulder allowed her to see that Christopher and her mother followed only a few steps behind.

As they neared the door to Graham's study, Graham turned to Alaina's mother and questioned, "Would it be ok to have a moment alone with your daughter, Lady Charlotte? You and Christopher would be just outside the door for only a few moments, and we would keep the door slightly open for propriety."

"That would be fine with me, as long as it is ok with Alaina," her mother smiled warmly at Graham, and then glanced at her daughter.

"That is fine," was all Alaina could manage, unable to meet Christopher or Graham's eyes.

Having gained Charlotte's approval for their semi-private tête-à-tête, Graham opened the door to his study, allowing Alaina to enter. He followed her, leaving the door slightly open.

Alaina looked around the duke's study, taking in her surroundings in an attempt to delay the discussion, if only for a moment. During the past few days, Alaina had observed the diversity of styles throughout the duke's country manse. It seemed that every parlor, dining room, and bedchamber had different décor, ranging from the overwhelmingly floral room she had just walked from to more serene surroundings. The house seemed to hold the characters of every generation of Ashford women, with very few truly masculine touches. It was this that made Graham's study stand in stark contrast.

The space was distinctly masculine, with dark leather chairs and rustic animal skin rugs scattered about the floor. Even with the large windows on the wall opposite the door, the darkness of the room meant that Alaina's eyes took a moment to adjust to her surroundings. As she looked around, she saw piles of papers, some on the large desk in front of the window, and others scattered around the room, on small side tables or on piles of books on the floor. A fire burned bright on the far side of the room, lending warmth. From her time spent with Graham, Alaina could surmise that he had little to do with the décor, but everything to do with the books she saw about, even a few they had oft discussed. The dark furnishings and hunting lodge style did not match Graham's charming and kind personality, but the controlled mess certainly transformed the study into a perfectly imperfect place.

Graham cleared his throat from behind Alaina. "This was my father's room before it was mine. I have not had a chance to change anything."

Alaina turned to meet his gaze, and smiled, crinkling her nose ever so slightly in amusement. "I do not think I agree entirely with your assessment; I see you in some corners."

"I imagine you mean the mess. My mother and Georgiana always say I should keep a tidier study," Graham responded, diverting his gaze ever so slightly downward, betraying a boyish nervousness he had not felt in some time.

"Not the mess, the books. But I find it quite charming, actually, giving the impression that someone human resides here. Otherwise, it might be quite unwelcoming." Alaina hoped she had not insulted the duke, especially with what she knew was bound to come next in their conversation.

Graham cleared his throat. "Well, I had hoped you might find my home in Ashford a charming place. Georgiana has a way of putting our best foot forward as well, which plays to my advantage." Graham segued, a lopsided and disarming smile finally gracing his face.

"Oh, I have most definitely been charmed by this place, your grace," Alaina assured him, tentative about what to say next.

⚜

Christopher moved away from the study door and went to stand on the other side of the foyer, afraid that if he eavesdropped any further, his heart would be torn from his chest. He watched the door intently, expecting that at any moment, the happy couple would burst forth to share the news. It took every ounce of willpower that Christopher had to stand rooted to his spot, resigned to offer his congratulations should that moment come.

It also, unfortunately, gave him time to consider all of his mistakes. By pushing away Alaina, and the idea of marriage, he was now convinced that he had put in jeopardy his very happiness. And even last night, he had been offered an opportunity to right everything, if he had just admitted to Alaina that his feelings for her overruled his reservations. That a vision of a lifetime with her had taken form in his mind, and could not be uprooted. All these things, Christopher had realized too late, and now he would have to stand aside for his friend, no matter the cost to himself.

Graham looked at Alaina more intently as the silence between them stretched, as if he wished for Alaina to continue speaking. When she did not, Graham was forced to break the silence. "But? It certainly sounds like there is a but in your statement."

Alaina sighed, feeling no better option than to forge ahead most directly. "But I fear I am not as charmed as I should be, or moreover, no more charmed than a good friend is when they learn pieces of a person they care about. I imagine that is what we are here to discuss?"

Alaina felt a little embarrassed to have stated such a sentiment, especially with no proclamations from the duke. She broke eye contact with Graham, and studied the bear's head on the rug closest to her.

"Well, I had hoped for otherwise," Graham stated, moving to stand near the fireplace, resting his arm on the mantel and staring into the flames. After some time, he turned again to face Alaina.

Chuckling, Graham sought to put her mind at ease. "Fear not, Alaina, I had hoped, but felt it was possible you did not feel exactly the same as I did. I assume there was nothing in particular wrong with our courtship?" The last question hung in the air uncomfortably, and Alaina watched a passing grimace cross Graham's face.

"No, your grace. I am afraid we cannot control matters of the heart so readily, that is all. You are wonderful and will find someone to share in the overwhelming kind of love that both of our sets of parents found, I believe," Alaina responded, hoping to sound genuine and sincere, for she truly valued her new friendship with Graham and his family.

Graham turned his head away again and said hollowly, "I thought I had, but it seems the past couple of days have set even my senses a bit on their ends."

Alaina was about to reassure the duke once more when the door handle smacked the wall as her mother rushed into the room.

"Alaina, my dear, we must leave at once!" Charlotte nearly burst as she flew halfway across the room to her daughter, clearly distraught.

"Mother, what is wrong?" Alaina asked, surprised.

Charlotte remembered herself, if only a bit too late, took a breath, and continued. "My apologies, Graham, but it is your father, Alaina. He has taken a bad tumble off his horse in Hyde Park. It knocked him unconscious, and he has yet to wake, based on the note we just received, but that was from the time it took the letter to get here. Things could be better or worse by now! I sent Christopher to find Evelina to pack, but we must leave posthaste. I hope you will forgive us, Graham."

Graham moved closer to Alaina and her mother and gave a short bow. "No forgiveness is needed. I will help to get you on your way quickly, however I can."

Trying to ignore the tinge of sadness in Graham's voice, Alaina expressed her gratitude. "Your grace, we appreciate your offer of assistance. If you would be so kind as to have our carriage readied, we should be able to embark to London within the hour."

Alaina hurried out of the room after her mother, her blood hammering in her ears. She fixed a vision of her father in her mind, hale and healthy, and forced it to stay. A trip to London would be long enough without thoughts of the worst.

CHAPTER 14

Alaina sighed and resettled herself in the chair they had set up next to her father's sick bed. It had been close to a week since Alaina, her mother, and her sister had raced to London to see to Edward. The Dowager Duchess Eleanor and Lady Georgiana had been outside waiting to say goodbye, assuring them of their support should they need it.

Alaina regarded her father, who looked to be sleeping once more in the massive four-poster bed. His condition had improved, having regained consciousness a few days after their return to London, but he still suffered from headaches and fatigue. Out of an abundance of caution, the doctor had recommended they keep a close watch. Even with a fair amount of blustering from Edward, who had insisted on returning to his normal activities, the ladies of the house had kept almost constant watch should his condition worsen. Eventually, Edward acquiesced to their presence and rested as the doctor had ordered.

Lost in thought, Alaina had missed the fact that her father had stirred from his afternoon nap, and she was surprised when he made a keen observation. "You look as if the world is on your shoulders, Alaina. Surely you are not so concerned for my health still. The doctor even proclaimed it will only be a few more days before I am up and out of this blasted bed."

Alaina jumped in her seat and looked at her father, whose eyes twinkled with the teasing she had heard in his voice.

"Papa, you are awake, and feeling well I see," Alaina chided, hoping to avoid any further prying.

"Now now, you cannot avoid my inquiry so easily," Edward said, only half-teasing, knowing his older daughter well enough to know something of import weighed on her mind.

Instead of rising to what would surely be an uncomfortable conversation, Alaina stood up and stretched her arms, trying to relieve the stiffness from sitting for long hours in a chair intended only for comfort during brief visits. She busied herself tidying the room. In truth, there was not much to tidy, and Alaina found herself standing at the foot of her father's bed with nothing more to distract her from her father's persistence.

Unfazed by his daughter's silence, Edward pressed on. "I had hoped to be regaled with tales of the garden party you and Lady Georgiana planned. So far, I have heard not one word. Even Evelina has been relatively mute, steering clear of any details. All I got from your mother is that your courtship with the Duke of Ashford is over, but, in truth, I know of nothing else. Was it really so bad?"

The last question hung in the air for only a moment, and Alaina responded, "No, it was a wonderful party; fun games, rides along the countryside, and the most magical, if a bit chilly, ball in one of the Ashford courtyards. Only a bit of mischief caused by Percy and Lady Barbara marred an otherwise pleasant stay."

"Lady Barbara and Graham's cousin? What on earth?"

Alaina waved her hand in dismissal, not wishing to cause her father any stress in his condition. "They were not invited, if that is your concern. They were the reason Graham had been called away from London, thieving, vandalizing, and terrorizing the Ashford Estate. I had a run-in with Lady Barbara, but I am fine, really. I am sure they have been appropriately apprehended by now."

"Then what happened with Graham?"

"Well, I was able to figure out that I did not love him and thought it unfair to continue with the courtship," Alaina explained, not wishing to share every detail just yet, if only to save her heart from speaking it out loud.

"But I was under the impression that you held some affection for Graham," Edward spoke softly.

Alaina turned from her father to face the window opposite his bed, forgetting that the curtains had been drawn to shut out any light as Edward slept. Frustrated in her attempt to appear distracted and nonchalant, Alaina turned back to face her father with a sardonic chuckle. "I suppose I would be required to explain everything?"

Edward pondered her question and took a soft approach. "It would be nice to know what has happened to make you so melancholy, but I know sometimes matters of the heart are difficult to discuss. Your mother thought I should give you time, and I have tried to do so, but the look in your eyes when I woke up worried me enough to ask. Can you blame me for being concerned?" Edward paused, searching his daughter's eyes, finding a lost look he had never seen before. At Alaina's shrug, he continued, "Besides, I am bored and stuck in this room. I need some entertainment. Come sit and tell me whatever is troubling you. *Please.*"

Alaina relented to her father's cajoling and came back to perch on the chair next to his bed, where she had passed so many worrisome hours. As she started to talk, she could feel the floodgates of her thoughts and emotions open. "Well, remember when we talked before and I mentioned being unsure of my future with the duke? I was able to discern my heart's desire, whom I love and see a future with, but I am unsure if he wants to share a life with me. I just know for sure that Graham is not the one."

"This other gentleman: I assume you knew him prior to the party? It is hard to imagine a whirlwind romance."

"Yes, Papa, I knew him before. I would not do something so rash." Alaina rolled her eyes.

"Love has no timetable, my dear, and I suspect you loved Christopher before you left for the country." Edward reached out for his daughter's hand, clasping it within his large sturdy ones for assurance.

Alaina, who had been staring down at her lap, slowly raised her eyes to meet her father's. "But how did you know who?"

"You are not very good at disguising your emotions, Alaina. Besides, what other gentleman did you know in that group?"

"None, but how am I to know if he feels the same?" Alaina asked the question that had been on her mind most of the past few days.

"It would be entirely up to him, but I imagine he would have given you something of a clue?" came Edward's assurance and question all rolled into one. There was no way of knowing if the man had made any proclamations to his daughter. It was tough to see one's child distraught over a possible unrequited love; it was one problem that he could not fix.

"Clues?! To think they would be so clear. From my first meeting with Christopher, he has been equal parts surly and taciturn, and yet…"

"Yet, what?" Edward asked softly.

"And yet, he looks at me as if I was his whole world, like he wants to know everything about me. He defends me when he has no obligation to do so. He is charming in one minute, and then ignores me the next," Alaina said, everything coming out in a tumble. She did not wish to share every detail, especially not the kiss they had shared, but she desperately wanted her father's advice. "We talked the last night of the party. He offered me some insight into his heart, told me he could not stop thinking of me, but then… then he refused to answer if the idea of marriage was ever in the cards."

Edward listened to his daughter intently, amazed at the emotions that played across her face, and all the small exchanges between her and Christopher that spoke of an all-encompassing love, one he had experienced with his wife, Charlotte. Finally, it was his turn to speak.

"Refused? It sounds to me that it is not a question of if he loves you, but if he is smart enough to share his life with you, and that is not something you can control." Edward paused, his expression growing pensive. "I am curious why he has not come to see you since you have been in London, or at least seen to my welfare as an excuse to call. Has he written?"

"No! I have received letters from Georgiana, Eleanor, and even Graham, but nothing from Christopher," Alaina burst, a sob wracking her body. Her sadness turned quickly to anger. "I did not even see him before I left Ashford to come back to London. We never got to finish our conversation! He must have been completely content to let me leave and never see me again. Perhaps he does not love me as I hoped. Perhaps I have misread everything!"

Edward's brows lowered, his face taking on an ominous look, but his words to his daughter were ones of reassurance. "I am sure there is some explanation."

Alaina scowled. "The first reason that comes to mind is that he does not feel anything for me."

Cresting the hill closest to the manor house on his estate, Christopher brought his horse down to a walk, for a much-needed break for rider and animal. In the week since Alaina had left Ashford and traveled to London to see to her father's welfare, Christopher had found it difficult to move on from what he thought was an amazing connection with the lady who had captured his heart. He had not heard the outcome of Graham's proposal, but had assumed its conclusion. Who would turn down the offer of marriage from a duke, let alone one so charming? After the news of Alaina's father, and their quick departure, it was not in Christopher's heart to stay at Ashford. He had quietly left a note for Graham, Georgiana, and Eleanor before departing for his own country estate, Waverley Place in Rochester, situated directly between Ashford and London.

A manor house stood at the end of a large, winding drive, covered by old trees that bespoke of the history of the property and house itself. Where Ashford contained a fairly new manor house, the old one having fallen into disrepair one or two generations ago, Waverley Place was built in medieval times with large turrets at each corner. The outer wall of the keep had long been reduced to a few sections of low walls surrounding the outer gardens, about half their original height. The old moat was left as a water feature, with lily pads and various other wildlife occupying the deep ravine. Where the entrance of the house stood, a more permanent bridge had long since been constructed, replacing the old portcullis that had once been lowered to allow for safe passage of the residents, keeping unwelcome guests safely outside the fortress. Inside the now-reduced curtain walls, the keep had been modernized and updated, but the main structure still stood as it had centuries ago.

As Christopher approached the side of the house, he had a clear view of the front bridge and drive, as well as a partially obstructed view of the gardens in the front of the house, where large rose bushes stood to welcome guests. In the summer, the bushes would fill with blood red, pearl white, and dusty pink blooms. At this time of year, though, the bushes resembled more of a tangle of thorns, but their size was still impressive and, in some cases, imposing. To the marquess, they meant he was home, even if this particular home had not been an overly happy one during his childhood years.

Christopher was about to dismount and walk his horse the remainder of the distance to the stables, tucked into a large crevice in the old keep walls, when he heard a horse racing down the pebbled drive behind him. Not able to see who approached around the bends in the long drive, Christopher cautiously made his way to the front of the manse to await whoever was making their way to Waverley. He had not been expecting company.

At the last moment, the horse and rider came into view, quickly galloping across the bridge and stopping just short of where Christopher had been waiting. It was clear that the rider and horse had been pushing hard, the stallion breathing heavily and frothing at the bit. Graham was breathing more easily than his horse, but a sheen of sweat on his brow gave away his effort, especially in the cool weather of March.

"Graham! To what do I owe the pleasure of this visit?" Christopher called out to his friend, surprised and curious about when he had started the journey, considering it was a full day's ride from Ashford. "I hope all is well? Shall we stable the horses and head inside?"

"Ho, Christopher! Greetings to you as well. I am afraid what I have come to say will be best shared outside," came Graham's flat response.

Christopher found it odd that his friend would be curt. Finding it difficult to remain nonchalant, Christopher forged ahead with a joking tone, or at least the best he could muster. "What is this? Is there trouble in paradise?"

Based on his own reaction to seeing his lifelong friend in the midst of his pending nuptials, Christopher had much doubt as to whether he would be able to tolerate the actual wedding. He had hoped to be given enough time to allow himself to offer a proper congratulations.

"Paradise? What in the world are you talking about?" Graham shot back, exasperated. "I was coming to see why you have not seen fit to visit Alaina in London at all in the past week. To be honest, I was not going to press the matter, but Georgiana insisted that I *deal* with this after she received word from Alaina on Edward's recovery in the past week, and their lack of visitors, as I am your closest friend."

"Why would I visit Alaina? It seems quite inappropriate given the two of you are now engaged." Christopher felt confused; *what in the world was his friend talking about?*

"Engaged?!" Graham exclaimed, raking his hands through his hair. "It seems I was blind to what was going on, but according to Georgiana, Alaina's letters always inquire after *you*."

Christopher studied his friend, for the first time questioning his understanding of events from a week ago. "But I thought… I heard her say she was completely charmed."

"And I expect that since you were eavesdropping, you heard that she was not as charmed as she should be, and did not think our courtship should continue. It seems she was not in love with me." At this last statement Graham relaxed a bit in his saddle, slumping his shoulders.

At a loss for words, wanting to comfort his friend, but also to celebrate his own good fortune, Christopher stayed mute.

"Well, are you not going to say something?" Graham stated quietly, willing his friend to snap out of his trance.

Still stuck in his assumed version of events, Christopher only mouthed, "not engaged."

"Yes, we have been through that," snapped Graham. "It is my mother's and sister's firm opinion that she is in love with you, and I am compelled to ask: what the hell are you doing *here,* wasting an opportunity with Alaina? I certainly would never have let her slip away."

Finally, Christopher was able to grasp what his friend was telling him. "I am truly sorry to have hurt you, my friend. I never intended to become entranced by Alaina, to be sure. I am not totally sure if Alaina would have me."

"Well, how will you know if you do not try?"

Graham's soft question seemed to light a fire within Christopher, making him feel as if he must talk to Alaina at once.

"I guess I should head to London," was all Christopher said before once again mounting his horse and turning back toward the bridge, intending to leave Waverley posthaste. Before getting up to full speed, Christopher turned back to his friend. "I guess I owe you a debt of gratitude, my friend. You will have to forgive my poor manners and the haste of my departure, but I have a long journey."

"Be ready for the day I shall call in the debt," Graham chuckled. "There is no need for forgiveness. I hear love can make you stupid and blind. It seems you have been afflicted with both."

Hearing the good-natured teasing in his friend's voice, Christopher relaxed a bit and acknowledged, "It appears I have been afflicted, as you say. Farewell, for now." Christopher spurred his horse up to full speed, quickly disappearing around the first bend in the drive, leaving Graham to contemplate the course of events.

It was unlike his friend to keep such matters from him, but then again, it was love, the strangest of phenomena. As Graham sat atop his horse, not quite looking forward to the ride ahead but eager to be home, it was clear to him that his affection for Alaina did not match the fervor he had just witnessed from Christopher. It was possible that the feeling of love had not graced the duke's life just yet. Graham had always thought that he would know if and when he met the love of his life, but now he was not so sure. Graham shook his head and smirked a bit, sighing as he made his way back toward home.

Having been shoved out of the house by Edward, with assurances he would be fine and would not do anything against doctor's orders, Charlotte, Alaina and Evelina found their way to the main shopping district in London, hoping the bustle would revive their spirits after so much caretaking. With nothing in particular they wanted to buy, the mother and daughters found themselves wandering, glancing in windows in case some wares should catch their eyes. It was an uncharacteristically sunny day, but with a bit of cold still in the air, Alaina found herself quickly worn out and in need of rest. Evelina had just spotted a hat that piqued her interest, when Alaina pleaded for relief.

"Please, you must allow me to return to the coach. It seems that I am more tired than I thought. You would not think that sitting for long hours and watching someone sleep would be so exhausting," Alaina reasoned, hoping her mother and sister would take pity on her and end the shopping outing early. They had each taken turns as caretakers for Edward, but, even in moments of solitude, sleep was ever elusive this past week; visions of Christopher haunted her as soon as she closed her eyes.

Seeing her sister's fatigue, Evelina acquiesced. "If you allow us a few moments to look at this hat, we can head to the carriage straight away."

Charlotte took a look at her eldest and, feeling a more immediate rest would be required, suggested, "Why don't you make your way to the conveyance now? It is just a few steps away from the shop, so you will be in view. The driver is waiting for us anyway. We should only take a few minutes, and then we can all go home."

Knowing that her mother was making an exception, Alaina was quick to jump at the chance for some peaceful alone time. "Thank you, Mama. That would be wonderful."

Alaina quickly turned on her heel and made her way to the door of the carriage, accepting the assistance of the footman as she stepped up into the conveyance and quickly settled into the interior. Assured of her daughter's safety, having watched her approach and the footman open the door, Charlotte turned and ushered her youngest through the portal of the milliner's shop.

In the carriage, Alaina relaxed into the bench facing forward, thankful for the blankets and the warming pan they had brought. The coals still maintained some level of heat, even after a few hours of window shopping. Covering herself with one of her throws, Alaina leaned her head back against the wall of the carriage and closed her eyes. It had certainly been an eventful season, with much more drama and stress than Alaina had expected or wanted. She was thankful that her father was on the mend, as evidenced by his increasingly cantankerous mood, seemingly sick of all the company after being fussed over for the last week.

Alaina was still reeling from the garden party, and lamenting the end of her courtship with Graham. She did not love him, that was true, but she held him and his family in affection, and she was sad to have lost that close relationship.

And then there was Christopher. Initially, she had hoped he would visit her in the days following her return to London. They certainly had some unfinished business to discuss. But as time passed, seeds of doubt began to drown out her hopeful spirit. She was convinced that at least by now he would have heard of the severed courtship, and would feel free to call upon her. Maybe he was just giving her time to be with her family? Or maybe it was that he had decided that he really preferred the bachelor lifestyle? In Alaina's mind, nothing made sense and, to be frank, it was starting to give her a headache.

Rubbing her temples to relieve some of the tension, Alaina heard a slight commotion outside the carriage, almost like someone calling or racing after a companion. Thinking little of it, Alaina kept her eyes closed against the daylight streaming in through the open window of the coach.

Alaina felt a shadow fall across the opening, blotting out the sun, and she heard the coach door snap open. Thinking her mother and Evelina had made quick work at the milliner's, Alaina opened her eyes, ready to greet each of them with a smile, only to find someone entirely different filling the doorway.

"Percy! What are you doing here?" Alaina exclaimed, having no trouble recognizing his narrow face and mean-spirited eyes.

Percy gave a lazy smile, and his eyes seemed to glitter with rage. "Lady Alaina, what a *pleasure.*"

He motioned, as if he was about to step up into the coach itself but then thought better of it. Alaina noticed that his clothes were rumpled, although they appeared to be of fine quality. She did not smell any intoxicants on his breath or person, so she had a hard time believing his appearance was due only to a night of carousing and a late morning rising. Seeing him outside her carriage door made the hair on her neck stand on end, and her heart beat faster; surely the man was not here to say hello.

"What do you want?" was all Alaina could manage without her voice wavering between rage and fear.

"Well, it is funny you should ask," Percy answered, his smile only growing more sinister. Reaching his hand into his pocket, he deftly removed a small pistol and pointed it at Alaina. The handgun was small enough to be blocked from sight on the street. "If you would come with me, please, I would have no reason to use this, *yet.* And do not get any ideas to run or scream, I am quite a good shot."

Swallowing hard, Alaina quickly considered her options and saw no means of escape. Gritting her teeth in frustration at having to cooperate, Alaina slid off the bench seat and cautiously made her way to the open door. Percy took a step back to allow her to descend the steps, but kept close to the carriage, so as to not raise an alarm on the street with the gun.

Stepping down to the ground, Alaina found it hard to hold her tongue. "I am not sure what you expect to accomplish by doing this, but it is sure to end in folly."

"My dear, you underestimate your value mightily. I imagine my cousin would be willing to pay a tidy sum to keep you safe, even if I find your *value* quite minuscule," Percy stated matter-of-factly. Choosing to remain silent, lest the information of her and Graham's severed courtship bring more danger, Alaina just glared.

Alaina looked around as much as she could, given Percy still largely blocked an escape route outside the carriage. She only saw the driver, who seemed to be similarly detained by a subtle knife wielded by a large, burly man who was clearly one of Percy's lackeys. His hair was cut super short to his head, and he had one golden earring, giving him the look of a pirate from a fantastical book. The back of the driver faced her, so she had no way of getting his attention. The footman who had assisted her into the carriage was conspicuously missing, most likely away for a break at an opportune time.

Looking up and down the street and seeing an almost empty thoroughfare, as the hour approached teatime, Percy took the opportunity to proceed with what Alaina surmised was an abduction. "If you please, follow me this way, my dear," Percy motioned for her to proceed down the sidewalk, away from the shop with her mother and sister.

Alaina walked slowly in front of Percy, hoping he would assume that her purposefully minced steps were merely ladylike, but she had no such luck. "Now, do not think you can hope to garner escape by slowing our procession. Remember the gun, darling." Percy almost whispered, even with no one about, so close to her ear that she could feel his breath. And then, as if she needed a reminder, he prodded her back with the pistol, which prompted her to speed up to at least her normal walking pace. He certainly was not going to make it easy for her to flee. In the distance, too far for Percy to be concerned with, Alaina noticed a pair of men walking quickly in their direction. It took a moment, but Alaina recognized the footman by his uniform, almost too far away to see his face clearly. The man trailing wore a peculiar top hat, not quite stylish, but black and distinctive.

Percy was still distracted by their slower-than-expected getaway, and being behind Alaina, he had still not noticed the men approaching. As they reached the street corner, Alaina lingered before attempting to cross, even though the street was fairly empty. Percy muttered something profane under his breath and pushed her forward, causing her to stumble and almost fall. This motion cleared Percy's vision, and he caught sight of the men. In the same moment, Alaina's footman pointed in their direction, and the taller man he had been escorting gave chase. Percy immediately gave up Alaina's capture in order to make a clean escape, turning the corner in an attempt to get away. The man in the top hat, who had still been a few shops away, called out, "Stop! In the name of the law!" as he raced after Percy.

It seemed unlikely to Alaina that the man in pursuit of Graham's cousin would have difficulty closing the gap. To her surprise, another gentleman, similarly dressed in the same topcoat and hat, stepped out from an alleyway just in time to throw Percy to the ground. A few moments later, the original man who had given chase stopped just short of Percy's prostrate form. Almost at the same moment the footman reached Alaina at the street corner.

"You alright, my lady?" he panted.

Alaina gave the man a quick nod, "Yes, I believe so. I must thank you for being quick, Benjamin."

"I am just glad to have made it in time. I was lucky to step away from the carriage before those bastards came upon Milton, or else they would have gotten me too. I ran as fast as I could to Bow Street. It was the only thing I could think to do." Benjamin puffed, having run almost the whole way there and most of the way back. His cheeks were quite a shade of red, from a combination of cold and exertion, his flat brown hair askew and partially covering his youthful face.

Both Alaina and Benjamin watched the two men in uniform peel Percy off the ground, having put him in handcuffs, and lead him back toward the street corner. As they approached, the lead pursuer called out, "Are you alright, miss? Your footman said this man had set upon you at your carriage. He feared the worst."

"Yes, I am fine. Thank you so much for coming so quickly," Alaina responded, taking a quavering breath before continuing. "I fear he was after money from someone who had been courting me until just recently, and hoped to hold me for ransom," Alaina responded, trying to ignore the shocked expression from Percy at this pertinent piece of information.

"What?! You lying bitch! She agreed to come with me to help my cousin," Percy yelled, sending spittle flying as he struggled against the two men's restraint. Annoyed with this struggle, the lead pursuer again subdued Percy with a quick cuff on the head.

"At gunpoint? I suggest you keep your mouth shut. You are not doin' yerself any favors," said the quieter of the two uniformed runners, before turning his attention to Alaina. "My lady, if you will allow us to properly detain this fellow, our superior can come to call on your family for a full statement later, so you can go home to rest."

Alaina, finally feeling the effects of the terror of the afternoon take hold, responded shakily, "Yes, I would find that agreeable. My family and I reside at the Norwich townhome on Berkeley Square."

Both of the uniformed men nodded in agreement and began to half lead, half drag Percy back the way they had come. As the group passed by Alaina and Benjamin, Alaina began to shake in earnest, and was barely able to square her shoulders in an effort to steel herself against total collapse.

Setting her jaw, she attempted to take command, refusing to fall apart in the middle of town. "Let us return to the carriage, Benjamin. I imagine my mother and Evelina are worried and I would like to return home."

"Yes, my lady," was all Benjamin could say before practically running after Alaina as she beat a hasty retreat to the carriage.

***

As Christopher rode into London later in the day, he noted the faded daylight. It had not yet gotten completely dark, as the days had gradually lengthened since the start of the season, and he was happy to have ridden the whole of his grueling eight-hour horseback ride from Rochester in daylight. Christopher brought his horse down to a slow walk and patted his neck. The large chestnut stallion had certainly put in a hard day's work, first the ride this morning, then the trip to London, with only a few stops for a quick rest and water. He would have to make sure that the horse had a good brushing and lots of oats tonight, and more than likely, a few days of rest.

"Thank you, Lazarus," Christopher muttered with gratitude, sure almost no other horse would have weathered the journey so well.

As the pair, man and horse, walked through the streets, both tired from the day in the saddle, streetlamps were slowly lit by attendants and full darkness encroached. Christopher found himself turning down Berkeley Square, where Alaina's family townhome was situated. Christopher wished to run up the steps of the townhome and declare himself, but thought, given the time, and his current disheveled look from riding all day, it would be best to wait until morning.

As he rode down the street, closer to the Norwich townhome, Christopher could feel the heavy chill in the air. The skies had been clear all day, but the clouds he could see rolling in overhead to cover the moon told him rain would start at some point in the evening. He was thankful to be in town and close to his lodgings, as he planned to head straight to the Rochester property a few blocks over on Bruton Lane. There he could rest and clean up before his call upon the Sinclair family in the morning. With the streetlamps lighting his way as he and his horse traversed the cobbled street, Christopher could make out the front of the townhome where Alaina was passing her evening, quietly, if he were to guess. A carriage was parked out front, signaling that there may be visitors.

Christopher was about to simply urge his horse back to a trot as he came to the front of the townhome, when the front door opened, and a few uniformed men stepped out into the night. Their distinctive top hats and military-style gray jackets and pants signaled them as the Bow Street Runners. The third man wore a wig and carried a ledger, much resembling a magistrate. The relative low crime in London meant that the runners were rarely seen out and about, and it gave Christopher pause. As the men climbed into the carriage on the street and rode away, Christopher brought Lazarus to a halt.

An overwhelming urge to check on the welfare of Alaina and her family made him rethink his earlier plan to avoid calling until morning. But what would they think of his appearance, and how would he avoid pouring his heart out to Alaina and begging her forgiveness for his delay in calling? Despite his trepidations, his need to be reassured of Alaina's safety won out, and Christopher swung down from Lazarus.

Leading his horse around the half-circle that served as the front drive at Norwich, Christopher tied him to a hitching post, since a short visit tonight was all he planned. He wanted to see to Alaina's safety, but wished to be more presentable when discussing their relationship and the possibility of their future. Christopher climbed the steps to the front door and was about to knock when the door was abruptly snatched open by Alaina's father.

Shocked to be looking at the earl instead of a butler, Christopher was at a loss for words, though Edward gave little opportunity to speak first. "What do we owe the honor, my lord?"

Christopher could not ignore the edge in Edward's voice. Clearly, he had not wished to be disturbed. "My apologies, sir. I was riding past your home and saw a group of Bow Street Runners leave in their carriage, along with an older gentleman who I assume was a magistrate. I had planned to call tomorrow but I felt compelled to see to everyone's well-being."

"Everyone's or just Alaina's?" Edward asked, an unintended edge in his voice. It had been a trying day, to say the least. Seeing the shock on Christopher's face, Edward took some pity on the young man. "Forgive me, it has been a trying day. To be honest, this is my first time out of bed since the fall, all because your best friend's cousin decided to kidnap Alaina."

"Kidnap? What happened? Is she alright?" Christopher rattled off questions, surprised at the severity of the mischief Percy wreaked.

Edward studied the young man standing only one step down from him. The lack of action on the marquess's part this past week had sowed small seeds of doubt as to his intentions, or maybe just his courage in acting on his feelings. "What brings you to London?" was Edward's next query, trying to avoid betraying Alaina's heart.

Christopher was not used to such direct inquiries and cleared his throat in discomfort. "Sir, I came back to see your daughter. It seems that there may have been a… misunderstanding between us. Although, like I said, I was not planning to call until tomorrow."

"Good. We will expect you on the 'morrow. Alaina, as you can imagine, took quite a fright and is resting right now. My wife and my youngest were also quite shaken when they came out of the shops to find Alaina missing and the driver sporting a bump on his head, with no footman in sight. I was in the front parlor after the discussion with the runners and the magistrate. I saw your approach and did not want to disturb the house. I expect Alaina will be happy tomorrow."

Edward turned back to head inside, and Christopher noticed the earl was wearing a dressing gown and was moving gingerly, holding his head as he moved to close the door.

"Of course, sir. I will be here tomorrow, in the morning. Are you sure there is nothing I can do to help this evening?"

Edward turned, standing a bit straighter and dropping his hand in a show of bravado. He had caught Christopher's thinly veiled implication, and it rankled Edward that this man was responsible for his daughter's doldrums, however much he expected that the marquess loved Alaina.

"The only thing I need from you, young man, is to call on Alaina tomorrow and to not disappoint her," was all Edward said before softly closing the door.

"I hope I can make her happy, my lord," Christopher said at barely a whisper, speaking only to the front door and wishing Alaina's father had more confidence in him.

CHAPTER 15

Christopher straightened his cuffs once more, not out of necessity, but to quell his nerves. As he looked out the window of his family's London townhome, he found that the day's weather was much as he anticipated. The evening's wispy clouds and damp air had given way to heavier rain overnight, ending in a gray and misty morning. The streets, having been doused in rain, had taken on a rather mucky appearance, promising to treat every rider to a full splatter of mud.

The weather matched Christopher's mood. After his encounter with the earl, nothing could quell the feeling of tension that had settled in the pit of his stomach. The only modicum of comfort was knowing Alaina was unharmed and safe at home.

Since leaving his estate, Christopher had been hounded by a sense of urgency to see Alaina and confess his feelings. He had been overwhelmed by the folly in not professing those feelings sooner. *Would Alaina even see him today, after all of his mistakes? Would she understand that he could not have overstepped the boundaries of friendship to pursue her? That even now, his fear of repeating his parent's mistakes weighed on him?*

Feeling the need to look his best, he chose a midnight blue topcoat with tan, close-fitting breeches. Going with his standard riding boots, which he had had cleaned and polished the previous evening, made him feel some level of comfort. His waistcoat was the same midnight blue and topped a crisp white shirt and cravat of the same white linen. Christopher's valet always made sure every piece of clothing was clean and freshly pressed, but given the gravity of the conversations today, Christopher checked Baldwin's handiwork so as not to leave anything to chance.

In an effort to call at an appropriate hour, Christopher had tried to make himself busy in his study, but found no matters of great importance, and thus ended up in his current position of studying the misty view out of that window. His contemplation of life was not limited to his present worries, but encompassed the whole of his life, as if the past that stretched out behind him was to determine the future that lay before him.

Both of his parents had died when he was young, his mother before he turned fourteen, and his father a few years later, both to fevers. Even before then, they had been distant, his father preferring to spend time at whatever estate Christopher was not currently residing in. Before her untimely death, his mother was always present in body, but not so in mind. At a younger age, Christopher had remembered more hugs and playtime from his maternal parent, but it had always seemed a distant memory. He had gotten used to the lack of interaction early on, throwing himself into his studies and horseback riding, spending most of his time with tutors or out of doors, until he went away to Eton, where he met Graham.

Christopher had not felt the emptiness of the loss of his parents in body or spirit quite so much until he visited with Graham's family on their first Christmas holiday from Eton. Graham had learned that Christopher would be spending Christmas at his Rochester country home alone, or if he was lucky, with his drunken father, and quickly insisted he needed company over the holidays. In truth, Graham had applied only minimal pressure before Christopher relented to travel to Ashford instead. Watching Graham and Georgiana tease and torture each other had made Christopher yearn for a sibling, and seeing their parents dote on them, as well as each other, made him yearn for the parents of his much younger years, when laughter had not been so scarce. Spending the holidays with Graham and his family became tradition, and he came to see them as family, as they did with him. The only downside was that they were not his true family, and it was quite possible, as they all moved on in life, that he would cease to be included in their large family gatherings. This thought, along with his blunder in not telling Alaina of his feelings sooner, weighed on him. In trying so hard to preserve his bonds with Graham's family, he had almost lost out on the chance to make a new one, a household of his own with the woman who occupied all corners of his mind.

Her family was much like Graham's, from what Christopher could see, and even if she had ended the courtship with Graham, Alaina may not want a life with him. He had been taciturn and unsure at every turn. That said nothing about the fact that without any nuclear family of his own, their life would be quiet, and in his experience, lonely. His closest relative was his cousin, Lord Charles Kendall, Baron of Newhaven. Charles and Christopher were close enough for cousins, and Christopher hoped they could find more time to visit one another, but Charles would one day have a family of his own, with responsibilities and commitments. Christopher wondered, *would he alone be enough?*

Christopher got up from behind his desk, where he had been blankly staring at piles of unopened correspondence and estate ledgers, nothing terribly pressing, and walked to the window to stare at the small but well-manicured courtyard behind his townhome. Looking at the clock on the mantel of the fireplace, Christopher sighed and tried to push all the doubt from his mind; it was time to go.

With the weather outside, Christopher elected to use his carriage, hoping to make it to the Sinclair townhome still polished. Accepting the outerwear from his butler before stepping out into the elements and into the coach on the street, he steeled himself for what was to come and hoped his heart would be fuller at the end of it.

"Who do you expect to join us? Hardly anyone knows you are out of your sick bed, and to be frank, your doctor would probably not approve of you receiving guests," Alaina said, mildly annoyed that her father had implied she make herself presentable for them.

It was her mother who responded. "Alaina, dear, after yesterday I insisted your father get checked by the doctor. He was by early this morning. Thankfully, it appears your father, even with yesterday's exertion, is free to resume normal activities. It seems logical that his friends may come to inquire on his health. He just knows you would want to look your best."

"Well, is there some reason you waited until breakfast to tell me?" Alaina motioned to the table laden with food. In truth, she was still not very hungry after her near abduction yesterday, and had already finished eating what she could stomach. The shopping trip gone awry had only added to her melancholy. With the hope of Christopher dwindling with every day, Alaina could only wish for their season in London to meet a swift end. While going home to her family's country seat would not erase what had happened, Alaina could more easily detach there from the unhappy memories of London.

It was Edward's turn to smooth things over with his eldest. "You were sleeping, sweetheart, we did not want to wake you. It should not be so hard to change, although if you would rather not, you do look charming as you are," Edward said, his look toward his daughter softening. Alaina looked winsome as always, but after a week by his side and her scare yesterday, Edward thought changing into one of her newer dresses may lift her spirits. And *he* knew who was supposed to call this morning.

"Fine, if you think it is best, but I honestly see no purpose. No one is going to come and visit *me*," Alaina huffed, stuffing her hope that a certain marquess would call deep inside. She stood up from the table and almost threw her napkin. She made a quick escape upstairs, knowing it would take her some time to complete the modification.

As Alaina made her way up the stairs, it was Charlotte's turn to ask questions of Edward, once their oldest was out of earshot. "Who could possibly come to call today? And why bother her to change, if you think they will be visiting you? She looks perfectly fine as she is."

"I agree, my dear. I just think she may feel better in something newer or different than the day dress she has been wearing the past week to help take care of me," Edward explained, and before his wife could question him further, Edward held out his hand. "And no, I cannot tell you who is to call, as I am not sure they will show. I just want to be prepared."

Charlotte stared at her husband obliquely, aware she would garner no further information. She had a few guesses, but did not see the point in voicing them. "Well, if Alaina should be prepared, perhaps I should help her."

As his wife left in much the same manner as his daughter a few moments earlier, Edward chuckled, hopeful that at the end of the day he would be forgiven for his secrecy.

Back downstairs after changing, Alaina sat in the front parlor and tried to focus on the book she was reading. Her mother had joined her upstairs and had been even more flummoxed by her father's behavior. Nonetheless they had both decided that one of her new day dresses, purchased for the garden party but never worn, was the perfect choice. The dress had a slim and simple silhouette, but the fabric gave the dress its interest. The skirt and sleeves were muslin, with subtle rose-colored stripes of varying widths running vertically down the length of the dress and sleeves. The bodice, save for an insert in the center imitating a full striped dress underneath, was made out of the emerald velvet fabric. It was the same material as her dress on the last night of the party in the country, and was fashioned like a short jacket with mock buttons on the front and a longer look in the back, similar to a spencer jacket. Alaina had yet to wear the dress because its unusual style made her doubt what impression it might make, even with the assurances of the dressmaker, her mother, Evelina, and Georgiana.

Her choice to wear it today was somewhat due to her mother's insistence not to waste the dress, and partly because Alaina felt that it was the right choice. The velvet of the dress elevated what would have been a very simple day dress, giving it more formality and flair. Unfortunately, Alaina's mood did not match what she wore. For the past week, she had been worried and focused on her father's health, and in moments of quiet had mulled over everything that had happened with the duke and Christopher. The more time passed, the more sadness and anger had overtaken her mood, the elation over Christopher's admission of attraction overshadowed by his lack of commitment.

Alaina sighed at the futility of trying to read. Placing her book on the nearest side table, she stood and slowly walked to the front window. She looked out at the dreary day and numbly noticed that not many people had decided to brave the cold and damp weather. Mostly it was just carriages traversing the cobbled streets, picking up muck and mud as they went.

One such carriage had turned onto her street and came to a halt outside her family's townhome. Alaina craned her neck to see who the visitor was, even though she knew the futility, the archway covering the front doorway blocking her view. Not able to see the occupants alight from the carriage, Alaina turned her attention back to the coach itself, hoping to find some clue as to who may be visiting her father. Edward had maintained that he was expecting no specific visitors, but the early hour of the call spoke of other circumstances.

Alaina wrinkled her brow, trying to place the coach, but with no luck. Though it was a sizable coach, with rich appointments and a well-maintained team of horses in front, there was no distinguishing crest or emblem to indicate who owned it. Not realizing how much time she had been staring, Alaina barely heard the greeting as the front door opened to allow the visitors to enter. Alaina heard no name as an announcement from the butler or in greeting from Edward, but she could hear their footsteps approach the parlor.

Alaina moved inward, away from the window so as not to be caught staring, and smoothed her hands down the front of her dress. Obviously, whoever was visiting was important to her father.

Edward was first through the parlor door and caught sight of Alaina. "Ah, Alaina, perfect. I was just going to show your guest into the parlor and see to refreshments."

A visitor for her? Alaina has little time to consider who it might be, when her father stepped aside to allow the guest in question to enter, to her astonishment.

"I trust you remember the Marquess of Rochester," her father smiled slyly, and Alaina realized he had known all along who would be visiting today. "I will leave you two to catch up on the events of the last week, while I see to a few things and some tea. Always know that Arthur is here to assist. He can hear you in the hallway, as long as the door remains open."

Edward disappeared through the opening. His message was clear; they were free to talk, but with little expectation of true privacy.

Alaina took a moment to collect herself and she clasped her hands together, afraid Christopher would see any emotion. Alaina forced her eyes to meet his, and she found a turbulent sea looking back at her. The orbs spoke of too many emotions to afford Alaina insights.

"My lord," Alaina said, not keeping the edge from her voice. "To what do I owe the pleasure?"

"Alaina, I…" Christopher started, and Alaina watched as he shifted his weight uncertainly, his hand scrubbing through his hair. "I fear I have…"

Alaina crossed her arms and strode toward the marquess. "You have come all this way and have nothing to say?"

"No, I do, it's just…"

"Just what? You find me unwilling to run into your arms the moment you show up at my family's home? After a week of no word from you? Not asking after even my father's health?" Alaina railed, advancing on Christopher until she was within an arm's length.

Christopher backed up a bit, his eyes wide.

"Still nothing to say?"

Christopher cleared his throat before he tried to continue once more. "I came here to say so many things, but right now, I am worried that none of it will matter, or that I may not even get all of the words out."

Alaina was surprised to hear the sadness in Christopher's voice, and although she did not want to let his behavior pass, she decided to at least let him speak. "Well, please continue. Nothing can be gained if you do not speak."

Christopher sighed, "I have behaved abominably, and for that I am truly sorry. So many things were left unsaid and unfinished between us, and once I thought you had become engaged to Graham, I could not bear to be around you any longer."

"Engaged?!" Alaina blurted.

It was Christopher's turn to be angry, and he gritted out. "Please let me finish."

With quick nod from Alaina, Christopher continued, "I had no intention of finding someone I felt drawn to this season, or any season in the foreseeable future. Graham's friendship was the only thing that pulled me out into society, and I felt a duty to help him in his quest for a wife. And then I met you, and you were infuriating! And smart, and kind, and beautiful. I found myself torn between my duty to Graham and a woman I could not resist."

A quick hand up from Christopher stilled Alaina once more. "Graham is my best friend, and I thought I would never let a woman get in the way of that friendship. Yet, at every turn, I found myself drawn to you, and I convinced myself that you only tolerated my presence. Why should you do anything else? You were being courted by the most eligible bachelor of the season, and I was just his friend. Even my attempts at wit ended awkwardly, or worse, in an argument. But I could not put you out of my mind, your eyes, our *connection*, even when I knew you belonged to another."

Alaina looked at Christopher. His steel-blue eyes appeared stricken, as if he had bared his soul and now awaited her response, but she still had questions. "But at the ball in the country, I asked you if your thoughts had changed, and…"

"And I gave no response," Christopher interrupted.

"No response is an answer of sorts!" Alaina countered, as she poked an accusatory finger into Christopher's chest.

"Not when a swarm of people interrupted me!"

"Well?" came Alaina's question, exasperation clear in her voice.

"Well what?" came Christopher's question.

Alaina groaned and stepped away from Christopher as she paced the length of the room. "What is your answer on the matter of matrimony, you addlepated buffoon?!"

No words ushered forth from Christopher's lips, but he placed himself in Alaina's path, causing her to stop short. Alaina pushed against his chest, her efforts futile. "Get out of my way! You forget I have given you no quarter!"

Christopher chuckled, but did not move as he said, "I am afraid that your habit of showing me no mercy is what has me so enraptured. You have made me see that marriage would not be altogether awful, but rather pleasant, if I had to guess. I cannot promise that you will not loathe me after a courtship, but I can promise that should you not, I will make you my wife."

"Ooohhh, you spout such beautiful words, but they are just words," came Alaina's response, but her voice had lost its edge. Christopher took a tentative step toward her and when she did not back away, he closed the distance between them completely, gently taking her in his arms.

Alaina reveled in the feeling where their bodies touched, the twisting in the pit of her stomach clouding her mind. Christopher's voice came to her softly, almost a whisper. "If you do not wish to explore our compatibility, my dear, I will leave at once, and I am sorry for any *frustration* I have caused."

"And if I do want to explore… our compatibility, I mean," came Alaina's voice, a bit breathless.

Christopher smiled, and lowered his head until his lips were only inches from her own. "Then I shall have to indulge you."

The couple remained as they were for a few moments, their breathing equally ragged.

Alaina was the first to break the silence. "Well, what are you waiting for?"

Christopher did not miss a beat. "You. I was waiting for you."

And with that Christopher brushed his lips against Alaina's, the featherlight touch starting a flame deep inside her. She could feel her body respond as Christopher deepened the kiss, slanting his head and pulling her closer to him. Alaina's feet left the floor, and it was a long time before either of them realized.

CHAPTER 16

Alaina beamed, and the brightness of her smile came only second to the twinkle in the eyes of the Marquess of Rochester. Christopher offered his arm, and Alaina happily accepted, making their way through the door to the grand staircase of the Leicester Ball, the announcement of their names only a distant sound, their eyes seemingly only for each other. They walked down the stairs and into their first official dance as a couple, a waltz.

After Alaina had agreed to a courtship, her mother and father had promptly shown up in the front parlor with tea, making Alaina suspect that they had been waiting just outside the door. Though Alaina knew that her father had some hand in their encounter that day, it was her mother that had been all questions. Christopher charmingly assured both Edward and Charlotte that Graham, though a little put out that his courtship had not yielded the desired results, had been most insistent on his friend visiting Alaina. Out of deference to

Graham, Alaina suggested they keep their courtship quiet to avoid any salacious rumors about the circumstances.

Christopher agreed to only visit at tea or dinner, and then they ventured forth on a walk in Hyde Park with her mother and sister as chaperones a couple of times. In true London fashion, rumors circulated that Graham was the jilted party, but these rumors were quickly drowned, as the news of the arrest of Percy made the rounds.

It was this very evening that Alaina and Christopher made their courtship official in the eyes of London society. Few people knew any details as to what had transpired to make their courtship come to be, but there had been a few whispers about jilted best friends and the like, which Christopher warned her to ignore. As Alaina and Christopher made one last sweep across the dance floor, she tried to put those rumors and thoughts out of her mind.

"You are worrying about something, again," teased Christopher, as he noticed Alaina's furrowed brow. They may have known each other for only a short time, but Christopher felt he could read her mind and thoughts. He knew she had worries about what society would think, but to him, the approval of the ton did nothing to dull or raise his happiness.

"My apologies, I do not wish to ruin the evening. It truly is magical, I promise." Alaina mentally shook off her anxious reverie and smiled up at Christopher. Where they had been most at odds with one another a few weeks ago, or at least unsure of the other's feelings, their time together in the past couple of weeks had done well to foster a connection that

Alaina had only dreamed possible. She could look into Christopher's eyes and feel safe and giddy and nervous all at the same time. Her stomach did flips when he looked at her, his blue eyes full of heat, despite their icy shade. The simple act of dancing made Alaina heady with anticipation, her skin burning where he touched.

Christopher led Alaina through the last turn, setting her apart from him and bowing to finish the dance. Alaina's eyes sparkled and she returned his bow with a deep curtsy of her own. The kiss they had shared earlier in the season, unexpectedly, after her run-in with Percy, played over in her mind. With the limited visits over the past couple weeks and the constant chaperoning of Alaina's parents, they had had no opportunity to reignite that particular flame.

Christopher offered his arm to Alaina so they could properly exit the dance floor, and took the opportunity to lean in. "The look on your face, my dear, makes me wonder if you can actually read my thoughts."

Missing his full meaning, Alaina was quick to reassure him. "No, I assure you it is solely due to my own thoughts. I fear our first kiss is on my mind."

Christopher let out a laugh, amused and endeared by her naiveté. Now that they were courting, he had much more delectable things on his mind than a simple kiss. Leaning in again, he got one last private statement in before they made it back to her parents at the edge of the dance floor. "I did enjoy our kiss, to be sure, but I had more on my mind."

The nearness of his lips to Alaina's ear, and the idea that he had something more than kissing on his mind, tripped something deep in her core, making it difficult to calm her breathing before reaching her parents. Of course, her mother decided to point such a thing out.

"Alaina darling, I hope you are not close to expiring, you are breathing quite heavily. Maybe that is too many dances in a row. Christopher, would you be a dear and get her something to drink? You seem to have nearly exhausted her with all the dancing," Charlotte chirped, unaware of her daughter's increased unease.

Christopher chuckled and took the order in stride, not sure what amused him more: Alaina's embarrassment from their conversation or her mother's worrying. "Of course, I will be right back."

As Christopher made his way to the refreshment table for punch, thankfully close by, Edward took the opportunity to correct his wife's assumption.

"Dear Charlotte, I fear Alaina's breathing may be due in part to her proximity to Christopher. Remember how young love used to feel?"

Alaina watched her mother consider her father's statement, and noticed that she almost seemed embarrassed herself. Her eyes went wide as she looked at Edward with a sidelong glance and then back at Alaina. Alaina groaned, mostly on the inside, and was about to refute both of her parents, when Charlotte caught sight of someone over Alaina's shoulder and her face lifted.

"Eleanor! How nice of you to seek us out in this crowd. I was unsure from your letters whether you would be able to join the festivities."

Alaina turned around to see the dowager duchess approach with a smile on her face, and in her eyes. The two friends met in an embrace, as though they had been lost to each other for years. When Eleanor and Charlotte stepped back from one another, Eleanor turned her affection on Alaina.

"Alaina, you look radiant, my dear. You must forgive me for hoping to have you as my daughter-in-law, but I was denying what was before my own eyes. Besides, Christopher is practically my second son, so I should think to see plenty of you."

Unsure of how to respond to such a conclusion about the future, Alaina smiled back at Eleanor and searched for words. Luckily, at that moment, Christopher returned with a glass of punch, pushing it into Alaina's hand and taking Eleanor's outstretched hand in his.

"Eleanor, I do hope you are telling no stories about my youth that might scare Alaina away," Christopher stated. As Alaina glanced askance, she caught the twinkle in his eyes and breathed a sigh of relief that such an encounter should lack any true tension.

Eleanor was quick to parry, "No story I tell would scare her away, although some recounting of your youth may make her think twice. However, those stories usually involved my son, which would not accomplish my task of keeping Alaina close to me." Eleanor looked at Alaina and winked.

"Speaking of your son, I assume he escorted you here?" Charlotte leaned in to inquire, hoping an encounter between Christopher and Graham would not ruin the evening.

"Of course, but as per usual, he has been waylaid by friends or acquaintances," Eleanor's response was easy. "As a matter of fact, he is approaching now," she continued as she half-turned to welcome her son to the group.

Everyone offered their greetings to the Duke of Ashford, Alaina and her mother a bit on edge in anticipation. Alaina clasped her hands in front of her in trepidation, but all nerves were quelled when the two best friends clasped hands in greeting.

"Good to see you out and about with such a lovely companion," Graham teased with a smile, winking at Alaina in an attempt to avoid sending a wistful look her way.

"It is good to see you out in society as well," Christopher agreed, truly happy that his friend should see fit to join them in public so soon after his own courtship had ended. "With Percy behind bars, I assume you are breathing easier?"

Graham smirked at this remark and conceded, "It is true I find myself with much spare time on my hands, and my tenants are pleased to say the least."

As the two friends continued to talk about the resolution of problems on the Ashford Estate, talking over repairs of the barn and other things, the ladies conversed with ease, catching up on any big news that was not already known through the gossip papers. Eventually, the conversation turned to Georgiana.

"I do hope to see Georgiana soon, now that you all are in town again," Charlotte mentioned in passing, expecting a quick and simple affirmation from Eleanor.

"We shall see when Georgiana is back in society. She has some of her own family matters to attend to. In truth, I am not quite sure of what they are," Eleanor responded, causing Alaina and her mother to raise their eyebrows.

As Charlotte and Alaina fumbled with what to say, someone who looked vaguely familiar to Alaina approached Graham and Christopher, clasping the latter on the shoulder in a friendly gesture. Christopher turned to meet the man, and his face lit up.

"Charles! I did not know you were back in town. Rumor was you ran off shortly after I made a short trip to Ashford."

"Yes, cousin, I fear I was hasty in my retreat to the country, but I am back now, and I hear you may have good news." Charles's vision shifted to rest on Alaina. She was unable to place his face still, but had a hard time shaking a sense of unease.

Christopher was quick to make the introductions. "Ladies, this is my cousin Charles Kendall, Baron of Newhaven. He is a country gentleman, with a barony just near my estate. Charles, this is Graham's mother, Dowager Duchess of Ashford, the Countess of Norwich, and her daughter, Lady Alaina Sinclair."

Alaina placed her hand in the crook of Christopher's arm, and joined the other ladies in greeting Charles. "It is nice to meet you, my lord. It is great to finally make acquaintance with some of Christopher's relatives," Alaina smiled sweetly, still not able to shake the feeling of disquietude.

Charles turned to the ladies, having long disengaged from Graham, and greeted each one with a short bow. "It is a pleasure to make everyone's acquaintance."

The pause in the conversation became longer than acceptable for Alaina, while she peered more intently at Charles. He was as tall as Christopher and quite nondescript for the ton, with blonde hair and light eyes. His build was slimmer than either Graham or Christopher, but he still looked athletic and not gangly by any stretch of the word.

Feeling the weight of her perusal, Charles shifted uncomfortably to one foot and cleared his throat. "Something amiss, Lady Alaina?"

Alaina realized everyone in the group had turned their eyes to her, aware of her odd fascination, and were waiting for her response. She giggled, hoping to dispel any awkwardness. "I am sorry Lord Newhaven, I fear I feel we may have met before, or at least you seem very familiar."

Alaina thought she saw a slight widening of Charles's eyes, but then he shook his head and laughed easily. "Dear maiden, we have never been formally introduced, but I would be lying if I said I had not noticed you prior to this evening. Maybe you just recognize me from a chance encounter in passing? And please call me Charles. We may be family someday soon."

Alaina was amused as Charles caught an elbow in the ribs from Christopher. "Watch it cousin, no flirting." Christopher chuckled, winking at Alaina to reassure her it was only in jest.

Alaina looked around the group, catching bemused glances, and shrugged her shoulders. "I must be mistaken."

The group fell into easy discussion, leaving Alaina to wonder if her mind was playing tricks on her. She could not shake the feeling that she had at least encountered Charles before, even if they had never been properly introduced.

❖

The breeze hit Alaina and Christopher as they rushed out the door. Both were dizzy from all the dancing and merriment, and giggling with excitement. There was a chill in the air, and attached to the ballroom was a balcony with gardens below for guests to enjoy a moment's quiet. Candelabras were set up on a few scattered tables to provide enough light at the outer edges of the balcony, with the light spilling out of the windows and doors illuminating the space immediately outside. It was at the outer edges of the balcony that the couple stopped their flight.

Out of breath from laughter, and with a heady feeling, Alaina looked into Christopher's eyes, which had taken on a midnight hue in the candlelight. She was barely able to get out a whisper. "Christopher, I fear I will expire from all this fun, truly." A small giggle punctuated her sentence.

"My dear, I highly doubt that," Christopher said, raising an eyebrow.

A few other couples were standing on the balcony, each focused on their own conversations, with nary an eye turned in their direction. This allowed Christopher to slowly pull

Alaina toward the shadowed edge of the balcony, near the staircase leading into the gardens. With a hand to his lips to stop any questions, and a twinkle of mischievousness in his eyes, Christopher pulled Alaina to the side of a large planter, shielding them from view completely. A walkway lay off to their side and Alaina could faintly make out the outline of a door that would probably lead to a servants' back hallway. After a quick survey of her surroundings, Alaina turned her attention back to Christopher, who was now standing close in front of her, the heat of his body radiating toward hers, making the cold in the air unnoticeable. A smile spread across her lips as she raked her eyes over his broad shoulders, up to his strong chin, lips, and then his eyes. By the time their eyes met, the rate of their breathing had picked up almost in unison. Christopher matched her smile with a lopsided one of his own. Christopher began to lean in, leaving room for a last-minute refusal, but hoping for none.

Seeing no hesitation from Alaina, Christopher brushed his lips to hers ever so gently, leaving both of them tingling from the contact and in anticipation of more. Christopher pulled back slightly to check on Alaina and found wide pools of umber looking at him in the moonlight.

Alaina struggled with a mix of feelings, and could not help the next words out of her mouth. "That was different."

Her statement surprised Christopher, leaving him momentarily confused as to what she was referring to. Then it dawned on him. "Yes, this kiss is different, but no less precious. I must apologize for my haste at the first ball, and my desperation in the parlor. I could not help myself then, and it was forbidden before, but now…"

"It is still technically forbidden." Alaina interjected, a giggle escaping her lips once more.

Christopher chuckled and put his hand up on the wall just above Alaina's head, unsure of what to do next.

After a moment of silence, Alaina whispered. "You know, I liked it. All of them were lovely."

Christopher met her eyes and was lost, his gentler manner torn asunder by his need. His lips joined Alaina's with a fervor surprising to both. Once she got over her initial shock, Alaina instinctively slanted her face and Christopher groaned in pleasure, drinking her in. His hand found the nape of her neck, without thought, supporting her head, while his other arm wrapped around her waist and pulled Alaina toward him. Their bodies connected and each felt heat crackling in the frosty night air.

Alaina's nipples puckered against the fabric of her dress as it met his muscular chest, and she felt a hardness against her belly. Christopher tested her lips with his tongue, and they slightly parted at the intrusion. Alaina found her hands moving up his arms to rest on Christopher's broad shoulders, one hand eventually finding its way to the nape of his neck, her gloved fingers burying themselves in his short hair. The couple seemed intent to explore with their mouths, but neither could ignore the warmth that started to radiate from their bellies, a deep throbbing in Christopher's loins and a pleasurable sensation between Alaina's legs, one very foreign to her, but delightful.

So lost in the moment was the couple that they did not hear the familiar voices coming their way until it was almost too late. Christopher, only slightly more aware than Alaina, suddenly pulled away from her and turned his head to listen.

Alaina opened her mouth in question, but a quick shake of Christopher's head caused the words to catch in her throat.

"I swear I saw them come out these doors." Alaina could hear her mother's voice.

"Well, my dear, your eyes are not what they used to be. I do not see them anywhere," came Edward's response.

"I do say children do move quickly," was Eleanor's reassurance, but if Alaina judged the tone right, she may have meant something else entirely.

"Shall we check the gardens? Just in case," came Charlotte's voice again, her tone a bit worried.

"I see no need," Eleanor responded quickly.

The chatter of voices now too close for an escape from their dark corner without ruin, Alaina felt Christopher's hand on the small of her back, guiding her quickly down the narrow path to the door she had seen, as he pulled her further into the shadows. Only when they were at the door did he feel it safe enough to whisper.

"This should lead you somewhere close to the ladies retiring room. Go there and fix your hair and collect yourself. I will go meet your parents and tell them you made your way indoors to refresh yourself."

Alaina nodded, too afraid to speak quietly enough, and turned to open the door. Christopher's light touch on her upper arm made her once again turn to face him.

"Be careful, my love," was all he said as he placed a quick kiss on the end of her nose, leaving her at the door in order to join her parents and Eleanor. Alaina watched Christopher retreat back down the dark corridor, his fingers raking through his hair before he disappeared around the planter.

Alaina, turned and clasped the handle of the door, praying for smooth hinges. Luckily, she was able to open the door without a sound and enter the small hallway inside. With the door quietly closed behind her, Alaina allowed herself to breathe, and quietly thanked the servant who maintained the door so well, and who had left it open in preparation for the party.

Allowing her eyes to adjust to the dim light of the hallway, Alaina quickly assessed that her best option was to move away from the ballroom, in hopes of finding another hallway perpendicular to the one she was traversing that would bring her out to the main hall and back toward the ladies retiring room. Alaina only had to walk a few feet before encountering such a hallway. Keeping to the carpet runner in the center of the hallway, in an attempt to mute her footsteps, she quickly turned the corner and saw an opening twenty feet ahead that looked like the main corridor, and she quietly celebrated victory. But Alaina had little time to revel in her success, as she heard a set of footsteps approaching and whispered voices. Afraid of being discovered, Alaina did an about-face, reaching the back hallway only seconds before a man and woman entered the space she had just vacated.

The back hallway was not carpeted, so Alaina stopped just around the corner, praying the couple would not come further, and at the same time hoping her footsteps had not been heard. It was not long before the couple's footsteps ceased and Alaina could better hear their whispers, letting out a trembling sigh of relief that the partygoers, from what she could hear, only wanted a secluded place to talk.

"What are you doing here?" came a low whisper, almost a growl, from the man. Alaina cocked her head to hear better, convinced that she recognized the voice.

"I was invited. I do not see the issue," hissed a woman, clearly perturbed by the man's line of questioning. There was a pause, and Alaina imagined the man, whoever he was, running his hands through his hair in frustration.

"Do you realize the ruin we both would see to be associated with one another; it would jeopardize all of our plans." The man restarted, this time more calmly.

Alaina could hear the woman's tone become softer. "And here I thought you would be happy to see me," the lady said. "No one will think we know each other, unless someone saw you pull me into this dark corner."

"You know I am pleased to share your company, my dear," came the gentleman's response, a bit lighter than before. Alaina heard a crinkling of fabric, and could only surmise that the couple was caught in a passionate embrace.

Alaina strained to hear more, but only caught a manly sigh once the rustling sounds stopped, and one final remark. "For tonight, let us avoid each other, and plan better so as to not show up at the same social events in the future. I fear that even the slightest connection between us might set things awry."

"Ok, darling, if you insist," came a beguiling response from the woman.

Alaina heard muffled high heels as the woman raced to the outer hall, followed in a few moments by more manly boot sounds, each retreating until all was quiet once again. Finally letting out the breath she had been unaware she was holding, Alaina quickly gathered herself and made for the main hallway, focused on reaching the retiring room before she encountered her own party. Something stuck in her mind, though. The voices seemed familiar, but with the whispers, she could not properly place them.

CHAPTER 17

Alaina awoke with a start, surprised to find herself trembling. She had been reliving the events of the evening, but her dream had ended with the two voices in the hallway. In her dream, they had gotten closer and closer until a sound like an opening door had interrupted, causing her to wake. Pushing back her tumbled mass of hair with her hand, she assessed her surroundings.

Alaina found her room was as she had left it before falling asleep. It must not have been too much later, as the moon shone in her window, still illuminating her dress, which she had slung over her dressing table on the far wall in haste. The fire in her fireplace still burned high, radiating warmth and a soft light throughout the room. Her bedclothes and blankets were quite mussed, speaking to the anxiety of her dream and the evening's events.

After finding the retiring room, she had put herself back together and quickly returned to the ballroom to find her parents, who were standing with Eleanor, Christopher, and

Graham. Her parents had seen no reason to not accept the story that she had somehow slipped past them, but she noticed peculiar looks from Graham and Eleanor, enough to make her uneasy.

Alaina scrubbed her eyes, but something still seemed off, and then she heard it, a sound much like the door opening in her dream.

Clank! It sounded like a door latch clicking, coming from the window overlooking the garden. *Clank!* There it was again.

Alaina groggily got out of bed and shuffled over to her window to peer out between the light curtains, drawn for privacy. As she was trying to peek through the curtains, a little concerned about what she would find, a quieter *plink!* sounded again against the glass, startling her completely. Fighting her trepidation, she gathered courage to open the drapes and peer out the window. In the darkness, Alaina could make out two tall forms below, but little else. One of the forms was picking up pebbles and aiming at the window, and the other was poised by the gate leading to the garden.

Before the figure closest to the window could throw another pebble, he seemed to notice that Alaina had drawn the curtains, and stood straight and waved, stumbling a bit as he did so. In the moonlight, Alaina was able to get a better glimpse of the man in the foreground, and breathed a sigh of relief, opening the window.

"Christopher? What are you doing outside my window at this hour?" Alaina whispered into the night air, her breath floating like a cloud in the chill.

With the window open, Alaina could see that Christopher was smiling at her in almost a leer, and was teetering slightly on his feet. Standing just a few feet back from Christopher, Graham leaned against the outside gate that led to the garden below, which apparently had been left unlocked against intruders. Graham appeared more stable, his cravat still in place, but clearly the two had been drinking, probably at their club once they had left the ball that evening.

"My lady, you must forgive me," came Christopher's reply, a little slower but still crisp as ever. "I was thinking of you and just had to see you before I fell asleep so I could hold your memory close."

Graham, who had been hanging back in indecision, stepped forward with his own explanation. "He could not be placated, Alaina. I suggested we simply walk by, and was surprised to see the gate open, so here we are."

Alaina giggled, "It is quite alright, I was just sleeping."

"Yes, I see that," Christopher's eyes lit on her attire and Alaina crossed her arms, trying to hide her nightgown. In her haste, she had forgotten to put on her robe and stood before both men clad in a serviceable, but light, white nightgown. Even in the dark she imagined they could see more than she preferred. Graham cleared his throat and shuffled back toward the gate.

Christopher seemed undeterred by his friend's discomfort and pressed on. "There is just something I had to tell you. It is just easier when I have had a bit to drink."

Christopher paused, looking up at Alaina in wonder for long enough that she felt compelled to prod, "And what is that?"

"I am in love with you," Christopher said.

Alaina shook her head. "You are drunk is what you are."

"Yes, I know, but I know my own mind. I love you."

Alaina gave a short chuckle. "You may know your mind in this moment, but what of the next? What of when you wake tomorrow?"

"You will be my everything, just the same," Christopher replied, placing his hand to his chest as if making an earth-shattering declaration, and then smiled as if satisfied by the exchange. He did not seem necessarily at a loss for words, but rather for what to do next. The hour was late, and it was increasingly likely that they would be discovered. Graham stepped forward and clasped his friend on the shoulder.

"It seems you have accomplished what you set out to do. It is best we be off before the household descends on us," Graham spoke softly to his friend, avoiding looking at Alaina.

"But what if I am not ready to go?" Christopher complained, loathing the thought of leaving Alaina for the evening. They had already been cut short earlier in the evening, and he was taking her presence in, enjoying the vision she presented in her nightgown.

"I imagine you can enjoy Alaina's company on the 'morrow if you so choose. You are a very lucky man," came Graham's answer, his voice tinged with yearning. He tugged at Christopher's arm, hoping to get his friend to go home before being caught without too much of a struggle. When Christopher would not budge, Graham glanced up at Alaina and she caught his wistful stare.

Christopher seemed to notice his friend's tone, and placed his arm around Graham's shoulder, as he had when they were boys getting ready for a cricket match.

"I do know, I am quite lucky," Christopher agreed, giving Alaina one last crooked, charming smile. "I guess we should be off."

Each gentleman touched his hat to bid Alaina adieu, and Christopher added, "Until the 'morrow, my love."

Alaina waved, smiling her own lopsided smile, watching them both walk out of the garden as silently as they had entered, after which she finally closed the window against the chilly night air.

Love! How amazing it was to hear. Alaina clasped her hands to her chest and twirled once, her nightgown flaring. She walked over to the fireplace in an attempt to warm up and replayed the event back in her mind. Suddenly, she stopped her musing, and the girlish smile faded, caught on Christopher's words. *What was he thinking, saying such words in his drunken state, at her window late at night, and in front of his friend no less? Words of love are meant to be shared intimately, and certainly not in a state of inebriation!*

A little bit down the street, Christopher and Graham walked on in silence, happy for the cool night air and the walk to clear their heads, each man in his own thoughts. It was late in the evening, and it was unlikely for the men to encounter anyone on the streets as they walked to their respective homes. A light fog had also descended, giving the night an ethereal feeling, making it easy for one to get lost in a train of thought.

It was Graham who broke the silence first. "You got close to getting caught tonight."

Misunderstanding his friend, Christopher forged ahead nonchalantly. "The whole house was asleep, and I was very quiet."

Christopher glanced over at Graham, giving a shrug and a look of inebriated confidence, then turned and kept ambling down the street.

Graham paused ever so slightly and shook his head a bit, in disbelief and amusement at his friend's lovesick foolishness. Christopher missed these exasperated gestures as he continued on, causing the duke to have to jog to catch up to him.

Hoping to get through to his friend, Graham tried a different tact. "You know, I have used that same door on the balcony to escape some ambitious mother trying to foist their daughter on me. It was many years ago, even before my father had died. I was not a duke yet, but I was going to be." Graham looked sidelong at Christopher, and although he had not stopped walking, Graham could see the wheels turning, the goofy smile eventually driven from his face. The years of friendship made it difficult for Graham not to get in one last jab. "I imagine servants use that door quite a bit, and keep the hinges well oiled. I would certainly be thankful for it, if I were you."

Christopher stopped. Graham stopped with him. A furrow creased Christopher's brow, and he turned his questioning stare to his friend. "Do you think Alaina's parents suspected anything?"

"No, but if I could discern something, it is only a matter of time. To be honest, I am surprised at you."

"What?" Christopher asked.

"Well, for one, acting so carelessly with your reputation and a lady's, especially one you are so fond of, is not like you. And then the spectacle outside her window just now was quite…" Graham could not seem to find the right words, but ended by shrugging his shoulders and giving Christopher a lopsided grin. "Well, something I would do. If I had better judgement myself, I would have stopped you."

Christopher scrubbed his hand through his hair and hit his top hat against his leg, letting out a sigh as he did so. "I know, I know. I am finding it difficult to imagine a few more months of courtship."

"Few more months? What are you waiting for?" Graham exclaimed, incredulous.

"Well, it would only be proper, and I still worry there might be rumors with the dissolution of …" Christopher stopped short.

"Of my courtship with Lady Alaina?" Graham finished, waving away Christopher's look of concern before continuing on. "I think you are in more danger of besmirching her reputation yourself."

Christopher felt chagrined. His actions were certainly ruled by lust, with no care of who saw. A few moments of silence passed between the gentlemen, before Graham gave in.

"Will you ask her to marry you already? Lord knows after tonight you want to."

"But I had everything planned out, that after the appropriate time…" Christopher started.

"Appropriate timing be damned! Besides, whenever did life work out as expected?" Graham chuckled.

"You are right, of course," chimed Christopher, and then he could not help but to tease, "besides, I would not want you getting any ideas."

"Do not you worry about me, old friend, though I cannot vouch for others," Graham responded, a bit miffed.

"Oh, I was only kidding," Christopher threw his arm around his friend.

Graham grunted, "I know that, but do not forget that it was supposed to be my nuptials we were celebrating. Not that I think things did not work out as they were supposed to, but they certainly did not work out according to *my* plans."

"And for that I am sorry," Christopher said quietly. The men continued through the misty night in silence, each in his own thoughts.

The next morning, Alaina awakened slowly with a smile on her face, remembering the words uttered by Christopher the night before, or really, earlier that very morning. Light streamed through the window just across from her bed, where Alaina had received the declaration of love, albeit a bit awkwardly, and quite unorthodox, with Graham present.

Her dreamy smile turned to a furrowed brow and a deflated mouth. Christopher had declared his love in an intoxicated state and had even admitted as much. *How did he ever think such a thing was appropriate?*

Alaina heaved a sigh and threw the covers off, crossing to the fireplace to stoke the embers and place a log or two on the newly generated flames. It was still early, and Alaina felt it unnecessary to ring for a servant to rebuild the fire when she was completely capable. Besides, she wanted some time alone with her thoughts before readying for whatever day it was going to be.

Christopher had promised to call this morning after breakfast when they were at the ball last night. Alaina had imagined a nice walk through Hyde Park or something of the like to give the young couple some modicum of privacy. Now she had doubts that he would show at all. Given the state she had seen him in last night, Alaina would not be surprised if Christopher had to sleep the morning away or at least lie abed recovering. And then what would she tell her parents? What if he did not even send word with an excuse?

Pulling a blanket from the bed and curling up in the wingback chair by the fire, Alaina contemplated all the possible outcomes of the upcoming day. *Christopher could have regrets at speaking his words of love in that manner, or altogether. Or worse, Christopher could have forgotten the interlude altogether.* After what felt like an eternity, Alaina settled it in her mind that whatever the day may bring, she would need to look her best, so she got up her resolve and rang for her lady's maid.

⚜

A few streets over, quite a bit later in the morning, Christopher groaned as he peeled his eyelids open to glare at a strip of late morning sun. He must have been careless in drawing the drapes last night, which was not surprising, given the revelry he had partaken in and the late hour he had returned home. Bits and snippets of the night assailed him in rapid succession; the ball, the erotic kiss on the balcony, the near miss in getting caught, the time at White's club with Graham, and their walk home after, with one very memorable detour. Christopher groaned again, pulling the covers over his head even if the current source of his frustration was not the offending sliver of light.

What had he been thinking? Christopher had no doubt of his feelings for Alaina, but was a little taken aback at how he had gone about telling her, and in front of Graham, no less. What must they think of him? His only hope was to make amends to Alaina as soon as possible.

Sitting up in bed, Christopher looked around his room. His head was hurting but still swimming in the libations of the previous evening, his stomach just a bit uneasy. Christopher took stock of his surroundings, noticing his boots strewn carelessly on the floor. Other than his shoes,

Christopher was wearing the same clothes of the previous night, his cravat and shirt loosened and disheveled, his coat wrinkled and a bit constricting. On his night table, he noticed a glass filled with some vile looking liquid, on top of a quick note. Easing off the side of the bed, Christopher gingerly made his way to the nightstand and lifted the glass, catching a strong whiff of alcohol before quickly setting it aside. He imagined the taste of the green liquid would test his stomach almost as much as the smell. Picking up the small piece of paper, he could make out Graham's scribble, truly amazed that after all these years his handwriting had improved so little.

> *Baldwin said you were "indisposed" when I stopped by this morning. Since it is such an important day, I told him to make you this to clear your head, or at least the contents of your stomach.*
> *-G*
> *P.S. Good luck today!*

Christopher could almost see the crooked, pitying yet mocking, smile of his childhood friend, accompanied by an innocent shrug of the shoulders.

Afraid of missing out on calling on Alaina before the lunch hour, judging by the light streaming in, Christopher considered the glass of noxious fluid. He sighed and picked up the glass, certain it would either save his day or ruin it, and downed the liquid in one gulp, with only a slight grimace and shudder as accompaniment. Christopher took a deep breath to await the effects and was surprised there was no immediate illness. Feeling a bit more confident, he made his way to the bell string to ring for his manservant, but stopped dead in his tracks and reversed course with eyes wide. A few quick steps to the thankfully clean chamber pot saw his stomach contents evacuated. Leaning his head back against the wall, after slumping to the floor next to the chamber pot, he finally felt steady enough to mentally curse his friend. What a way to start the day.

⚜

After a surprisingly short time, Christopher found himself walking briskly toward Alaina's family home, a few blocks over from his own family townhome. The turnaround after the illness had been remarkable and Christopher had been quick to bathe and dress in new clothes, hoping he no longer smelled of cigars and brandy. The fog from the previous night had burned off at first light and the day was bright, with amazingly clear skies. The weather was still chilly, but the warmth from the sun held a promise of the coming spring. Christopher turned the last corner onto Berkeley Street and saw his destination up ahead, just a few houses further on the left. His eagerness to see Alaina was met with regret of the encounter the previous night, his steps slowing as he traversed the final distance. Christopher ascended the front stoop of the Norwich townhome and rapped the knocker on the door. The hour was just shy of eleven, and he hoped he had not come too late.

The Norwich family butler, Arthur, stuck his head out of the door, and upon recognizing the marquess, opened the door fully to allow Christopher to enter. Doffing his hat, gloves, and outer cloak, Christopher handed them to Arthur, who, sensing the young man's nerves, smiled ever so slightly.

"I assume you are here to call on Lady Alaina?" Arthur asked, not needing or expecting an answer other than an affirmation.

Christopher nodded his head and then thought better of it. "Yes, I mean, no, at least not right away. Perhaps Lord Sinclair is available first?"

The butler gave an amused snort, a bit out of character, but he really could not help himself. "The earl is working on his books and told me he does not wish to be disturbed until after lunch. Lady Alaina is in the front parlor, if you would like to see her."

And, as if Arthur could conjure Lady Alaina by speaking her name, she appeared at the door of the parlor, just past the foot of the stairs. "Hello Christopher. Should I feel miffed that you came to see my father and not me?"

Christopher met Alaina's stare and was surprised to find it reflected the same worries he felt, even if she had tried to infuse a teasing tone into her statement. Alaina looked just as he had remembered in his dreams. Her hair was swept up in a simple loose collection of perfect curls on the crown of her head, tendrils escaping around her temples, making her look more like a nymph, especially with the light from the parlor at her back. She was dressed in a simple day dress, cream colored with green brocade accents on the shoulders, wrists, and around the waist. Christopher thought she would look perfectly at home in a spring garden, and with only a few weeks to warmer weather, he smiled, able to conjure up such a vision. With the most fervent hope that he had not been silent too long, Christopher walked toward Alaina.

"My dear Alaina, I had hoped to see you just the same, but thought it might be prudent if I talked to your father first."

Alaina furrowed her brow in confusion, and then a thought entered her mind, making her smile, partly in joy, and partly in chagrin for being so dense; at least she hoped he meant to discuss the subject of marriage with her father.

Alaina backed into the parlor to allow Christopher to enter. As Christopher passed Alaina to enter the room, her scent, a mix of soap and roses, washed over him, causing a familiar clenching in his belly as he relived their passionate kiss from the previous evening. A quick marriage was maybe best; his friend certainly had not been wrong about that.

Arthur poked his head into the parlor, keeping his amused stare as muted as possible. "I will let your father know that the marquess has arrived, although he did say not to disturb him until after lunch."

At this statement the butler closed the door most of the way, leaving only a sliver open to the hallway: a way to keep within the bounds of propriety while giving the couple some privacy.

Christopher looked at Alaina in surprise. "Are you sure that leaving the door like that will not make your parents angry?"

Alaina shook her head and came to stand squarely in front of Christopher, who stood in front of the fireplace. The placement of a pair of chairs close to the fire meant Alaina had to stand close to Christopher to look at him, or at least his chest. Christopher looked down at her, her head upturned, and seemed ensnared by the deep brown eyes that looked warm and inviting in the light.

Christopher, feeling his attention driving to thoughts of more fun exploits than a conversation about his embarrassing display, cleared his throat and tried to start. "I had hoped… I would like …"

Christopher was unable to muster the right words and averted his gaze, but Alaina was undeterred. "What do you want, Christopher?" she said in almost a whisper.

As Christopher met her gaze, all he could think of was the vision that filled his heart. "You, my love. Ever since you flayed me at the refreshment table."

Each of them stood there, entranced by the other, Alaina amazed at what she felt and could see in the depths of Christopher's steel-blue eyes. Without much thought to the surroundings, Christopher took one step toward Alaina, closing the remaining distance between them. Alaina could feel Christopher's breath at her temple, and he could feel the heat of her body. He ached to gather her in his arms.

With Christopher's height, Alaina had to crane her neck to meet his eyes, ever-changing like the sea. Her mind was a tumble of thoughts, the first being the feeling of the kiss they shared last night. Alaina could feel her heart in her ears; a warm feeling washed over her. Christopher leaned in and Alaina's heart leapt as their lips connected in a soft touch, Christopher just brushing his lips on hers. Alaina's hands moved up to his neck without thought, causing her to lean into his body. Only one statement escaped her lips, "Me, huh?"

No verbal response came from Christopher, as his response to her question was to crush her to him, his lips turning to allow a deeper connection, his tongue tracing her lips. The couple did not hear the faint approach outside the door, but snapped apart as the door hit the wall and reverberated, opened rather forcefully by Alaina's father, Edward. The butler stood just behind with a look of chagrin, almost apologetic.

Edward considered the two young people, obviously having just disengaged from a very improper kiss, and tried to keep his mirth hidden. They would certainly be married, but he knew it was expected to have some self-righteous anger. "So, I hear you needed a word with me, marquess? It seems I may be too late in my ability to object."

And with that, Edward strode into the room and closed the door, Alaina and Christopher giving each other sheepish smiles.

Chapter 18

After walking in on Christopher and Alaina in what could be assumed was not the first passionate embrace of their courtship, Edward had discussed the terms of the engagement and eventual marriage with Christopher rather quickly. The younger man had no real demands; love certainly did that to a person. It was Edward who had one demand: the length of the courtship would be long enough to allow for a proper wedding, no exceptions. And, in an attempt to avoid conflict with his wife, Edward convinced Christopher to hold off on any formal proposal to Alaina until Charlotte and Evelina returned from the shops, which happened luckily right after the contract had been signed.

The midday celebration over the impending nuptials spilled into the afternoon tea and then into the evening meal. By the end, Alaina and Christopher were elated, blissful, and exhausted, with no time throughout the day to talk or have any moments alone, most likely by the earl's design.

Against his better judgement, and at the coaxing of his wife, Edward allowed Christopher and Alaina to occupy the front parlor at the end of the evening to say their goodbyes. This time the door remained completely open to the hallway, leaving no room for privacy.

The front parlor was warm from the fire that had burned all day, just recently stoked by Arthur, but the light from the afternoon was gone. Candles had been lit and a lantern sat on the table between the two chairs situated directly in front of the fireplace. The glow of candles gave the feel of a bedchamber, or at least some setting more intimate than a formal front parlor used for receiving guests. Once they were left in their own company, Alaina and Christopher automatically came together closely in front of the fire. No outward passion could be observed, it was only boiling under the surface, but an element of tenderness and hope for the future had taken its place.

"I fear they do not trust us," Alaina whispered, motioning to the door.

"Well, if it justifies their actions, I have to keep reminding myself the door is open, else I will continue what I started this afternoon," Christopher half-growled, only partly in jest.

Alaina looked away slightly. Christopher could not see her fully in the dim light, but he felt her embarrassment. Trying to keep the tenderness of the moment, Christopher gathered Alaina's hands in one of his own, putting the knuckle of his free hand under her chin, forcing her to look him in the eye once again.

"I feel so lucky to be here at this very moment, but I also owe you an apology," Christopher probed Alaina's eyes and sighed, finally able to broach the real reason for his hurried visit and proposal.

Alaina drew her brows together in confusion. "Apology? Doubts already?"

"No," came Christopher's quick answer, a little more brusquely than he intended. Frustrated with himself, he dropped Alaina's hand, turning to face the fire and raking a hand through his tousled hair, almost blonde in the firelight.

It seemed the best he could muster was a muted apology said to the flames. "I should never have said the words I said in the state I was in last night, and for that I am sorry."

"Oh," was Alaina's response, such a small word that seemed to fill the space between them.

Realizing his mistake, Christopher turned back to face Alaina. She was quick to put up her hand to stop further explanation. They were engaged to be married; if Christopher did not love her now, it mattered little, as long as there was hope for the future.

"I do not think you understand my meaning, please let me get this out," came Christopher's plea. Seeing the glitter of tears in Alaina's eyes spurred him. "You see, words of love should be exchanged in times of joy, untainted by drink, or company. For goodness' sake, I could not even make them private. What I mean is that they should be special, given in an intimate moment, like now."

At the end of his explanation, Alaina's lips trembled ever so slightly up in a smile.

"I love you, my dear Alaina. I fear I have loved you since we first met. I had been denying it ever since that moment. And I feared not saying the words for one moment longer would be my downfall. It was unfortunate that I needed the confidence of drink to express my true feelings. Will you forgive me?"

Alaina giggled. "There is nothing to forgive, I am just glad to hear the words again. I love you too, my darling Christopher."

And with their declarations in the air, their lips met in a tender kiss, heat seeping from their bellies and spreading through their bodies. After only a moment, Christopher pulled away, placing his hands on Alaina's arms in order to set her a safe distance from him. Christopher could see Alaina's eyes were glazed over with passion even in the candlelight, and had to force himself to maintain decorum.

"It is getting late. I should be going," Christopher said, giving a quick bow as a way of forcing courtly manners on the moment and on himself.

"You make me yearn for our wedding. I get the feeling kisses like these can lead to good places," Alaina purred, aware that her words could lead to added embarrassment with her parents; but what she felt at his touch made her yearn for something more.

Christopher groaned, and pulled Alaina close in his embrace once more. She could feel a hardness on her belly and knew he felt the same.

"You, little minx, have much to learn, but know that I yearn for the wedding night as much if not more than you."

Christopher landed a passionate and hard kiss on Alaina's lips, and although it was brief, it communicated that his statement was in fact true.

Coming up a little breathless, Alaina was barely able to get out the words, "It is getting late."

"That it is," Christopher added, and with one last kiss, this time on the tip of her nose, he left by way of the parlor door and then quickly out of the front door of the townhome, thankful for the cool night air.

Alaina could still feel all the places Christopher had touched with his hands, his lips, his body, and took a breath to steady herself. The wedding certainly could not come soon enough, even if she had no idea what was truly in store past the kissing.

⚜

News travelled fast in society, and even before the proper announcement, Alaina and Christopher had received a wide variety of congratulations, invitations to dinner, musicales, and other social engagements. It was always expected that Alaina and a chaperone of some sort would accompany the marquess, so whomever had proffered the invitation could learn about the couple, either to feed the gossip, or to gain favor.

The Rochester estate and title had long been held by gentlemen who preferred privacy over ambition, happy to maintain the success of the title without expanding it, at least through overtly political means. Alaina learned that until Christopher's late father, who had taken to excessive drink at a young age, there had been no real scandal, or none at least that captured the attention of the ton for more than a few minutes. In fact, the Rochester line had been so boring that the family situation, or lack thereof, had never garnered much attention at all.

With a family that was so close, Alaina had been eager to learn about Christopher's, and was sad that he had no close relatives to share in his life. Alaina found herself asking questions, largely that Christopher could not answer. Christopher did not remember much of his father before his mother's death at all, as he had always been away at whatever Rochester estate that Christopher and his mother did not occupy. Christopher admitted to Alaina he had realized that the absence of his father was probably what kept his mother from being completely withdrawn. The few times the old marquess was in attendance, mostly holidays, Christopher recalled awkward and forced family dinners. After his mother passed, Christopher was often only in the company of tutors and servants. The occasional forced family dinners became more and more unbearable, as Christopher got older and became more aware both of his father's drunken and belligerent behavior as well as its worsening impact on the late marquess's health.

It was not until he went to Eton that Christopher made any friends his own age. Graham was his roommate by chance, and they became fast friends, even as Graham pulled Christopher into mischief.

Not even Charles, Christopher's cousin, older by a few years, had seen fit to engage much with his younger family member while they both attended school, only extending basic courtesies, as required. When Christopher had been younger, it had seemed personal. After the passing of his father, Christopher learned of the bad blood between the late marquess and his uncle, Charles's father, the second-born son, but had never learned the cause. Over the years, their relationship had not much improved, even without the presence of the previous marquess. It was only with the death of Charles's father, and Charles's own ascendence to his barony, that Christopher and Charles became friendly, still only seeing each other on occasion, but more due to circumstance than lack of desire to engage socially. Christopher had come to value his cousin's company and humor, and accepted his invitation to a quiet dinner at the rented townhouse his cousin currently occupied. Alaina convinced her mother to join them for propriety, all of them leaving from the Norwich townhome together.

As they wound their way by carriage to Charles's home in the city, Alaina tugged at her gloves. Charlotte, who was seated next to Alaina, seemed oblivious to her distress, but Christopher, who was sitting opposite, watched her on their short ride, unsure of how to ease Alaina's trepidation.

"Alaina, my dear, it matters not to me how you and Charles get along. Besides, you seem to get on well with most people," Christopher attempted to assure her.

Alaina, who had been absently biting her lip while she fidgeted, looked up to meet Christopher's eyes, and he could see the plea in them. "I just want to get along with your family. Charles and I met ever so briefly at the Leicester Ball, and I cannot shake a feeling that he does not like me."

"Nonsense. Charles has always been a bit odd. I am sure he was just struck by your beauty," Christopher said, adding a jaunty smile to hopefully brighten the mood.

Alaina heaved a big sigh and glanced back down at her lap, not placated by Christopher's assurances. Charlotte took this moment to reach over and squeeze her daughter's hand.

"Alaina, Christopher is right. I will grant you that Charles seemed a bit odd, but I am sure it has nothing to do with you," Charlotte said, giving Alaina and then Christopher a smile only a mother could dole out.

The carriage pulled up in front of a modest town house on a busier street than Alaina was used to. Christopher had mentioned his cousin was a baron, and had to rent accommodations when he came to town. That meant they were currently on the outskirts of where nobility respectably lived. The street was still overwhelmingly safe, and the houses lining the street were well kept, but smaller. Occasionally, one would see a stray dog wander the streets, or an overly drunk gentleman, maybe even a member of the lower-level nobility on a bench or curb, all of which Alaina was not used to seeing.

Christopher's cousin was a baron, a title that had been in the Kendall family for several generations, either remaining with cousins or second-born sons. Christopher explained this meant that Charles was able to claim a decent income and investments. The money and property were not as extensive as the marquessate, but enough to rent the best townhouse on the street. As a baron, Charles had to keep his staff in the country to keep an eye on the surrounding property, including a farm and tenants, so he hired staff every London season he was in residence. As Alaina, Christopher, and Charlotte prepared to alight from the carriage, one of these newly hired servants opened the door.

"Good evening, ladies and gent. The baron had me come greet you at the coach instead of waiting by the door. No footman tonight," came the gentleman's greeting, ever so slightly less refined than the typical staff at the front of the house, but genial and warm.

"Good evening, we appreciate the help," came Charlotte's reply, taking the lead in leaving the carriage, as she accepted the hand offered in assistance and stepped down from the carriage.

Christopher alighted from the carriage and handed Alaina down, quickly turning to the man. "Thank you, sir, we appreciate the help." Alaina murmured her thanks as well.

The group made their way up the short flight of steps and into the small foyer at the front of the townhome, where the man waited to take their cloaks and hats. Alaina could not shake her dread over the upcoming encounter with Christopher's cousin. *What if Charles really did not like her? Why did Charles seem so familiar?* She pushed these thoughts to the back of her mind and attempted to make conversation to ease her discomfort.

"So, sir, are you originally from London?" Alaina asked.

The stand-in footman looked directly at Alaina, and let the silence stretch as if he was considering his answer. "Yes, ma'am, born an' raised."

The weight of the man's stare made Alaina squirm, as her tongue refused to work. The footman's eyes narrowed, and he straightened his coat, as if readying for some sort of rebuke, but he was cut short as their host made an entrance.

"Ho there, cousin!" came Charles's voice from the back of the hallway, his footsteps quickly closing the distance between himself and his trio of guests, clasping hands with Christopher briefly before addressing the ladies.

"I am so glad you could join me here for dinner. I must apologize for my modest home. I had not originally planned to attend the season, so when I changed my mind last minute, I was stuck with scant few options. Thankfully, I have my man, Felton Reid, to help me when I have guests. You ladies absolutely liven up the place with your beauty," Charles exclaimed, his words overly bright, as he motioned to the footman, whose glower had subsided, at least for the moment.

"Ah yes," Christopher remarked with a chuckle, "I fear one must be overly prepared for the season. I am happy you were able to find suitable lodgings and join the scene here in London."

Alaina found that she could not help herself as she countered, "You know, my dear, it is amazing how you have changed your tune. If I had to guess, when I met you, I would have thought you would give up your place here in London never to see the city again, or any of its occupants."

Christopher smiled sheepishly, and shrugged. "I find myself reformed. It seems I met a captivating young woman who made the city sparkle like I never expected."

Alaina thought she caught Charles narrowing his eyes, as he did the other evening, but then Charles chuckled without missing a beat. "Of course, dear cousin, it seems that ladies always have a hold over us, no matter how hard we try."

Alaina could not determine if his last comment was meant in jest, as she watched a hard look cross Charles's face, and sought to assuage whatever malice might come as a result of the banter. "Oh, Charles, us ladies are not so bad, I assure you. Stick with me, and I can steer you clear of the bad ones."

Charles seemed to break out of his trance, an easy smile crossing his face again. "Of course, of course. I just meant that love does strange things, mostly good." And then he gave Christopher a conspiring look before continuing, "Now, I have invited you to dinner, so please follow me."

Charles motioned for all of them to follow him down the narrow hallway, chattering about the house, its history, and even the weather. Christopher and Charlotte joined in as well, while Alaina fell silent and half-listened. It had been the same when she first met Charles; Alaina had an inkling of something just beneath the surface. She had worried it was some dislike for her that Charles was hiding, but now she could not shake the feeling that neither Charles nor his employee were very happy with their visit.

The pre-dinner drinks did much to ease Alaina's nerves, making way for a pleasant dinner. Easy conversation about any and all topics seemed to flow as freely as the wine, but Felton suddenly appeared as dessert was being laid on the table, and quickly made his way to the head of the table where Charles was seated, laughing at some story Christopher had been recounting about his time at Eton.

Charles's man leaned in to whisper to Charles discreetly and after a moment, Charles' smile faded almost directly into a scowl.

"Felton, I told you I was not to be disturbed. Did you mention I had guests?" Charles queried.

"I mentioned you were occupied, but she insisted," Felton replied, handing Charles a calling card and placing a pot of ink and quill down on the table. When Christopher's cousin raised his brow, Felton answered the unspoken question. "She refuses to leave until you respond."

Charles quickly scrawled something on the calling card, no more than a few words, and sent Felton away, leaving the inkwell awkwardly on the table in his haste. Charles seemed distant, and after a moment of silence Christopher felt the need to ask, "Everything alright, I hope?"

Shaking his head, Charles plastered a smile once more on his face, this time without the light of laughter, and shrugged. "Everything is perfectly fine. It just seems I have a fervent admirer."

Christopher chuckled, "Love can do strange things."

"I am afraid so. She is most persistent and unconventional, bordering on reckless. It seems of late, nothing will shake her attentions," Charles lamented with a rueful half-smile.

"I take it that you do not return her ardor?" Christopher asked, his voice soft and gentle.

"Ah, well," Charles started as he cleared his throat. "I fear I cannot condone her methods in seeking me out at all times of day."

⸙

After dessert, which was short-lived by anyone's standards, Charlotte begged to return home, claiming a headache, so all three of Charles's guests departed, the carriage rumbling down the almost empty street. The early crowd was already abed, while the parties of nobility stretched long into the night. A fog had settled on London, with the warmer days of spring heating up the city, and the still cool nights making for damp and chilly evenings.

It was in this fog that a cloaked figure made its way toward the waterfront, keeping to the shadows, cautious in stride. The salty air mingled with the fetid smell of the Thames, and the stale smell of ale, as the figure approached and entered the unnamed saloon closest to the docks. Sailors knew the place by many names, none of them official, but all of them apt: The Blind Sailor, A Place with No Name, and lastly, The Meetin' Spot.

The cloaked one felt this last name to be both the most fitting and a taunt of sorts. Walking through the half door at the supposed front of the establishment, the cloaked figure's senses were assaulted by the din of mostly drunk sailors and their paid or unpaid companions for the evening. The smell of the place had already wafted onto the cobblestone streets, but was much more intense inside, with an added stench of unwashed flesh and thick smoke.

This place was not intended for bawdy activities, with no rooms for it, but served merely as a place for sailors to either start or end the evenings without venturing too far from their posts on the docks. Its location and relative unpopularity among the more boisterous crowds also made it a popular place for anonymous, if not discreet, discussions, no patrons really caring about the business of others. It was little more than a shack with a long rough-hewn bar on one side of the room and only a few sets of tables and chairs for larger groups. Tonight, the crowd was lighter than usual, the first batch of ships having arrived earlier in the week, and the younger sailors preferring the more cosmopolitan scene of London proper. This left only a few people strewn throughout the tables, and some at the bar, leaving plenty of room for the hooded newcomer to sidle up to the bar without incident, taking a seat on a high stool.

The lone barkeep lazily made his way to the figure, not particularly interested or bothered by their presence, other than the fact that he thought it was unlikely the person would order anything. When he came face to face with the would-be patron, he was surprised to see such a winsome visage beneath the hood of the cloak.

His gruff exterior softened, but remained suspicious, as he asked, "Would you like anything, miss, or is it my lady?"

A snort came from the cowl of the hood. "Nothing please for now. I will order in a moment, sir."

A few folks further down the bar looked up at the refined speech, narrowing their eyes in attempt to focus their blurred vision, unable to determine the exact source. They quickly gave up their quest of discovery and went back to drinking, but not without the bartender taking notice.

"You know, people here care not a whit for why you are here or who you are. It is more the threat of something unknown that can cause trouble," the bartender said quietly before moving along, leaving the lady to contemplate.

Clearly, he had been speaking of her hooded presence, and wishing to not garner any more attention, or worse, curiosity, Lady Barbara relented and pushed back her hood. Her dark hair was sedately tied back in a knot at her nape, her pale skin glowing in the soft light of the bar, giving her usually appealing face a more severe look. No one seemed to bat an eye in her direction, as all those looking for company had already found it, while all the others were there for the drink. Lady Barbara waited for what seemed to be an interminable amount of time, hearing the tick of an imaginary clock in her head as she sat alone at the bar.

She did not hear the approach, but she did recognize the voice of the man next to her. "Lady Barbara, what is it that you want?"

Barbara whirled in her seat to see Charles Kendall, a scowl on his face. Barbara softened her expression and motioned to the chair next to her. "Please sit, my dear. We have much to discuss."

A few moments passed before Charles decided to sit. "So, what is it that we have to discuss with such urgency? I had to end my dinner with my cousin early."

"I have to say, I had thought you would welcome my company a bit more than that," Barbara prodded. "When I first met you, it was all smiles and sweet nothings; now you are a veritable grouch."

"You seem to conveniently forget that when we first met, your attention was set on Percy. After his arrest, I foolishly believed your change of attentions to be based on a true connection," Charles growled. "Now it is clear to me that you just found another opportunity. And I feel that your ambition outreaches reason."

"It is for both of us, my dear," Lady Barbara countered.

"Do not 'my dear' me. What do you want?"

"I have something that could prove useful, and I thought to pass it along," Barbara said nonchalantly, as she removed a pouch from her cloak, a *thunk* sounding as she placed it on the bar.

Charles was quick to grab the proffered satchel, opening it only enough to peer inside. He raised an eyebrow. "How did you get this? And what exactly am I supposed to do with it?"

Lady Barbara considered her answer for a moment and decided on flattery. "Charles, you are smart, I am sure you will put the trinket to good use. As for how I came into possession of it, Percy was useful in his way, even though he ultimately failed in his endeavor."

Charles snorted, "Do not bother with flattery, I know you have picked me out only to serve your purpose, and your brother preyed on my shallow pockets and my proclivity to cards to ensure that I went along with your plan. And I must say, the man has an uncanny ability with cards, one that cannot be attributed solely to good luck, as he claims."

Lady Barbara sighed, softening her demeanor, as she placed her hand on Charles. "My dear, my plan ensures we both get what we want, money for you, and…"

But before Barbara could finish, Charles spat out, "There is no need to explain it to me as if I were a child!"

"Very well, Charles," Barbara replied smoothly, unaffected by his outburst. "Let me know when you have a plan."

The chair scraped the floor loudly as Charles stood up, and executed a crisp bow. "Good evening, madam. I will be in touch."

Sometime later, Lady Barbara exited the dockside hole-in-the-wall, hoping for a quick trip back home by foot. She readjusted the hood of her cloak for more anonymity and set off with wary confidence.

A thick fog had settled on London, making for a more anonymous, but uncomfortable, walk. Barbara's footsteps echoed unnaturally in the night, each step bringing with it random sounds from the fog that startled her, only to prove an errant cat or rat wandering the streets in search of the day's leftover scraps or a warm place to sleep.

Soon, though, a more constant cadence reached her ears, one she quickly identified as footsteps. A quick look around gave her no peace of mind, as the fog masked the identity of their source as well as the direction of her company on the long quiet streets. Frozen for a moment, Lady Barbara heard the steps grow louder until a dark figure coalesced in the night. With no time to run, Barbara hoped the man was just out for a stroll in the night and cared not a whit of her presence.

Unfortunately, the dark figure, cloaked by midnight cloth, seemed on a collision course with her and was closing in at an alarming rate. Suddenly too afraid to move at all, Lady Barbara awaited her fate with eyes wide in terror. Her would-be assailant stopped just short of Barbara, leaving little space between them. She craned her neck to see who lay within the cloak.

A gasp was the only thing that escaped Lady Barbara's mouth before the cloaked figure picked her up and smothered her screams with their gloved hand. Lady Barbara struggled against her captor to no avail and was dragged into the fog, the sound of her muffled screams lost to the mist.

Across town, the Norwich townhouse had settled into relative quiet as the clock on the mantel in the front parlor chimed the eleventh hour. After dessert at Charles's home had turned awkward, Charlotte had claimed a headache. Christopher had made his quick apologies and suggested that they retire for the evening. Alaina wondered if her mother's headache was feigned or due to the true discomfort of the moment. The exchange between Charles and his manservant butler, Felton, had been unsettling at best, the identity of the lady in question still unknown. Even the carriage ride had been quiet, each occupant mulling over the evening.

Back in the townhome, Alaina and Charlotte seemed to relax, playing easy hostesses to Christopher. Edward and Evelina joined them in the front parlor for tea and biscuits. The men added a bit of brandy to their cups and soon the tension of dinner was forgotten. Laughter echoed in the parlor, filling the space with warmth and life, the happy couple exchanging a heated glance now and again as discussions steered toward wedding planning and life after the blessed day. Charlotte and Evelina took it upon themselves to set a schedule for the wedding planning; Christopher and Alaina just enjoyed the moment.

With such excitement, Evelina and Charlotte eventually excused themselves for bed, leaving Edward as chaperone. However, the brandy which had at first been enough for boisterous laughter, now led to a more mellow tenor, causing Edward's eyes to close in rest. Edward was positioned in front of the fire, which still burned high, although signs of waning could be perceived, the crackles of the logs becoming lazier. Christopher and Alaina moved to a settee closer to the window, far enough away that a chill from the glass window could be felt, but with the fire at their backs, it was still cozy. A small table had been moved in front of them where a small chess set was currently in use. Christopher and Alaina tried to remain focused on the game, but it was clear their nearness to one another was overtaking their attention.

"You know, my dear, it is your move, has been for quite some time," Christopher teased.

In an effort to distract Alaina further and for his own pleasure, Christopher took her hand, kissed the knuckles gently, then turned over her hand to trail kisses on her palm and the inside of her wrist. Ensnaring Alaina's gaze, Christopher flashed a roguish grin. Heat crept up her arm and she was immensely grateful for the dim light of the hurricane lamp. Alaina was both exhilarated by the feeling in the pit of her stomach and unable to control the hitch in her breath. A heat seemed to reach all corners of her body, emanating from deep within her.

Alaina's distraction was so great that she temporarily forgot the presence of her father mere feet away in the wingback chair by the fireplace. Edward had chosen the chair facing away from the window either by chance or on purpose, and with Alaina and Christopher faced outward toward the window, it was unlikely Edward would see the exchange. Even still, Alaina looked over her shoulder quickly to ascertain his awareness. The tension she felt eased only a fraction when she saw his closed eyes in profile and heard a soft snore accompanying his even breathing.

Alaina turned a pointed look on Christopher. Trying to appear stern proved difficult and Alaina eventually gave way to a smile and giggle, which made Christopher chuckle as well.

Alaina attempted to pick up where they left off, moving her rook recklessly on the board in order to just keep the game going. "Well it seems, my dear, it is now your turn."

Christopher heaved an exaggerated sigh, moving his pawn to capture her rook. "Well, if I had to guess, you are letting me win, or is it that you are distracted?"

Alaina pulled her hand forcefully from his grip and whispered, "Will you stop?"

Christopher put up his hands as if to signal his concession, and they played the game in silence for a few moments. It was Alaina who once again started the conversation, "It is nice to meet your family, although I fear that your cousin may not have taken much of a liking to me."

The abrupt change in conversation seemed to catch Christopher off-guard, but it was not long before he responded, "Fear not, Alaina. I expect that he was half-distracted by the lady who interrupted dinner."

Alaina mulled over Christopher's assurances and found it difficult to accept them, but could not find anything concrete in her mind to provide evidence to the contrary. Alaina gave a quick shrug of her shoulders. "I must admit that there is nothing to contradict your assessment, so I will allow that you may be correct."

Christopher once more recaptured Alaina's hand, a chuckle escaping him. "I know I am correct, my dear. Fear not, I am sure that Charles likes you, and even if he does not, I do not care. It is just recently that Charles and I have truly reconnected."

"I do wonder why your families were so at odds," Alaina commented.

Christopher sighed. "I was too young to realize all that happened between my father and my uncle, but there was one season in London where I remember a row after some night at a ball or some social event. I was supposed to be abed, but I could not sleep and waited for my parents' return. I was excited when I heard my aunt and uncle's voices as well, but partway down the stairs to greet them, I heard yelling. I do not remember ever seeing my uncle after that night. My father became surly and withdrawn, taking to drink more and more often, and my mother receded from society, from everyone. I rarely saw her smile after that day, and she refused to ever attend a season in London again. For nine years after that, my parents lived as strangers, and then she died from fever."

"Did you hear any of what happened?" Alaina asked.

"I was only five at the time, but I heard the words 'common whore' thrown about a bit before my aunt and uncle stormed out of my family's townhome," Christopher recounted. "My father was silent after they left, but I could hear my mother pleading with him. I did not stay to witness the aftermath and retreated to my room. I fear I did not sleep well, if at all, that night. Reflecting on it many years later, my best guess is that my mother had some affair. I know we are all awed by our parents when we are young, but I truly could not reconcile what I knew of my mother with that type of accusation."

"What was your mother like, before everything with your uncle?"

Christopher smiled as if reliving happy memories. "I was so young, but I still remember her laugh. She was so happy, so carefree. Even my father seemed infected by it. It was the only time I ever heard him laugh; my earliest memories were of my mother and father laughing together. To see such a change in both of them was confusing, and my father refused to talk of it ever, even after my mother passed."

Alaina threw her arms around Christopher. "Oh, my darling, how awful."

Christopher reciprocated the embrace, his arms enveloping Alaina and pulling her close, but a clearing of a throat intruded, snatching each back to their original seats.

Alaina was too embarrassed to look around, but Christopher turned to meet Edward's gaze, the latter having just awoken. Edward was just turning in his seat to see the couple, causing relief to flood Christopher, thankful Edward had not witnessed their closeness. He did not wish to mar what had been a beautiful evening.

"It seems I fell asleep. Perhaps it is time to end the evening. Will you both forgive me?" Edward yawned, his voice still carrying the sound of sleep, its deep timbre crackling a bit as he talked.

Alaina had regained her aplomb and turned to her father, waving her hand in dismissal. "No forgiveness needed, the hour certainly is late."

Edward took in the sight of the couple, the chess game largely unfinished, and smiled knowingly, giving a warning, "I do hope my slumber did not cause either of you to forget the game of chess. Perhaps my snoring was too loud?"

Christopher chuckled, understanding the implication, and then laughed more heartily after catching a glimpse of Alaina's confusion. "No, sir, we had just gotten to talking about the wedding and our excitement for summer so we can be man and wife."

"Ah, yes, I remember those days. Charlotte and I were also excited for our nuptials. But there is so much planning to do for a wedding, the summer still does not give us much time," Edward stated, matter-of-factly.

"There is always a special license that can be procured." Christopher pressed his luck.

"No daughter of mine will need such a thing. Besides, her mother would be heartbroken to not plan a large celebration," was Edward's response, choosing to ignore the implication of a special license. "Young love is so much fun, so many stolen kisses and moments of joy. Well, I remember this one time at the Darby townhouse where Charlotte and I... Let's just say, we enjoyed being out in society and married. It always amazes me how many dark corners of balconies and secret hallways are out there, positively unseemly."

Christopher and Alaina caught each other's eyes, surprised their actions were so transparent to her father, but Christopher found amusement as well.

"It certainly would be unseemly if it were true, although I have yet to find such things," Christopher stated, the overly bright tone giving away his lies, but Edward seemed, or at least acted, as if he did not notice.

"Well, I should be going, it is very late," Christopher started, but before he could finish Edward continued, "And you have a lot of planning and a long engagement ahead of you."

Alaina giggled, "That we do, but it will be so much fun."

CHAPTER 19

Alaina smiled as she looked out an east facing window at Waverley, the Rochester country estate. The morning light draped everything she could see in a warm glow. The weather was perfect for the couple's wedding day, and Alaina was more than eager to join together with Christopher in holy matrimony. She was ready for the ceremony, and had some time to reflect on the past couple of months.

Their engagement had been fun, exhilarating, and oh-so-sweetly frustrating. The wedding planning had stretched only two months into the early summer, but Alaina and Christopher thought the wait interminable. With fewer balls and dark balconies at the end of the season, there had been only a few stolen moments to tide the young couple over until after the wedding. After one such encounter in late May, Christopher thought he might have to swear off seeing Alaina altogether, for fear of what public spectacle he might cause in the throes of passion.

On that particular occasion, Christopher had found a private alcove, not too far from the Sussex townhome ballroom, where a stolen kiss had turned impassioned, crushing Alaina's silk dress roughly against Christopher's more hearty attire, causing telltale wrinkles, but thankfully no snags. As Christopher trailed kisses from her lips to her collarbone and to the swell of her breasts above her dress, both of them had been swept away in the moment. He seemed to have more than two hands, all roaming her body with clear and frantic intent. With Christopher's hand on her derriere, he pulled her full against the length of him, exposing the full extent of his desire, a hard and hot brand pushed against her lower belly. Unfortunately, just then a familiar voice had broken through their cocoon.

"Where do you think they have gone?" came Charlotte's query, Edward giving a non-committal grunt in response.

Such a simple question had acted like a bucket of cold water, breaking the couple apart in a hurried attempt to repair their appearance and calm their racing hearts in time for Charlotte and Edward to round the corner. Partially shielded by the curtains, Christopher had remained out of sight while Alaina rushed to join her parents, making some excuse of being lost on the way to the ladies retiring room.

It was Christopher's reaction that made Alaina cherish the memory. Even with the inopportune interruption, Christopher had uttered words of love and left her with an affectionate peck on the tip of her nose, before taking a large step back into the shadows and raking his hands through his hair in an attempt to gather himself.

The memory made Alaina chuckle almost silently, but loudly enough to catch Charlotte and Evelina's attention. Each saw the wistful look in Alaina's eyes and were loath to interrupt the reverie, but felt the need for a good-natured teasing.

"You know there are only a couple of hours until we have to call you Marchioness. It is too late to back out now, you know," Evelina was the first to venture into the conversation.

Alaina rolled her eyes, but it was Charlotte who countered the notion out loud. "If I had to venture a guess, I would imagine Alaina cannot wait for the end of the day. I remember that wistful look, young love."

"Thanks, Mama," was all Alaina had to say before turning her attention back toward the window, this time with a more focused eye to the grounds of Waverley.

Charlotte and Evelina had originally suggested a wedding in London, citing the ability to invite all of society. An added bonus was the lack of requirement to house everyone for what was to be quite a celebration. However, Christopher had been adamant about being married at his family's country estate.

In addition to being an ancient fortress with a moat, mostly for show now, the Rochester estate was still an operational castle in at least one sense of the word. A small abbey was on the grounds, attached to the manor house behind one of the remaining castle fortress walls. The stature of the abbey spoke to a time when each fortress was its own living and breathing city, housed behind stone walls, Waverley being no exception. Time had seen most of the main walls demilitarized, as the need for fortresses for protection dwindled. In some places, walls were removed, or additional gates were added for function. The abbey maintained a pastor and a small staff to see to the religious needs of the estate, performing weddings and logging births and deaths of those who lived in the keep and the surrounding area, including tenants.

According to Christopher, he had seen little utility of the abbey until this moment. Looking down at the wedding preparations, Alaina smiled and had to agree; getting married here was splendid, certainly outshining any wedding they could have planned in the crowded city of London.

From her set of rooms, given to her and her family in the week leading up to the wedding, Alaina could see the rose bushes curl around the inner wall on the west side of the manor house, and tents erected in the vast courtyard to provide shade or shelter depending on the weather. The tents themselves were colored to match the roses, in shades of red and pinks and greens, giving the courtyard, once used for battle preparation, an almost fantastical air. Just at the edge of her vision, Alaina could see the largest tent setup, with tables and chairs enough for one hundred people, a small wedding gathering by the standards of the ton, but a perfect size for the marquessate.

Alaina knew that beyond that tent was the abbey, waiting for her and Christopher today, and she sighed with pleasure. "Well, it seems it is close to that time," Alaina said, turning from the window to face her mother and sister, both beaming from ear to ear. "Shall we make our way to the abbey?"

Charlotte was blinking back tears as she nodded, when a knock at the door sounded.

Anne, Alaina's lady's maid, who had been hovering in the corner of the room, her preparations long finished, rushed to open it, allowing Edward to enter. His eyes filled with tears of happiness and pride, barely able to get out the words, while presenting his arm to Alaina. "Shall we? We certainly do not want to be late."

<hr>

Christopher stood near the altar at the end of the aisle in the small abbey. It was almost more of a chapel, with simple but sturdy pews on either side of a short aisle, only twenty or so feet from the front door to where he stood. Christopher knew more space stood behind the wall used as a backdrop of the altar, mostly records from its inception to the present, but the space for guests was limited.

Christopher shuffled his feet, and looked around the room. The stained-glass windows gave the abbey a surreal presence, the color splashes falling on the flowers attached at the end of the pews, the faces of the guests, and the walls, making everything a kaleidoscope. Given its size, not all one hundred guests were present for the actual ceremony; only the closest relatives and friends were in attendance. The main door straight down the center aisle had been opened to allow in the mild summer breeze, as well as a view of the proceedings for the rest of the guests standing outside.

Luckily, the weather was sunny and nearly cloudless, meaning all the festivities could occur outside with no issues of weather. The sun was still on the eastern side of the manor, given the morning hour, and would soon be overhead, making the tents set up outside the abbey a requirement for a comfortable summer wedding celebration.

At approximately the eleventh hour, a side door opened, and Graham emerged, making his way to the altar where Christopher stood and clasping his friend on the shoulder in a reassuring gesture. A quick nod between friends was all that was needed to signify things were about to begin.

Christopher retrained his eyes on that side door, one he knew led down a narrow hallway that connected to the manor. What once allowed priests to pass safely to the keep without detection during raging battles now allowed Alaina to traverse most of the length of the house without causing any stir among the guests.

First to arrive at the door were Charlotte and Evelina, dressed for the day in happy shades of mauve and pastel pink respectively, to match the roses that were in full bloom all over Waverley. As they made their way to the front pew, a murmur could be heard rippling through the guests, who all turned to the door in anticipation of the bride's arrival.

Edward stepped through the side door first, stopping to turn and offer his arm to the soon-to-be bride. As Alaina stepped fully into the light, all eyes were transfixed by her beauty, but none more so than Christopher's.

Her dress was matched perfectly to her personality, deceptive in its simple silhouette but more complex and unique upon closer inspection. The cut was only slightly fuller than everyday wear, but the train that trailed behind gave it extra body, embroidered with a variety of roses in the lightest of pink to match the most delicate blooms in the surrounding gardens. The empire waist was accented with the same embroidery, and was perfectly complemented by slim sleeves reaching just above Alaina's elbow.

Christopher's eyes took in the whole vision, lingering on Alaina's bosom, modestly covered for the wedding, but its full pertness revealed by the close cut of the dress. Her head was covered by a full long veil, but through the gauzy fabric, Christopher captured Alaina's eyes and smiled what he thought was a flash of a debonair grin, but ended up being one of pure unadulterated joy, without pretense. He imagined her lustrous dark hair piled high on her head, tumbles of curls, specially tended for the day, perfectly placed in rivulets down her back.

As Alaina walked down the aisle on her father's arm, it was as if only she and Christopher were in the abbey. She could see that he had dressed with extra care, just the same as she. To her, he looked resplendent in a dove gray ensemble, perfect for a sunny summer day, almost like a rain cloud holding a quick summer shower. The breeches were tucked into tall black riding boots, as was usual for Christopher; no fancy shoes, even at such an important affair. They were clearly Christopher's best, but riding boots all the same. A crisp white shirt and vest tapered to a trim waist, where the breeches sat, well fit but not overly snug. An overcoat of the same gray color accentuated Christopher's broad shoulders; his height made him an imposing presence, but to Alaina, he very much looked like her knight in shining armor.

Edward delivered Alaina to the altar, where the pastor, whom Christopher and Alaina barely noticed, too smitten and in awe of one another, mumbled some words. Edward responded, looking between the couple one last time before patting Alaina's arm and placing her hands into Christopher's outstretched ones.

One final step up and Alaina was perfectly in front of Christopher, his steel-blue eyes shining brightly into her own. Christopher was overwhelmed by the love shining through the warm pools of umber and honey beneath her veil.

All the while, the pastor continued his speaking, Alaina and Christopher mumbling their replies when necessary, and the small congregation replied in kind.

"Will you support this couple on their journey of matrimony?" *Yes,* came the reply.

"Will you, Christopher, take this woman to be your wife? To have and to hold for the rest of your life."

"I do."

"Will you, Alaina, take this man to be your husband? To have and to hold for the rest of your life".

"I do."

Before too long Christopher lifted Alaina's veil, tears glistening in his eyes, Alaina's eyes reflecting the same emotion.

"You may now kiss the bride," came the pastor's voice, clearer than before in Alaina's head.

Christopher took a slight step toward her and leaned in, brushing his lips against hers. As they kissed gently in front of their closest friends and family, Alaina's head filled with impressions; Christopher's cologne, a clean scent, the smell of flowers decorating the small abbey, the sunlight pouring through the stained-glass windows splashing color on every surface, and the memories of times passed and anticipation of what was to come this very night. The kiss was light and gentle, but promised more, setting flames burning in both husband and wife. In the last moment, Christopher moved his head side to side ever so slightly, causing Alaina to follow and respond to his featherlight caress, before drawing back and smiling down at her as her eyes fluttered open again. An applause and cheer erupted, and the pastor smiled at the couple.

Staying close to Alaina, Christopher whispered, "That will have to do for now."

The low rumble in his voice gave Alaina a pang of anticipation, and she wished no one would notice the passion bubbling just below the surface. She knew she would need to keep her actions in check for at least the remainder of the celebration.

For now. Once it was their wedding night, all bets were off, and though she was nervous, she was excited for the world beyond the kisses of their courtship.

"Shall we?" Georgiana asked.

"Shall we what?" Alaina countered with her own question. In truth she had not been listening intently, or much at all.

"Shall we make our way to the refreshment table?" Georgiana queried. "I am quite parched myself."

"Well, if you are in want of refreshment, how am I to deny my guest?"

"Guest and closest friend, I hope," teased Georgiana, taking Alaina's hand and tucking it into the crook of her arm. "Now come along, time to deliver you to your mooning husband."

By the refreshment table were a few tables on each side, allowing guests to sit and enjoy a repast or just rest. The opposite side of the long tent, where Alaina and Georgiana were currently standing, was partially under one of the bigger oak trees in the back courtyard, shielding the tent from the full effect of the day's heat. On the end of the tent closest to the back of the manor, a small quartet of musicians played softly. The other end of the tent opened up to the lawn where other smaller, but equally lovely, tents spotted the courtyard and guests stood in loose groups enjoying the festivities. Christopher stood nearest the courtyard and was intently watching as Alaina approached.

Both women made their way through the crowd, Alaina acknowledging a congratulatory greeting from time to time. Even though the distance was short it took a few moments to make it to Christopher and Charles.

"Lady Georgiana, how nice of you to fetch my wife for me on our wedding day," Christopher teased, a twinkle in his clear blue eyes.

"Hello, husband. It seems ages since I have seen you," Alaina giggled.

Charles tipped the glass of sherry he had been holding and downed its contents in one gulp, catching Georgiana's attention, if not the young married couple's.

"Young love, eh?" was Georgiana's best statement on the matter, causing a snort or grunt or some such sound from Charles. Georgiana seemed unfazed by his lack of enthusiasm and continued, "Well, I for one am happy for Alaina and Christopher, they seem so much in love. And what a beautiful day they have to celebrate their union. It is absolutely refreshing to see a love match and not some feat of ambition from one party or the other."

Charles had procured another glass of some liquid and was beginning to drink, when it seemed to get lodged in his throat. Coughing and sputtering, Charles looked between all the members of the small group, holding a hand to his chest in an effort to right himself. Christopher wore a look of concern, while Alaina stared in shock. Georgiana grabbed a glass of water from the refreshment table and handed it to the suffering man.

Before any of the rest of the group could inquire as to Charles's well-being, Eleanor approached and laid a hand on Georgiana's untethered arm. "Georgiana, dearest, have you seen your brother? There is just someone to whom I must introduce him."

"Mother, he is probably hiding, able to perceive your intentions as such," Georgiana said, earning a stern look from the dowager duchess.

"Georgiana?" Eleanor tried again, this time a bit more forcefully.

"Fine, mother, I will help you find him," Georgiana relented, disengaging from her friend's arm and placing Alaina's hand in Christopher's outstretched one.

As Georgiana and Eleanor walked toward the lawn, in search of Graham, Eleanor's words could be heard, "Well, he cannot pout forever …"

Christopher grinned, a little lopsided, hearing that last comment. Eleanor would never change. Christopher turned his attention back to his cousin and was surprised by his state. Charles seemed distracted, his eyes unnaturally trained on the liquid swirling inside his small crystal glass.

A clearing of Christopher's throat was enough to capture Charles's attention, causing him to finally look up from his glass to meet Christopher's eyes with an almost blank stare.

Christopher asked, "Are you alright, Charles?"

Charles waved his hand. "Oh that? I just forgot how to swallow for a minute, nothing a glass of water and a few minutes cannot fix, I assure you."

Christopher clasped his cousin on the shoulder and smiled broadly as he glanced lovingly at Alaina. "Well, I for one am happy you are here to celebrate with us. Right, Alaina?"

Alaina only had eyes for her husband. "Yes, we are so happy you could join us."

"To the happy couple," Charles raised his glass and put down its contents quickly, forcing a smile onto his face afterwards. "Shall your union be long and full of joy."

Chapter 20

The moon peeked through the trees every so often as the phaeton, pulled by a single chestnut mare, made its way through the winding path on the outer edges of the Waverley grounds. The country night was quiet in comparison to London, but alive with the sounds of crickets, owls, and rustling leaves, punctuated by the steady clip clop of hooves muffled only slightly on the packed dirt path.

Alaina sighed as she leaned into Christopher's arm, feeling the muscle flex under her touch. As he steered their small vehicle around a large bend and into an opening, a hunting cottage came into view that was tucked into a copse of large trees. The front of the slate-roofed stone structure led to an open field dotted by a few trees and shrubs. The glass panes of the cottage were quite large and glowed with a soft light, revealing the crosshatch pattern making up the windows.

Emerging from the trees, Alaina could see all the stars in the sky accompanying the moon to light their path, the smell of roses still strong as they rode through the night.

Alaina sighed dreamily and asked, "So who lives there?"

"Well, we do, my dear, at least for the time being," Christopher answered, pulling his arm out of Alaina's grasp in order to place it around her shoulders, bringing her closer.

Alaina cocked her head in order to catch a glimpse of Christopher's profile, a frown of confusion marking her brow.

Before she could inquire as to what he meant, Christopher chuckled and continued. "I figured with all of our guests, and the amount of interruptions I have endured from your family and our friends in the past, it would be best that we ensconced ourselves somewhere private. This hunting lodge has been on the Rochester property for generations. My father had a groundskeeper who liked the accommodations, but now it is just kept for my seasonal use. I had some servants prepare it for our stay, but as of now, we should be completely alone."

"Is that why you were in such a hurry?" Alaina teased.

"Of course. I have been thinking of little else this past week, or really these past months." Christopher turned to grin at her, as he pulled the phaeton into a small stable to the side of the cottage.

When they came to a full stop, Christopher dropped the reins for a moment to gather Alaina in his arms, placing a tender kiss on her lips, brushing them lightly with his own before deepening the kiss, crushing Alaina's body against his.

Alaina felt her nipples harden as her soft, full chest rubbed against his hard muscular one. Christopher parted his lips ever so slightly, using his tongue to trace lightly around the opening of Alaina's own lips. A small sigh escaped her, and Christopher let out a moan, slanting his lips across Alaina's and delving into her sweet mouth. He put his arms under her knees and behind her back and lifted her from the bench of the phaeton and onto his lap. Alaina could feel the hard heat under her soft bottom, and the connection created a warmth of her own between her legs as they continued their kiss.

The horse nickered gently, sensing the inattention of both passengers, and Christopher reluctantly pulled back to look at Alaina in the dappled moonlight. "It appears I have some duties to attend to before we can proceed."

Flushed, all Alaina could answer was, "And so it seems."

Christopher leaned his forehead to Alaina's and sighed, lifting her effortlessly back onto her seat on the bench beside him.

As Christopher climbed down, turning back to lift Alaina quickly to the ground before tethering the horse and putting the phaeton away, Alaina mused silently on the day, all perfect in her mind; the church, the party on the lawn, and dinner.

By the end of the evening, Christopher had pulled Alaina aside and told her he had a surprise. Begging their guests' forgiveness, to a round of loud whoops, Christopher had half-dragged her in excitement to the stables, revealing the mode of transportation, laden with a basket and a small trunk, before exclaiming that they were going on an adventure.

Alaina smiled to herself, giddy. She watched as Christopher deftly shouldered the small trunk in one hand and picked up the basket with the other, having already taken care of the horse with grains and water for the night, before turning toward Alaina.

"Ready?" Christopher motioned, with a swift jerk of his head, toward the path leading to the front door of the hunting cottage. Alaina followed along, eager to see what the inside held for them. As she walked, she watched Christopher's strong, broad shoulders carry their burden easily, her eyes making their way down his back admiringly.

Christopher paused at the front door, placing the small trunk down on its end and setting the picnic basket on top, while he removed a key from his gray overcoat. When the door was opened, Alaina could see the soft glow of a candle set just inside the front door on a small table. Christopher turned to Alaina and, with a mischievous glint in his eyes, swept her into his arms in one swift motion.

They crested the threshold. Just inside, Alaina looked up to meet Christopher's gaze. She wasn't sure what was to come next; Charlotte's fumbling attempt to provide insight, without actual information of use, had made Alaina smile. She had not had the heart to tell her mother that she had some inkling about what was to come, even if she did not possess the entirety of the information. Alaina only hoped she was correct that it had something to do with that feeling in the pit of her stomach.

Christopher released Alaina's knees, keeping one arm behind her back. Holding her chest close to his own, her legs slid down the length of his body slowly, coming to rest almost a foot from the floor. Their bodies were now pressed against one another, Alaina's arms clasped together behind Christopher's neck. Their faces were only inches apart, their breath becoming more ragged. Alaina was not sure if it was her heart she felt or Christopher's.

"It seems we are truly alone, and, as a married couple, now completely free to do as we please," came Christopher's voice, soft and sensuous, the sound caressing her body as well as his hands could.

Alaina took a few moments to find her own voice, but eventually responded in kind, "So it seems, *finally*."

That last breathy statement set the coals that had been smoldering, almost since they had met at the refreshment table, completely aflame. Christopher crushed Alaina's lips with his own as he sought to take advantage of their newly wedded status. Remembering himself and his young virgin wife, he slowed his fervor, turning the kiss into a slow caress, brushing his own lips across Alaina's from side to side, his tongue tracing the outline of her lips slowly.

Alaina was both pleased and surprised to find her body reacting without thought; Alaina and Christopher belonged with each other and were bound for life, the bonds that could not be broken by law sealed by the union of their bodies, the consummation of their vows fast approaching.

The sensation Alaina felt in the pit of her stomach blossomed with each caress of the lips, each flick of his tongue across her lips and in her mouth, making her legs feel as if they might collapse to the ground if she was forced to stand at that moment. Christopher started to move his hands in concert with his tongue and lips, caressing her shapely and trim back. With a will of their own, Christopher's hands moved even lower to cup Alaina's soft bottom, squeezing and pulling her body even tighter to his own, which seemed to grow more and more taught with each passing moment. Forgetting their meager luggage outside, Christopher kicked the door to the cottage closed in one quick motion, neither of them seeming to notice the loud bang and rattling that the heavy door caused as it abruptly shielded the couple from the world outside. Across from the table in the small entryway was a long, largely unadorned wall, leading to a stairwell at the center of the house.

Christopher pushed Alaina against the wall and deepened his kiss, his tongue darting in and out of her softly opened mouth. A moan escaped Alaina's throat as she felt Christopher's hard manhood press against her belly. Unsure of what to do, Alaina shut out her mind and let her body take over, her legs opening and encircling Christopher's hips. Even through her skirts, Christopher could feel the heat emanating from Alaina's womanly core. The friction of their bodies caused a dewy wetness to form at the cleft between her legs. Christopher, whose hands had remained on Alaina's torso for support, began to explore more freely, with some of her weight supported now by the joining of their hips. His hands roamed over her bodice, Alaina's thin waist almost swallowed by his large manly hands. Christopher's palm and then fingers caressed her bosom, her nipples puckering even under the fabric, eager for his touch.

Unsatisfied with touches between clothing, Christopher moved his hands to the back of Alaina's dress, deftly undoing the long row of buttons before loosening the garment from her shoulders. Alaina understood Christopher's unspoken intent and uncurled her arms from his neck long enough to free herself from the sleeves, the dress coming to rest at her waist. Her chemise and corset, drawn tight and low over her breasts, strained at the motion, a rosy peak becoming exposed in the frenzy. Christopher used his thumb to move the delicate fabric to reveal and capture one breast in his hand, rolling it around and capturing the taught nipple with his thumb and forefinger. Alaina squirmed with pleasure.

The wall no longer seemed the optimal spot for their tryst. Christopher captured the back of Alaina's knees, one in each hand, to keep her legs wrapped around him as he walked down the hall and through the door to the study. Christopher closed the space to a settee with long quick strides, setting Alaina down gently before standing and frantically doffing his overcoat, waistcoat, and cravat, untucking his shirt before pulling it easily over his head. Alaina had not remained seated, wishing to rid herself of the dress, chemise, and corset pooled at her waist, making quick work of the task. As Christopher emerged from under the tail of his shirt, he was met with a most wondrous sight. Alaina stood before him, close enough to touch, in just a garter, stockings, and elegant shoes, silhouetted by the fireplace. Christopher was thankful for the preparation of the cabin before their arrival. Alaina's breasts were firm and high, the peaks still taught from his earlier caresses. Her waist was slim, her derriere and legs strong and full, and the ivory color of her skin almost shimmering in the firelight. Her hair was still dressed on top of her head, some chocolate curls making their way down her back, and some escaping their stays to frame her face. Her eyes shone in the low light, their depth threatening to swallow Christopher, her lips swollen from their kisses, and her face as beautiful as any could imagine.

Alaina bit her bottom lip as she took in the sight before her: Christopher bare chested, his broad shoulders rippling with sinewy muscles, tapering to a flat belly. A light furring on his chest came to a line before disappearing into his breeches, which were tight on his narrow hips, giving away the fullness of his erection. His cobalt blue eyes seemed to burn with the reflection of the fire, setting off the color of his hair. His eyes took in the sight of her, his strong nose and jaw as handsome as ever. Alaina could see his chest rise and fall at an ever-increasing rate as they stared at one another.

Their eyes locked for only a few moments before their bodies came together with renewed fervor. Christopher found Alaina's breast again, rolling her nipple between his fingers while he captured her bare bottom with his hands. His hands roamed from her breast to her hips, before one came to explore Alaina's cleft of womanhood. Alaina jerked uncontrollably with pleasure, Christopher pleased to find Alaina slick and almost ready for him.

Alaina's hands explored his body, starting at his shoulders and tentatively moving to the top of his breeches, instinctively putting her fingers inside the top of his trousers to gently stroke the tip of his manhood. Christopher moaned his own pleasure, capturing Alaina's mouth with his own.

Reluctantly, he caught Alaina's hand, pulling it out of that sweetest spot, afraid he might spill his seed right then. All he could mutter was, "Not yet, my sweet," before he guided her once again to the settee, settling himself between her thighs.

Christopher showered her with kisses, starting at her brow and moving down her body, stopping every once in a while, to kiss her. As he felt Alaina relax, Christopher moved his radius of kisses lower and lower, capturing and nibbling her nipples, causing Alaina to arch her back, before moving to her lower belly. Caught in the moment, Alaina barely noticed as Christopher's kisses moved to her thighs and then hovered over the small tufts of hair covering her womanhood. Finally aware of his intent, Alaina met Christopher's eyes and breathlessly whispered, "Wha…" a moment before he parted her hair and captured her with his mouth, causing a shock to emanate through her body, her head rolling back against the seat in rapture.

Christopher's tongue started a slow rhythm, flicking a nub she had been unaware of until this moment, occasionally tracing the whole of her womanhood with his tongue. Alaina's panting and moaning was uncontrollable, giving Christopher all the feedback he needed to quicken the pace of his tongue, pausing every few moments to suck on her. Alaina started to feel something build deep inside of her, almost like a tingling, but warm, spreading out to touch every corner of her being. Christopher kept his mouth in place and reached up to cup a breast in his hand, playing with Alaina's nipple. At this change, Alaina became frantic to reach whatever crest awaited her, and she thrust her hips almost instinctively toward Christopher, feeling her body tightening. The warmth overwhelming her body sent tremors throughout her limbs as she cried out in ecstasy and collapsed back onto the settee, opening her eyes to see Christopher's smiling face.

"You are a vision, my dear, more than I could have ever hoped. Now it is time for you to please me, if you want," he said, standing only briefly to remove his breeches, boots, and socks, never breaking eye contact with Alaina, her eyes still glazed with passion.

When his breeches lowered to reveal his manhood, fully erect, Alaina felt unsure of what was to happen next, but felt compelled to touch him as he had touched her just moments ago. As he settled between her thighs yet again, this time fully naked, Alaina reached out to take his blade of passion in her hand, amazed at the hardness. Leaning forward, Alaina tentatively came in toward his member, pulsing with heat, to place her lips on the tip. Christopher let out a groan of pleasure, as he regretfully placed a hand on her shoulder.

"My love, there will be plenty of time for that, but I shall have you now. I want to be man and wife, in truth. Do you trust me?"

A swift nod of her head gave him his answer. Alaina leaned back again, pulling Christopher with her. Christopher lowered his lips to Alaina's as he positioned himself at her entrance, moist and ready for him. He regarded her for a moment before he slowly entered the folds of her womanhood, pausing to take things slow, mindful that it was her first time. Alaina felt the pause and looked up at Christopher. He was looking down at her tenderly, as if waiting for something. All she knew was that it was not enough, and she placed her hands on his taut buttocks, pushing ever so slightly.

"I need… more," she uttered.

Christopher felt his restraint give way, as he plunged fully into Alaina, feeling her tightness envelop him with ease, the passage made wonderful by her readiness. Propped up on his arms, he paused only a moment before he started to move, slowly, coaxing her body into rhythm with his own. Alaina began to meet his hips thrust for thrust, tilting her own upward to allow him to fully sheath himself as he moved in and out. A familiar blossoming of heat started again from her lower belly as the joining of their bodies continued, the rhythmic motion increasing in speed. Christopher hungrily ensnared Alaina's mouth, each moaning their own pleasure until it seemed they could go no higher. Each of them saw the heavens, Alaina arching her back and Christopher spilling his seed deep within her womb.

The glow after was cozy and enveloping, the fire keeping their glistening bodies warm as they drifted to sleep in each other's arms.

A short time later, Alaina awakened to a chill on her back. After a mildly confused moment, she realized she was still mostly disrobed, her only protection against the cool air of the room her garters and the heat of Christopher's body. Snuggled against his side in what seemed a natural position, her leg draped over his and a hand on the center of his chest, Alaina could feel his rhythmic heartbeat and breathing under her fingers, and marveled at the preceding intimate encounter, wondering how long they may have been asleep. Trying not to wake Christopher, Alaina craned her head over her shoulder to see if the fire was still burning bright. The flame had dwindled to a flicker, providing only minimal heat for the room. As Alaina pondered if she should wake Christopher, for her bottom *was* quite chilly, she felt him stir next to her.

"Well, that was not exactly how I envisioned our wedding night. I thought I would at least be able to make it to the bedchamber," came Christopher's deep but groggy voice, a chuckle punctuating his statement, sounding almost incredulous. "I fear, though, I have no regrets about how anything happened."

Alaina giggled and placed her chin on Christopher's chest in order to meet his gaze before she responded in kind, "I am quite astonished we ended up in your study. From what little I knew about the whole event of becoming man and wife, it always seemed to involve a bed." She paused and chewed her lip, unsure of how much she wished to share about her current predicament with her new husband.

Christopher's brow furrowed a bit, "What is it, my dear? Are you sore? Was I too rough?"

"No, no, nothing like that. It was… wonderful, truly. I am just… well, a bit cold and in need of the facilities," came Alaina's response, embarrassment causing her words to fade as she spoke.

Christopher tried to contain his mirth and chastised himself for being so unconcerned with what his young wife might need after. "Well it seems we both got quite wrapped up in the moment. I can have you upstairs in just a moment, where we can draw a bath and warm up, and you can use the facilities."

Christopher stood up, stark naked, and swept Alaina into his arms before heading out the study door and walking to the stairs. Alaina was not quite sure if she would ever get used to the view of a naked man, even one such as her husband. In an attempt to hide her embarrassment, Alaina leaned her head closer to Christopher's neck, reveling in the comfort of such a position. Feeling his laughter more than hearing it, Alaina pulled her head to look at the one, who seemed to carry her up the stairs with ease, in confusion.

"Do not worry, you will get used to me naked. I do not much like sleeping or bathing in clothes. I have certainly committed the vision you present in those garters to memory, but I fear I am greedy and wish to see you just as you are at every opportunity. I hope you do not run and hide." Christopher seemed to sense the source of her embarrassment.

"Well, if that is what you say, husband, then I believe you. I do not mind seeing you naked anyhow. You are quite magnificent, my love." Alaina answered in kind, amazed at her new boldness and the comfort she felt nestled in her husband's arms.

Having crested the top of the staircase, Christopher took a sharp left and confidently strode down the short hall to a set of double doors. Using one hand to open them, he stepped inside what Alaina assumed to be the main bedroom. A large four-poster bed stood against the far wall, serving as the room's centerpiece. An area rug adorned the slightly rough wooden floors to provide warmth. A fireplace was situated directly across from the bed, and a copper tub was placed on the large hearth. A set of doors could be seen just beyond the firelight.

Christopher settled Alaina on her feet and whispered in her ear, "You should not tell me I am magnificent, it might just feed my ego. Now, the leftmost door is the privy closet. Take a few moments to do what you need, while I go get our luggage. Some smitten and distracted man left it outside on the front walk. I will be back to pour a bath that we can *both* enjoy."

Before Alaina could respond to the banter, Christopher had made his way out into the hallway. Alaina caught herself admiring his retreating form before mentally focusing on her very urgent need for relief, and scurried to the closet. She had her doubts about sharing a bath, but was intrigued by the prospect.

"I do not see why you had to put the whole pitcher of water down my back, you got water everywhere," Alaina mused as she crawled into bed next to Christopher, having finished mopping up the hearth with the towels Christopher had gathered for their bath. "I only had a little soap on my back, nothing to constitute a full dousing."

Christopher just shrugged his shoulders and flashed a puckish grin, clearly amused by the whole affair of the bath. Despite Alaina's protests, Christopher had insisted they share the bath, even offering to help her wash.

But what started as help ended in fondling and a fair amount of chicanery and then finally a wet floor. Alaina had been a little perturbed at first, but then decided to play a game of her own, slowly drying the hearth fully naked, even with Christopher's insistence that cleaning up the mess could wait. Alaina contemplated if she would even don a nightgown from the trunk they had brought along, while Christopher begged her to come to bed.

His long wait was rewarded though, when Alaina emerged from behind the screen in the corner of the room in a slip of fabric he could barely classify as a nightgown. The fabric was a dark color of some sort, difficult to exactly discern in the low light of the fire, and was almost completely sheer. The sleeves buttoned from her shoulder and gathered at her waist, in the style of a cotton nightgown. Embroidery of flowers seemed to wind around her body, starting from the shoulder and pooling at the floor. A large slit that ended at the top of the thigh allowed for free motion as the gown hugged Alaina's curves.

This particular slit was where Christopher found his hand drawn to, gently stroking the exposed thigh and roaming under the gown, moving ever closer to the cleft of her womanhood. Alaina nestled against his side once again, this time under the covers.

"Now, this is a bit more of what I envisioned," Christopher murmured against Alaina's hair. "Us actually in this bed to consummate the vows of love we took earlier today."

At that moment, the small clock on the mantel chimed the hour of twelve.

"It seems, my love, that we missed out on your vision for the day," Alaina stated, smiling against Christopher's chest.

"Oh well, in my mind it is still the day until we fall asleep," Christopher countered, his other hand having found her breast, barely concealed by the gossamer gown.

Alaina squirmed at his touch, feeling a tingling begin to grow once again between her legs. Her hand moved down Christopher's chest to slowly encircle his manhood, now hard and ready for her touch.

A little breathless she countered, "Well, we did fall asleep once already."

"I guess you are right, but we were not in bed. And, I do not want this day to end."

"Neither do I," came her response, and with that Christopher captured Alaina's mouth with his own, sliding his hand fully under her nightgown, ready to show her the heights of passion once more, amazed that he could feel so complete, so fulfilled.

CHAPTER 21

Time seemed to both slow down and flash by as the young couple reveled in their newly obtained unity. The hunting cottage, tucked into the back corner of Waverley, provided Alaina and Christopher privacy; privacy to explore, to learn, and to just be. Almost as if the weather predicted the first week's activities, the sky was gray and the environment was wet, inhospitable to do anything out of doors.

Alaina and Christopher took advantage of this time to explore the benefits of the large four-poster bed in the main bedroom, as well as what unique and evocative opportunities could be found around every corner or at least in every room, revisiting the study a few times to relive and even reinvent memories. On the settee, this time better equipped with a blanket to keep away the chill that followed, Alaina and Christopher shared themselves in body and in spirit, whiling away the hours talking after lovemaking. Many nights ended with Alaina and Christopher sharing a bath in front of the fireplace, their evening repast of simple rations, easiest for them to prepare without household help, lying mostly unfinished on a table beside the tub.

Time not spent exploring the more intimate moments of marriage was spent in quiet domesticity. Christopher cared for the horse at regular intervals, Alaina tidying while he did so, and each of them contributed to making or preparing food, hands wandering in the process. Hopes and dreams for the future were shared in whispers, with giggles or a serious mien. Both Alaina and Christopher were ever surprised and warmed by the depth, intellect, and vision of their other half, and yet also unsurprised by these qualities in their choice of partner.

When the rain cleared later in the week, Alaina and Christopher took a ride in the same phaeton they had used to traverse the path to the hunting lodge. It was a meandering journey to explore the outskirts of the estate, in part to enjoy the weather, and in part to better familiarize Alaina with the grounds.

To Alaina's surprise, they headed on the path away from the hunting lodge, deeper into the woods that surrounded it.

"Are we still on Rochester land?" Alaina questioned as they rounded another bend in the gravel path.

"Yes, my dear. Never fear I shall wander us into danger," Christopher smiled, soaking in both the bursts of sun through the dense canopy and his wife's nearness, her arm gently tucked inside his elbow as he steered the conveyance, her thigh pressed up against his own. They rode along a few minutes more before the trees began to thin and Alaina could see a field ahead.

Christopher spoke almost as if he anticipated what her question would be. "Alaina, my love, this might be my favorite part of the estate, although you have made a compelling case to move the hunting cabin to the top. There is little else I have seen to rival this, and we are here at the perfect time of day."

As Christopher spoke those words, the sunlight broke through the trees and Alaina beheld a wonderful sight. Lines of trees seemed to go on for miles, a fence to the right of the path surrounding what Alaina could guess was an orchard. So early in the season it was not the scent of ripe fruit that greeted them, but one of flowers and promise.

"Apples, I presume?" Alaina smiled.

"Apples," Christopher stated plainly, a boyish grin gracing his chiseled face. "I guess it is nothing so spectacular, but I used to come and spend much of my time here; it was peaceful, I guess, with shade enough to read under, and a ready snack depending on the time of year."

Alaina giggled and snuggled closer to her husband as he slowed the conveyance beside a gate to the orchard. Christopher regretfully disengaged himself from Alaina only for enough time as was required to step down and turn. Alaina followed quickly behind, making her way to the edge of the bench of the phaeton, where Christopher plucked her down by the waist as if she weighed nothing, setting her down in front of him so their bodies touched. They both seemed captivated by the other, their eyes locked and smiles shared.

Alaina's clean scent of roses drifted to Christopher, and he was reminded of an earlier encounter. "You know, when I handed you down from the carriage at Graham's estate, I could barely imagine anything so wonderful as this moment. I will admit though that you interrupted my thoughts, when you tested my reflexes that day."

"I tested *you?* I fear you caught me off guard. Kissing me and then never mentioning it again, immediately going back to the brooding bachelor. I dissected every comment, every closeness, every touch. I felt I may go mad," Alaina said, the teasing tone in her voice lightening her statement. "Besides, there is no way you imagined this very moment."

Christopher turned his head to the sky in laughter, thankful for his life, and the quick wit of his wife, before settling his eyes back on Alaina's face, seeing the love he felt reflected back at him. "You are quite right, my dear, but maybe a moment just like this one. I love you."

And with that he softly kissed Alaina, their bodies melting together as they stood in each other's arms, time standing still. When Christopher pulled back, it was with a pang of regret, but that was soon overshadowed by his excitement. Ignoring the knot in his belly, he clasped Alaina's hand in his own and pulled her through the gate of the orchard, excited to share his thoughts, his joy, and his life with her.

⁕

The sun was setting over the field when Alaina and Christopher made their way back to the hunting cottage, both content and at ease with the world. Christopher had shown Alaina the sprawling apple orchard, explaining the different varieties, which trees gave the best shade, and even showing her where he had fallen from one tree in search of the best apple, sure he had broken some bone when he had not. Alaina reveled in the opportunity to learn all there was to know about her husband, his joys, his memories, and even his hurts.

Christopher opened up about his childhood, his father who was almost never home, and how difficult it was when his mother, so happy and full of life, had turned so closed and melancholy after a rift had opened between his uncle and his father. Then Christopher's heart had broken even further when his mother died years later, putting his father into a constant state of drunken moroseness. After that, he saw little of anyone until Eton, where he met Graham and ultimately became a member of his family.

A common theme was Christopher's value of family and disappointment in his own. His parents had been absent much of his life, both emotionally and physically. Christopher's connection to his cousin had been severed by some rift between his father and uncle. The relationship with Charles had only healed in recent years, since both patriarchs had passed away. Where some people may have become bitter from experience, this seemed to make Christopher acutely aware of his own friends, some of whom were practically family, and their needs.

Alaina, by comparison, had little to lament in her life, save for the embarrassment she experienced early in her first season in society and some unkind remarks or insinuations, much of which her parents had shielded her from. Nonetheless, both listened to the other's hopes and fears, and goals and regrets, with equal empathy; they knew that better knowledge of each spouse was required for a happy union and future life full of joy.

Alaina sighed contentedly, the day beautiful and wonderful, with the man she loved. She snuggled closer to Christopher, safely ensconced under his arm as they made their way up the winding path through the trees.

As they approached the back of the hunting cabin, darkness was descending, and Alaina was immediately unsettled by the sight of what had been her and Christopher's safe haven the last few days. One of the windows on the second floor stood ajar, the slight breeze causing an eerie creaking of its hinges as if to warn the couple away. By the stables, Alaina saw that the earth had been disturbed by something resembling horse hooves, but the jumble of markings made it impossible to determine how many horses, or riders for that matter. The chestnut mare pulling the phaeton nickered as they approached and Alaina realized, distracted as she had been, that she had hardly noticed Christopher alert at her side. It seemed he was equally unsettled.

In silence, Christopher pulled the phaeton alongside the large stables, but not inside, and turned to Alaina with a finger to his lips, his stern expression almost lost in the receding light. Christopher climbed out and helped Alaina down, looping the reins of the horse quickly around a nearby fencepost, to allow for a quick getaway should they need one.

Coming around the stone pathway leading to the front door, Alaina followed closely and quietly behind Christopher. She glanced around his broad-shouldered torso as they walked, finding the door to the cottage carelessly ajar. Alaina shivered as they slowly approached the open portal.

Christopher motioned for her to stay put while he retreated inside, gone only a few moments before reappearing through that same portal. Alaina jumped, unaware until that moment of how afraid she was that someone other than Christopher would walk out, or that he would be hurt.

"Let's go." Christopher firmly clasped Alaina's hand, waiting for her feet to catch up to his as they quickly made their way back to their conveyance.

"What's wrong?" Alaina asked as she settled on the bench, Christopher pulling the horse and phaeton back onto the gravel path, this time toward the main manor house.

"I am not sure, but I certainly did not leave the window nor the door open. And to my knowledge, there is only one animal who can enter a latched portal." And with that they rode back to the manor house in quiet, hopeful of more security, but both upset that their seclusion and bliss had been violated just shy of a week into marriage.

"See that the cabin is cleaned and secured," came Christopher's voice from the lower level. Alaina could hear him talking to his butler, Baldwin.

"Yes, sir. Any idea who would have intruded?" came the even timbre of Baldwin, who had been the butler of Rochester estate for over a decade.

"Unfortunately, no, Baldwin. I will keep you apprised if I hear anything," Christopher sighed, sounding defeated.

Alaina descended the rest of the stairs, having paused midway to listen to the conversation not out of suspicion, but out of worry. She could almost see Christopher pinching the bridge of his nose in frustration and it made her heart lurch. As the early morning sun played along the wall during her descent, Alaina wondered how early Christopher had gotten up to see to the hunting lodge. Alaina knew her husband had been awake well past midnight, and she had awoken this morning to find him already gone from their bed.

The trip back to the manor house from the hunting cabin had been largely silent and tense. Arriving around the dinner hour, Christopher had been surprised, but a little thankful, that all their house guests, even their closest family and friends, had seen fit to return to their own homes. Alaina felt a pang of absence that her family was not there to greet her, but was also thankful for the peace after an unsettling evening.

Rounding the final corner into the front hall, Alaina saw Christopher, alone and staring off in the general direction of the cabin, his eyes glassed over with thoughts that Alaina could only begin to guess. At the sound of Alaina's footsteps, Christopher turned to meet his approaching wife and could not help the smile that came to his face, although it was a little less bright than usual.

Alaina's simple day dress of ice-blue damask complemented Christopher's more rugged riding attire that he had donned early in the morning to inspect the grounds, including the hunting cabin, for any signs of who had intruded on his estate. Even with that weighing on his mind, it was hard to ignore the vision his wife presented.

"Alaina, my dear, I hope you were able to get some restful sleep," Christopher said, his voice straining to sound normal and nonchalant, and failing exceedingly.

"Well, I think we were both restless last night, but after you left the bed early this morning, I think I got at least a couple hours of exhausted sleep. Where did you go?" Alaina asked, yawning uncontrollably as a sort of punctuation.

"Out to survey the property, just a little restless, considering," Christopher shrugged.

Christopher weighed how much of his concern he should share with his wife, considering how little he really knew at the moment. It was most likely a random passerby who had taken advantage of the vacant but warm place to stay, only to be scared away from the premises by their untimely arrival. Still there was something nagging about the lack of evidence he found in the house; he would have felt better to have come across a poor soul by the fire, surprised by an intrusion. In his mind, it had to be someone planning to not get caught, or at least someone with a lookout. The lack of light or warmth in any of the fireplaces was odd as well. Nothing seemed to sit right in Christopher's mind, but there was nothing he could put into words.

"Maybe once the groundskeeper takes another look at the cabin he will find something that gives us a clue about who is to blame for the break-in and why. Until then, there is nothing more we can do," Alaina offered, the words not providing much comfort to Christopher.

A half-smile came across Christopher's face, another failed attempt to act nonchalant. By all accounts, he had expected his young wife to be in hysterics. He knew his own mind was almost in such a state, and yet here she was, trying to comfort him. How truly blessed he was to find one with such strength, intelligence, and beauty, both inside and out. If he was so lucky to share a long-wedded life with Alaina, Christopher knew they would face times such as these just like now, as an unbreakable team.

In an effort to shake the pall hanging over them, Christopher took Alaina's hand and placed it through the crook of his arm, and he smiled down at her. "Shall we at least pass the time with a tour of the manor house? I am sure there are some corners you have yet to explore."

Alaina answered with a gentle squeeze of his arm, a soft warmth of pleasure creeping up from the neckline of her gown. "Well, I would be remiss in my duties as mistress of the house if I did not know every corner *intimately*."

"Well, let us begin then, shall we, my love?" Christopher winked and led them toward the west wing of the house, through the hallway under the grand staircase. The parlors on this side of the house were less used and left mostly alone by the staff except for weekly cleanings, a perfect situation for how Christopher planned on passing the day and distracting them both.

———————————⚘———————————

Through the remaining part of the morning, Alaina and Christopher explored much of the quiet side of the house, mostly parlors, studies, and libraries that stood unused. Along the way had been stolen kisses, and soft caresses that turned into passionate embraces, until both of them had been swept away, but thankfully not before closing the doors to the peacock parlor, at least that is what Christopher had dubbed it as a child. It was decorated by some previous marchioness in teals and purples, a screen painting of a group of peacocks taking part in a mating dance gracing the long wall of the room. Some of the furniture had been covered by dust cloths, and Christopher had hastily removed one to reveal a small sofa that Alaina and he promptly fell onto, their hands clasping at buttons in order to quickly free themselves of clothing.

A sharp rap sounded at the door, bringing Alaina and Christopher back to their senses, or at least a vague awareness of their surroundings. Christopher gritted his teeth as he pulled back from Alaina, who was quickly trying to repair her appearance.

Christopher looked down at Alaina after refastening his breeches and found her still struggling to right her chemise and bodice, the latter still gaping indecently in front, revealing thinly veiled peaks. Alaina's hair was also quite askew. His loins still hot and hard, Christopher steeled himself before plucking Alaina from the sofa by her waist and setting her on her feet in front of him. Christopher left little time for her to be confused before he turned her around and quickly righted her bodice, fastening buttons and smoothing the fabric of her skirts down over her petticoats, both of which he had been seeking to move out of the way before they were rudely interrupted. A quick kiss on her neck did little to ease the strain of the interruption, but it was hardly something he could avoid doing when presented the opportunity. As Alaina, having regained more of her senses, fixed the hair that had escaped from her gathered twist with some scattered pins, Christopher replaced the dust cloth and walked to the door, checking one last time that both of them were respectably clothed before opening the door, revealing Baldwin and the groundskeeper, Thomas.

"What is it?" Christopher blurted, not intending to sound brusque, but failing in his current state. He cleared his throat. "I take it you have found some information at the hunting cabin?" His tone softened a bit.

The groundskeeper glanced into the room to find Alaina standing only a few feet away, seemingly unsure of where exactly she should be. Baldwin's face remained staid as he recounted to Christopher, "Well, my lord, we found things, but we are not sure what it means."

"Well then, what is it, Thomas?" Christopher asked.

The groundskeeper shuffled his feet uncomfortably and looked at Baldwin in almost a plea for help.

Baldwin shuffled his feet, but his expression did not change. "Well, my lord, we are not sure how much you might want to share with the marchioness."

Alaina moved beside Christopher, and he responded, "Whatever you have to say, you can do so in front of my wife. It may put her mind at ease."

The couple let both men into the room, stepping to the side of the door. Baldwin and Thomas entered and stood in the center of the room while Christopher softly closed the door.

"Ok, out with it." Christopher stated evenly.

"Well…" Thomas started, "it is just that …" His stuttering frustrated the butler.

"It appears as though the only part of the cabin that was disturbed was the study. Nothing is missing, but the ledgers seem disturbed," Baldwin explained.

"The ledgers in the hunting lodge are old, at least by a few years. Why would anyone look at those?" mused Christopher, almost to himself, as Alaina watched quietly.

Both men shrugged, and Thomas finally found his words. "We have no idea. We hoped you may know."

"I have no further insights than you," Christopher responded, mulling over the implications of a person poking around his estates' financial records, even old ones; nothing pointed to a passing traveler in need of shelter. Turning toward the windows flanking the peacock painting, Christopher thought about what to do. After a moment, he turned back to both men.

"And no one has found a trace of anyone on the wider estate?" Christopher asked.

"No, sir. We have sent riders in all directions, but they have found nothing of consequence. Other than what was directly around the lodge, there were only a few sets of tracks, but they look like wildlife. Whoever these people are, they are exceptionally good at staying hidden in the woods and covering their tracks when they choose," Thomas replied.

"I will ride out again this afternoon to see what I can find. There has to be some trace of them on the grounds," Christopher sighed. "I appreciate both of your efforts."

Both men took the marquess's last statement as a dismissal and quickly shuffled out of the room. Christopher hung his head and raked his hand through his hair as Alaina moved to embrace him. As he wrapped his arms around his wife, Christopher whispered, "I am so sorry, my love."

Alaina pulled her head back to gaze at her husband, a quizzical frown playing across her face. "Why would you have a need to feel sorry?"

"My most fervent hope is to have you safely ensconced in our marriage bed for at least a month," a playful smirk half-touched Christopher's mouth. "But it seems I must root out whatever bandits may be galivanting around Waverley instead."

A huff escaped Alaina as she nuzzled once more into her husband's arms. "Dear husband, whatever this is, it is not your fault. And whatever is going on, we will face it together."

Chapter 22

Graham flicked the spittle from his coat and tried not to make a face of disgust as he listened to the warden, Jeremiah, explain how he thought 'Lord Percy' was wrongfully accused and how his heart ached to see him here in such a state.

"…Surely you's being family and all. I could'n think of a better person to let him write to…" Jeremiah prattled on as Graham smiled tightly.

Having had enough of the man, and having trouble stomaching the smell of the Newgate Prison, Graham tried to politely interject. "Mr. Jeremiah, I do appreciate the aid you have provided to my cousin; his letter seemed quite urgent. Percy's circumstances are dire. May I see him?" Graham's impatience only slightly colored his tone.

"Why, sure thing, my lord…" Jeremiah smiled, seemingly pleased with how the morning was going. Surely, with a high-bred lord showing up at Newgate, he thought he could gain something extra. "Well, I have been helping Lord Percy, these long weeks, and I learned of his innocence, taking extra time from me own and money from my pocket for better food for him. Percy said if you would come, I may get some compensation for me time and help."

Graham cocked an eyebrow and took out his heavy purse, counting out a few gold sovereigns and handing them to the warden, who practically licked his lips at the thought of the ale or food he could buy with that coin. It wasn't that Graham minded paying a man for his time, but he got the impression Jeremiah often preyed on family seeking to help a relative. Luckily, Graham had no issues where it came to the depth of his pockets, and his curiosity had been piqued by Percy's letter.

Jeremiah securely pocketed his money on the inside of his waistcoat, one that looked to be of the most recent fashion, Graham mused, standing in stark contrast to the surroundings of the prison, including even the warden's office they were currently occupying. Giving the pocket one last pat, setting the coins jingling, Jeremiah smiled a toothy grin at Graham and motioned to the door at the back of the office, which led to a set of alleyways and cell blocks. Graham followed Jeremiah, as he removed a large ring of keys and unlocked the door leading to a tight hallway just behind the warden's office. The ceiling was lower than the front entrance and office, causing Graham to lower his head and stoop his shoulders ever so slightly. He followed the warden closely as he led them through a maze of hallways.

Jeremiah seemed to prattle on endlessly, without need of input from Graham or pretty much anyone else, Graham surmised. Graham crinkled his nose at the increasingly musty air they encountered as they made their way through the bowels of the Newgate Prison. It was all Graham could do not to try and stifle the stench with his hand. Jeremiah seemed unconcerned.

One final turn, and Graham was met with another assault on the senses, this time in the form of sound. Large wooden doors flanked this hallway, and from the clanking, moaning and general din, Graham imagined them to be overfull of fetid prisoners from all walks of life, kept at some interminable interval awaiting trial, execution, or, in the lucky case, the end of their confinement. Jeremiah stopped about halfway down the hall, outside a door identical to all the others, and started the arduous task of searching the large keychain for the key to unlock the door.

Understanding the meaning of such an action and not wishing to truly meet his cousin face to face, Graham placed hands on Jeremiah's forearm to stop him. "Jeremiah, he may be my cousin, but I think anything that needs discussing can be said through the window on the door," Graham stated, motioning to the small, grated window at eye level, where a man of average height could converse without too much effort. Jeremiah moved to speak through the opening as he rapped soundly on the door.

"Hey, Lord Percy," Jeremiah almost bellowed to be heard over the noise of the hall. "I gots yer cousin here to speak wit' ye. He comes just as ye said he would."

Jeremiah stepped back from the door, seeming confident the occupant of the cell had heard him, and motioned for Graham to take his place. He walked a few paces down the hall, as if to give them privacy.

Graham moved closer to the door, but had to stand to the side to allow enough room for him to lean down and talk through the grate. The stench was not as bad as the rest of the cell block, but it still had a musty quality, causing Graham to involuntarily wrinkle his nose. He suddenly realized the reason for the warden's distance was not to provide them privacy.

"Dear cousin, I thought you might never come to see me," came a gravelly voice resembling Percy's normally snide tenor, punctuated by a cough. Clearly time spent at Newgate had taken its toll on the duke's cousin.

"I daresay, I did think more than twice about not coming," Graham said as he cocked his head to the side, gaining a small sliver of a view of his cousin through the grate on the door.

Percy's hair and beard were long and greasy, his eyes taking the wild look of a caged animal. His face did not appear as gaunt as Graham had expected, and the duke thought Jeremiah and the promise of a visit from a duke may likely be the cause. Graham could not see Percy's clothes, but he expected they would show the same level of filth as his hair and beard. Clearly there were limits to any warden's sympathy, even Jeremiah's.

Percy took a long pause before speaking again. "So, I see that either your curiosity or your good heart got the better of you," Percy said, a sly smile slowly curving his lips, despite the circumstances.

"Actually, cousin, I am afraid I am here against my better judgement. But, if I had to pick a reason, I would begrudgingly admit I was curious. Your message was quite cryptic," Graham quipped, as he removed a piece of parchment paper from his pocket, unfolded it and started to read, "*Dearest Cousin, My stay here at Newgate has taken its toll, please come at once. I also have information that you may need.*"

Percy chuckled for a few moments before a wheezy, rasping cough racked his body. Eventually, Graham heard Percy take a drink of something and clear his throat, before he continued, an edge in his voice. "I had hoped that you would have some care for my welfare."

"What do you want, Perceval?"

"What anyone in my situation would want, to be free. And that can always be achieved with money."

"And what would that serve me?" Graham asked, aware that helping Percy would be to his own detriment.

"Well, I hear you are on the outs with Lady Alaina," Percy stated.

"We are no longer courting, if that is what you mean, but there are no ill feelings. That fact has been known for some time, but given your incarceration, it is curious how you came by it," Graham responded.

"Lady Alaina did say something of it herself, but I did not believe her. However, there is someone who religiously wrote to me of the outside world, someone who I thought would champion my defense," Percy continued cautiously. "That stream of letters halted entirely, until a couple of weeks ago."

"You are making no sense. Maybe the prison cell has taken more than your good health," Graham said, but Percy continued on with his story, seeming to not notice the duke's interjection.

"And when the letters started once more, they spoke of a scheme involving someone you hold dear."

"I told you, Alaina and I are nothing more than friends, if that."

"Yes, I know the sting of rejection, *again*, must chafe for you, but the lady is not the center of the scheme, though… she is involved," Percy said, a chuckle rising in his throat once more. "This time because she is entangled with your best friend."

"Are you saying the marquess is in danger?" Graham railed, facing the opening of the cell door to find his cousin's grotesque smile through the small opening in the door. He did not wait for an affirmative answer from Percy; the smile told him. "Who is the source of this information?"

"Well, I am sure you would like to know that, would you not?"

The worry and rage that had been boiling just below the surface for Graham bubbled up, and his hand shot through the small opening, barely clearing the grate. He found purchase on the front of Percy's shirt, pulling him flush against the door. "You had better tell me who is to blame, or I shall ensure you are moved to even more unpleasant accommodations."

Jeremiah turned at the sound of the scuffle and made to advance toward the cell, but Graham released Percy and stepped back from the door, waving the man off, hoping the guard would allow Percy and him to finish their conversation. Jeremiah held his place, though a frown marked his face.

Graham could hear a grunt from the cell and Percy's gravelly voice was the first to break the silence. "Temper, temper, Graham. You really should have a better hold of yourself."

Graham's next statement came out as more of a growl. "Percy, you had better start talking or I will talk to the warden. Now, who is it that is behind this scheme?"

"I will admit that I do not know who the ringleader is, but Lady Barbara wrote to tell me how she had been lured in by the wrong kind of person, and convinced to participate, until one evening she was knocked unconscious, waking to find a void in her memories," Percy explained, sounding as if he may spit from anger. "Even in her letters I could hear her mewling about being the wronged party, even as I sat here in this cell, cast off by her as soon as I found myself in trouble."

Graham chose to ignore his cousin's self-pity. "Has Lady Barbara recovered her memory?"

"Cousin, you may have been able to get some information out of me with threats, but I fear additional information will cost you. See, you have a need and so do I."

Graham chuckled. "I fear you have overplayed your hand, Percy. I am a perfectly free man, and can glean what information I need from her." Graham turned to Jeremiah and bellowed so as to be heard over the din, "Warden, I fear my time with my cousin has come to an end, can you see me out?"

Percy extended his hand through the opening in the door, and yelled as Graham strode past the warden, who practically ran to keep up with the duke. "Cousin, where are you going? What about me? I give you everything you want, and you turn your back on me! You will pay for this!"

The way out of the prison was a blur of turns and babbling from Jeremiah, who was late to realize the folly of his association with Percy. The only thing clear to Graham was that he needed answers!

⚜

"What was that, my dear?" Alaina asked, embarrassed, her mind having wandered to their intimate activities that morning on the east side of the house in their newly christened parlor, this one decorated with peonies.

She and Christopher had taken to having their morning meal on that side of the house over the past couple of weeks, in part for the view and the early morning light, and in part for the privacy of the room, far from the hustle and bustle of the heart of the manor. This morning had been no exception, their breakfast and tea cold and long forgotten as they shared a tryst on a nearby settee. It was lucky they had righted their appearances well before the kitchen maid came to clear away the hardly touched breakfast tray.

"I would ask about your daydream, but from the look on your face it seems we are both remembering the same event," Christopher responded, looking at Alaina over the records of the Rochester estates spread out on the large desk at the center of his study. "I was asking if you would fancy a ride this afternoon; we will keep it at a relaxed pace, just something to enjoy the outdoors. But we could forgo it in favor of other activities."

Alaina, who was seated near an open window facing the grounds, was seriously tempted by another afternoon of lovemaking, but desperate for some fresh air after a week of rain. She could smell the roses and yearned to be outside.

"I fear if we waste this beautiful day, the world may see fit to treat us to another week of summer storms," Alaina teased as she met her husband's eyes, losing a little of her resolve to make it outside today.

"I feel you are quite right, my dearest Alaina," Christopher remarked, closing the book he had been pouring over and standing in a quick motion, making his way around the desk and over to Alaina. Christopher offered his hand as assistance and Alaina smiled affectionately as she placed her hand in his and stood.

As Alaina and Christopher were making their way to the door of the study, intending to make it to the stables after a change of clothes, Baldwin came through the door in a haste, almost colliding with the couple.

"I beg your pardon, my lord, my lady," the butler hurriedly stated, taking a step back to the door of the study, acting a bit chagrined at his haste.

"No apologies necessary, everyone is in one piece, Baldwin," came the quick reply from Christopher. "What has you moving with such purpose?"

"Well, my lord, a missive came from London, sealed with the duke's family crest," Baldwin held out the letter to Christopher, where it was quickly plucked and opened.

Alaina and Baldwin waited as Christopher read the note, no one bothering to speak as they watched a frown mark Christopher's face. The hush in the room stretched until Alaina could take no more. "What is it, Christopher?"

"I am not sure," he started to reply. "The person who wrote this letter claims to be Graham's steward, but there is no signed name."

Alaina huffed in frustration. "Well, what does the letter say?"

Christopher looked up from the letter and looked at Alaina. "It says Graham has been in an accident, and is asking for me in London immediately."

Alaina reached out and snatched the letter from Christopher's hands, quickly reading it herself. "But there are no details! How grave is this accident? When did it happen?"

Christopher reclaimed the letter and took one of his wife's hands and squeezed. "Darling, please calm down. I am sure the letter was written in haste. But I fear that means our newly wedded bliss will be cut short. I have to go to London tonight, or really as soon as a horse can be readied."

"Just you?!" Alaina exclaimed. "You think I would let you go alone? Who knows what state Graham is in at the moment. If anything, I can provide an extra set of hands and should be there for Eleanor and Georgiana."

A sigh escaped Christopher's lips. "My dear Alaina, I fear it may not be safe out on the road later in the evening. I would not want to put you in danger. Besides, I need to move fast, and that is best done alone on horseback."

"And it is better if I stay here, alone?"

Christopher sighed. "It is the best option. I have men I can set to guard the house. I cannot guarantee your safety on the road."

Alaina took a deep breath, and calmed her voice, changing tact. "And you would take such a risk? Like all of your early morning rides alone? I will not have you taking such a journey without me. Besides, you could need me once you get to London."

A half-smile touched Christopher's lips. "I fear I will always need you, my love."

"So, then it is settled." Alaina quickly stated.

"What is settled?"

"I am going with you to London, but I shall have to follow along in the carriage," Alaina responded. "I would not think to slow down your pace, but it would not be too difficult to follow."

"But..." Christopher started, but was quickly interrupted.

"But what?" Alaina said, allowing no time for further argument. "It is the perfect solution; we can both go to London to see to Graham's welfare, and you have no need to fear for my welfare if I take the carriage. Like you said, we must be on the road as soon as we can; I will head up to pack a few things to see us through the week."

Alaina quickly was out the door and up the stairs before Christopher even turned to Baldwin to make plans for their last-minute trip to London.

Christopher gathered Alaina's face in his hands as he gave her a parting kiss. "I will only be a few paces in front of you, darling, in case anything should happen."

"Nonsense! I shall not have you slowing your pace for me," Alaina admonished, her breathy response lacking weight. "You seem to have a sufficient retinue accompanying me to keep me safe on the trip to London, but I fear that leaves you sorely lacking."

Christopher shook his head. "A lone rider gains little attention, a conveyance, however…"

This earned a huff from Alaina. "Fine, fine, you have made your point. It will be close to midnight when we arrive in London at this rate, and I am anxious to be on our way."

With a final peck from Christopher on the tip of her nose, the marquess stepped back to close the carriage door. "I will see you in London, dearest."

"I will see you in London, and we will see that your friend is well tended to," Alaina reassured Christopher before a final, "I love you."

"I love you," Christopher repeated before finally tearing himself away from his wife. There was a niggling feeling down the back of his spine as he turned toward the groom holding his horse and quickly mounted it. Turning only once more to salute the carriage, he set off down the front drive. The faster he and Alaina got to London, the better he would feel, his worry for his friend at the forefront of his mind.

Alaina watched as the sun, now low in the sky, skipped through the trees, playing upon the seats of the carriage to match the galloping pace of the horses. Once more she stuck her head out of the side window and found the familiar form of her husband, now far down the road, almost out of sight. In the fading light, Alaina found it difficult to assure herself of his continued well-being, but she found solace in knowing that he did not turn back and thus was safely on his way.

Resettling herself on the cushions of the carriage, she closed her eyes and tried to calm her thoughts. As much as she had pushed to convince Christopher that she would be fine on her journey, the pit of her stomach was a roiling mess, and she tried once more to convince herself everything would be fine. Alaina took a few deep breaths and tried to focus on the pounding of the hooves and the swaying motion of the conveyance, hoping to find herself in London when she next opened her eyes.

———————— ❧ ————————

Graham banged on the door of the Finch townhome, hoping his second round of knocking would not go unanswered. After rushing home, Graham had pressed his mother for information on Lady Barbara and her family, not least of which was where they lived. He needed answers before leaving for the country to warn Christopher and Alaina.

Graham finally heard a click sound from behind the door, and the portal was pulled slightly inward to reveal an older, stylishly dressed woman, exhaustion clear in her eyes.

Before the duke could open his mouth, the lady spoke tersely. "Who are you?"

Graham executed a shallow bow as he took off his hat and introduced himself. "I am the Duke of Ashford, my lady. I was hoping to speak to Lady Barbara Finch."

The lady did not open the door wider, but Graham watched as her eyes widened and then narrowed. "She is not receiving visitors."

Graham watched as the lady moved to close the door. Desperate, Graham stuck his boot in the door and tried once more. "Please, my lady, I would not come if it were not of grave importance. I feel Lady Barbara may have information to help a friend of mine. I promise to only stay a few minutes."

"I fear my daughter no longer has certain memories. She has been recovering from a fall and a hard hit to the head," came the woman's response.

"I had heard of her misfortune, and I am sorry. I hope she recovers fully," Graham stated, hoping to placate the elder Lady Finch. Unsure if it would help him gain entry, Graham offered a bit more, only fibbing slightly. "My cousin, Percy, told me of her troubles, and wished me to check on her."

Lady Finch sighed and pulled the door inward. "Like I said, Barbara remembers little of the last couple of months. It pains me to admit that I have let her keep up some correspondence with that criminal, no offense intended, your grace. It has been the only thing that has raised Barbara's spirits as she recovers. And I am sure she would want to be of help to you. Please come in."

Graham stepped inside and was immediately surprised to find the interior of the home to be in stark contrast to the sunny day outside, the foyer and hallways almost pitch dark, with the only points of light the sconces on the wall.

Lady Finch only paused to close the front door before making her way silently down the dark hallway. With no invitation, Graham assumed he was supposed to follow and fell in behind the lady as he tried to make polite conversation. "I fear I was terribly abrupt in my greeting. I assume you are the lady of the house."

"I am, my name is Lady Jane Finch, and my husband is Lord Samuel Finch. We have had seldom few visitors with my daughter still convalescing, so please excuse the state of the house," was the woman's response as she made her way into a room almost as dark as the rest of the house. Only small slivers of light streamed in through openings in the curtains.

Graham's eyes adjusted, allowing him to see a slight figure near one of those openings. Upon closer inspection, the woman in question was in her nightclothes, a robe providing sufficient modesty.

"Barbara, dear, I hope you have the energy for a visitor. He comes with word from Percy," Lady Jane said softly, gaining the attention of the one by the window.

Lady Barbara turned from the window, and Graham watched as a look of shock and then anger crossed her face briefly before she turned a wane smile on her mother. "Mother, could you see that our guest has tea and biscuits. I am so *thankful* he is here to bring me news of Percy. I would like to show him gratitude for his visit."

The duke was astounded when Lady Jane quickly acquiesced to her daughter's request, leaving them alone in the room.

With a strength belying someone unwell, Lady Barbara spoke first. "What do you want? I know it is not to tell me how your cousin pines for me. He was quite rude in his last letter, so much so that I burned it; I could not have my parents reading such filth. So, I will have it out now."

Graham mulled over his approach for only a moment, just now realizing he had come to Lady Barbara's family townhome without much of a plan. "Percy told me you are knowledgeable about some scheme that puts my friends in danger."

"You mean Lady Alaina and her husband the marquess?"

"You know that is who I mean," Graham gritted between teeth, his earlier interaction with Percy making his patience short.

"Well, I fear that my memory is quite *unreliable*. One minute I can remember something and the next I cannot," Lady Barbara said benignly, before she continued, "But there are *ways* to help it along."

Graham shook his head and scoffed. "Well, if it were not for the lover's tiff you are currently in the middle of, I would say you and Percy were made for one another."

"We are not!" Lady Barbara burst, a moment later holding her head in her hands as if in pain. "We may have been once, long ago, but not anymore. Now if you have nothing to offer, I will insist you leave immediately."

Graham looked at the woman, remembering the torture she had wrought on Alaina, and the trouble she caused with Percy at Ashford, and reluctantly removed his remaining change purse. He was perturbed to have the need for so many bribes in one day. A loud *thunk!* sounded as he tossed the coin purse onto the table next to Lady Barbara, who finally removed her head from her hands to look for the offending sound. She hefted the coin purse deftly in her hand and then turned her eyes back to the duke.

"So, you want to know who would have it in for your friend and his new wife?"

"Yes," Graham snarled, "I hope you have sufficient motivation now."

A sly smile crossed Lady Barbara's face. "Yes, I do believe I have remembered enough."

A pause still hung in the air when Graham became inpatient. "Well, who is at the center of things?"

"Christopher's cousin, silly," Lady Barbara huffed, "It seems like every son of a second-born is out for as much money and power as they can get, and at any cost. It helps to motivate them if they are in a bit of debt. My brother finds them easy targets for his own schemes. It is easy to lure them into a game or two to start, and then they can't stay away. Money is a powerful motive for anyone."

"So what, Charles is in a bit of debt to your brother, Richard. Why would he want to hurt Christopher? How could he even make that a reality?" Graham questioned.

"I told you *why*, but how may cost you extra," Lady Barbara spit.

Graham felt a rage build up, but he kept it leashed, only allowing himself a single threat. "I suppose I could take it to the authorities that you were in league with Percy and Charles and are an accomplice to their wrongdoings. That I found you trespassing on my estate, setting fire to my property. Vandalizing and causing consternation among my tenants. The list of offenses is impressive, but I had it in my mind that you were merely a pawn. I had thought that with Percy in Newgate, we would all be safe."

"There is only your word!" Lady Barbara practically shouted once more, wincing as she did so. "Besides, I am a victim of a crime in my own right."

"You will find that my word can count for a lot when it is lent to the right ear. My family has a long history with the crown. If you doubt me, so be it, but I dare you to test me,"

Graham stated coldly, his voice flat and direct. "Was it Christopher's cousin who attacked you?"

"What?! No!" Lady Barbara exclaimed. "Or at least not that I can remember. The last I recall was meeting him to discuss our future, and then nothing…"

Graham watched as Lady Barbara stared off at nothing, as if trying to recall what had happened, but he was impatient for answers. "So, you have not explained how Charles would be able to hurt Christopher and Alaina."

"You may have only yourself to blame."

"What is that supposed to mean?"

Lady Barbara chewed her lip, as if contemplating whether the duke would see his threat through, but then she spoke. "When was the last time you saw your family's ring? The one with the crest? How easy would it be to lure them away from the safety of their manor home with that seal?"

For the second time that day, Graham found himself disengaging from a conversation without proper farewells. He barreled through the dark hallway and foyer, taking little note of Lady Jane Finch as they passed one another. Graham numbly made his way out the door and onto his horse, as he set a course for the country and hoped it was not too late.

❧

Crack!

Alaina bolted upright in the carriage and struggled to understand her surroundings as the conveyance careened to the left and crashed onto its side at an awkward angle. Alaina landed against the window, her arms barely providing any cushion for her abrupt stop, her head knocking against the pane of glass.

As Alaina struggled to keep the impending darkness in her head at bay, she heard scuffles outside of the carriage, which was now completely cloaked in darkness, and listened to a bevy of short pistol *pops!* The door opposite Alaina was snatched open and a lantern filled the inside with light. Alaina attempted to scramble toward the door closest to her, absolutely sure the person with the lantern was not there to help. A piercing pain ripped through her head at the motion, making her woozy, as her hand feebly tried the door handle, and she felt her hair yanked back.

"You will not escape so easily," the voice rasped, close to her ear. Her mind worked overtime as the familiarity of the voice tickled it. "Now, where is your husband?"

Alaina tried to turn and push away from her attacker, but the man held the nape of her neck in an iron grip, and she whimpered in pain, "I do not know where my husband is."

"Nonsense! You know exactly where he is; it was supposed to be him traveling to London," came the voice once more, a shiver making its way up Alaina's spine.

"I am telling the truth," Alaina stated, hoping her confidence would keep Christopher from this man's pursuit. "I am the only one traveling to London."

A growl escaped the man, and he moved to exit the teetering carriage, dragging Alaina behind him. However, she was not to be so easily taken. She reached out to find some purchase, kicking her legs in an attempt to be free.

"Enough!" came the roar from the man, still not clear in Alaina's vision. He came around with his other hand with vicious intent, driving the butt of his pistol down on her head, the lantern hanging from his arm the only point of light before darkness closed in on her.

Chapter 23

Christopher stood up in his stirrups and attempted to stretch ever so briefly before resettling low in the saddle, the breakneck pace of his horse kicking up clumps of earth as they raced down the road in the darkness. He glanced back to find the road empty, which was not surprising, as he had lost sight of Alaina hours ago. Christopher had been adamant they stay close, but Alaina had been most insistent that his pace not slack for her. His sole reassurance in that regard was the men he had left to protect her. Surely, no lone brigand would be able to overcome them. Shaking his head and clearing it of worry, the marquess refocused on the road ahead of him, and almost missed a lone rider traveling at an equally hectic pace before it was too late.

Both of the riders brought their horses up short, and barely missed the other, causing each man to slow his pace. Christopher wiped the sweat from his brow and sought to quickly apologize to the other rider before heading on toward London once more, when recognition dawned on him.

"Graham!" Christopher exclaimed, as he gulped air and came to a complete stop.

"Christopher?" came the duke's response, the other man equally out of breath.

"What on earth are you doing out of bed, let alone riding like a banshee at this time of the night?" Christopher questioned, his brain not computing finding his friend on the road.

"I could ask the same of you, I guess. I was coming to see to you and Alaina's welfare," Graham responded.

"We were coming to see to yours. According to the letter, you had a nasty accident, but I can see we have been deceived."

"And for that I am sorry… It seems your cousin has a need for funds and found a way to purloin my ring to lure you away from home. Who knows what he intended?" Graham replied.

Christopher was given no time to react before a faint echo found them. *Pop! Pop! Pop!*

Without another word to Graham, Christopher took off in the direction of the sound, back toward Alaina, and prayed that his ears had deceived him; he had been convinced that his nagging worry had been unfounded, and yet now his fear for his wife made bile rise in his throat.

Christopher was quick to realize that another horse was galloping beside him, his friend needing no explanation to follow. It seemed an eternity that Christopher and Graham rode back toward Waverley, around several bends, before they came upon a fallen tree. Each rider brought his horse to a halt and picked gingerly around the massive trunk splayed across the road. They found their way around the stump that, even in the dark, seemed to be cleanly cut at the base. As they found their way to the other side, both men's eyes settled on the carriage and a collection of bodies, the horses still tied and tangled within the branches of the tree, but otherwise unharmed. Only a faint light shone from the post of the driver's seat, and a soft groan could be heard.

Christopher and Graham quickly dismounted and located the man, the driver, stuck under the front corner of the conveyance.

"Nicholas, what happened?" Christopher rushed into questions, as he and Graham gently moved the man out from under the carriage, taking care not to move him too quickly. Graham stepped away to survey the interior of the coach and rushed back to Christopher.

"I am sorry, sir. The tree fell in the road and before we knew it, a cloaked rider was on top of us," the driver stammered. "The man had a couple of pistols and dispatched with those of us that moved to stop him. And then he dragged Alaina with him. The last I saw they were headed into the woods."

"Alaina is not inside," Graham interrupted, confirming Christopher's worst nightmare. At a quick nod from Christopher, the duke moved to check on the other men around the carriage.

Christopher stood and raced to the tree line. "Alaina! Alaina!" He turned this way and that, frantically searching for any sign of his wife and her assailant, but saw nothing amiss, and heard no sounds out of place. He ran around the carriage in his search, his breath ragged, and eventually came to rest near the upturned wheels of the carriage. Christopher's throat was hoarse from his yelling, and a feeling of helplessness threatened to close in around him.

After a few moments, Christopher felt someone take hold of his arm and he turned to find Graham. "Christopher, I cannot see any sign as to which way they might have gone. I fear that to go out into the woods alone will be fruitless and dangerous."

Christopher was loath to admit it, but his friend was right. It was his first instinct to go after Alaina at once, but without knowing what he exactly faced with his cousin, or where they had gone, he felt that idea could lead to an unpleasant end for both him and his wife. At the very least, it could end with a fruitless search and precious lost hours. Eventually, Christopher nodded in agreement, and Graham released his arm.

"Nicholas is the only one to survive," Graham said, his tone bleak. "And he needs medical care. Not to mention, we are sitting ducks ourselves. We can regroup at Waverley, and recruit some more men to help. I promise we will recover Alaina and make sure all of those responsible pay for their wrongdoing."

A grunt came from the marquess, and he returned to the driver. "Nicholas, the duke and I will get you help. I fear moving you without a proper litter, but I do not want to leave you here. Do you think you can sit in a saddle?"

Nicholas pushed his way onto his elbows. "My lord, I think I can sit on a horse, but I fear your delay in helping me may see some harm come to the marchioness."

Christopher sought to allay the man's fears as well as his own. "The duke and I know who took her, and I believe they will keep her alive to get what they want. If we get back to Waverley, I can send out men to see where they have gone."

Graham had broken the horses free from the coach and was bringing one back for Nicholas. A fair amount of effort from the marquess and his friend saw the driver atop the horse, and they made their way to Waverley at a slower pace than before. As they traversed the road, Christopher kept his eyes sharp for any sign of people in the woods, but only inky blackness met his eyes.

Alaina slowly opened her eyes and tried to focus on the lit taper in front of her, unable to focus on all of her surroundings just yet. Her head throbbed, due to the blow from her assailant, but she was intent to take in her surroundings. The candle sat atop a desk, which she realized was actually the desk in the study of the hunting lodge. Alaina was astounded at how long she had remained unconscious. Without moving too much, she realized the settee had been moved toward the desk, almost to rest alongside it.

From her position on her side, facing the front of the desk, Alaina could see nothing more than the single candle and a faint outline of books on the shelves behind the desk.

Afraid to move quickly, unsure of her physical state and loath to alert her captor as to her alertness, Alaina slowly turned from her side to her back. She took note of her tied wrists and ankles, and an ache in her hip. Alaina's head throbbed as she moved, the small exertion making her aware of how vulnerable she was. Even if she could somehow get her ankles untethered, Alaina doubted she would make it very far before collapsing again. She hoped that with some time, her head would cooperate.

Moving just her eyes, Alaina probed the room, seeing mostly shadows, but discerning that no one else was with her. It was bizarre and terrifying to be in the lodge under the current circumstances, when Alaina held such fond memories of her early wedded days with Christopher here.

Just outside the door, she could hear a pair of footsteps, each one pacing rapidly, as two men argued.

"I told you that the marchioness was the only one in the carriage!" Even with a yell, Alaina could determine this was the man who kidnapped her, and yet she could not place the voice.

"She is not who I was aiming to surprise! I swear this scheme finds folly at every turn," came a lower voice, muffled by the door.

"Well, you can still use her as a bargaining chip."

"With someone well on his way to London? It will take days! And the servants are bound to notice someone taking up residence here."

"If you had just asked the marquess for funds when you had the chance…" came the first voice, in a more pleading tone.

"Silence! I have told you before, he did not acknowledge my request for an audience," came the second man, his voice sounding clearer as he walked toward the door of the study. "Now, I am going to check on our injured marchioness. You had better hope that she does not succumb to her injuries, or it will be the gallows for the both of us, if we are lucky."

The last statement came to Alaina clearly, and her brain was slow to put the pieces together as Christopher's cousin crossed the threshold. Alaina's eyes went wide with shock and her heart hammered in her ears. Alaina had always pushed her feelings of unease away, but it turned out Charles was more dastardly than she had ever imagined.

"Charles?" Alaina squeaked out, almost unaware of speaking out loud.

Christopher's cousin started at her exclamation, not having expected an awake prisoner, but he recovered quickly. "Why, yes, my dear. I was worried that Felton had delivered such a blow, you might never wake up, giving me little hope to barter with your husband. But I am relieved to see he was not so rough."

Again, Alaina's mind was slow to catch up. "Felton?"

Charles huffed, seemingly annoyed as he walked behind the desk, took a seat and stated, "Yes, Felton, Mr. Reid, my *helper*, if you will. I have always said he was too hot-headed to deal with matters such as these. I do apologize for his rash action."

"Rash action?" came a voice from the door of the study, and Alaina recognized Felton Reid's voice, his tone even more slimy and malevolent than it had been on their first meeting. "I fear, *my lord,* it is just the fact that I did not happen upon the marquess that has you upset. I believe the word you used was folly."

Alaina heard Felton walk into the room and round the desk, where he entered into her vision, the look in his eyes more sinister than she could imagine, the edge in his voice clear and dangerous.

"Come now," Charles rejoined with a half-chuckle. "I was only saying that in jest, truly; your plan worked out just as well as any."

A silence fell upon the room as the two men stared each other down, and Alaina felt that she was stuck inside a powder keg with the fuse already lit. It was an effort to remain still, Alaina's head throbbing uncontrollably as she strived to stay in a more upright position. Eventually, Charles turned to her. "Felton has ambition to start his own trade of contraband or something, and I want to rise above the position that was purchased for the cast-offs of the Kendall family."

Felton was fast in his reproach. "Ye swindled me into thinking I could make a profit selling goods from your trading company under the table. It was only after I had *dealt* with a few of your business partners that I found out yer business was little more than a sham!"

"It could be more if I had even a fraction of the money of a marquessate!" Charles bellowed.

"It could be more if you decided to not piss away yer money on gambling!" Felton returned Charles's ire.

"That is a mere pittance of what we could earn!"

"We?! What about ye and the lady?" Felton screamed and moved closer to Charles, leaning over his chair in a show of physical power.

Alaina watched as Charles's demeanor changed, softening under Mr. Reid's pressure. "Can we just agree that Lady Alaina is a way to satisfy both our needs?"

Felton took a deep breath and stood once more, turning his glare on Alaina before asking. "How long until we send word to the marquess?"

"I figure we can wait until the morning to deliver a note as to the terms. By then, Christopher will be worried enough to accede to any of our demands and should be in London," Charles asserted.

The fog that had plagued Alaina since waking up in the study had started to lift enough for a well-placed glare. "You both are despicable. Why, you are no better than Percy," Alaina quipped.

This time it was Charles's turn to stare daggers at Alaina. "My dear, if you value your life, you will not compare me to Percy."

At this, Felton hurled a taunt. "Still smarting from being the second choice of Lady Barbara?"

"Enough!" roared Charles, and Felton and Alaina fell obediently silent.

A thud sounded somewhere upstairs, causing the party of three to jump in unison. When silence followed, the two men shared a look. Charles nodded, and Felton left the room to investigate. Alaina met Charles's eyes with an unspoken question, and he shrugged. "This old place makes the strangest noises, but one can never be too careful. I am sure Mr. Reid will return shortly. Your husband will receive our demands in the morning and, if he agrees, your captivity should be short. We shall endeavor to at least act civilly."

Obviously, her fate was tied to Charles's good graces, and she decided a tight smile and mute nod would best suffice.

"You never could make it through a window soundlessly," Graham stated flatly. Sneaking into the hunting lodge window was what he least expected from his impromptu trip to the country. They had precious few moments to prepare once they had seen Nicholas to a bed and sent other servants to check on the remaining staff with the coach, though there was little hope for them. Christopher had been restless and convinced Alaina had to have been taken somewhere close, and a quick ride found the occupied hunting lodge.

Soon enough, the measured creak of the staircase sounded, almost too slow to pick out from the other noises the old house made. Graham and Christopher were in the bedroom across from the landing and had, in unspoken concert, moved toward the door, keeping to the large rug under the four-poster bed to avoid noise. With Christopher against the wall next to the door, and Graham in the corner with the door's hinges, they waited as they listened to the explorer check the first bedroom, and then the second.

The door handle was tested on the bedroom of their choice, and as it was slightly turned, and the door slowly opened, Christopher was quick to cock and aim his pistol directly at the one who entered within a split second. Graham followed up behind the intruder, the sound of the gun cocking close to the man's ears. Christopher was surprised to recognize Felton Reid, Charles's manservant, butler, and man of miscellaneous other talents, it seemed, but he quickly recovered his aplomb.

"Alright, Mr. Reid, where is Alaina? Tell us and we might let you live," Christopher growled, low and guttural.

Felton started, as if surprised to find anyone in this creaky house, and Christopher was happy that they had maintained their element of surprise. Felton held his silence, and Graham pressed the muzzle of his pistol to the base of the manservant's skull.

"My friend asked you a question," Graham asserted. So intent were the friends on their own weapons that they failed to see Felton's own weapon until it was too late.

Bang! Bang! Two shots rang from upstairs, sending Charles and Alaina almost clear out of their seats. Alaina's head had cleared some, but her attempt to stand in reaction to the gunshots made her lightheaded and, feeling the weight of her head and ankle tethers, she soon sat back down. Charles seemed more capable and intent on an explanation for the commotion he heard, and was only steps out of the door to the study when he was stopped short.

"Christopher? Thank heavens you are here!" Charles quickly pivoted, from captor to captive. "My man has gone off the rails and has been keeping me hostage in an attempt to extort money from you, my dear cousin. He even set a trap for Alaina."

"Liar!" Alaina exclaimed, but Christopher was already a few steps ahead of his cousin.

Christopher pointed his pistol directly at the end of Charles's nose, pushing him back into the study, and assessing the scene around him. An ugly bruise marred the perfection of Alaina's temple, a raised welt partially disfiguring her face.

"Are you ok, my dear?" Christopher asked, not changing the sights of his gun, and continuing his advance on Charles. In a few steps, Charles was forced to again sit in the chair at the study's desk, this time with none of the smugness.

Alaina met her husband's eyes with elation and fear and touched her fingers lightly to the contusion, wincing. "I am as ok as I can be. It hurts, but I am otherwise unharmed."

Assured of his wife's health, Christopher turned his eyes back to his cousin, not once moving his pistol off its target. "Lucky for you, cousin, my wife appears to have survived your manhandling with just a bump and bruise. Otherwise, you would already be dead."

"But it was not me!" came Charles's plea, but before Alaina could present another counterargument, they all heard a bang of the door against the stopper and the subsequent ricocheting vibrations of the large wooden panel.

"You bastard," came a snarl from Mr. Reid, who was resting on the door jamb for support as blood slowly dripped onto the floor, seeping through his jacket.

Christopher surveyed the man, amazed he had survived the altercation upstairs. He had been unconscious only moments earlier. His right arm hung unnaturally at his side, blood streaming from his fingertips, and his left arm folded inside his outer coat. Christopher assumed it was an attempt to stem the blood from his shoulder.

Felton finally worked up the strength to stumble into the room, walking unsteadily in the direction of the desk and settee. Alaina managed to find enough strength to move off the couch and over to Christopher, who had stepped into the corner of the study to stay clear of Felton.

Felton's wheezing filled the study. "You said we could both find better fates with a simple kidnapping, but now I find myself with blood on my hands again for you while you try and save your hide at my expense. At every turn, you have thwarted my ambition: you lied to me about the success of your business, and then you put Lady Barbara over me like a lovesick swain. So in cahoots you were with the lady that I had to remove her from the equation! And now you try and convince your cousin that you are the innocent party!"

Charles seemed paralyzed in his seat even as Felton closed in on his position. "You harmed Lady Barbara?"

Mr. Reid shouted, "I had to! You would have handed over everything I did, everything I earned, to satisfy your love, or lust, for her."

"But it was not like that. I do not even love her, you have to believe me!" came Charles's plea.

Mr. Reid now stood less than a foot away from the chair Charles occupied, and sneered. "I have certainly met a lot of two-faced blokes in my life, but you, sir, take first prize. Say goodbye."

And with that, the hand in his coat came free to reveal a pistol, and another volley of shots rang out in the hunting lodge.

To Alaina and Christopher's surprise, Mr. Reid crumpled to the floor, and yet a blossom of blood could be seen on Charles's white shirt, exposed by his jacket, just where his heart would be. A quick glance at the door revealed that Graham had somehow made it down the stairs and reloaded, all while dragging his wounded leg. He slowly lowered himself to the floor almost in a complete slide, as Christopher stepped over Felton's body to get to his cousin, being sure to check that the man was actually dead this time, the hole in Felton's head leaving no room for doubt.

Charles was sputtering by the time Christopher got to him. "You know, you always had it so easy," Charles struggled, blood and spittle spraying as he talked. "Never had to worry about anything, never worried about money, never had a vice, you even got lucky when you married a woman who actually loves you. Even had a mother who was honorable, though I doubt you know much of that."

"What?" came Christopher's question, the marquess feeling powerless to stem the flow of blood from his cousin's chest.

"You were too young, really," Charles started, coughing a bit, as blood splattered his lips. "My father found a love note in my mother's things, some London season when we were young, and she somehow convinced him that she was helping your mother hide an affair. Your father refused to believe him, each brother accusing the other's wife of infidelity. Turns out it was my mother's own deceit and shame that tore this whole family apart."

Stunned by the deep family secret, the only word Christopher could muster was, "Why?" It seemed he had misjudged Charles's character entirely. And to think, he had always wanted Graham and Alaina to form a close bond with his remaining family member. How foolish he had been.

"Why kidnap my wife and hold her for ransom?" Christopher asked again.

Charles choked, coughing up blood as he tried to answer. "Every man has ambition and vices. And I was unfortunate to be surrounded by those with bad ideas of how to achieve my goals, money and power," came the answer, so simple, and yet perfectly summing up the mayhem he had wreaked. It seemed that humans were always reduced to basic, uncomplicated reasons and motivations, no matter how complicated the situation appeared.

And with that Charles took his last breath, an anticlimactic gurgle before his body gave way to the damage wrought by Mr. Reid's close-range shot.

A hush fell over the room and Graham struggled to remain upright against the doorjamb, closing his eyes against the pain. Christopher surveyed the carnage, still in shock at what had transpired in so short a time, and at what he had learned. Tears of terror and relief flooded Alaina's eyes, and she brought her hand to her chest in an attempt to steady her beating heart. She closed her eyes, and a tear escaped onto her cheek as she quietly sobbed.

"We really do have the worst pair of cousins, Christopher," Graham said, breaking the silence. "I will be the first to admit that I always disliked Charles, but never could figure out why. Now I can at least put to rest any guilt I had."

Alaina was first to react to Graham's injury, and she scrubbed away tears as she made her way over to the duke to provide aid. "I would have to agree with you on that account, Graham." Alaina stated, touching his arm as Christopher applied pressure to the wound on Graham's leg.

Graham turned his glassy eyes toward Alaina and studied her face for just a few moments before turning his attention back to his friend. "You know I would only take a bullet for you or your lovely wife. You owe me now."

"And how should I repay you?" Christopher questioned.

"I am sure my love story will be something grand with highway heists and such, so I will call in the favor then," Graham said weakly, attempting a smirk to Christopher and then Alaina, before fainting from the pain and loss of blood.

Alaina grasped Christopher's arm in worry, but Christopher was quick to reassure her. "He has just passed out from exertion. From what I can tell, Graham has lost a fair amount of blood, but not too much. The wound is largely superficial. We do need to get him back to the manor house as soon as possible and get him proper medical attention."

Christopher left to bring the wagon that was kept in the stables of the hunting lodge as close to the front door as was physically allowed, thankful that there were still horses to hook up to it even after all the commotion of the evening.

Once Graham was loaded in the back of the wagon, through no small effort, Alaina settled in next to Christopher, worried for their friend, but reassured by the strong steady breathing she could hear and the makeshift bandage they had fashioned out of handkerchiefs and strips of linen from one of the bedroom's sheets to slow the bleeding.

Christopher was quiet for most of the drive back to the manor house, darkness still shrouding the estate as they wound around the winding path. His worries for his friend, his wife, and his adoptive Ashford and Norwich families were at the forefront of his mind. Christopher also wrestled with his grief. His cousin may have been at the heart of what happened, but they had grown up together, and reconnected as adults. It was tough to reconcile the Charles who had kidnapped his wife with the one he thought he knew. He had always seen ugliness in people like Percy, overt and in the open, *but how was he to protect his loved ones from the people who were like his cousin, Charles?*

A quiet knock sounded on the door, and Graham called out, "Come in." He attempted to sit up more in bed and was perturbed when a twinge of pain kept him from doing so.

Graham watched as Alaina and Christopher entered his room, his friend bearing a tray with afternoon tea. They had insisted he take up residence at Waverley until he was completely healed, but after a week, he was already wishing to be home.

"Graham, we thought you might like some refreshments," Alaina said softly.

"Yes, thank you, Alaina," Graham responded, and he huffed in consternation as she went about fluffing pillows and fussing over him before she took the tray from Christopher and placed it in front of him.

"Still wishing to be home? You have not even rested a week here. Surely our company is not so terrible?" Christopher questioned.

"I just prefer to be home, 'tis all," Graham answered. "At least you both have somehow convinced my mother to restrain herself from making a visit. I could not fathom what it would be like to deal with her tending and yours."

A brief look passed between Christopher and Alaina, but before Graham could inquire, Christopher spoke. "Well, I for one am happy that the doctor says you should make a full recovery."

Graham grunted and felt unnecessarily constrained in bed. It was infuriating!

"I told Christopher that we cannot keep you here," Alaina said. "And that when the doctor gives the ok to let you travel, we shall see you safely home."

"I can see myself home," Graham responded, his tone cantankerous.

"Nonsense, it will be some time before I let anyone travel completely alone," Christopher challenged.

The statement hung in the air as the three of them relived the events of a week ago. Graham could not help but ask, "How is Nicholas doing?"

"Well," Christopher replied, "He is up and about a bit, and is being just about as ornery as you when he is asked to rest."

"I suppose you have informed the authorities?" Graham continued on his line of questioning. After a week, he still had no idea how things were resolved. According to Alaina and Christopher, no news was so important as to threaten his recovery.

"Ah, yes, funny you should mention that," Christopher started, but then paused as Alaina shot him a glare. "Darling, I cannot keep the sheriff from him forever."

"Will you both stop treating me like an invalid and just tell me what is happening?" Graham implored.

Alaina waved her hand in Graham's direction. "Go ahead and tell him if you must."

"Well, it took a few days for us to sort through everything. Charles and Felton wrought so much destruction that the sheriff has been visiting every day with more questions, more information. We have been delaying his speaking to you to allow you to recover," Christopher said.

"Why the worry?" Graham asked.

"I am not worried about what the sheriff will do. He knows you only shot Felton in an attempt to save him from shooting anyone, including yourself, and that you suffered grave harm in the process. But… the delay in his official report has set tongues wagging."

At this point, Alaina interjected, "There really is no *need* for you to speak to the sheriff, Graham. He has admitted such, especially with Christopher and me as witnesses. But with everyone shouting 'murder', the sheriff feels a certain pressure to formally interview you. You know, to put everything to rest, finally."

Graham let out a groan, and fell back into the pillows. "What a mess."

"Indeed," Christopher agreed. "You know, I was telling Alaina that our early married life has not gone at all to plan. I am sorry you have been dragged into our mess."

"What are friends for, if not to help when there is need?" Graham asked, rhetorically. "Well to say the world's plan, at least at this particular moment, is shite would be quite an understatement in my opinion."

Alaina and Christopher released a breath they did not know that they were holding and chuckled ever so slightly. They certainly could agree on that sentiment.

A sound of a carriage coming down the pebbled drive of Waverley caused the three friends to shift their attention. Not long after, the sound of the front door opening and closing echoed through the halls, and they all heard a familiar voice.

"I asked to see my son! The duke, where is he?" Eleanor's concern was palpable even from a distance.

Heeled footsteps sounded across the foyer, up the stairs, and down the hall. In just a few moments, Eleanor practically crashed through the door. Her shrill greeting almost made Graham wish it was the sheriff.

"Graham! How are you, my darling son?" Eleanor asked, not waiting for a response as she crossed the room and assured herself that her son was indeed alive and well.

Disengaging from her ministrations, Graham smoothed down his hair. "Mother, Alaina and Christopher wrote to you that I was perfectly fine, and that there was no need for you to come. What are you doing here?"

"Not to come? Do you think them so callous as to keep a mother from her son? I would have been here sooner, but I was visiting Georgiana in Cornwall and just returned yesterday," Eleanor responded. "Besides, you are bedridden, so 'perfectly fine' is not an apt description. I can stay with you until you are well enough and then I can escort you home."

The last statement from Eleanor caused Christopher to laugh. "Well, Graham, if I know Eleanor, you will be home before you know it, just as you wished."

Alaina giggled as well, and soon the friends were all laughing, leaving Eleanor to wonder what was so funny.

Epilogue

Alaina moaned deep in her throat, a warmth starting to spread from her center outward through all of her limbs. Christopher paused in his exploration of her womanhood to trail kisses up her torso, ending with her breasts, capturing the dark nipples in his mouth to suckle and tease with his teeth. Alaina, caught up in the rapture of the moment, missed the smile that curved on Christopher's face as he watched her enjoy their interlude.

As Christopher made to resume his tongue's caress of Alaina's womanhood, he was stayed by Alaina's hand.

"Where do you think you are going?" Alaina asked, leveling a passion-glazed stare at her husband as he regarded her from his current position on her lower abdomen.

"To finish what I started," Christopher answered, his grin turning to a more rakish smile as he reveled in his wife's beauty.

"Well, when have I ever been one to stop you in that endeavor?" Alaina teased, and Christopher chuckled, quickly making his way back to the tufts of hair covering her most private areas and once again capturing her in his mouth.

Christopher's tongue traced the edges of Alaina's inner core, now slick with excitement, and revisited the nub over and over, bringing her to the very precipice of ecstasy, before sending her over the edge, the sound of her pleasure making him harder than he could have imagined.

Alaina, catching her breath, looked up at her husband with a gleam in her eye and sat up on the four-poster bed where they were currently ensconced. Christopher sat back on his heels to regard his wife, and was now amazed to find her making her way with intent toward his manhood. He rolled his head on his shoulders as her mouth placed a kiss on the tip of his member.

"I let you finish, and now it is my turn," came his wife's voice, her breath hot, before she brought his length fully into her mouth. In any other moment, Christopher would have countered with something witty, but he was himself engulfed by the passion of the moment, letting his wife's mouth work its own type of magic.

"Daydreaming again, my dear?" Christopher asked, breaking Alaina's memory of their exploits from earlier in the day, just after breakfast. Alaina averted her face from her husband, and Christopher caught the look. "Remembering this morning, are we?"

"Why, my dear husband, my mind seems to have wandered."

"Well, what if *my* hands wandered in the same direction as *your* mind?" Christopher questioned, feeling his pants tighten. With this question, Alaina seemed to remember their reason for being in the study.

"When did you say he was coming?" Alaina asked, turning toward Christopher. He had been seated at his desk, pouring over ledgers while she read in an oversized chair by the fire, when he had noticed her far away gaze and had heard a moan of contentment.

It was turning out to be a rather cold day and the only place Alaina could keep warm in the Rochester townhome was in Christopher's study. It was not like he minded, but Alaina was sure he was used to more peace and quiet while he worked, or at least a view that did not drive him to distraction.

Placing his quill back into the inkwell, Christopher looked up from his desk and smiled at his wife. "It is supposed to be today, my dear. There is no need to fret."

"I am not fretting, just reminding myself," Alaina said, turning back to her novel.

Almost a year had passed since they had last seen Graham. Their only contact with him, aside from a single, unplanned visit, had been through letters. Christopher had hoped his friend might join their holiday celebrations, but some last-minute personal business had kept Graham away. With the season due to start in a few weeks, Graham had finally sent word that he would be in town and planned to call on them soon.

Alaina placed a hand on her slightly protruding stomach and began to worry again. Although there had only been goodwill between the three of them during Graham's short convalescence at Waverley, Alaina could not help but think his long absence from Christopher's life had something to do with her.

"You are doing it again. There is no need to fret, everything is as it has always been," came Christopher's voice.

Alaina met her husband's eyes and offered a weak smile. "Yes, I know. He just did not formally visit last season in London, even though he was in town."

Christopher chewed on her statement a bit before responding with a shake of his head. "If I had to venture a guess, there were other reasons he failed to call."

Just then, they both heard a commotion in the front foyer, and a short moment later, the person of the hour walked through the door, resplendent in his finest evening wear.

"Graham, nice of you to come calling, finally," teased Christopher, who pushed away from his desk to greet his friend with a handshake that turned into a quick embrace.

Alaina watched the pair and smiled; nothing seemed out of place to her eye. The only real difference was the walking stick Graham carried, which to a less astute observer might have looked like a mere prop, but Alaina could discern a slight hitch in his step. She stood up and smoothed her skirts, approaching the two friends who had already amicably fallen into conversation.

Graham turned at her approach and gave a slight bow before pulling Alaina into an embrace as well. "Alaina, how nice to see you again," Graham said as he pulled back to gaze into her eyes. "You must forgive me for not calling sooner. I have been bent on getting rid of this limp. The country air seems to do me good."

"No apologies necessary. It is wonderful to see you again, your grace."

"It is Graham, you must use my given name," the duke stated good-naturedly, turning to Christopher. "You should remind your wife I took a bullet for her; no more formalities."

Christopher chuckled and Alaina shook her head.

"Truly, I meant no offense," Alaina stammered. "It has just been so long."

Graham waved his hand in an effort to dispel the tension. "No apologies needed; I have been away a long time. I am just happy to visit my good friends and see their expanding family."

Graham smiled as he watched Christopher put a protective and supportive arm around Alaina, her hand dropping to her stomach, barely noticeable through the fabric of her skirts. The couple murmured their thanks to Graham, happy to be able to share their news with an old friend.

"Now, from your letters you have some interesting stories of your own," Christopher nudged, causing Alaina to furrow her brow in confusion.

"Well, I will tell you my tales as soon as you explain why you choose to keep your cousin's deeds hidden?" Graham offered.

"That is simple; his debt and his deeds would have hurt my children, even if just in rumors. His character had no bearing on my decision, abhorrent though it was," Christopher answered simply, aware Graham already understood from his correspondence that Charles had racked up debt and had used every trick to stave off debtors' prison, including Christopher's name and the marquessate, before he was able to execute the attempted extortion scheme. Christopher had seen it best to pay the debts and be done with everything. Had his cousin been alive, Christopher might have let Charles rot in Newgate with Percy, where they could commiserate about their ill fortunes as men of the peerage, away from ears that would care.

"So, what are your tales? You made it sound like something important," came the question from Alaina after a lengthy silence had settled in the room.

Graham chuckled and shrugged. "Well, I am officially in London for the season. Maybe this time I will have better luck with love?"

His question may have been rhetorical, but Christopher felt the need to clarify. "I take it, by your confidence, that you already have a lady in mind?"

"You could draw that conclusion," Graham answered, a bright smile gracing his face.

"Do we know her?" Alaina asked, unable to contain her excitement.

"Yes."